The Unseen

Carol O. Riordan

WESTBOW
PRESS®
A DIVISION OF THOMAS NELSON
& ZONDERVAN

WestBow Press books may be ordered through booksellers or by contacting:

WestBow Press
A Division of Thomas Nelson & Zondervan
1663 Liberty Drive
Bloomington, IN 47403
www.westbowpress.com
1 (866) 928-1240

ISBN: 978-1-5127-5362-2 (sc)
ISBN: 978-1-5127-5363-9 (hc)
ISBN: 978-1-5127-5364-6 (e)

Library of Congress Control Number: 2016913400

Print information available on the last page.

WestBow Press rev. date: 09/16/2016

Dedication and Appreciation

I would like to dedicate this book to my family and friends for always believing in me and encouraging me! I am blessed to have all of you in my life!

Thank you, Tim, for allowing me the time to finish this project and for supporting me, financially and emotionally, as I completed it.

Thank you, Luke, for your consistent encouragement to finish my book and for the ideas you gave me which were pivotal to the plot!

I want to thank my Mother, Mary, who is now in Heaven. You always believed the best about me and encouraged me in everything I ever wanted to do. You are the best friend I've ever had!

I want to thank my father, Mason, who always told me I should write a book. I finally took your advice and I hope you can read it in heaven.

And thank you to my friend, Kathy Hancock, who read and edited this book several times. I couldn't have done it without you!

Thank you to Jim and Susan Clark for your support and for endorsing my book. You are dear friends!

And I want to thank Arianna Daniela Parisi for using her artistic flair to design the cover.

I am grateful to Naomi Fraher who edited the final manuscript on a professional level.

I am also thankful for my dogs, Sugar and Cooper, who sat patiently with me at different times throughout this endeavor.

My utmost thanks go to The One Who saved me and set me free!

May HIS Name be glorified!

Prologue

T he story I am about to tell you is hard to believe. I wouldn't have believed it myself a year ago. Over the past year my beliefs dramatically changed beyond anything I could have ever imagined. You are about to read about these life altering experiences. I felt obliged to share them.

Though I wanted to share these unusual events that changed my life, my primary purpose in writing this story was to offer a warning to those reading it. As the story transpires, the warning will become clear. I hope you will read this story with an open mind and a desire to know the truth. Truth never changes–we are the ones who have to change.

It is increasingly apparent to me that our life experiences do not always support our long held beliefs. We can encounter 'potholes' on our path we never expected and these obstacles can totally redirect our lives. This unexpectedly happened to me during the past tumultuous year I spent in the town where I grew up.

This manuscript is a compilation of months of unbelievable occurrences I experienced while writing a story for my magazine. And even though I am a journalist, I would have never written this unusual story unless I felt an obligation to do so. I am putting my career and reputation on the line by publishing this book.

Although my life revolves around words, I had never considered writing a book—that is until now. If this book doesn't read like a bestselling novel, I ask that you would overlook my haste and perhaps my lack of skill in putting it all together. Since I felt a sense of urgency, I may not have given it the time and detail it deserved. I was not as concerned about being on The New York Times Best Sellers List as much as I wanted to publish this book as quickly as possible because of its urgent message.

Due to the unusual nature of this story, I ask you to read the entire book before you make your final judgment. I have discovered there is only one Truth, and it does not change based on your belief. Your inability to believe will not change the Truth but it will limit your life. The Truth is what sets us free.

If you fit into the category of people who only believe what they can experience with their senses, I can relate. I was one of those people. My definition of reality is no longer determined by the litmus test of what I can see, hear, touch and feel. My horizon has been expanded beyond the natural realm.

With that said, I will give you a little background about myself. My name is Henry Pike, and I live in Fort Worth. I work for an on-line magazine, one of the first in Texas. The magazine is called *Ragweed* and our fan base enjoys reading about the more unusual stories in Texas. We appeal to what many would call the "fringe population" of this great state.

I love my job and have been doing it for almost eleven years. I have worked for other magazines and one newspaper, all of which would be considered more traditional publications. Working for *Ragweed* has been the job of my dreams and I love it. It is exciting and challenging.

The best part of my job has been traveling throughout this vast land to learn more about Texas and her people. Texas has always been my one true love, and I know her well. There are few places in Texas I haven't visited, which is saying a lot when you consider Texas has almost 260,000 square miles of landmass.

It is exhilarating to hit the open road as I travel to various locations on assignment for my magazine. It is when I feel most alive. I am often on the road for weeks at a time but I never grew tired of traveling like most do. I rarely thought about going home. Home did not offer the same sentiment for me as it does for most. My newly renovated townhouse is nice but void of warmth. My job was my life and I believed it was all I ever wanted or needed.

Though I love Texas, there was one place I told my editor I never wanted to go and he had always respected my request. But everything changed about a year ago when a mystery began brewing in the small city where I was born. So, when Sydney considered who to send to cover the story, he chose me. He decided my issues with my hometown should not interfere with my job.

My editor erroneously believed I might have some connections there since it was where I grew up. What Sid did not know was I hadn't been back to my hometown for almost 30 years. I had no reason to go back because I had no family there and no friends. But Sid persisted and insisted until finally I relented. So began my journey into a world I never imagined.

This story originally began as an article for *Ragweed*, but as the content exceeded the boundaries of a magazine, it turned into a book. For me, this very well might be the work of a lifetime.

In this book I reveal a world I did not know existed. You probably were not aware it exists, either. Since I experienced it first hand, I believe I have a message for everyone. I hope and pray you will benefit from what I learned.

This story takes place in Abilene, the place of my birth.

Chapter 1

As I began packing for my trip to Abilene, I couldn't help but wonder what I was getting myself into. I hadn't been able to focus on anything else since I agreed to do the story. My mind had gone into overtime, reeling with memories of my miserable life growing up in Abilene and anticipating what could be awaiting me there.

Sid didn't understand what he was asking me to do. He thought it was a small enough town where I was bound to know people who were affected by the tragedy unfolding there. He wanted me to act like a professional and put aside my dislike of the place so our magazine could get this story. But Sid did not endure what I did.

He was not the one ridiculed and shunned throughout adolescence. He didn't have to endure the nightmare I called "high school" and then have to come home to another one—my dad. My hesitation in returning to Abilene stemmed from a past I was trying to forget, not relive.

Sid didn't understand, and I didn't have the energy to explain it to him. And, because I wanted his respect, I was embarrassed for him to find out just how pathetic I was. So I decided to just give in and go. I knew it wasn't as big a deal as I had made it. He wasn't asking me to go to the moon—just one-hundred-and fifty miles away.

After I graduated from high school, I left Abilene and never went back. My mother had passed away in the middle of my senior year. She would have been the only reason for me to return. My sister had moved away a few years later to attend a college in Lubbock. And my dad...well, my dad was not a good enough reason to go back. He passed away a few years back. I did have pangs of regret because I rarely called him, much less saw him. But, in my opinion, that's what he deserved.

Remembering my sad childhood was not helping me get ready for the trip. Nevertheless, the memories kept flooding my thoughts—the taunting, the ridicule, the rejection. When I escaped Abilene, I didn't look back. I wanted that place to stay in my rear view mirror forever. But Sydney was my boss, and I really liked my job.

The story coming out of Abilene was like none in recent years. I had been reviewing the news reports and releases from the past few months. The disappearances, the lack of clues, and the prevalent fear was unnerving.

As a writer for various publications, I had been exposed to some pretty scary situations. I had been in danger many times when covering certain stories, like the time I did an article on the Texas mafia or when I tried to uncover the mystery behind the unexplained lights in Marfa (I almost had an encounter of the third kind with a rattle snake).

There were the stories I had investigated that revolted me, like interviewing a serial killer in Dallas or doing research on the prevalence of the sex trade in Texas. I felt I would never be able to remove the stain they spilled on my soul. All of these encounters just added to my already jaded view on life.

But nine people missing in West Texas was hard to contemplate. I knew to some extent what I faced when I did the story on the Texas mafia, but I had no idea what lay ahead in Abilene. No one had any idea what happened to these people. It had been almost a year since the first victim vanished with no trace. Then every few weeks it seemed like another one would vanish.

The story had been in all the papers and on the news so often that everyone was well aware of the situation in Abilene.

My editor thought it would be interesting to get up close to the people there and write about it from their angle. He also hoped I would be able to talk to some of the families affected by this tragedy. And because our magazine caters to those who are interested in the unusual and bizarre stories that happen in Texas, it seemed like a logical idea.

I did not think the story would take more than a week if I could find a few people who would be willing to talk to me. I knew the town had been inundated by the press, so I doubted they would be thrilled to talk to another reporter. I knew they must be tired of talking and just wanted some answers--something no one had been able to give them. But all I had to do was find one or two people who would give me an interview and I would be out of there, hopefully for good.

The logical explanation for these disappearances had to be a serial killer or lunatic on the loose. Even so, it was quite unusual that no one had been able to find any clues to any of these people's whereabouts. Nothing. How could that be in this day and age? Every law enforcement agency and federal investigator had been there for months and could not come up with any answers. It was a puzzling situation.

My curiosity was stirred by this mystery in Abilene. I had always loved mysteries as a boy, and because I had few friends and a lot of free time, I read a lot of books. Books were my best friends growing up. They were always there when I was lonely.

As a boy, I was often alone. I seemed to have an inability to relate to my peers. The kids on my street only wanted to play ball, collect horny toads, or build forts. I was not athletic, which excluded me from many of their games.

But I did like horny toads, which were little lizards with soft bellies that were prevalent throughout West Texas when I was a boy. I once had a whole colony of them I kept in a box until one of them spit blood at me. It was at that juncture where I released them all and never touched one again.

Forts were very popular back in my day. The house I grew up in was very close to a pasture where I could literally look out my window and watch cows chew their cud. Our neighborhood was still being developed so there were numerous empty lots behind our homes. These lots provided the location for forts and many battles.

Due to my limited experience with forts, I construed how they were built by watching through my window. Large holes were excavated out of the hard, red clay prominent in West Texas. The children would use the excavated dirt to build a fortification around the hole. The hot Texas sun would bake the dirt making it very hard. These forts provided the protection needed when pretend battles erupted with kids from other neighborhoods.

The neighborhood children rarely asked me to join them for any of their bustling activities. But the few times I did attempt to join them, I ended up getting hurt or being teased, so I found the company of a good book much more desirable than that of my peers. I was fort-less and friendless. I was a lonely child who would become a lonely man.

I would have loved to have been more athletic, but God decided to do something different with me. I was small, frail, and wore glasses. Back then, none of that was cool. I was an easy target. And because I was short and skinny, I fit well into the high school lockers where I frequently found myself placed by a disgruntled jock. Growing up in a school that worshiped its athletes did not make it an enjoyable experience for me.

My appearance and lack of athletic skills caused me to hate everything about myself, which was the only thing I had in common with my father. He was never proud of his slight son. He was a big, burly man, and he did not relate well to his creative, gentle boy who preferred reading and writing over watching a football game. We did not fit well together.

Because I intensely disliked my father, I didn't want to be anything like him. My father would often call me a "mama's boy," which I was. I preferred her ways over his. But it did bother me when the boys at school would call me "a sissy" because of my slight frame and gentle ways. I often believed I was wrongly cast in life as a boy.

Though I struggled with my identity and the rejection I felt from nearly everyone I knew, there were rare moments of joy

I remember from my youth. One of those memories actually involved my father.

My father seemed to have a lot of friends, which surprised me since I did not find him very likeable. One of his friends decided to give away his piano and my father readily took it because he enjoyed music. But instead of him taking lessons, he decided I should. This idea surprisingly appealed to me so I was delighted. But, my father couldn't do something nice without diminishing it. He revealed his true intentions, "If you can't throw a ball, maybe you can at least play a tune."

He found out there was a man close by who offered lessons for a low price, so he set me up to take lessons from this guy. Brian would come to our house and teach me every week. I was really starting to enjoy the piano and would play for hours at a time. I could feel my father's pleasure when I played. Things were better between us for a while. But those good feelings didn't last long. Brian told my father he would reduce his fee if I would come to his house for lessons. My father always loved to save money so I began taking lessons at Brian's house. But that discount came with a price.

I quit the piano a few months after I started taking lessons at Brian's house, and my father was very upset with me. He called me a "quitter" and told me I would never amount to anything. He could not have known how much I loved playing the piano. After I quit taking lessons, I never played again.

The only gift I seemed to have was I could write. And write I did. I poured out all of my teenage angst into journal after journal. Stacks of these journals are gathering dust in my attic, but I don't need them to recall the pain of my past. It has always remained with me.

Chapter 2

My journey back to Abilene began on a Sunday so I could settle in before starting the drudgery of setting up appointments the next day. I never liked contacting people without having some connection with them, but fortunately, I did have one contact Sid gave me. I hoped this man would be helpful in connecting me with some of the families of the missing.

The drive to Abilene was not one I was looking forward to, even though I usually enjoyed driving. Texas is a huge state and my job often required driving long distances, which for me meant a lot of time alone. For most of my adult life I had lived alone, worked alone, and been alone. I thought that was how my life would always be, because that was pretty much how it had always been.

Over the years, I had learned how to appreciate my experiences on the road, even though I had no one to share them with. Perhaps that was why I enjoyed writing. It was my way of sharing my life and my experiences with others.

But, as much as I liked driving, I had never enjoyed the boring drive between Fort Worth and Abilene. There are few distractions to relieve the tedious ride, unless of course you like mesquite trees, cows, and truck stops. My heavy foot had retrieved a few tickets for me on this route–compliments of some of the small towns along the relentless road.

And, talk about relentless, if you happen to be going in the wrong direction at the wrong time on Interstate 20, you will have black spots in front of your eyes for hours after facing the West Texas sun. There is nothing to block it and often sun visors are inadequate to keep it out of your eyes.

Driving past Weatherford brought back the memories of enduring this road as a young boy. Back then it was Highway 80 but it wasn't as boring. The smaller highway managed to engulf a few little towns and amusements along the way. My favorite spot was in Weatherford where we would often stop for lunch. Next to the restaurant, there was a rock store with barrels of beautiful, gleaming, polished stones. I would rummage through them trying to find the perfect, shiny rock. My mother would usually buy me one or two and over time they evolved into quite a treasure of stones. They are also stored in the attic next to my journals.

My family would often drive to a little town called Idabel which was in Oklahoma. We would go there to visit my grandparents and it usually took the majority of the day. The boredom of the drive was minimized for us by sleeping most of the way in the back seat. My father kept himself awake by puffing on his cigarettes, and drinking coffee while talking on his CB radio to all the truckers. After a few seconds of "10-4" and "Copy that", the truckers would then tell my dad what he really wanted to know, where the highway patrol were lurking so he could avoid speeding tickets.

Thinking about those trips helped distract me long enough to get to Ranger. I stopped at a popular truck stop, the Car-C, where I could get some coffee and take care of business. From there it would only be a few more hours to Abilene. That wouldn't have been so bad if I wasn't dreading my destination so much.

The best thing about Interstate 20 is it takes you around Abilene so you can continue on your way without going through the town. I had managed to by-pass Abilene for the past 30 years so I practically had to force my car to take the Abilene exit. I quickly found my motel which was conveniently located right off the highway.

As I pulled into the parking lot of my temporary home, I found myself wishing there was someone in Abilene I could call and meet for a beer. I couldn't even think of one person. If I did have any friends left in Abilene, I was not aware of them. I had lost touch with everyone I had gone to high school with and that was a conscious decision.

Those of us who survived high school together were glad to have each other back then, but we didn't make any great effort to stay in touch. It was a part of our lives we wanted to put behind us.

I was sure Sid would have been surprised to learn the startling fact– I knew no one in Abilene. I didn't have the heart to tell him. Thankfully, he did have the one connection for me. A man who worked in the police department in Abilene had written an email to our magazine telling us how much he enjoyed our unusual take on Texas. Sid called him and asked if he would be willing to speak to one of our writers for a story and he agreed. I was relieved when Sid gave me his name; otherwise, I'm not sure where I would have even started.

When I checked in at the front desk, the man asked me how long I planned to stay. I told him I thought no more than a week, but I wasn't sure. Little did I know then that I would be in Abilene for much longer. It was probably best I didn't know.

My plan was to settle in my new room for the night so I would be rested for the next morning when I would meet my contact. I wanted to make a good impression. The room was nice enough, and I thought about taking a short nap. I turned the TV on and plopped on the bed for a few minutes. The bed was soft but I was too restless to sleep. Mexican food was calling to me so I decided to gratify my stomach and check out Abilene to see how much it had changed.

I drove down South 1st looking for my favorite fast food Mexican place where I frequently ate in high school, but I didn't see it. I decided to do a U-turn and went down North 1st to look for it but it was nowhere to be found. I was concerned it might have closed down.

As I drove down North 1st, I went past the place where a very popular drive-in restaurant had once been. It was the place to be seen on a Friday or Saturday night if you were a teenager. They were famous for their square burgers and pink cookies, but even more famous for providing high school kids with a place to hang out. Teenagers would drive their cars around and around the drive-in for hours, seeing friends and flirting with new ones. From a safe distance, I had witnessed the ritual of the cars circling the popular hangout and I desperately wanted to join the fun.

One night I convinced my friend to come with me and try this teenage ritual. What did we have to lose? I drove my parent's Pontiac around the place a few times eager to see who we might meet there. We soon realized it didn't carry the same exciting interaction for us as it did for our peers. When people saw who we were, they would just look past us, hoping to see someone more desirable in the car behind us.

The only friend I saw that night was the one sitting in the front seat with me. After we drove around the drive-in a few more times, we realized we were just wasting gas. We could sit on my couch and get the same amount of social interaction.

The urge for Mexican food was growing, so I decided to keep looking for some. I went to the downtown area to see if anything might be open there. I was happy to see some familiar businesses and was especially glad to see my favorite movie theater.

The Paramount had survived the fate of some of the other buildings which once populated the small downtown area. I used to love going to the movies there. What was most special about the beautiful theater was the unusual ceiling.

If you looked up, above the ornate interior architecture and the large movie screen where velvet curtains would part for the movie and close during the intermission, you might be surprised to find a reproduction of the night sky. White, wispy clouds could be seen floating by scattered star-lights as they twinkled in the theater sky. The 'sky' would grow darker when the movie would start and brighten when it would end. This theater sky was quite unique back then and would fascinate movie goers of all ages. The place was magical.

As I continued to drive around the downtown area, I was getting desperate for some tacos. I finally stopped someone on the sidewalk and asked where I might find some good Mexican food. He gave me a name of a restaurant on South 14th so I decided to try it. He was right. The food was wonderful.

When I came out of the restaurant, I felt full and content. I looked up into the night sky and felt a cool Texas breeze drift over me. This small, natural act created a twinge of happiness within me. This surprised me because it wasn't a feeling I had often—especially in Abilene.

Based on that fleeting moment of happiness, I decided to take a drive around town instead of going back to my motel. I drove past McMurry University and remembered going to some activities there as a boy. Every year at Homecoming, they had cool teepees and Indian villages set up with a lot of fun things to do. I would pretend to be a cowboy and run around the place shooting my imaginary gun.

Since I was thinking of cowboys, I decided to drive across town to Hardin Simmons University and see their campus again. I loved their Cowboy band. Our magazine covered them once when they were going to New York City to march in a parade there.

As I looked around the campus, I could see the college had expanded and had added some beautiful buildings. It looked like things had really picked up for Abilene and their universities. There are three universities in Abilene, all associated with different religious denominations.

I decided to check out the other university to see how much it had changed so I drove east on Ambler, passing the spot where one of my favorite hamburger joints once resided. They had such good food. I have often wondered why food doesn't taste as good to me as an adult as it did back then.

Abilene Christian University was my next destination on my college tour. They had built so many buildings since I had last been there, it didn't even look like the same place. I was impressed with the modern buildings and artistic sculptures they had added.

It would have been wonderful to have gone to any of these universities, as they were all well respected schools, but I decided to leave after my mother passed away. I couldn't bear the thought of living at home without her. I knew if I was going to college, I would have to do it on my own, and it would not be in Abilene.

As soon as I graduated, I left and went to a small college in Fort Worth. It catered to those who wanted to pursue writing and journalism. I had to put myself through school, but I did it. My sister was lucky enough to get a scholarship a few years later to a college in Lubbock. It seemed like things always worked out for her.

As I drove around Abilene, it occurred to me that there were a lot of good things about the town. If high school had been a better experience for me, I might have stayed. It wasn't the town I hated—it was my life.

There was one last place I decided to go before heading back to my motel. I shouldn't have gone because the memories started flooding my mind as I got closer to the house. I sat outside my childhood home on E. N. 10th and remembered what it was like to live there. It all came back in one big wave of emotion.

The house looked like I felt—haggard and run down. It made me sad to see it again especially in such bad condition. It looked like college students or wild animals had been living in it. In my opinion, there was not much difference between the two.

The house seemed to be vacant as there was no sign of life inside or out. The exterior needed a paint job and the fence appeared to be falling down. The gate was hanging by one hinge. Bushes were overgrown and the lawn looked like it had not been mowed in weeks. It was a mess.

It was a tenuous decision to get out and walk around the house. Everything in the backyard was in disarray. The memory of my dog, Lassie, came to me and I could picture her running around the yard. It made me sad as I wondered how she survived being our dog.

The porch in the back was full of junk and there was no path I could see to the back door. I was also aware it probably housed many spiders and possibly some snakes. I went around to the front and peered through a window where a curtain parted just enough to see inside. But when I looked through the curtains, all I could see was darkness. It seemed my house was always dark inside. Little sunlight ever found its way into any of the rooms. The only 'light' that shined in my home was my mother.

As I stood by the dark window, I closed my eyes and tried to remember what it was like to live there. I could almost hear the yelling that once echoed through the walls of the house. There was little laughter or happiness growing up there.

With a deep heaviness in my spirit, I got in my car and drove back to the motel. In reflecting on my tour of Abilene, I realized I should have skipped the old homestead.

The awareness was slowly seeping in—writing this story in Abilene would entail facing my past at every turn. I always felt I should face the 'demons' from my childhood and find some reprieve. But instead, I had just resigned myself to their inescapable presence. It seemed they would raise their ugly heads at inopportune times throughout my life. I didn't know how to rid myself of them so I just managed them the best I could.

Of course, I didn't literally believe the demons were real. I used the term loosely as a description for memories that tormented me. But this belief was one of the many that would become obsolete as I was about to encounter the 'real deal'.

Chapter 3

The next morning, I went to the lobby for my complimentary breakfast. As I ate, I took out the list of the missing people Sid had given me before I left. I inspected the list noting the difference in their ages, the brief description of who they were, and what precipitated their disappearance.

It was apparent, after reviewing the list several times, that these people had nothing in common. They ranged in age from twelve to seventy-seven. They were not the same ethnicity or religion. They were male and female. They were from different areas of Abilene and had diverse occupations. This disparity was not what you would expect to find if you were dealing with a serial killer.

These discrepancies were something I wanted to bring out to the police officer I was scheduled to meet with that morning. I wondered what his thoughts were on the unusual differences in the victims.

The police sergeant came out with an air of confidence. Something about him made me very uncomfortable. He was a large, robust man, with a bald head and a handlebar mustache. From the wrinkles etched in his face, I surmised he had weathered quite a few storms in his lifetime. I imagined his years on the police force had something to do with his appearance. He put out his hand to shake mine, and I wondered if his handshake would be as strong and confident as he appeared. It was.

"Good morning! I'm Sergeant Bardon. It's a pleasure to meet someone from *Ragweed*. I do enjoy your magazine. I can't believe some of the fruity stuff that goes on in Texas, right? I'm sorry, what was your name again?" he asked.

"Henry Pike." I saw his confusion and realized he didn't recognize my name. I quickly explained, "I write my articles under a different name. I use 'Oh Henry' as my pseudonym. I borrowed the name from one of my favorite authors. I added an 'h' to the 'O' to make it my own and to be funny."

It was obvious he didn't get it or think it was funny. "Oh yes, 'Oh Henry'. I believe I have read some of your articles," he said, almost like he was trying to convince himself. "Now, how can I help you, Oh, uh, I mean, Henry?" There seemed something very familiar about this guy that made me uneasy.

He invited me into his office and asked me if I'd like any coffee or water. I told him I was fine. I got to the point and proceeded to tell him what Sid was looking for, "My editor wants to be able to connect with a few of the victim's families, to get their perspective on the investigation, and whatever else they'd like to share with our readers."

The Sergeant didn't say anything so I waited, hoping I hadn't said anything wrong. I knew everyone around Abilene was on edge. Then, he bent down a little like he was going to tell me a big secret. "I actually know two of the families involved. I've been going to church with them for years. They are pretty gun shy at this point about talking to anyone, but maybe I could convince them that you are from a reputable magazine."

I stared at him in disbelief. How easy could this be? Two families were more than enough to interview, and I could be out of Abilene in a few days. I was trying to contain my excitement.

"Oh, that would be nice," I calmly uttered, trying not to give away how thrilled I was. "When do you suppose I could speak to them?"

He thought about it a minute and said, "Don't move. I'll call them right now." He quickly got up and left the room. I assumed he didn't want me to be privy to his conversation.

I couldn't believe my luck. I thought it would take several days just to connect to one of these families and even longer to try to convince them to talk to me. I never dreamed it would be as simple as this. I was beside myself thinking how quickly I could get the story done and get out of town.

Sergeant Bardon strode back in with a look of concern. I knew I shouldn't have jinxed myself thinking this was going to be easy.

"I just talked to one of the families—I don't want to give you their name just yet until they agree to talk to you." Then he thoughtfully added, "And, just so you know, we don't call them 'victims' around here. We refer to them as 'missing'," he said condescendingly.

I nodded my head.

He continued, "They are hesitant to give another interview. They have been approached by so many in the media and the few times they had agreed to an interview, the reporter had misquoted them and said things that were hurtful to their family. So basically, they don't trust anyone in the media."

He explained, "You must realize we have been swamped by reporters and people from those gossip magazines. But I did tell the family I had read several things you've written and you're not like most journalists. They said they'd have to think about it. I called the other family but they didn't answer."

It seemed clear this was not going to be as easy as I had hoped. I got up to leave. "I understand, Sergeant Bardon," I said with resignation. "I appreciate you trying."

He got up, too and looked at me like he was puzzled. "Now just wait one minute. What kind of attitude is that? Where is your tenacity, man? Don't give up. You always have to expect some road blocks in life. I'll get you in to see them. Don't worry. I'll be in touch."

As he turned to go back into his office, the obvious occurred to me: why hadn't I told him I was from Abilene? That surely would make them more trusting of me. So, before he could shut his office door, I said, "Oh, by the way, I forgot to mention I'm from Abilene."

He spun around like a top when I said those magic words and told me to come right back in to his office and have a seat. He told his secretary to bring us some coffee, and I drank it, even though it was lukewarm.

It was like I pushed a button inside his brain when I said I was from Abilene. He seemed much more interested in what I had to say. He started asking me questions about how I got into journalism; what college had I attended; what high school.

When he asked me which high school I had attended, I barely answered. Sergeant Bardon suddenly became even more animated, because of course, he had gone to the same high school, too.

"What year did you graduate?" he asked with great anticipation. I was almost afraid to answer. It was not surprising to learn 1975 was the exact same year he graduated. He walked over to me and gave me a bear hug. This was a response I certainly didn't expect from someone I went to high school with. And I was surprised by my reaction to his gesture. I flinched when he came near me and grabbed me. It was embarrassing but he didn't seem to notice.

He asked me what activities I had been involved in and hardly gave me time to spit out, "Well, I was an aid in the library, and I was in the literary club."

Then it was his turn, and he couldn't wait to tell me everything he did in high school: football, basketball, and of course, baseball. It was no surprise to me he was an athlete because he was a big guy and he had probably been in good shape when he was young.

I told him I couldn't place him, and, no surprise, he couldn't place me either. It was a large high school with about five-hundred in our graduating class so it wasn't that unusual to not know some of your classmates. But I was surprised I couldn't place him since he was apparently so popular.

He was trying hard to remember me, too, assuring me he would. He told me he would be looking through his year book that night. I was so thankful I had not succumbed to my mom's pressure to get my senior picture made. I wanted to forget about those years rather than commemorate them. I also didn't want to tell her I doubted anyone would ever look for my picture. But, as it turned out, it didn't matter in the grand scheme of things. She passed away before I graduated and never knew.

My mother was the only one who cared what I did in school, and was always proud of my writing awards. I went through the graduation ceremony mostly to honor her. My father had to work, and my sister didn't care about coming, so I went alone. I pretended my mother was in the crowd cheering for me as I walked across the stage.

I would just tell Bardon that I was a non-conformist back then and refused to let them take my picture in high school. My name would still be in the yearbook, underneath a blank box where my picture should have been. But there would be no accomplishments listed underneath my name like there were under the other seniors.

We exchanged phone numbers and he told me to call him any time. I left feeling a little more hopeful.

Since I had some time to kill and nothing else to do, I decided to go to the public library and see if I could find an old yearbook from my high school. I wanted to see if it would jog my memory to look at some old pictures of Sergeant Bardon. Boy did it ever.

Chapter 4

The West Texas heat was hotter than usual for that time of year. Unfortunately, the spring and fall can sometimes feel like summer in Texas. I always wanted to live somewhere with actual seasons, but I ended up in Fort Worth, which isn't one of those places. I looked forward to sitting in the air conditioned library.

The library was always a comfortable, safe place for me. My mother would often drop me off there when I was a boy. It was a refuge for me to get out of my house and my life. I could easily lose myself in whatever story I was reading. I loved mysteries and would often solve them before I finished the book. I would usually identify with the hero and tried to imagine myself in the story. But I knew even back then, a fantasy was the only place I would ever be a hero.

The library was very nice and inviting. The librarian was very friendly and asked me how she could help me. For some reason, I mindlessly told her I was doing a story on the missing people in Abilene. Immediately her facial expression changed from friendly to *get out*! I realized then I couldn't blurt out to people why I was in Abilene. People did not think kindly of all the reporters and journalists who had beleaguered the town for interviews.

I decided to backtrack and ask her if I could see the old high school annuals, which was the real reason I had come in.

She pointed in the general direction where they were, which wasn't very helpful, but I thought it best to leave.

As I walked in the direction she pointed, I saw the aisles where I had spent a great deal of my childhood. The fiction section was brimming with books, and I entertained the idea of checking one out. I reminded myself I wasn't on vacation; I had a story to do. I amused myself by thinking I should try to solve a real mystery instead of reading a fictional one. The story in Abilene was certainly the mother of all mysteries.

Another librarian asked me if I was lost. She kindly directed me to the yearbooks and explained they were on DVD's for space sake. I thanked her and went to the room where they were kept. The man behind the counter gave me the year I asked for, after explaining how to use the DVD player.

I sat down and was prepared to be wowed by Sergeant Bardon's antics and awards in high school. It didn't take me long to find him and it didn't take me long to recognize him, either.

After looking at two or three close-up pictures of Sergeant Bardon, his youthful face was coming back to me in a nightmarish fashion. Thirty years disappeared before my eyes as Sergeant Bardon's weathered face morphed into the youthful bully who had plagued my life in high school. Sergeant Bardon had lost his hair and his large, bushy mustache had disguised his identity while sitting in his office; but as I studied his yearbook picture, there was no mistaking the fact I had just spent the past hour with my greatest nemesis.

I hadn't recognized his name initially either, because everyone called him "Bubba" when we were in high school. Since I didn't participate in any extracurricular activities, it was the only name I knew him by. I had never been in a class with him, fortunately, so I never heard anyone call him by his full name—Joseph T. Bardon, Jr.

Sergeant Bardon was the bully of bullies who had tormented me mercilessly throughout my high school years. His cruel words and actions had beleaguered me throughout my life. I fought back tears as I remembered the degradation he perpetrated.

When "Bubba" and the football team weren't on the field, I was the one they enjoyed kicking around. They would bump into me or push me every time they saw me in the hallway. I would go flying along with my papers and books. Few people ever stopped to help me and no one ever reported their abuse.

They would get entire classes to start coughing every time I walked into a room. And a friend finally confessed to me, after he and several others denied me access to the boy's bathroom, that he had been threatened by Bardon to not let me use any of the bathrooms in the school. I learned to hold it in, like I did my feelings.

It was Bardon's evil grin I would see just before he would slam the locker door in my face. Then I could hear him snickering as he and his buddies waited close by for the janitor to eventually let me out so they could degrade me even more. Their taunting laughter still echoed in my soul.

The humiliation I felt back then flooded my mind again, as I remembered trying to walk to my class with some fragment of dignity after being released from my locker. Their actions and words methodically removed my manhood, like that of a neutered puppy. How could I have any pride when I was the joke of my high school?

My mind was reeling from this shocking discovery. I felt nauseous and put my head down on the table. Was this a sick cosmic joke? Of all the people in the world, Bubba Bardon had to be the contact Sid had for me. The one person who had made my high school years a nightmare had become the very one I was dependent on to get the story I was sent to do.

Everything in me screamed to run away. It was my usual way to deal with conflict and was the main reason I had left Abilene. I never wanted to see Bardon again. He tainted every memory I had of high school and of Abilene.

The decision was made. I was going home. Sid would never have to know the truth. I could tell him no one would talk to me, which seemed likely if I lost my one and only connection to the families of the missing.

I felt an urgency to get out of Abilene before Bardon could figure out who I was. I couldn't face him again. There was no way I would consider working with this demented bully, job or no job. I could not imagine trying to be nice to him just so he would help me get a story. He did not deserve my kindness or respect.

This unbelievable predicament had to be one of life's evil tricks. I had to wonder why things never seemed to work out for me. I was so disheartened by this revelation that I went back to the motel and collapsed on the bed. This unexpected bombshell had sapped all the energy out of me. I quickly fell into a deep sleep.

Chapter 5

A young girl is trying to say something to me but her words are muffled. I couldn't understand what she was saying, but I could see the desperation in her eyes. She was young and small and I wanted to help her. She appeared to be behind some type of curtain or veil. I tried to run to her, but I could barely move my legs. My feet felt like they were encased in thick mud. Looking down, I expected to see mud, but instead I saw beautiful grass under my feet. Nothing was stopping me.

She started crying, "Help me! Please, help me! I need to get home." I desperately wanted to help her but I could barely move. I kept inching towards her. I yelled at her that I was coming to help, but it was like she didn't see me or hear me.

Where were her parents? Where were the police? Where was Sergeant Bardon when you needed him? With each agonizing move I got closer, but by the time I reached her a wall had appeared out of nowhere. I could no longer see her. I banged on the wall and yelled, "I'm here for you! Can you hear me? I'll help you. Just tell me the way to get in," but there was no response.

As I turned around to try and find someone to help me break the wall down, I bolted upright in my bed. My cell phone was ringing. It took me a minute to figure out where I was. I then realized I had just had a crazy dream but the little girl in the dream seemed very real. My heart was racing and sweat was pouring off my body as I tried to calm myself down and get my thoughts together.

My phone was still ringing. When I checked it, I could see Sergeant Bardon's name gleaming in the dark. The reality of who this man was came flooding back to me like a slap in the face. I couldn't answer it. I hoped he would just leave me a message. He was the last person I wanted to talk to and yet, he was the one person I needed to talk to if I wanted to keep my job.

Slinging cold water on my face helped. I walked over to the clock in the room and couldn't believe I had slept so long. My nap had turned into a 4 hour marathon. I must have been more tired than I realized.

As coherency began seeping back into my foggy mind, I became aware of a new resolve surfacing in my heart. I felt totally different about everything. I wasn't sure if it was because I actually got some sleep or because of the crazy dream I had. Whatever the reason, my energy level was soaring, and I felt like I had to do the story.

Perhaps the dream had been a sign to me. I knew from the list Sid gave me that one of the missing was a little girl. I didn't really believe the girl in my dream was literally the missing girl, but somehow, the vivid image of her calling to me for help put things in perspective for me. It gave me a renewed strength to endure Abilene and Bardon.

It was farfetched to think I could actually help find these people, but someone would figure it out eventually. Why couldn't it be me? I had done some investigative reporting in the past and had helped solve a crime. I literally saved a little boy's life just by asking a few questions no one else had.

It happened about fifteen years ago, when several young boys were missing in the Dallas area and the latest victim had just been reported. I was working for a newspaper then, and was sent over to one of those pizza party places to talk to some of the workers. The parents had given a party for the little boy at the party place only a few nights before he disappeared

When I arrived, there were only two or three people working because it was mid-morning and they were cleaning up after the party the night before, getting ready for the next onslaught. I knew the police and detectives had interviewed them, but I hoped one of the workers would still be willing to talk to me.

I stopped one of the teenage boys and asked him if he remembered the boy that had been reported missing. He did remember him, and had been one of the workers assigned to help the parents with his party. He said they were very nice people, and all of the kids were well behaved. He assured me that was not typical of most groups.

His name was Mike and I could tell he was shaken by the boy's disappearance. He said, "The father tipped me and the other worker very generously. They were all really nice. And then a day later, I saw on the news the very same boy had been reported missing. I couldn't believe it! It made me sad that this could happen to such nice people."

The missing boy had not made it to school that day, and no one knew where he was. I asked Mike if he had seen anything unusual that night or the next day.

Mike told me, "I hadn't noticed anything unusual that night. I even helped carry some of their things out to their car. I didn't notice any strange people around." He said he told the police the same thing.

"But there was one thing I didn't tell the police," he confessed. "I found the receipt of the boy's party in the janitor's room the morning after the party. The boy had not been reported missing yet, so I didn't think much of it. I had gone in to ask Jim why he hadn't cleaned up the mess from the night before, but he wasn't in there." Mike explained that every once in a while Jim would go on a bender, would call in sick, and not show up for a day or two. He knew Jim must have come in because he found the receipt in his room, so he was surprised he hadn't cleaned up.

He continued, "Jim has worked here several months. He keeps to himself, but he seems like a nice guy and he usually does his job. One night Jim and I were the only ones here and he told me he had a drinking problem. He asked me not to tell anyone, so I never did."

I asked him, "You didn't tell the police investigating the case?"

"No. I didn't want to get Jim in trouble for missing work. He told me those things in confidence, and I wouldn't feel right if I told on him. I thought he might lose his job," Mike reasoned.

When I asked him if he had told the janitor about finding the receipt, he told me he hadn't. "Do you still have it?" I asked. He did and brought it to me. On it was the last name of the little boy who was missing and his father's name who had signed it using a credit card. It wouldn't take a genius to use that information to figure out where they lived.

Mike was hesitant to let me take the receipt because he felt like he was betraying Jim, but he finally handed it over. I took it to the police and told them what the teenage worker had said. They knew Jim had not been working during the party, so they hadn't questioned him. They quickly got a subpoena to sweep the janitor's room and the apartment he lived in. There they found the missing boy tied up to a pole still alive.

Jim was arrested for the seven other boys who were not so lucky. After he had been convicted and imprisoned for a year or so, I had started working at *Ragweed*. When my editor, Sid, found out the part I played in the capture of Jim, he asked me if I would consider interviewing him. I really didn't want to, but since I was new at the magazine, I decided to do it.

Arrangements were made, and I stepped into the cold cell where he was cuffed. I was glad he didn't know the part I played in his capture. When I sat down, he looked at me and smiled, "Sorry I can't shake your hand." Then he rattled his chains and said, "But you can see I'm a little tied up." I was thankful for those chains because I didn't want to touch the guy.

Other than the chains, he seemed like a normal person. I tried not to think about what he had done as I began my questions. He was kind of excited about being interviewed, and I assured him we were not a big magazine. I told him we were on-line and if he had access to a computer and some money to pay for a subscription, he could read the article after I finished it.

Then I proceeded to ask him the typical questions like: where was he from, what was his home life like and how did he get into serial killing. (Note to reader: I am sarcastic) And then I asked the magic question, "What caused you to pick certain boys?"

His face and his words suddenly became animated as he began to explain his demented reasoning in great detail. He smiled as he talked about each boy, and how he looked for boys who had what he called "a light" inside them. This was not the explanation I expected, but I sat spellbound as he talked about each boy he met with this quality. He summed it up by saying, "I wanted the light they had."

Then, I remembered he had not been working the night the boy had his party, so I asked him why he had taken him. The monster looked at me with cold, calculating eyes and said, "I came in later that night to clean up, and I saw his picture on a poster they still had up for his party. When I saw him, I knew.

"The next day, I found him," he said with a smile. "I even talked to him for a few minutes when he was walking home from school. He was kind to me even though he seemed nervous. His parents probably told him to be careful around strangers. We talked a few minutes about his school and his teacher. I could see the 'light' in his eyes. The next day, I met him again, but this time, he came home with me. He didn't want to, but I convinced him. He is the only one who got away. But, I'll find him again one day."

As he finished his devilish oratory, he looked at me and smiled like he was pleased with himself. It appeared he had no remorse for the evil he had committed. If there is a devil, I think I met him that night.

All of the sudden I started to feel very nauseous. I had to get out of that room. I didn't say anything else to him or look back. I felt like I was about to throw up all over him. It would have been a just payment for having to listen to his demented story.

I picked up my notes and knocked on the door, hoping someone was there to get me out of the cage with that animal. It was beyond disturbing, and I'll never forget the stench that wafted up into my nostrils right before I left. It reeked. I was surprised I hadn't noticed it when I first walked in.

As I thought about that interview, I wondered if the same type of evil lurked in Abilene.

Chapter 6

Since I was wide awake at 8:15 in the evening, I wondered what I should do. The night was still young, and I had a lot of energy. I knew I should call Bardon back but it was going to take everything I had to do it. I had to play nice with this bully to get what I wanted. There was no choice. If I didn't, I would have no credibility with these families. Life is so full of irony.

I comforted myself by thinking, after I finished the story, I could tell him exactly what I thought of him. But until then, I would have to push all of that anger back down into my gut where it had been festering for years. I had to do what I had to do to get what I needed.

Bardon seemed glad to hear from me when I returned his call. I assumed from his reaction he had not figured out who I was in high school yet. He told me he had spoken to the other family and they had agreed to talk to me. I was relieved, and I thanked him half-heartedly. After all, it was the least he could do for me.

He gave me their names, address, and phone number and told me to give them a call the next morning. After we hung up, I decided to get some more Mexican food and think about what I was going to say. I knew I had to make a good impression. This would probably be my one chance to get this story so I had to ask the right questions.

Fried quesadillas with refried beans and hot sauce has always given me clarity of mind. I sat with my notepad and some iced tea, thinking about what I'd say to them. I knew I had to come off as caring and compassionate.

After coming up with some good questions, I felt prepared so I went back to my motel and watched a mindless movie until I fell asleep. The next morning I grabbed some breakfast, and then gave the family a call. They were gracious and we set up a time to meet.

My new resolve did not keep me from having a horrible feeling that Bardon was going to somehow sabotage everything, like he had done so often in my past. The old feelings from high school were coming up like vomit. I had to keep pushing them down so I could get the interview done.

After ringing the doorbell, I could hear someone rustling around inside. I took a deep breath and was glad when they finally opened the door. I put my hand out and introduced myself, "Hi, Mr. and Mrs. Smith, I'm Henry Pike with *Ragweed*."

The man gingerly took my hand and limply shook it. "Hello, I'm Dennis and this is my wife, Janet. Please come in," he said in a polite southern way, but I was sure this was the last thing they wanted to do.

We sat down and Janet offered me some sweet iced tea but I told her I was fine. Dennis said, "Sergeant Bardon told us you are different from all the other reporters. He told us he reads your magazine and really likes it. It's on-line, is that correct? I don't get on the computer much. I have never taken to all this technology. What I'm trying to say is, I'm sorry, I've never heard of your magazine," he explained as nicely as he could.

"Well, you're certainly not the only one, Dennis." I was trying to bring some levity to the conversation because the mood was beyond somber. "We are small but our readership is growing. We do stories about the unusual things that happen in Texas. Of course, what has happened here is more tragic than unusual. I'm sure you agree." As soon as I uttered those words, I regretted it.

Dennis started to say something, but Janet interrupted him. "I'm sure you know Mr. Pike, our town has been through a lot. We know you are just trying to do your job, but we are tired of questions. We want some answers, but no one has been able to give us any."

It seemed like Janet was playing interference for her husband. She continued, "But we are willing to sit and talk with you for a few minutes. Now, what would you like to ask us, Mr. Pike?"

I was appreciative to get another chance so I chose my words carefully. "Tell me about your mother, Dennis?" I asked cautiously.

He began, "My mother, Mary, is seventy-seven, in good health, and is a wonderful person. She is always doing something for someone. She would never hurt anyone and has no enemies." I noted he spoke of her as if she were still alive.

Janet also contributed her thoughts about Mary. As they went on and on about this lady, I realized they were trying to convince me that this should not have happened to Mary. She should not be included in this category "the missing." Their mother /mother-in- law did not deserve this because she was a wonderful woman. I wondered if they thought the other people did deserve it.

Dennis' mother had lived close to them, and they went to see her nearly every day. Mary has another son too who lives in another town. He and his family often came to visit and they all got along very well.

"My mother was very active in Abilene. She volunteered in her church and worked part-time with an agency that provided emergency care for children who needed temporary housing. They used licensed foster families to take in these children since they did not have a literal building to house them. The agency was called, 'The Shelter from the Storm',", he explained.

Dennis added, "My mother helped in the office and with fund raising. She was always busy with this organization. She felt like she was making a difference. The board and director always appreciated her help. But a few months before my mother went missing, the director stepped down and the board started looking for a replacement. In the meantime, they asked my mother if she would step in as a temporary director, but she felt she was too old and inexperienced to do a good job so she declined."

"They felt they needed someone quickly so they hired a young social worker with little experience. She was very prideful. She didn't let her lack of experience keep her from being bossy. The young girl had the college degree, but not the compassion this type of work requires. She treated my mother like she was in the way," Dennis concluded.

"My mother tried to impress on this young director the need to recruit more foster families because they had lost several with all the transition. But she did not want any advice from my mother or anyone else. She was often out of the office, and no one knew exactly what she was doing. My mother would pick up the slack in the office when she could, even though she was only there part-time."

Dennis continued, "One night, a young mother called, desperately needing a place for her young daughter to stay. My mother happened to be in the office later than usual because she wanted to organize some files. The young mother told my mom she lived with her boyfriend, but he was growing increasingly angry about having to watch her little girl when she had to work at night. The mother was afraid he might hurt her. This young mother asked for immediate housing for her daughter because she did not want to leave her alone with him again."

Dennis added, "This was precisely what the Shelter had been set up to do—take in children in emergency situations. But, because the volunteer foster homes had been dwindling, there were only a few homes and they were at capacity."

I nodded that I understood, and encouraged him to continue.

"My mother knew she shouldn't make any decisions without talking to the director, so she put the young mother on hold and tried to call her, but there was no answer. She left a message telling her it was urgent."

"In the meantime, my mom asked the mother if there was any one the little girl could stay with that night until she heard from the director. The young mother screamed at her, 'No, that's why I called you!'"

"Before mom could say anything else she hung up. Mom tried to call her back using the caller ID but she didn't pick up. She tried several times, but couldn't reach her. My mother kept thinking she should have offered to take the child herself even though she wasn't licensed. We tried to tell her that wasn't her responsibility, but she wouldn't listen to us," Dennis said, sadly.

"My mother felt horrible about what had happened, and told us later that night she felt like she had failed everyone. She feared the worst for the child, and the next morning, her fears were confirmed," Dennis lamented and shook his head.

"On the news the next day, it was reported a little girl had been beaten to death by her mother's boyfriend. When my mom heard the news, she knew it was the same little girl. Not only did he kill the girl but he also killed her mother. Her body was found in an alley not far from their apartment. That's when my mother called me hysterically crying. She was sobbing, saying over and over, she had caused the death of a little girl," he recalled.

"I had never heard my mother so distraught. I couldn't even understand half of what she was saying. I rushed over to her house and found her devastated, crumpled up on the floor. She told me what happened, and I tried to tell her it wasn't her fault but she wouldn't accept that. She had decided to take the blame, and I couldn't change her mind," Dennis revealed.

Dennis and his wife went on to explain how The Shelter soon closed down after that. "The police found the phone number for The Shelter on the young mother's cell phone. Everyone knew she had reached out to The Shelter but it was obvious no one helped her. The reporters asked my mother for an interview, but she refused. The director was happy to be on TV, but could give no reasonable explanation why they didn't help this young mother. After her interview, the funds dried up and now there is no one to help these people."

"The Shelter shut down, and so did my mother. My mother became a different person. She had always been joyful and outgoing, but she seemed to slip deeper into a depression every day. We felt we were losing her. She lost her will to live. She seemed to just want to die," Dennis said sadly.

"We tried to get her help but she refused. We thought about committing her to a hospital until she could recover but we put it off. We kept thinking she would come out of it. We were wrong," Janet added.

They said every time they would visit Mary the shades would be drawn shut and it would be so dark in her house. Mary would just sit in a chair or lay down most of the day. Things would be a mess everywhere. This was not the Mary everyone knew.

When they would come over, they would clean the house, leave food for her to eat, and open the shades, but the next day they would find them closed again. They also discovered she was throwing most of the food out.

One day Mary did not answer their calls so they rushed over. Janet continued, "We rang the doorbell but no one answered. The door was locked but we had a key. We went inside but she was not there. Her car was in the driveway, her wallet was on the dresser, and nothing was missing–except Mary."

They quickly reported her missing. Dennis explained, "She would never leave without telling someone because she knew we would worry."

I then learned that Mary was the first person of the nine to be reported missing in Abilene. But at the time, they had no idea she would be the first of many.

As I stood up to leave, Dennis added something I thought was significant. "When we went inside her house, everything was just like it usually was except for one thing–the shades were open."

Chapter 7

Dennis and Janet expressed to me their frustration over this case and the way it had been handled. They felt the investigators had not provided any plausible answers for them or the other families. They told me a few of the families had taken matters into their own hands.

The Smiths had joined together with some of the other families and hired private detectives. Three different detectives had been employed by this group over the past year, but none of them could uncover any clues as to what happened to their loved ones.

They said two families had gone to the extreme measure of hiring mediums who claimed the spirit world would uncover the whereabouts of their loved ones. But so far, the spirit world had remained mum.

Dogs were also employed to follow the scent of some of the missing people, but the handlers were amazed when the dogs started running around in circles after only a few moments. The dogs seemed as baffled as the investigators. It was as if these people vanished into thin air.

These futile attempts began to conjure up the idea of a possible alien abduction. Janet and Dennis were surprised many in this religious town started to believe that might be the explanation. These theories brought in their own weird proponents. UFO enthusiasts started showing up soon after these ideas leaked to the press. And there were other bizarre notions arising as well, like spontaneous combustion and people falling through worm holes. All of these theories sounded ridiculous, but there was no evidence to the contrary.

The Smiths told me Abilene had become a circus after the fourth person was reported missing. The religious fanatics seemed to crawl out of the woodwork from every part of the country. They preached their theories and beliefs to anyone who would listen. Some believed God took these people and some didn't, depending on which group you talked to. Some churches in town supported the fanatics, others didn't. It was chaotic.

They told me about one woman who held up a sign that made all the newspapers. It simply read, "This has God's fingerprints all over it." When a reporter asked her why she thought this, her reply was, "God has no fingerprints."

"These fanatics were hurting business in downtown Abilene and some of the businesses had to shut their doors until things calmed down," Janet explained. "Some businesses were demanding action to get these street-preachers and sign-carrying lunatics out of their area. Volunteer police had to be hired to help contain the pandemonium in Abilene."

"But it seems like things are starting to get back to normal finally. It has been a while since anyone has been reported missing. The drama is subsiding, as are the fanatics," Dennis concluded.

When Dennis finished his remarks, I knew the interview was done. I felt like they had given me exactly what I came for. They gave me valuable insight into what people were experiencing in Abilene since Mary and all the others had vanished. I appreciated their kindness and thanked them for their willingness to share their story with me.

When I got back to my room, I did a search on the various people who poured into Abilene when the reports about the missing were publicized. Footage posted on the internet revealed some of the strange people who came and there were many. I wondered if there might be a clue amidst all of this chaos.

Reading so many mysteries had taught me that the answer is often right in front of us, but everyone misses it because it is too obvious. Apparently everyone had missed it so far. I realized I had as good a chance as anyone to find that elusive clue. I became determined to at least try.

But in order to put some of the pieces together, I would need to talk to more of the families, which would also mean talking to Bardon. Because of my intense dislike of the man, he had become my greatest obstacle in pursuing this story. But the reality was painfully clear; if my story would have an ending, I needed Bardon. He appeared to be my only resource in getting in touch with the other families. It seems there is no justice in this life. I knew I was going to have to swallow my pride yet again.

I had swallowed my pride so often in the past; it wasn't that hard to get it down anymore. I didn't have much occasion to have any pride in myself. My father never had any pride in me. He knew I was being tormented by bullies because he would see my torn clothes and black eyes when I would come home from school. I would lie to him and tell him I fell down in PE, but I'm sure he knew what was really going on. He probably sympathized more with the bullies than he did with me. I think I could have handled the ridicule from my peers if my dad had been on my side.

My father always thought the worst about me, but my mother always thought the best. She was probably the only reason I survived those years. She worked as a secretary for a lawyer and often got home late. I could usually clean up enough before she got home, so that she wouldn't notice the black eyes or bruises. I didn't want her to worry about me. She was always so tired and I didn't want to add more stress to her life. When she got sick my junior year of high school, we then understood why she had been so tired.

My mother often told me how happy my father was when she told him he was having a boy. I could only imagine when that joy turned into shame as he slowly realized his son would not be making touchdowns or hitting homeruns.

If I had been able to play football or basketball or any ball in high school, my father would have been thrilled, but heaven decided not to bestow me with such attributes. I was too small to play football and too short for basketball. I had no athletic ability whatsoever. I did try to take up tennis, but no one would practice with me on the team, so I eventually just quit.

All of the sudden, my sad memories of my childhood were jolted from me as the rubber on my tire started flapping against the asphalt. I had been so lost in my thoughts, I wasn't paying attention to the road and probably ran over a nail or something.

I was on the corner of Butternut and South First, but I didn't see anything close by that was open. I managed to pull my car off the road and sat there wondering what to do next. I felt like a wimp since I really didn't know how to change a tire. I figured if I walked a little ways, I'd see a gas station or someone who could suggest a tire store.

As I started walking down Butternut, I tried to remember what might still be there from thirty years ago. I finally saw a building with a huge sign in front. It had letters on it, but no name. I wondered if it was some type of radio or TV station. There were a few cars parked out front, so I knocked on the door, but no one answered. Then I tried to open the door but it was locked. I rang the doorbell, hoping someone was there.

In a few seconds, a young woman came to the door and spoke through the speaker, asking me what she could do for me. I told her I was stranded on South 1st and was from out of town. She told me she would call a friend of hers who was a mechanic, and he would come and help me. She couldn't let me in because she had to go back on the air in a few seconds. I realized then it was a radio station.

While I waited outside for the mechanic, a cool Texas breeze blew through my hair and wafted over me. It was always a nice reprieve from the hot Texas days. It didn't take long for the mechanic to arrive. He drove up in a pickup and was a nice looking, friendly, young man. He told me his name was Tim, and I introduced myself. I told him I had a flat on

South 1st but wasn't very handy at changing tires. Tim told me to hop in his truck, and we drove to my car.

He got out his tools and started jacking up the car. I was embarrassed to be a middle aged man and not know how to change a flat. My dad had certainly never shown me how to do it and the one time I had tried, I ended up bending the rim of the car.

Tim looked in my trunk for a spare and fortunately, there was one in there. I'm not sure how it got there but I assume it was in there when I bought the car. Tim talked as he worked, and asked me about myself. I told him I used to live in Abilene, but had lived in Fort Worth for about thirty years. I told him I wrote for an on-line magazine and was doing a story about all the disappearances. Tim told me he couldn't believe what was happening in his hometown.

I asked him about himself and he told me he had lived in Abilene all his life. He had gone to the same high school I had. I told him I hoped he had a better experience in high school than I did. Tim confided he had some problems with bullies before he graduated. Some people had written crude posts about him on social media. But, he told me he had someone that helped him through those years.

It was apparent who he was referring to, so trying to be funny, I asked Tim, "Tell me, did that someone part the halls and make a path so you could walk through unscathed by your enemies?"

He laughed and said, "No, but He did help me to learn how to love my enemies and be kind to them." He went on to say, "Some of the meanest kids back then ended up becoming good friends of mine."

As he continued telling me what a saint he was, I thought to myself I wouldn't want any of the bullies I went to high school with to be friends of mine no matter what. I didn't want to prolong the conversation, so I thanked him and wanted to be on my way. I was hungry, tired, and didn't want to hear a sermon. I offered to pay him but he refused. He said, "My pleasure, Henry. If you need anything, feel free to call." Then he gave me his cell number. To be polite, I put it in my phone.

The young man was nice but naïve. I thanked him, and went on my way. I was grumpy and tired, so being kind was the last thing on my agenda. And I didn't need a lecture from someone half my age. If he wanted to be nice to mean people who did not deserve it, then he was a better man than I was.

My motel room looked very inviting after such a long, frustrating day. I left the TV on and put on the sleep timer so it would shut off in an hour. But if I had stayed awake a little longer, I would have heard that another person had just been reported missing—number ten.

Chapter 8

Sid called me at seven AM. "Have you heard the news?" he asked, with unusual excitement.

I groggily informed him I had not.

His excitement turned to irritation. "How can you be in the epicenter of the biggest story of the century and not know what is going on?"

At that point I was annoyed. "What are you talking about, Sid?"

"Another person was reported missing last night, Henry! I just assumed Sergeant Bardon might have let you know. I also assumed you might already be on this, finding out all you could before the rest of the media arrives. That was what I was hoping to hear, but obviously I was mistaken," he said with disappointment.

"Well you know what they say about those who assume," I replied. He didn't find that amusing, but it was the best I could come up with in the moment. I didn't want to tell him I was asleep when he called and hadn't listened to the news. I also didn't want to explain that his precious contact, Sergeant Bardon, was my long lost enemy. "I'll get on it now, Sid, I promise."

Sid was incredulous, "I'm finding this out with the rest of the world, Henry, when I should have found this out from you!" I didn't remember ever hearing him so angry. I assured him I was doing all I could. He told me—in no uncertain terms—I had better.

"We could have put this breaking news into our next edition which goes out tomorrow, Henry. It would have been perfect. We would have been one of the first to report on it. But now, we will just be one of many," he lamented. I knew I had failed Sid by not getting on the story as soon as the news came out, but there was little I could do at that point to rectify my blunder.

After being lambasted by my boss, I thought the day couldn't get any worse. I knew I had to call Bardon so I took a deep breath and made myself call him. He answered, "Bardon, can I help you?"

"Hi, Sergeant Bardon, it's Henry Pike. How are you today?"

"Not that great, Henry. Things are crazy here as you can imagine. I really can't talk. What do you need?" he said with some degree of irritation.

I tried not to convey how nervous I was. "I can only imagine what all of you are going through with another person disappearing. Was this someone you knew?"

"No, I did not know him personally. I knew who he was. He was...is a very prominent person in Abilene. He had been a dentist here a long time. Dr. Darby never returned home last night, and no one has seen him. He still might turn up, but considering all that's going on around here, I'm thinking the worst."

"I'm sure you're not the only one, Sergeant. Have the experts taken over the investigation?" I asked. I knew that was probably a sore spot with him because they had taken over all the cases months ago and the local police were not included in many of their efforts.

"What do you want, Henry? I have to go," he said abruptly.

"I'm sure you do, Sergeant Bardon, but I was wondering if you could help me to get in to see that other family you mentioned. One interview is not going to be enough for my story," I explained cautiously.

"Are you crazy, Pike? Do you not know what is going on here? Bedlam has broken lose on this town again and you're asking me to help you with some stupid story? I have more important things to do than hook you up with another family. How many more do you have to talk to before your story is done anyway?"

The way he spoke to me pushed every button I had, which apparently unlocked all of the anger I had stored up for years. This anger produced defiance in me that I didn't know I was capable of. Any fear I had of Bardon left as I boldly stated, "I want to talk to all of them, Bardon. If I get a chance to put all their stories together, I think I might be able to help them."

Bardon didn't say anything at first but then he burst out laughing. "You think *you* can help them?" he asked incredulously. "What fantasy are you living in, Pike? We have had the best minds in the world here trying to figure out what is going on, and you think you can do a better job than they have? Thanks for the laugh, Pike."

Bardon continued expressing his contempt for me, "By the way, Henry, I looked you up in the high school year book and I remembered who you were in high school. You were a pathetic loser back then and it doesn't look like you've changed much. Go home, Pike. You left Abilene a long time ago so what happens here doesn't concern you. You're not welcome here anymore."

With that, he hung up. I felt the sting of his words. He obviously had not changed, either. He was still a condescending bully. I wasn't sure why I had been so daring in what I said to Bardon, but it did feel great to stand up to him for once. It was like a shot of adrenaline.

But the high quickly wore off as I considered my plight. My job was on the line and I had just lost the best connection I had. I should have kept my mouth shut. When would I ever learn? It never pays to stand up to a bully.

Chapter 9

After my interchange with Bardon, I wondered if I had any options left. The option which made the most sense was to just pack it in and leave. I had lost my only connection in Abilene, and I had been told to leave town by a police officer.

The thought of telling Sid was not pleasant. I knew how mad he'd be at me for giving up. Then I thought about how mad I'd be at myself for giving up. And then I thought about the little girl in my dream. What if she was the little girl who was missing? What if she really was crying out to me for help?

My conversation with Bardon kept playing over and over in my head. I thought of the things he said to me and of all the things I should have said back to him. I was never good at thinking on my feet and usually cowered under the words of strong, belligerent people. I couldn't believe my horrible luck that Bardon was my only connection in Abilene. The cosmic forces seemed to always be against me.

Bardon was doing the very same thing to me he did in high school; he was ruining my life and I was letting him. If I let him get his way this time, I would never forgive myself. I knew I had to stand up to him if I was ever going to have any self-respect at all. He had slammed the 'locker door' in my face for the last time.

I felt empowered by these thoughts, and decided I would stay in Abilene for as long as it took to get the stories I needed. I knew the whole idea was a long shot, but what did I have to lose?

After making the decision to stay, I had to make a plan on how to proceed. The first thing I needed to do was buy a new tire for my car. I looked in the phone book and found a tire store close by. While they were putting the new tire on my car, I tried to call Dennis and Janet. After calling them several times with no answer, I decided to just show up on their doorstep. They answered the bell after looking out their window and seeing it was me. They seemed glad to see me and invited me in. I was relieved.

They immediately asked me if I had heard the news about the latest person missing, and I could honestly say I had this time. I asked them if they knew the dentist, Dr. Darby. They seemed surprised, and asked me how I knew his name because they had not yet released his identity. I told them Sergeant Bardon told me. It was the perfect answer because it was true and gave the appearance he was still on my side.

It seemed we were off to a good start, so I decided to take a chance and tell them what I was hoping to accomplish by seeing them again. I told them about the dream I had about the little girl. I told them how it had impacted me to the point of wanting to do anything I could to help find the missing people.

They were intrigued by the dream. They both felt it held significance as I described how the little girl was trapped and was begging me to help her. I tried to convey the compassion I felt for her.

I concluded by saying, "My heart was pounding and I woke up drenched in sweat. The dream seemed so real. I could not shake the effect it had on me and that was when I decided I needed to do more than just write about the missing; I want to help you find them. I think that could happen if I had the chance to talk to the other families. With their stories, I can hopefully put all the pieces together and figure out what happened to them."

Then I told them the story of the serial killer in Dallas, and how I had helped solve that crime. I told them I had always been good at solving mysteries and had thought about becoming a detective. I assumed the more they knew about me, the more they would trust me.

Dennis looked at me like I was crazy, and asked incredulously, "What are you saying, Henry? Do you really believe you could do a better job than all these experts with all their modern technology and scientific methods? We have had some pretty impressive people here trying to figure out what happened to our loved ones."

At that moment Janet interrupted him and said, "And they haven't got a clue. They haven't found hide or hair of these people, Dennis. What would we have to lose if Henry tried to figure this out? He certainly couldn't do any worse."

I appreciated Janet stepping in and supporting me. I continued my request. "I'm asking for a chance to try, but I can't do it without your help. I doubt any of the other families would talk to me without your assurance that I'm not a typical reporter just trying to get a story. They need to understand I want to help them."

He and his wife looked at each other and then at me. Janet looked in my eyes and said with all the sincerity she could muster, "We'll help you, Henry. I just know you were sent here for a reason. I told Dennis that the first time I met you. You are the only one who has ever really wanted to help us. And that dream you had is like a confirmation to me."

Dennis was shaking his head like he still wasn't sure, but I was amazed she believed in me. This woman, I didn't even know, thought I was sent to help them. This was certainly a new experience for me.

I asked Janet what she thought I should do next. She told me not to worry. She would try to contact the other families and then get back to me. I hoped it was before Sergeant Bardon talked to them. If he did get to them first, Janet would probably change her mind about me being a godsend.

There was no doubt; Bardon would do anything he could to stop this effort if he found out about it. My only hope was she, and hopefully Dennis, would connect me with the others before Bardon discovered our plan. I had to avoid him long enough to talk to these families, and then I could be on my way.

With Bardon looming in my head, I tried to impress on Dennis and Janet the sense of urgency I felt. I knew at any minute Bardon could burst in and ruin this thing for me. If he found me anywhere near these people, there was no telling what he might do. A locker might seem tame compared to a jail cell.

Chapter 10

I t had been two days since I had spoken to Dennis and Janet. After I left their home, I felt encouraged because they seemed onboard with my plan to talk to the other families. But I hadn't heard anything from them since. I could only think the worst. I had probably blown everything by alienating Bardon. I could only imagine what he would say to Dennis and Janet if they told him about our plan—my plan.

While waiting to hear from them, I watched TV, slept, and ate fast food for breakfast, lunch and dinner. I knew I was going to gain weight if I kept up that lifestyle. On the third day, I couldn't stand it any longer and had to get out of my room. I didn't know where I was going, but I had to go somewhere. My biggest concern was that I might run into Bardon.

I decided to eat breakfast like a human, so I went to a restaurant on Interstate 20. As I ate breakfast, I read the newspaper while keeping one eye peeled on the door, in case Bardon might walk in. I realized I might be worrying too much about running into him. I had a right to stay in my hometown. I hadn't done anything wrong, but I knew he could make my life miserable if he found out I was still in Abilene.

After finishing breakfast, I decided to drive around Abilene again. I thought about going to the mall. I had never been to the Abilene Mall, since it was built after I graduated. I would have liked to walk through it and see all the stores, but thought it might be too risky to be around a lot of people.

When I was young, there was only one small mall in Abilene called Westgate. It had your basic stores, and I went there often with my mom. Our small mall was totally adequate for all our shopping needs, but there were families in Abilene who were more well-to-do, who went to Dallas to do their shopping.

As a boy, my favorite store was Thornton's Department Store. This store had everything you could think of. They had clothes, toys, tools and TV's. The first color TV I ever saw was there. I stood in amazement as I watched TV in living color. I knew my father was too frugal to ever buy one. I was thankful we even had a black and white model.

But the best thing about Thornton's was Christmas. This store knew how to make childhood dreams come alive at Christmas time. They always made sure Santa came to Abilene in style. I got to see Santa come to town on several occasions. Once, he came on a fire engine with its sirens blazing, and another year he came on a helicopter. It was always exciting to see how Santa would arrive each year. His entrance never ceased to delight the children and the parents.

Thornton's always had great window displays at Christmas which could have competed with any of the ones in New York City. Going to see their holiday decorations was a family tradition for everyone. It was truly a magical place.

The store was famous for saying their address after their name—"Thornton's 4th and Oak." That famous address now belonged to the Abilene Police Department where I met with Bardon. The magic was definitely gone.

It was interesting seeing the new places in Abilene. I drove down South 1st and fondly remembered a pizza place that used to be on that street. The entrance looked like a cave on the outside and it was pretty dark inside, too. I would often imagine bats hanging from the ceiling as we ate. It was a very unique restaurant back then. I loved that place.

As I continued my journey down South 1st, I didn't see many stores or places I recognized. I took the Winters Freeway exit and headed towards the Abilene Mall. This part of Abilene had really built up since I had lived there. It was almost like a different town. This appeared to be where most of the new stores and restaurants were. I sailed right pass the mall and took the exit for Buffalo Gap.

There are several small towns on the outskirts of Abilene, but Buffalo Gap was always my favorite. I had gone to their historical village several times as a kid on school trips. I had also gone there a few years ago to cover their famous Chili Cook-off. Even though it was close to Abilene I didn't have to go there, I just drove to Buffalo Gap for the day and then turned around and went home. It was seven hours of driving but it was worth it, even though I had heartburn for a week. Those cowboys sure had a lot of fun making their chili and it was pretty good to boot.

After driving around Buffalo Gap, which took about three minutes, I tried to think of somewhere else to go. It seemed like I had all the time in the world, but nothing to fill it with. Driving around Abilene and the surrounding area was not offering the distraction I had hoped. I started thinking about my last visit with Dennis and Janet and replaying my conversation with them. Didn't they remember I said it was urgent for me to talk to the others?

As hard as I tried, I could not stop my imagination from thinking the worst. And the worst case scenario would be Bardon talking to Dennis and Janet. I could only imagine what he would say to them: "Don't talk to that guy, Henry. He's a pathetic loser. His nickname in high school was 'Putrid Pike' if that tells you anything. We knew back then, he would never amount to anything."

I replayed those words over and over in my mind. Bardon was probably right; I was a pathetic loser. Who was I kidding thinking I could solve this case? I would be lucky if I could finish the article I came to do.

It looked like the bully from my past may have beaten me again.

Chapter 11

The suspense of wondering why The Smiths had not called was killing me. I finally gave in and called them. The call did little to alleviate my anxiety because they didn't answer. I should have been grateful because I would have sounded desperate if they had. While I listened to their message, I took deep breaths before I calmly said, "Hi, this is Henry Pike. I had hoped to have heard something from you by now. Let me know if there are any problems with what we talked about. I do hope to hear from you soon. Thank you."

Then all I could do was sit back and wait to hear from them. With each hour that passed, I grew more anxious and paranoid. The only explanation of why they hadn't called had to be Bardon. I was becoming obsessed with what he might have said to them. I had to do something to fill my time.

Out of the blue, the idea of bowling rolled into my head. It was one of the few things I was good at when I was younger. I used to go to the VFW bowling lanes when I was a child. My dad was a veteran, so if he ever did anything remotely fun, it was going to the VFW. Occasionally, we had even bowled a few games together, but it never ended up being a good father/son memory.

My father seemed to delight in pointing out every little thing wrong with my bowling techniques, as well as everything else I did. Sometimes his criticism would escalate if he was in a bad mood, "Your eye-hand coordination is terrible. You got that from your mother's side. You are both awkward and clumsy. You're certainly no athlete and you can't even bowl." Never one to mince words, my dad just spoke whatever happened to glide into his brain. And his thoughts were never positive.

I never expected to be a great bowler, or anything else for that matter. But, when I'd go bowling without my dad— like on a rare night out with a friend— I was pretty good.

As I remembered how I used to enjoy bowling, I decided it might be fun to do it again. I realized Bardon might be a bowler, but if I went during the day, he would most likely be at work. I decided to take the risk.

Then it occurred to me I was still letting a bully rule my life even to the smallest detail like whether to go bowling or not. This made me angry. I was a grown, middle-aged man, still afraid of a bully from my childhood. It was pathetic. I decided then and there, I would no longer worry about Bardon and go wherever I wanted to go.

So I went bowling. Unfortunately, the VFW bowling alley was not there anymore, but I remembered another bowling alley I had gone to a few times when I was in high school. I was happy to see it was still there so I went inside. It was like walking back in time for me.

No one was at the counter when I walked in, so I decided to walk around the familiar lanes. I looked up on the walls where pictures hung of those who had once graced those lanes in years past. This was Abilene's legacy of superior bowlers. There were several who had managed to accomplish the elusive "300 Game". As I scanned the names, the only one I recognized was Michael Oden.

Michael was a few years younger than me, so I didn't know him personally. But I had seen him bowl several times in a few local tournaments and he was an exceptional bowler.

I would never forget one night as I was getting ready to play a game, I saw he was actually in the lane next to me. It made me a little nervous to play next to someone who was so accomplished.

After my third frame, he walked over to me and asked if he could give me a pointer. I told him I'd be honored if he had any suggestions for me. He showed me the right way to hold my hand, and how to follow through as I released the ball. I bowled three strikes after that. This guy knew what he was talking about, and it was so nice for him to take a few minutes to help me. I would never forget his kindness.

I was impressed and happy for him when I heard he went pro a few years later. He seemed like a nice guy, so I was rooting for him. But then I saw his obituary on-line a few years later, and was surprised to learn he had died so young. He was only 46. It made me very sad.

As I continued to walk around, I felt a familiarity emanating from the bowling alley. It was the first place I had gone inside where I had actually spent some time as a young boy. I was surprised to find it was a nice feeling.

The man returned to the counter and saw me wandering around. He asked if he could help me, and I asked if I could bowl a few games. He teasingly said, "I believe we could arrange that." I chuckled. He asked me if I was from around Abilene, and I decided to risk telling him why I was there.

He asked me if I had talked to Bill Major. I looked at him with a puzzled look and he went on to say, "Bill's son, Elias, was reported missing about 3 months ago." I remembered reading about this young man on the list Sid had given me.

The man started telling me about Elias. "That boy loved to bowl. He came in a lot and was pretty good. I think he might have been one of the best in Abilene. His father, Bill, would often come in to watch him. We became friendly over time. The man is so heartbroken since Elias went missing. He's called here a few times to see if I have heard anything, and asked me to call him if I ever did. It's so sad what's going on in the world today."

I told him I had not talked to Bill but would certainly like to. I asked him if he had Bill's number, and was surprised when he readily gave it to me. It occurred to me to ask him if I could use the phone there. It was a smart move because Bill immediately picked up when he recognized the number.

Bill seemed hopeful when he answered. I knew it was a deceitful move on my part to use the bowling alley phone. I tried to calmly explain who I was, "Hello, sir. My name is Henry Pike, and I was just talking to the manager here at the bowling alley. He was telling me what a special boy Elias is and what a good bowler he is. (I was being careful not to use any past tense words) He said you would often come in and watch him bowl. I used to come here and bowl, too, when I was in high school."

He still hadn't responded. I knew I would lose him soon if I didn't quit beating around the bush and tell him what I wanted. "I was wondering, sir, if you would consider meeting me and tell me more about your son. I have already talked to one family here who has a loved one missing. You see, I am writing an article about them. I was hoping you might allow me to write something about Elias." Then I held my breath.

He seemed somewhat hesitant, but he finally agreed to see me. "I guess we could meet. How about one o'clock tomorrow?" We agreed to meet at a fast food place near his house. I couldn't believe how well that worked out. Apparently I didn't need Bardon to get this story. I was glad my urge to go bowling had worked out so well.

The manager took my money and told me what lane I'd be bowling in. After putting on the cheesy shoes and finding the perfect ball, I bowled one of the best games of my life. After I finished the second game, I was feeling pretty good about myself.

I had a bite to eat and then, with great boldness, I went to the Abilene Mall.

The mall was nicer than I expected. There were stores I recognized, though I had done little shopping in my lifetime. As I walked around looking at the nicely dressed people, I realized it wouldn't hurt to improve my appearance.

I went into a department store and looked for some nice slacks and shirts. The lady was very helpful, putting together a few combinations for me. I went into the dressing room to try them on. Before I could close the door to my stall, someone ran past me so quickly it was like a blur. It startled me because

I knew logically no one could move that fast. I went into the stall and started to undress but I couldn't quit thinking about the weird thing I had just seen. It was unsettling, so I decided to just purchase the items without the effort of seeing how they'd look on my skinny frame.

The lady was surprised I didn't want to try them on, so I gave her some flimsy excuse that I had to be somewhere soon. I asked if she had seen anyone rush out of the dressing rooms. She looked at me puzzled and said, "You were the only one in there, sir." She then looked at me strangely and said, "You look as white as a ghost, sir. Are you ok?"

I caught a glimpse of myself in a mirror nearby and realized she was right. I left feeling eerie about whatever it was I had just seen.

The sun was hot and I was tired after my brief shopping spree. I went through a drive-in and got an iced tea and felt much better. As I sat in my air conditioned car, I wondered what I should do with the rest of the day. The only thought that came to me was to park somewhere close to Dennis and Janet's house and see if Bardon or someone else might show up. It would be like an impromptu stake out. It seemed like a good idea at the time.

Chapter 12

I t was around five PM when I decided to do the stake out at Dennis and Janet's house. I figured they would be home since it was dinner time. I would have loved to join them for dinner. It had been a long time since I'd had a home cooked meal, but I doubted they would be giving me an invitation. I went back through the drive-in and got another fast food meal.

After arriving about a block from their house, I settled in to eat my greasy feast. Their car was in the driveway, so I would wait and see if they went anywhere or if anyone came to see them. It was kind of fun at first. But after two long, boring hours, the novelty had worn off. I was weary of the stake out and the thought of sitting in my air conditioned motel room grew more appealing by the minute. And I needed to go to the bathroom.

Then another uncomfortable thought came to mind. What if someone saw me sitting outside on their street for hours, and decided to report a strange car in the neighborhood. I could just picture a police cruiser coming by and asking me for ID. It wouldn't take long for Bardon to find out I was still in town.

Just as I was about to give up, they came out of the house. They looked around like they were suspicious someone was watching them. I slumped down in my seat as they got in their car.

When they backed out and started down the street, I turned on the car and inched forward hoping they wouldn't notice me. I could see they made a left turn, so I waited a minute before I made the left. I didn't see them at first because they had sped up, but I caught up to them and saw them turn onto the Winters Freeway.

The freeway made it easier to keep an eye on their car because of the flat terrain. I could stay far enough behind to see them from a good distance. I also had the advantage of being on a well-traveled highway so they would not notice me, but that advantage soon ended when they took the Potosi exit.

It would be harder to remain inconspicuous on the Potosi road since it was less traveled. The darkness had settled in and I knew my headlights could be a problem as I tried to keep them in view. I wasn't sure what to do because I realized they would eventually figure out I was following them. We were the only two on the road at that point. So at the next house, I turned into the driveway.

After sitting there a few seconds, I turned off my lights and backed out. I knew it was dangerous to drive that way but I had no choice. I caught up to them and kept them in sight. Several miles down the road, they turned on to another road. I saw the dust churn up behind their backlights and realized the road wasn't paved.

A few minutes later, I saw their car turn into a small parking lot. There was just enough light to see a few cars in the lot with a little building next to it that looked like an old church with a short, broken steeple on top.

Since I knew their destination, I could find a spot to leave my car and walk down there. I pulled into a recess just past the road they turned down to the church. That way, if anyone else was coming, they hopefully wouldn't notice my car. I cautiously walked towards the building to see what was happening there.

The night sky suddenly grew darker as clouds covered the stars. My biggest concern, as I carefully inched my way to the building, were rattlesnakes as they tend to be out at night. I walked slowly towards the little building. When I got closer, I could see the building looked a little dilapidated. I was surprised anyone would go inside. There was a faint light glowing in the windows.

As I was about to try and peer into the window, two bright lights started coming towards me. I got down quickly, hoping no one saw me. Then, I heard a car pull up into the gravel parking lot. I stayed down which was good because within the next minute, another car pulled up and then another one.

After a few minutes, I got up and realized my hand was bleeding. I had hit the ground so hard one of the rocks cut my hand. I had nothing to put on it, so I hoped it would stop soon.

The windows were low enough I could look inside if I stood on my tiptoes. I slowly rose up to get a view of what was happening inside. I could not imagine what type of meeting would be going on in this dilapidated church in the middle of nowhere.

As I looked inside, I could see about twenty people sitting around a table. There was a small lantern on the table, which eerily illuminated all their faces. I couldn't tell what they were doing, but it gave me the creeps.

Chills were starting to go up and down my spine as I considered what kind of meeting this might be. Then out of the depths of the night, I heard a scream that did not originate from this world. It made my heart stop. I plopped quickly down on my stomach, hoping no one heard me gasp.

The light went out in the church which made it even darker outside. I crawled on my hands and knees as fast as I could on the gravel, which hurt a lot. As soon as I got to the road, I started running. I wasn't sure what was going on, but I was not going to stay to find out.

As I fled to my car, I stumbled in the dark several times. By the time I reached my car, I had several cuts on my hands, torn my pants and my knee was bleeding. Even so, everything would have been OK, except for the unbelievable fact—my car wouldn't start.

Chapter 13

The car made a clicking noise each time I tried to start the ignition. I couldn't believe what was happening. It had never happened before. As I desperately pleaded with my car to start, the few horror movies I had seen replayed through my imagination in vivid color. I kept looking in my rear view mirror to see if any zombies were coming to pull me out of the car.

It was apparent the car was not going to start. That was not good. As I pondered my situation, I realized I might be spending the night in my car. The thought of being out in the dark, in the middle of nowhere, was not acceptable. There had to be someone who could at least come and get me, but I wasn't sure I could even tell them how to find me.

I thought about calling the police. They could probably find me using the GPS signal on my phone. But after calming down and thinking about it rationally, I knew Sergeant Bardon would find out. So, I scratched that off the list.

Then Tim, the mechanic, who helped when I had a flat tire, came to mind. He gave me his number and I had fortunately put it in my phone. He would probably be my best option. I did feel bad asking him to come out so late to wherever I was, but he said to call him anytime.

Unfortunately, when I tried to call him, the dreaded words popped up on my phone—NO SERVICE. Of course, why should I have service out in the middle of nowhere when I really needed it? And then the final, horrible realization came—my battery was very low. My phone would soon die and I couldn't recharge it. As I realized my phone would soon die, I wondered if I might, too. Then I really panicked.

As I slumped down in my seat in despair, I knew I had to do something. I couldn't just sit in my car all night. I wondered if I should ask the people in the church to help me. As I thought about it, I knew it would ruin any chance I had to get an interview with them, since Dennis and Janet would realize I had followed them there. And I wasn't sure I wanted their help, since I had no idea what they were doing in that creepy meeting.

As I sat in my car trying to figure out what to do, I decided I could put my situation to some good use. I knew a good reporter would go back and watch the church. Perhaps if I stayed longer than a few minutes, I could figure out what they were up to. I gathered my wits about me, and went back to the road leading down to the church. I could see they had put the lantern back on. I decided I was close enough and watched the church from a safe distance.

I checked the time before turning off my phone to save the battery. It was 9:33. I wondered how long satanic cults usually meet.

It seemed like another half hour or so, before I saw anything happen. The light went out inside and lights were coming on in the parking lot. I watched as each car left and then headed up the road towards me. They couldn't see me because I was standing off to the side and it was dark. But just to be sure I hid behind a Mesquite tree. They didn't all leave at once. One would leave and then a few minutes later, another car would leave. It was like at an airport where the planes are spaced a few minutes apart.

After the last car left, I hurried back to my car. I didn't want to be outside all alone. But just as I was about to get in my car, I looked up and saw the clouds dissipate. It was like the heavenly curtains had parted to reveal the vast Texas sky. There had to be millions of twinkling stars stretched out across the heavens. I had never seen anything so beautiful. My fear vanished as I gazed into the sky. The sight took my breath away. I hesitated to get in the car because I just wanted to take it all in. I wished I had decided to include the moon roof when I bought my car.

But reality soon set in, as it always does, and I didn't want to be standing out there all alone, so I got in the car. I tried the ignition once again but the car still wouldn't start. I had to accept the fact I would be there all night. At least I didn't have to worry about freezing to death. I cracked the window a very little bit and laid down in the back seat. The best way I could pass the time would be to sleep. I would turn my phone back on in the morning and call someone, hopefully.

As I tried to get comfortable, I couldn't help but wonder what kind of weird meeting Dennis and Janet and those people sitting around the table were having? Was it some kind of cult? Hopefully, no sacrifices were required. This might be another story I could get while in Abilene. Maybe I had uncovered something no one else knew about. My mind was starting to race. And, just maybe, this secretive group had something to do with all the missing people?

After spending at least an hour turning and wiggling so I could find some comfortable position in my mid-sized sedan's back seat, I finally drifted off to a fitful sleep.

It seemed I was asleep only for a few minutes when I was suddenly awakened by something banging on my car door. My mind started racing as I tried to contain the terror that was inching its way into my heart. I slowly rose up and looked through every window but no one was there. I tried to peer down to the ground to see if someone was on the ground, but I couldn't see anyone or anything.

Something was hitting my car and it was getting louder. My heart was racing as I frantically kept looking through each window hoping to catch a glimpse of the culprit, but there was nothing but blackness. I realized someone could be under my car, but there was no way I was opening my door to find out.

Then the scratching started. It sounded like something sharp was going back and forth etching its horror onto my car's exterior. And with each nerve wracking scratch, my panic was becoming uncontrollable. I didn't know how much more I could take before having a heart attack.

I fumbled around looking for my phone because I was calling for help. It took forever for it to come on and when it did, I could see it was 5:33 in the morning. I punched in 911 but the message NO SERVICE popped up again. I had forgotten there was no service. I tried again hoping it might work in an emergency but it didn't.

The panic was growing and thoughts were flooding my mind that this was it for me. I could vividly imagine being disemboweled by some dessert monster only to be found by a wicked cult the next day. Or maybe I would never be found and my name would be added to the growing list of the missing. Perhaps this was the terrifying monster capturing all those who were missing. Did he eat them and leave nothing behind? All I knew for sure was I didn't want to be 'number eleven'.

Even though I didn't really believe in God, I figured He might be the only one who could hear me out in the middle of the wilderness, so I desperately screamed with all I had, "God, please help me!"

My eyes were shut tight as I let out my plea. As I shuddered from my fear, I noticed the scratching had stopped. Perhaps my scream had scared it away? I was afraid to open my eyes to see what I might face. But as I slowly forced my eyes to open, I saw there was a faint light in the sky and a man was tapping on my window. It was light enough to see his face. He was an older man who wore a brimmed hat from the last century. He didn't look dangerous, so I rolled the window down just enough to talk to him.

"Howdy there, mister. Are you OK?" he asked. "I was driving into town this morning and I saw your car on the side of the road. I wanted to check that everything was OK?" he said with his very strong Texas drawl.

I couldn't think of a time I had ever been more glad to see someone. He seemed to be a normal enough person, so I decided I could trust him. I opened the car door and got out. I told him, "Yes, I'm OK, but I don't know what's wrong with my car. I was driving out here last night and got lost. When I stopped to check my GPS, my car died."

He just stared at me and I knew he was wondering what I was doing out there. I told him I thought it might be the battery, so he walked to his truck to see if he had his jumper cables with him.

As I watched him walk to his truck, the horrible memory of the banging and scratching came back to me. I walked around the car looking for the ugly scratch marks that a key or a tool—or a claw—might have made. As I studied my car from one end to the other I saw that, other than being caked with dust, it had no scratches on it and no dents. How could that be? Did I imagine it—or dream it? I was beginning to think the stress of the story was getting to me.

The old man cleared his throat and I realized I had been so caught up in my car's condition, I had temporarily forgotten about him. I told him it had been a long night and I was very tired.

He told me he couldn't find any jumper cables in his truck, but motioned towards my driver's seat like he wanted to give it a try. I nodded that he could get in. I gave him the key and he put it into the ignition. It started like a dream. He revved it up a few times and then looked at me like I was stupid. I said sarcastically under my breath, "Maybe all it needed was a good night's sleep."

I felt like a fool and wondered if the old man believed anything I had just told him. I thanked him and offered to pay him, but he refused. He told me he was just glad to help.

As he walked off, it occurred to me he might know something about the church down the road. I asked him what kind of congregation met there. He turned around with an irritated look and asked, "What church are you talking about?" I pointed down to the area where the church was. He replied, "Nobody has used that building in over fifty years."

Chapter 14

The old man walked off shaking his head. I felt foolish asking him about the church, but apparently he had no idea it was still being used. I called out and thanked him again for helping me, but he just waved without turning around.

I got in my running car and was thrilled to leave that crazy place. The first thing I did was plug my phone in to the charger. I couldn't imagine how people ever survived without them.

As much as I hated to, I knew I should take a closer look at the church. I had to see if I could find anything to indicate what kind of meeting they were having. I drove into the parking lot of the church but kept my engine running. I was nervous about getting out, but I wasn't going to learn much sitting in my car.

The building was even more dilapidated than it appeared the night before. I walked around the perimeter first and could see parts of the outside walls were missing. I went past one of the windows and saw blood on a rock next to the wall. It made me nervous until I remembered it was probably mine.

After closer observation, It looked like the building was about to fall down, and I couldn't believe all of those people were willing to risk their safety to meet there. But I was about to risk mine, too, because I knew I had to go inside.

I walked back around to the front door and went up the broken steps into the church. The front door opened into a small foyer. There was a small open closet near the entrance. The most noticeable item in the open closet was a shovel. It had obviously been used because there was dirt caked on it. Right next to it were some rubber boots and a crumpled pair of gloves on the floor. I had to wonder what they had been used for—to dig a hole for dead animals which had been sacrificed or maybe to dig a grave.

The rest of the foyer was just old and dusty. One of the doors to the sanctuary was leaning by the wall and the other was propped open. I walked inside where there were old, broken down pews, and some chairs strewn about. It certainly didn't look like a meeting had taken place there the night before.

I walked over to the broken down podium and stood behind it. I tried to imagine the pastor standing there pleading with the country folk to get right with God before it was too late.

As I looked around, I saw a table leaning against the side wall. It was a folding table from this century. This must have been the table they had been using. Then on a shelf nearby, I saw a lantern. I took it down and could tell there was some oil in it. The table and lamp would indicate I did not imagine the night before. After the dreams I had been having the last few nights, I was getting a little foggy on what was real and what wasn't.

The chairs were a mystery though. All of the people seemed to be seated, but there didn't appear to be enough useable chairs in the building to seat everyone. And the pews were as rotten and broken as the building itself so I couldn't imagine anyone sitting on them.

The church seemed like an unlikely place for so many people to gather. I could see high school kids hanging out there or young kids daring each other to go in the scary church. But for adults to come inside this place and have an actual meeting was bizarre. There had to be a reason for their great secrecy and willingness to risk their lives to meet there.

At that point, I decided I had tarried long enough in the abandoned church. I also wanted to be sure my car was still running. I jumped in and took off, glad to leave the creepy church and the terrifying night behind.

The first stop I made when I got into the City limits was a fast food restaurant. I was starving and very thirsty after being trapped in my car all night. I couldn't wait to take a shower and clean all the dirt and blood off of me from the night before.

I had hoped to do some research after cleaning up but I was just too tired. I needed a nap so I would be more coherent for my one o'clock appointment with Bill. I had to hope he would give me something I could use for my article.

Then it occurred to me, he might have been at the church. I knew I couldn't ask him because then he and the others would know I followed Dennis and Janet out there. But somehow, I had to find out the secret that called those people there. I was pretty sure it had to be connected to the missing people in Abilene.

Chapter 15

Bill stood up to shake my hand when he realized I was his one o'clock appointment. I asked him if he wanted to get a hamburger or something and he said he might like some ice cream instead. That sounded really good, so I joined him.

We sat for a few minutes licking our ice cream as it dripped down the cones. I felt a little lost for words. The best icebreaker I could come up with was to tell him I had grown up a few blocks from where we were sitting. That seemed to put him at ease. He asked what it was like for me growing up in Abilene. I told him it had its ups and downs, but I didn't elaborate.

He told me he and his family had moved to Abilene from Mineral Wells when his children were young. "Elias was just starting first grade when we moved so it worked out well for him. My oldest son was in fifth grade by then, so it was a little harder for him to readjust to a new school. But it didn't take him long to make friends because he joined the band and the football team. They sure had a lot of activities for an elementary school."

"My daughter got involved in the choir and loved it. They really put on some great shows for us. Elias was never as involved but he loved his teachers."

Bill seemed more at ease when I told him, "I went to Taylor, too, when I was a boy. It is a great school."

He continued, "I lost my wife a few years ago. I didn't think I could survive losing her, but I did, and Elias was one of the reasons. He moved in with me soon after his mother died. He never wanted to go to college and that was fine with me. I don't think everyone has to go to college. Elias' brother and sister went and they ended up doing something entirely different from what they majored in. All that money down the drain." He shook his head in frustration.

Bill went on with the historical account of his life, "I never went to college myself and I did OK. My wife and I had to work hard for a while but we got by. We had a nice house and two cars. What more does anyone need?"

I asked him what he did for a living. He said he was a retired postman. "I became a postman in Mineral Wells, and then transferred to the Abilene Post Office. It was a great place to work. I met the nicest people on my routes. Never had any problems—no disgruntled customers and no dogs ever chased me," he chuckled.

Bill paused for a moment and said, "Henry, I don't want to bore you to death with my life. I just don't get out much anymore, and it sure is nice to have someone to talk to."

I assured him that was why I came. He said, "That's mighty nice of you to say, but I know you'd rather hear about Elias." He was right, but I wasn't bored listening to him. He seemed like a lonely man who needed a friend. I could relate.

Bill continued, "Elias is a good boy. He did get into drugs for a short spell. He started smoking that marijuana nonsense in high school. I didn't realize it until a policeman brought him home one night and told me that he caught him and two other boys smoking in a park. He said he wouldn't press charges but would the next time he caught him. I was grateful for that and told Elias he was going to have to change his ways. He didn't."

"I found out a few months later he was into some harder drugs, and it broke my heart. I just couldn't understand why he was doing this when his brother and sister never did. I think it broke my wife's heart too. It wasn't too long after we discovered the extent of his addiction that she had a heart attack. She hung on for a few days. Elias was so upset. He spent nearly every moment with her before she died. I think he might have blamed himself for her stress, and I would have to say, it probably was what did her in. I know she would never want him to think that, but I know he did anyway," Bill said sadly.

Bill seemed like he was about to get choked up, but caught himself and went on, "Elias really changed after his mom died. He moved back in with me. He stopped hanging out with those friends who were a bad influence on him. It seemed to me he was trying to start over. I thought everything was going to be OK." He smiled, but I knew it was to mask his sadness.

"Not long after he moved back in, he started bowling again," Bill explained. "When Elias was in junior high, he learned how to bowl from a leader in his youth group. He was pretty good at it and he seemed to enjoy it. He was never good at football or baseball, so I think it made him feel good about himself to do something well." I shook my head in affirmation because I could understand.

Bill continued, "He met some nice guys there and they formed a league. He went at least twice a week and he really enjoyed it. I would go down and watch him whenever I could."

Tears were forming in his eyes as he continued talking about his son. "I was so proud of him and told him several times. He didn't seem to like it when I'd compliment him, but I wanted him to know. One night, I went to his apartment to ask him something, but he wasn't there. I searched everywhere for him but he was nowhere to be found. I called some of his friends and no one had seen him or had any idea where he might be. I waited until about three in the morning, and then I called the police."

"I'm not sure, but I think there were about five people declared missing by then. I didn't even think about that when I called them, but it was the first thing the police thought. They didn't waste any time coming. They went through his room and his car, but didn't find anything they thought was significant. I was kind of relieved because I sometimes wondered if he had completely given up the drugs," Bill explained.

"But the thing that didn't make any sense was that he had packed a small bag like he was going on a short trip. He hadn't told me anything about going anywhere. His wallet and his keys were on his dresser and his car was still in the driveway, but he was nowhere to be found," Bill said.

After Bill said this, I thought of Mary and how they found her keys and purse in her home and her car in the driveway. It was like they both just vanished out of their homes.

"The police looked through his bag briefly, but didn't find anything. They interviewed all of his friends and anyone Elias had ever known. Nothing. Not one single person had any idea he was planning a trip or could even guess where he might be. Why would he not tell anyone?" He asked like he thought I would know the answer.

As Bill finished telling me everything he could think of about Elias, I asked him if it would be alright if I looked through his apartment and his overnight bag. He seemed surprised but agreed to let me. I told him he could watch me and he told me that wasn't necessary, but I insisted. I knew he was relieved since he didn't know me.

Bill told me to follow him to his house. He didn't live too far from where we met. We pulled up to a nice house and he showed me where Elias' apartment was as we stood in front of his home. They had turned the garage into an apartment many years before when Bill's mother was unable to live alone. She had lived there for around eight years before she passed away.

I asked him how long Elias had lived there. He told me he had lived in the apartment about two years. "It was right after Elias' mother died when he moved back in with me. He told me he'd rather pay rent to me than to somebody he didn't know. I think he did it because he was trying to get away from those friends of his who were a bad influence. I was glad for whatever reason he decided to move back in. It was nice having him close. It seemed like Elias was finally getting his life together, and then he was gone."

Bill asked me to come inside. The house was nice, but musty. The curtains were drawn shut and it felt depressing inside. It seemed like a typical home where a lonely man would live —things thrown about, dishes in the sink, and dust everywhere. It made me feel at home, unfortunately.

He told me to follow him as he walked down a hall to Elias' apartment where the garage had once been. There were two entrances to the apartment—one from the outside, and one from inside the house.

He pulled the key out of his pocket to open the door when he noticed a picture of Elias on the wall. He took it off the wall and showed it to me. It was his graduation picture from high school. I commented that he was a nice looking boy. Bill shook his head in agreement. He then took another picture off the wall which was of Bill's family. It was obviously an old picture because his children looked like they were in their teens.

As Bill opened the door to Elias' apartment, a wonderful fresh scent greeted me. The only thing I could compare it to would be fresh roses. The aroma was very strong. I asked Bill what type of air freshener he used and he said he didn't use the stuff. I was shocked because the apartment had been closed up and no windows were open.

He made the comment, "If you had smelled dirty socks when you walked in, then I would have understood." As he said this, some tears fell down his cheeks and I knew he would do anything to smell those dirty socks again.

We sat down on the bed where Elias' suitcase was open and neatly packed. He said, "When the police went through his suitcase, they pulled out the clothes and just left everything out on the bed like it didn't matter. I folded everything back the way it was— the way he left it."

I looked at Elias' dresser where a picture of his mother and father were prominently placed on one side. On the other side was a picture of him and his siblings. They were more recent pictures than the ones Bill showed me. And next to one of the pictures were Elias' wallet and the keys to his car.

I asked Bill where Elias' car was and he told me it was still in the driveway waiting for him to come home and drive it. I looked down at the suitcase and felt uncomfortable rummaging through it with his father watching me. I asked him if he was sure it was OK, and he assured me it was fine.

The suitcase was like an overnight bag one would use to pack the bare essentials. I carefully took out the folded underwear and undershirts. Then, I removed a pair of shorts and two t- shirts. There was a small bag that had shaving cream, a razor, deodorant, and a toothbrush inside it.

I moved my hand around the sides of the suitcase to see if there were any hidden compartments. At first there didn't seem to be anything out of the ordinary, but then my fingers stumbled on a small flap underneath what seemed like an imperfection in the lining. I played with the flap a little until I was able to pull it up just enough to reveal a little hole. I reached in with one finger because it was so tiny. I felt something and had to tear the hole a little to pull out a little bag of pills. I asked him if he knew what they were and he had no idea.

It was surprising no one else had discovered the pills. Inside the bag was a small piece of paper. I opened the bag and pulled the paper out. On it was written these words: "A wise son brings joy to his father, but a foolish son brings grief to his mother." I looked at Bill and his eyes were glistening. I realized this new discovery had broken his heart once again.

Chapter 16

Bill told me I could take the bag of pills, but he wanted to be the first one to know what they were. And he specifically asked me to not tell the police. It was probably illegal, but I agreed with his request since contacting the police would involve Bardon. I told Bill I would take them to a friend of mine and would contact him as soon as I knew anything.

The only way I knew to find out what the pills were, without raising suspicion, was to take them to another town. I had planned to go home anyway, since I had been gone for a while. I needed some time away from Abilene. I was not sleeping well, and the strange dreams I kept having were taking their toll on my mind and my body. There were too many things I couldn't explain, and it was causing my rational mind to go into overdrive.

I called Sid and asked him to contact Perry. Perry, the pill pusher, as we affectionately called him, had been a drug dealer for many years before he straightened up after supposedly finding Jesus. He had become a good resource over the past few years for situations like this. I told Sid I needed the results as soon as possible, and I would bring the pills to him that night. He told me he would call him.

Sid also told me he'd like to meet with me while I was home. His request concerned me because I knew he was frustrated with my performance on the Abilene story. We decided to meet when I got in later that day.

As soon as I packed some things, I stopped by the motel office to let the clerk know I'd be gone a few days. I began the boring trek home to Fort Worth. As always, I tried to distract myself from the boredom by remembering some of my past trips.

When I passed the small town of Baird, I remembered the first trip I ever took without my parents. There used to be a passenger train in Abilene, and my scout troop took the train all the way to Baird, which is about a thirty mile journey. We felt so grown up. We rode the train to the station in Baird, where we ran around for a few minutes, and then jumped back on the train to go home.

As I was about to head back to the train, I saw something gleaming out of a gumball machine. When I got closer, I saw what appeared to be a diamond ring glistening through the glass. I knew my Mother would love the ring, so I put the only nickel I had into the slot. Out came the ring and some gum in a plastic egg like container. It was quite a bargain for five cents.

Later that day, I gave it to my mother, and you would have thought I spent thousands on it by her excitement. I found the ring in her jewelry box when going through her things after she died. She always treasured whatever I gave her.

The memory made me smile because I rarely saw my mother happy. But that was one day I knew I had made her happy, and it was worth all the money I had.

My thoughts came back to earth and I thought about the pills I was bringing to Sid. I knew they would probably not offer any clues about the missing, but it may give some insight into what Elias was dealing with. I would have been happy to bring some good news back to Bill, but the piece of paper in the bag seemed to indicate Elias felt badly about whatever he was doing.

When I pulled into my driveway in Fort Worth, I felt sad there was no one there to greet me. No one even knew I had been gone for almost two weeks, except for Sid. Loneliness was something I had dealt with all my life, but it seemed lately it was hitting me harder than usual. I thought of Bill and how he seemed very lonely, too. I decided I'd have dinner with him when I got back to Abilene.

After cleaning up and putting some wash on, I called Sid to see if he was ready to meet. I met him at a restaurant close to the *Ragweed* office which consisted of one big room. We didn't really need much office space, since most of us worked from our homes or on the road. Sid was really the only one who used the office.

Sid seemed upset when I saw him, which made me uncomfortable. Over the years, we had developed a nice rapport with each other, but that seemed absent for those first few minutes. We asked for a table for two, and he ordered a beer. I waited for him to tell me the reason for our meeting.

After we ordered, he asked me how I thought the story was going in Abilene. I told him it was challenging because it was hard to find people willing to talk. But I was happy to tell him I had completed one interview and was working on another.

He looked at me with piercing eyes and told me, "Sergeant Bardon, one of the few fans of *Ragweed* we know of in Abilene, is no longer a fan. He sent me a scathing email, and told me he thought you were inept and had bungled up an interview he arranged for you."

Sid was noticeably upset but was trying to speak calmly, probably because we were in a restaurant. "Sergeant Bardon told me you interviewed a couple he had arranged for you to meet and he couldn't believe the things you said to them. You told them you needed to talk to all the families because you believed you could solve this case?" Sid asked, incredulously. Before I could answer, Sid continued, "Bardon couldn't believe your audacity to think you could solve a case that no one else in the world has been able to solve."

Sid paused for a second, but before I could say anything again, he continued his rampage. "Sergeant Bardon thinks you are out of touch with reality, Henry. He told me he was embarrassed that he had referred you to them. What were you thinking, Henry? Have you lost touch with reality?" he asked.

My worst fears were realized as he revealed all this to me. So, the wondering was over. I knew for certain Bardon had spoken to Dennis and Janet and had bad-mouthed me just like I thought he would. But apparently, he was not content to just ruin my relationship with them, he was going after my job, too.

"Sid, I know I probably misspoke when I told them that, but remember I solved the case involving the serial killer a few years ago? I know it's a long shot, Sid, but somebody has to solve the case in Abilene, right? Why can't it be me?" I whined.

"Henry, it's not going to be you," he replied seriously, "because you're off this story." I looked at him in disbelief. He continued his upsetting diatribe, "And let me remind you, Henry, you were not sent to solve a *case*, you were sent to do a story. I don't think I'm even going to use what you've written so far. I know now it was a mistake to ask you to go to Abilene. You were right, Henry, you were not the person for this assignment."

His words were a crushing blow. I could feel any confidence I had drain out of me. I was totally blindsided by his words. My first inclination was to give up like I had done so often in the past. I felt so defeated by his lack of confidence in me.

Sid looked at me like he was disgusted with me. It reminded me of the way Bardon would sneer at me right before he would push me into a locker and slam the door shut. The image of Bardon's face was just what I needed to get my resolve back. I decided then and there Bardon was not going to win again.

The defiance which rose up in me was noticeable to Sid. He looked at me puzzled as I confidently said, "Sid, I realize what I said to that family was not wise. But, things have changed since I first got there. I believe I am the right person for this assignment. It's hard to explain why, but I know I was sent there for a reason."

"I also know I can make this story appeal to a wider audience than we usually have. This is the biggest story of the decade and it will put *Ragweed* on everyone's laptop. This will interest the world—not just people in Texas. Don't take me off the case, Sid. Give me another chance," I pleaded.

"Henry, somehow you've gotten way too involved in this story. I'm taking you off the Abilene story, and I'm sending you to Georgetown. There is a group of fanatics gathering there in a few days. They advertised the event and invited people to join them to pray for rain."

Sid continued, "This should be interesting to our readers, Henry. I want you to talk to some of them and find out why they think praying will bring rain. Try to peg the ones who seem a little crazy. That always makes the story more interesting. This will be an easy assignment. I think you need some down time, Henry." Sid seemed like he had made up his mind.

My response was immediate and not well thought out, "NO, Sid! I'm going to finish what I started in Abilene. I now have another contact there. He is really opening up to me. His son is one of the missing, and he is the reason I needed Perry's input. I found some drugs in his suitcase the authorities totally missed."

"Are you out of your mind!" he yelled. Several people turned and looked at us. Sid quieted down, but he continued to lambast me. "First of all, you should tell the police about this, Henry. And why are you rummaging through a missing person's bag? I'm not sure what to think about you anymore. You have always been so sensible and respectful. Now it's like you've become a harebrained detective instead of a journalist. It seems like you have lost all your senses, Henry."

Sid warned me, "Henry, if you go back there, you're fired. You are giving our magazine a bad name and we don't need that kind of publicity. We barely have enough subscribers to pay our office rent now, and Bardon was one of those paying customers. He told me if he found you were harassing any of the families again, he would arrest you. Is that what you want?"

"Of course not, Sid. But I never thought you would be one to back down from a story, even after being threatened. Are you going to let this bully push you and me out of this town and off this story? Where is our free speech, Sid?" I asked.

I knew I had made a good point when he stopped talking and looked at me with a shocked expression. There were few things Sid hated more than people who tried to block the media from reporting the truth. It seemed like he hadn't even considered Bardon was trying to shut us out of the story. He didn't know Bardon the way I did.

"Do you really think that's what he's doing, Henry?" Sid asked thoughtfully.

"Yes, Sid, I do." And then I explained some of my history with him. "Bardon found out we went to the same high school and graduated the same year. When he looked me up, he realized I was someone he despised in high school. He thought I was a loser then, and he told me the same thing a few days ago."

"Bardon was the biggest bully in my high school and he made my time there a nightmare. I didn't recognize him at first because I hadn't seen him in thirty years, but after looking at some old pictures, I knew it was him. Even so, Sid, I was still willing to work with Bardon, but he was not willing to work with me."

Opening up to Sid seemed to soften his heart towards the whole situation. He was also bullied in high school and the last thing he wanted was to be bullied again. An attitude of defiance rose up in him, just like it had in me. Sid spoke a little more calmly, "I understand now. I'm sorry I doubted you, Henry. Go do the story, but use caution because I have no doubt this oaf would arrest you if he got the chance. And I don't care who Bardon is, he's not going to tell me how to run my magazine."

We shook hands and I felt like we were back on the same team again. We now had a common enemy, and we would stand up to him together. I left with a greater resolve and more confidence than ever. This story was mine. I had fought for it and knew I would do it justice. And no one, especially Bardon, was going to stop me.

Chapter 17

After taking care of some bills, doing some wash, and watering my plants, I left Fort Worth the next day and was back on the road to Abilene. This time I felt excited to get back to my hometown, which was something totally new for me. The miles flew by as I drove back to Abilene, which was also a first.

My talk with Sid was so encouraging. I felt like a new man since I had the total backing of my boss. It gave me more courage to know I would not be facing Bardon alone if I ever ran into him again.

Sid had given the pills to Perry, and he had called Sid the following day. Perry told him the pills were new on the market and had the same effect as amphetamines, but were amplified many times over. They were dangerous and had caused several people to have heart attacks. I wondered if that was what happened to Elias. Even if it was, it would not explain why no one could find head or tail of him.

After hearing this information, I dreaded having to tell Bill what his son had in his bag. I knew it would tear him apart to think Elias was either taking these drugs or selling them.

As soon as I settled into my room, I called Bill to see if he'd like to have dinner. He asked me point blank if I found out what the pills were. I told him I had and would tell him at dinner. He insisted I tell him right then.

"They are something akin to amphetamines, Bill. They are relatively new on the drug scene. They are very strong and have even caused a few deaths." I was somewhat relieved to get it over with. He didn't say anything for a moment, and then told me he would see me later at dinner. I was surprised he still wanted to meet.

We met at my new favorite Mexican restaurant, which happened to be Bill's, as well. I knew it was somewhat risky to go out to such a popular restaurant. I could easily run into Bardon or The Smiths, and they would surely tell him. But, I was becoming more and more defiant in my attitude towards Bardon.

Bill shook my hand when we saw each other at the restaurant. I felt uncomfortable at first, since I had been the bearer of such bad news. We ordered some food, and I was at a loss to know what to say. I knew he was probably thinking about this new revelation regarding Elias. After dinner, we had some coffee, and he asked me out of the blue if I thought Elias was using or selling.

It seemed best to minimize his worries as much as possible, "It was such a small bag, Bill. I doubt he was doing either. Perhaps a friend had asked him to check out the pills and he may have had second thoughts? Maybe that's why he had the note in the bag—to remind him how much grief his past use had caused. There is no point in torturing yourself and wondering about it, Bill. How is it helping you to think like this?"

He agreed with me and said, "I know, Henry, but I don't know how to stop thinking about it."

As he said those words, I suddenly saw something just above his head. It almost looked like a small dark hat, but it was moving. I jumped up and told Bill not to move. I knew he was totally alarmed wondering what in the world I could be reacting to as I stared at the top of his head. I told him to stay very still as I got up and slowly inched towards him, staring intently at his head.

I took a few steps towards him, and then saw, whatever it was, fly off his head and out the door. I had no idea what I had been staring at? I didn't know whether I should even try to tell Bill what I thought I saw. I knew he would probably think I was crazy. I was beginning to wonder if I was.

As I realized how bizarre this incident was and how my reaction to it was probably just as bizarre, I knew I had some explaining to do to Bill. I had to somehow minimalize what had happened so I told him, "Bill, I think I must have been hallucinating from lack of sleep, because I thought I saw something moving just above your head. It may have been a big, flying insect or a bat or something else but, whatever it was, it's gone now. I'm so sorry I alarmed you."

Even though I tried to downplay the whole incident, he didn't buy it. I could tell he thought my behavior had been nothing short of crazy. He stood up and took some money out to put on the table. He mumbled he had to be somewhere early the next day and needed to go home.

I knew he was lying and was shocked by my strange episode. I had to think fast or I would lose the only connection I had left in Abilene. I stood up and told him, "Look, I know what I just did was kind of weird and I can't really explain what just happened. But, in my defense, there seems to be a lot of weird things going on in this town. Could you please give me the benefit of the doubt? I need you to believe me and know I am here to help you."

Bill glared at me, but he slowly sat back down. I was grateful and sat back down, too. He said very seriously, "Henry, I don't know why, but I like you. I was beginning to think of you as a friend and no one needs a friend more than I do. But just now, when you looked at me like you were seeing a ghost or something, I couldn't take it. You were acting like a nut, Henry. I need a sane person in my corner, not some idiot who believes God took my son or some aliens beamed him up. I don't need people around me who chalk everything up to the supernatural. I need real answers. I can't handle any more of the craziness that has surrounded me for the past few months. Do you understand what I'm saying?" he asked.

"Yes, Bill. I understand and I'm not crazy," I said hopefully.

Bill continued, "Do you understand what it's like to lose someone so precious to you, and then have people coming at you all the time thinking they have the answers. But they didn't have any answers, Henry. Their theories were absurd and their words only hurt. I truly couldn't take it anymore. I thought things had finally calmed down and everyone would leave me alone, but then you showed up. You seemed like a nice guy who cared about me and my son. I thought I could trust you. But now, I'm not so sure. Please tell me you are not a crazy lunatic."

I was relieved he was giving me another chance, but I knew I had to say the right words in that moment or forever lose any possibility of him trusting me. "Bill, I am no crazier than any other person in this world. I don't even believe in the supernatural. I pride myself on being a realist. So you don't have to worry about me. I am as pragmatic as they come. You can trust me when I say I don't believe in ghosts or anything I can't see, touch, hear, or smell. You can ask anyone who knows me, I just report the facts."

Bill smiled as he recognized those words from an old TV show. He paused for a moment and then said, "OK, Henry, I guess I'll give you another shot. I'm sorry about my reaction. I have been around 'crazy' too much lately and I need some normalcy in my life."

I told him, "No problem, Bill, I can only imagine what you've had to put up with. I'll do my best to be as *normal* as I can be," I said and smiled. I think he was relieved. "Can I ask you something, though? Were you referring to anyone specific when talking about these lunatics?"

"Oh, there were several characters I've had to deal with. As soon as Elias was reported missing, they started coming. They found out where I lived and they wouldn't leave me alone. And, of course, the media joined them. It was a three-ring circus for a while. Things are quiet now and it's a relief. That's why I wasn't sure I wanted to talk to you," he paused and then said, "But I'm glad I did." Then he looked at me and said with a smirk, "I think."

I chuckled a little, and then asked him if any of those characters stood out to him. He said one of them did. "I never really met him, but he was one of the street preachers downtown. For some reason, Elias liked this man. Elias was working in one of the office buildings there, kind of like a 'gopher'. He did a lot of coffee runs. He hated the job, but was looking to get into the company on the ground level." He hesitated and smiled, "He probably should have gone to college."

"This guy was usually in the same place every day, in front of a bank on Pine Street. It was about a block from where Elias worked, so he and his friends would take their lunch and listen to him. He said they mostly did it to make fun of him, but Elias thought some of the things he said made sense."

"I think the man believed he was some kind of end time prophet or something. But as crazy as he sounded, Elias seemed very affected by what he said. I didn't think much of it because I figured Elias would grow tired of the man. But he didn't. For a while, Elias was always telling me things the guy preached, and I would usually make some snide remark about it. One of the things the man said was, 'Our words are like portals to the supernatural'. I asked Elias if he was starting to believe in all of this superstitious nonsense."

"Elias said the man kept warning people to be careful what they would speak over their own lives or those of others. This preacher seemed real caught up in what people say," Bill concluded.

"I didn't listen to Elias even though he wanted to share the preacher's words with me. Instead I just dismissed the things he told me about the preacher. I couldn't believe my intelligent son was so taken by this homeless lunatic. What I wouldn't give to go back and truly listen to what my son had to say," he said thoughtfully.

"After Elias was reported missing, I went to Pine Street and tried to find the guy but he had left by then. I know people were getting tired of him preaching on the streets because there were a lot of complaints. I think he was arrested several times," Bill said.

I asked him how he knew that and Bill said, "Some of the families were talking about it when we all met together one night. The City had paid for a therapist to meet with all of us to help us deal with our loss. I only went to a few of the meetings. I didn't know what to say, and I couldn't handle listening to all their grief. I had enough of my own to deal with."

"Many of the families had heard of this preacher downtown, but they thought he was just a crazy, homeless guy. A few of them heard he had been arrested as a suspect in the case. But the police didn't find anything to hold him for so they released him. I heard he lived in an abandoned building somewhere," Bill rumored.

As Bill continued to talk, it occurred to me how significant it was that many of these families were aware of this street preacher. And, it also occurred to me that Bill might be able to put me in touch with some of these families. I asked him if he still met with the families.

He looked like he was surprised and said, "I just told you, Henry, it was too much for me to listen to all their grief when I had so much of my own. I only went a few times."

When he said that, I felt bad because it appeared I hadn't been listening. I guess I hadn't been. I was thinking of how I could use Bill to get an interview with one of these families. I felt bad and told Bill I was sorry and hoped he would continue his story.

He said, "There's not much more to say, Henry. I know I talk a lot, so I don't blame you for not being able to listen to everything I say."

I reassured him, "I am very interested in what you're saying. I just haven't been sleeping well lately so my mind tends to wander." As I said that, I remembered the church and wondered if Bill had ever been there. I asked him where the families would meet for these counseling sessions. He said they usually met in one of the church basements.

"In town?" I probed.

"Yes, why would we go to another town?" he asked.

"I was just wondering, Bill." I knew then he was probably not aware of the group that met at the church in the country.

As Bill continued to recap his last few months, I realized this street preacher had to be a significant character in this story. I asked Bill, "Do you happen to remember the name of this man who was preaching downtown?"

He shook his head and thought for a minute, "It seemed like people mostly referred to him as a preacher or a prophet," he said, "and some even called him a crazy homeless guy. I saw something about him in the paper. I don't think they were sure of his identity, but I think his name was Michael or something like that."

I knew in my gut, I had to find this preacher, prophet, homeless person or whatever he was.

Chapter 18

After dinner, I went back to my room and searched for any articles about any recent arrest of an itinerant street preacher in Abilene. It wasn't too hard to find. But his name was not Michael, it was Micah, or at least that's what he called himself.

The picture of him looked pretty pathetic. He was unkempt and had long hair and a beard. I was surprised anyone would listen to a guy like this. He must have been very charismatic to draw anyone at all.

The article basically said he had been questioned in the disappearance of some of the missing people but they found no reason to hold him. He had also been arrested several times for disturbing the peace. They said it was not clear what his actual name was or where he was from. The article wasn't very helpful, but at least I knew what he looked like.

The next search I did was on the events in Abilene leading up to the first disappearance. From what I understood, Mary was literally the first person taken, but they didn't realize it at the time. By the time the fourth person went missing, the police concluded someone must be taking these people.

Abilene was busy during the months right before people were reported missing. There was a film festival going on and one of the churches was having a fair. There was the Chili Cook Off in Buffalo Gap, which a lot of people from Abilene attend. I found some pictures on a news feed of the various activities.

The Art Walk had taken place a few weeks before Mary disappeared, so I went through some of the pictures of that event. Abilene has a lot of cultural events for a small city. I was impressed to see all that happens throughout the year. I wasn't sure what I was looking for, but I thought I might see something out of the ordinary. Whoever was taking these people may have been at some of these events.

It was kind of sad to see the pictures of these people who seemed so carefree and happy, blithely unaware of the evil lurking nearby. No one had any idea what was about to descend upon this peaceful town that had been called one of the best places to retire in America.

I happened to glance at the hotel clock and noticed it was after three AM. I had been so lost in what I was doing I hadn't realized how late it was. It was rare for me to be that focused where I would be oblivious to the late hour, but I felt like I was onto something. I was so intent in my search, I hadn't even thought about eating or sleeping.

The awareness of the late hour made me realize how tired I was. I had to stop to get some sleep or I wouldn't be able to function the next day. I got up to brush my teeth and as I did, out of the corner of my eye, I saw something move above me. And in that same fleeting moment something pounced on me from the ceiling. A scream came out of me I had never heard before.

I ran out of my room in my boxers. Something was on my neck and I felt like it was trying to choke me. I frantically tried to grab it and throw it off—but there was nothing to grab. It was like a transparent devil had attacked me. It seemed to have no substance, and yet I could feel it. I was yelling in desperation trying to get it off.

A person in the next room heard me scream and came out. I ran to him and asked him what it was that had jumped on me. He was a large, hulking man and I felt certain if anyone could get it off, he could. I told him something was on my back and I couldn't see it but I could feel it. He grabbed me and turned me around several times like a top.

The man turned me around to face him and looked me over one more time and said, "You must have had a nightmare because there is nothing on you. I've looked at you from every angle and if there was something there, it's gone."

I looked at him in disbelief because I knew I was wide awake when it happened, so I was sure I didn't dream it. I tried to explain that to him, but he didn't buy it.

"Look, I've had things like this happen to me and they seemed so real, but I'm pretty sure this was all in your imagination. Or maybe I should ask you, what did you have to drink tonight?" I told him I had a few beers, and he smiled as he said, "Apparently, a few too many."

I apologized and felt foolish to cause such a commotion. A few others had come out of their rooms to see what was going on. The man said, "Don't feel bad. You can ask my wife, I've had some pretty crazy dreams and she had to talk me down from them. I was so convinced they were real but it was all up here," as he pointed to his head. "I was in Iraq for a while and it messes with you. People just aren't meant to experience some of the things we've experienced. Did you serve anywhere?"

It would have been great if I could have said "yes" but I couldn't. I had no excuse for what just happened. I thanked him for his service to our country and to me. I retreated back to my room. I was afraid to go back in, hoping whatever had attacked me had left. I checked every closet and under the beds, but nothing was there. What was going on with me?

I thought about going somewhere, so I wouldn't have to stay in my room, but I couldn't think of anything open at 3:30 in the morning. There didn't appear to be any other option except to stay in the room until later.

I was creeped out and knew I couldn't go to sleep after what had happened. I put every light on in the room and lay down on top of my covers. I would start to doze off then catch myself. I went over and over what I had just experienced. I knew I was wide awake when it happened. It was no dream.

After staring at the ceiling for at least half an hour replaying the wide awake nightmare, I decided to get up and make better use of my time. If I wasn't going to sleep, then at least I could finish what I was doing before the incident.

I opened my laptop and went back to the search I was doing right before I was attacked. It gave me chills to see the pictures again because all I could think about was what had just happened. The more I thought about it the more terrified I got. I realized thinking about it was not helping my search, but it seemed I couldn't stop myself. Every time I'd try to look at the pictures, an eerie feeling would come over me.

My thoughts were distracting me from the search, but I kept trying to push through. I had such a strong feeling I was going to find something significant if I kept looking. There had to be a clue somewhere in all of these events that everyone had missed. I went through the pictures one by one trying to make my bleary eyes focus. And then I saw it.

As I was scrolling through the pictures again for the Art Walk, I saw a group of people looking at a reproduction of a famous painting depicting a recognizable scream. This painting was an abstract of the original abstract which made the scream even more pronounced.

The crowd standing around the picture was small, and the photographer shot the group from several different angles. One picture was taken from behind the crowd and one from the side and the other shot was directly at the crowd as they gazed at the picture to get their reactions.

His face stood out to me from the crowd. His hair was shorter and his beard was groomed but there was no mistake— the preacher/prophet/ homeless guy was there in the crowd, but he certainly didn't look homeless. He was nicely dressed and looked like a normal person. As I studied the picture of the shot taken from behind the painting, it looked like he was staring right at me. I felt chills go up and down my spine as I realized this was the clue I was looking for. He had to be the villain in this story.

Chapter 19

I t was around four AM, when I discovered the clue I believed everyone else had missed. Even though I had a sleepless night and spent most of it terrified, I had still managed to stumble onto this startling discovery. This street preacher had to be the culprit in the mysterious disappearances! I couldn't wait to share this exciting bit of information with Sid. His faith in me would certainly be renewed.

The date the picture was taken of Micah was before Mary disappeared. This was significant because it meant he was in Abilene before the disappearances started. I had a feeling it would be hard for him to explain how he had become a homeless lunatic within a year. I knew this discovery was very significant and I also knew I should tell the police. But I don't always do what I should do.

I knew if Bardon found out I was still in Abilene and still working on this story, I would probably end up in jail. And knowing him, he would take what I had uncovered and make it look like he was the one who discovered this missing clue. I knew I couldn't tell the police.

This revelation was exciting. I wanted to continue my search to see if Micah might have attended other events. But my eyes were blurry, and I knew I couldn't continue my search without some sleep or some coffee. Sleep would have been my preference, but I knew I'd have to settle for the coffee.

Then it dawned on me that truck stops stay open all night. Why hadn't I thought of that before? I decided to venture out of my room, which was almost as scary as staying in the room. Once I made it to my car safely, I drove down Interstate 20 to see if I could find a truck stop.

When the rest of the world woke up, the first thing I was going to do was find another motel. I knew I would never be able to sleep in that room again. And hopefully, whatever attacked me would not follow me.

After driving a few miles on Interstate 20, the neon lights of an open truck stop caught my eye so I pulled in. I brought my laptop with me and hoped they had Wi-Fi. I needed coffee badly if I was going to continue my project, but the main thing I wanted was to feel safe again.

The truck stop was hopping for such an early hour, and I was thankful to be surrounded by other people. I finally did feel safe for the first time since the dark menace had attacked me. Being in a safe place also made it easier to think about what happened. I couldn't even imagine what it was that had pounced on me. Nothing about it made any sense.

I also knew it wasn't the first time I had seen such a thing. It was very similar to the dark shadow I had seen on Bill's head except mine was much larger. And I wondered why Bill couldn't feel the moving presence on his head, but I could definitely feel the spirit that had attacked me. And I recalled the dark blur that zoomed past me in the department store. I was relatively sure it had to be the same type of creature. I knew whatever these things were, they were real, even if they didn't fit my definition of 'real'.

Even though I was in a safe place, I still couldn't concentrate on the story. The dark apparition had totally unsettled me. I wasn't sure how I would ever be able to sleep soundly again. Fear was coming back on me.

The waitress came over to take my order. I was surprised by how friendly she was. It boggled my mind how someone could be so pleasant at such an ungodly hour. She poured my coffee and asked where I was from. I told her I lived in Fort Worth but used to live in Abilene.

"What are you doing up at this hour? Are you a truck driver ... or just a driver?" She laughed at her question even though it wasn't funny.

I decided there wouldn't be much harm in telling her the truth, so I told her the real reason I was in Abilene. As soon as I did, she sat down across from me to tell me she knew one of the people who had disappeared. "Actually, my son knows him but I am familiar with the family." My ears perked up as she continued telling me the details in her strong Texas twang.

"We just couldn't believe it when we heard the news. That boy was only twenty-four. He had grown up with my son and they had graduated from high school together. They were friends but they had grown apart after Carl went off to college. My boy, Joe, decided to stay in Abilene because he got a good job here. I was glad he did because my husband and I had just divorced. I guess it was selfish of me, but I liked having someone at home. My girl got married a few years ago and she lives in Odessa," she explained.

As she continued her endless dialogue, I was having a hard time focusing on her litany of words because I was so tired and distracted. The only thing I could appreciate about her presence was the possibility she might be a connection to another family for my story. I knew I wasn't listening and would have no clue how to respond if she ever stopped talking.

"My son ran into him just a few weeks before he went missing. He hadn't seen Carl in a long time and thought he was still away at college. Carl told him he couldn't handle the pressure and had decided to move back home. He also told my son he had met this girl he really liked... But then, my son said Carl got real quiet. He whispered to Joe that he was afraid for his life."

My ears perked up and my focus returned as she continued, "Carl told my son that he had gotten into some really weird stuff because of his new girlfriend. He said they would spend all their free time playing some type of video game. Carl said the game was kind of satanic but he was OK with it at first because he really liked this girl. But then, he started feeling real uncomfortable about this game."

CAROL O. RIORDAN

The cheerful waitress got off track for a few minutes talking about how bad video games were in general but then apologized and continued, "Carl said he believed he was being followed all the time, but when he would turn around, no one was there. He was having horrible dreams and couldn't sleep. He wanted to stop playing the game, but his girlfriend would call him a wimp whenever he complained. Carl liked her so he kept playing the game to make her happy, but he told Joe he felt like he was going crazy."

All I could think about, as she went on and on, was the dark, shadowy thing that had attacked me only a few hours before. I wondered if it was the same thing Carl had been afraid of. I was curious how many others were experiencing attacks from these creatures.

"Carl told my boy he would sometimes wake up in the middle of the night and there would be someone looking down at him. Can you believe that? That would scare me to death," she exclaimed.

She then proceeded with her detailed story. "Carl was tired of being afraid all the time so he finally told his girlfriend he had had enough. Carl said his girlfriend didn't seem that upset when he broke up with her. She was so involved with that game he believed it had become her reality. Can you believe that? Those games should be outlawed," she stated emphatically.

"I thought maybe Carl was making this stuff up, but Joe said he seemed very disturbed. Joe was worried about him and then, just a few days later, he was reported missing. Do you think his girlfriend might have done something to him? That was the first thing I thought," she concluded.

I asked the waitress if she knew the girlfriend's name and she said her son would probably know it. "I'll call him in a little while. He won't be up for another few hours."

This sounded like a great story for my article, so I was willing to wait around until she got the name from her son. A few hours later, the waitress woke me up. Apparently I had fallen asleep with my head on the table. Drool had pooled underneath my mouth, and a piece of toast was imbedded in

92

my cheek. I was probably snoring, too. I'm sure I was quite a sight for all the truckers.

The waitress seemed hurried, "I hate to wake you up, sir, but my shift is almost over. I wanted to let you sleep for a while because you looked really tired. Here is the name I told you about." With that she put a piece of paper in my hand and left.

As I watched her walk out the door, my mind started to recollect the story she had told me and the name she was referring to... I unfolded the paper in my hand and I saw the name, "Teresa Royale". This was the missing man's girlfriend, so I knew I had to talk to her. I opened my computer and searched for her name. There was no phone number listed, but I found an address.

I drank the rest of my very cold coffee, started for the door, but then remembered I hadn't paid my bill. I left a large tip and wrote "thank you" on a napkin. I drove back to the hotel, so I could check out of my room. I had no idea where I'd go but I knew I had to find a place on the other side of town, as far away from my old motel as I could get.

As I pulled down the mirror in my car to comb my hair, I almost gagged. The night before had taken its toll. I looked frightening and didn't smell too great, either. I realized I couldn't go see this unsuspecting girl the way I looked or smelled, so I either had to find another motel before seven AM or just risk taking a shower in my haunted room. The likelihood of finding a room at this hour was not high, therefore I decided to take the quickest shower of my life.

The clerk at the desk was surprised I was checking out after I had told him the day before I'd probably be there another week. I told him things had suddenly changed—which was true. I put the girl's address in my GPS and hoped to catch her before she might leave that morning. The GPS indicated her house was almost twenty minutes from my location.

As I drove to her place, I went over what I would say to her. This was a chance to get another story for my article, so I had to take full advantage of this opportunity. I pulled up to what the GPS said was her address, which was a little out of the City limits. I was taken aback at how unkempt the house was. There was trash out front, and paint was peeling on the outside. It looked like no one lived there.

I hesitantly got out and stepped onto the creaky porch. On one side of the porch there was a broken porch swing hanging lopsided from one chain and on the other side was a broken rocking chair on its side. I knocked on the door. I waited and knocked again, but still no answer. I was almost relieved and turned around to go, but the door creaked open. I turned around and saw someone peering at me from behind the door. It was a young woman and she yelled out at me, "What do you want, mister?"

She sounded similar to what I would imagine a hillbilly would sound like. I wasn't sure what to say but decided to go for it and told her I was looking for a Teresa Royale. She bellowed back that she didn't know a Teresa Royale and to get off her property.

I couldn't just give up so I said, "I work for a magazine, ma'am, and I am doing a story on the missing. I heard Teresa's boyfriend was one of the missing people. I want to honor those who are missing by writing about them, and I thought I might find Teresa here as this was the address I was given." I was surprised that I had come up with such a great idea on the spur of the moment.

She didn't speak for a moment, but then she opened the door, "OK, I guess I'll talk to you, mister. I'm out here all alone today, so I just don't tell every Tom, Dick, and Harry who comes knocking on my door who I am."

I told her I understood and reached out my hand to shake hers saying, "It's nice to meet you. I'm Henry. I work for an online magazine called *Ragweed.*"

She didn't take my hand but looked at me for a minute, and then opened her door wider and said, "Well, come on it then."

It was surprising she was willing to trust me and let me into her house when she was all alone. I told her it would be fine if we just talked a while on her porch. She said, "It's too dusty and hot out here. Just come on in, and I'll make us some coffee."

I did not want to go inside the house because it looked as dilapidated as the old church did near Potosi, so I hesitated. She responded to my reluctance, "Look mister, if you want to talk to me then come in. I'm not going to stand out here all day."

It was obvious—I was more worried about my safety than she was about hers.

Chapter 20

The thought of going inside the woman's house was not a pleasant one. I knew I had offended her by suggesting we talk on the porch.

She sneered at me, "So, I guess you think you're too good to come into my house. What are you afraid of? I don't bite." At that point, I knew I had no choice but to go in.

The house looked like I expected it to. The living room area was a mess with cans and wrappers strewn about. There was a stench in the room that was undefinable. It seemed like a combination of sweat and vomit. As I was wondering how long I could hold my breath, she asked me if I'd like some coffee. I quickly told her I had several cups already. Then, she asked me if I'd like anything to eat and I lied saying I wasn't feeling well, which was becoming more and more a reality by the second.

I was afraid to sit on the couch as it looked filthy and I wondered if the dirt could seep through my pants. She sat down on a chair across from me. She was a pretty young woman but was as unkempt as her home. I struggled to gather my composure as she seemed annoyed with me for turning down all her hospitality.

"So do you live here alone?" I asked nervously.

She replied, "I have two brothers who also live here."

"Oh, are they here now?" I asked innocently trying to make conversation.

"Why, are you afraid they'll come out and grab you? Or maybe you're just hoping we are alone so you can take advantage of me?" She smiled and got up. I was terrified she was going to come and sit by me, but she didn't. She needed a light for her cigarette.

"This won't bother you, will it?" she asked, not caring if it did.

"No, it's fine," I responded. It wasn't, but I wasn't going to cause any more issues.

It was a struggle to think of the right words to say to this woman as she was misconstruing basically everything I said. I asked her if she worked somewhere and she seemed annoyed. "No, not presently. I was laid off from my job a few weeks ago," she responded.

"Oh, I'm sorry. What were you doing?" I thoughtlessly asked.

"What do you mean, 'what was I doing?' It wasn't my fault they blamed me for a customer's stupidity," she said indignantly.

I wanted to kick myself. "No, that's not what I meant. I wasn't asking why you were laid off; I was asking what you did as a job." I tried to correct the misguided question.

"Oh." There was a short pause as she took a hit on her cigarette. "I was a bartender at a place not far from here," she informed me.

"Oh, I see," I replied. "And what did your boyfriend do for a job?"

"Carl was a bouncer for our club. That's where I met him. He had made lots of enemies because he didn't put up with any cursing or fighting. He was a good man. He always treated people fairly, and he was especially thoughtful of the ladies who came to our place. He was a real gentleman—not like the other 'low lives' that came in there all the time," Teresa said.

As she went on about what a good man Carl was, I saw her casually wipe away a few tears. I knew she didn't want me to see she was choking up, but it was clear she was. I wasn't always the best judge of people, but she didn't seem like the type who would kill her boyfriend. She appeared to really miss him.

She continued, "Carl and I were together for about six or seven months, and I thought we'd probably get married one day. I know he loved me and I loved him. I was hoping he would take me out of this pigsty and we would buy a nice house in town somewhere. We talked about it a lot, so I know he was planning to ask me soon. But then a few months ago, he just disappeared. No one knew where he was or what happened. He left here one morning to go to his other job in town. He worked as a janitor in an elementary school and at night, he worked in the club."

"So he left that morning and he never reached his job? Did they call you looking for him?" I asked.

"No, they called his mother and she called me. She doesn't like me and never has. I never did anything to her, but she just doesn't think I am good enough for her son. And she has always been jealous of me because Carl spent so much time here. He hated being home. His mother was always criticizing him and yelling at him. He got tired of it so he spent most of his free time here even though we didn't have much free time," she explained.

"What did you guys like to do in your free time?" I regretted asking the question the second it came out of my mouth because I knew how it sounded. But my intention was for her to tell me about the satanic game they played. But of course she misconstrued the question.

"Well, what do you think we did?" She giggled and I squirmed.

"'I'm sorry. I meant like other things. You know." I couldn't help it, but I started blushing and she noticed. I started feeling more and more uncomfortable and wished I could just run out to my car and forget this interview.

"I think I know what you mean, Mr. Henry." She smiled and looked like she felt sorry for me.

I started to correct her and tell her it was "Mr. Pike" but decided it didn't matter. "What did you do for fun when you were just hanging out in the house?" I prodded. The longer I sat there, the more I felt like I was going to vomit. Either the conversation was making me sick or my lie about feeling sick was coming true.

"Are you uncomfortable, Mr. Henry? I bet I could make you feel better," she purred.

"I don't think anyone could make me feel better right now. I feel like I'm going to be sick," I said as I gagged a few times. I didn't want to vomit on her floor, but I honestly doubted anyone would notice.

I got up to leave and she said, "We used to play a game together."

With her sudden revelation, I suddenly felt a little better so I sat back down. "Can you tell me a little more about it before I go?"

"Sure I could," she replied. "Carl didn't really like the game, but I thought it was fun. It was a video game I picked up in one of those stores that resells games. It's called 'The Misfortunes of Willy'. It's a stupid name but it is a lot of fun to play."

"How do you play it?" I asked.

"Would you like to play it or do you feel up to it?" She asked.

"Maybe I could just watch you play it." I said, relieved she was finally going to show me this game that had scared a grown man so badly.

She seemed agreeable and went over to an old TV which had a huge screen, but was like an old projection set. She turned it on and pulled out the controllers.

It booted up and there was a weird display as it began. The circles on the screen started turning faster and faster, going in and out so that watching it was making me even queasier. I told her maybe it wasn't a good time for me to watch it, and she assured me it would start in a few seconds. I agreed to stay a few more minutes— mostly because I never wanted to come back again.

Then some evil looking clown from the game started talking and it welcomed all who were brave enough to play. Then it shifted to an old run down house out in the middle of nowhere. Teresa was the only player and her character in the game was running across a field towards the house. As she ran, something was swooping down trying to attack her character. She had some sort of weapon in her hand that she used to fight it off.

Her character fell and something like a snake slithered up to her and started biting her. She pulled something out of her arsenal that she apparently had won in an earlier game and killed the creature.

She then made it to the house and went in. But, as soon as she went in, it was apparent something was inside the house with her. It was very dark, but you could hear something moving around in the house.

As she tried to get some type of light out of her bag of weapons, a gust of wind came out of nowhere and put the light out. She instantly lit it again so the room was illuminated and we could see what she was up against. In the corner of the room, close to the ceiling, there appeared to be something attached to the wall which looked like a huge bat. A dark, ominous form was looking down at her. It seemed like it was about to pounce on her.

As I stared at the TV screen, everything in my being knew. As unimaginable as it could be, the villain in her video game was the same creature that had attacked me. My mouth must have been open as she turned to look at me. She saw my horror as I looked at the screen and she said, "Mr. Henry, 'the souch' wants you to play. Please come take the control."

I couldn't take my eyes off this creature and it seemed like it was staring right back at me. I got up quietly to leave as his eyes followed me. This was too much for me to take in. I spoke to the girl without taking my eyes off the screen, "I'm feeling much worse. I have to go." I started to back out of the house still looking at the screen.

Teresa said again, "Mister, please come take the control. He's waiting for you."

I looked at her in disbelief. "What are you saying? This character can't talk to us. What did you say its name was— 'the slouch?' This thing can't see us," I said, hoping beyond reason I was right. "This is a game. A game I don't want to play. I have to go," I said, in disbelief.

She looked at me and said as seriously as she could, "He will come after you again if you don't do what he says. I know from experience, Mister Henry. Please just come and play. Once you do, you can get free of him. He'll leave you alone if you can beat him at the game."

This couldn't be happening. How did she know that thing had attacked me? There was no way she could know that. Fear was rising up in me. I told her emphatically, "I told you I have to go. I'm going to be sick. Thank you for talking to me and showing me the game, I think, but I have to leave now."

She looked at me and shook her head. "I feel like something happened to Carl because he wouldn't play along with 'the souch' anymore. I don't know for sure but please don't take a chance," she pleaded.

Once again, I was dumbfounded this girl could believe something happened to her boyfriend because he refused to play this stupid game. I looked at her in disbelief and said, "Teresa, you really need to get a life."

When I spoke those words, I knew I made a mistake. Her concern turned to anger and her words seemed out of character for her. As she got angrier and angrier, the voice coming out of her changed and evolved into what sounded like a man's voice and the words were vile. "You know what you can do with your story, Mr. Pike. Get out and don't blame me for what is about to happen to you. I tried to be nice to you. You think you're so smart. You're about to see who you are dealing with."

At that point I realized two things: I wasn't dealing with Teresa anymore, and whoever or whatever this was, knew my last name. I gathered my things and started for the door. I turned once more and thought to ask Teresa if she wanted to get out of this house of horrors. But she was not looking at me. I looked up at the screen, but the thing she called 'the souch' was no longer there.

Chapter 21

My mind was reeling from what I had just experienced in Teresa's house. An evil character in a video game that could see me and talk to me did not belong in the world I was familiar with. I no longer had to wonder why Teresa's boyfriend was so frightened by that video game. As I sped away from her house, I kept looking in my rear view mirror hoping no one—or anything— was following me.

The image of that 'thing' was terrifying. It not only could see me, it knew my last name. And somehow it was talking to me through Teresa. I kept processing it over and over in my mind and it all kept coming up the same—it could not be real. There was no logical explanation for this disturbing experience.

I had no idea what this creature was, but I knew it was not from a world I was familiar with. I had never wanted to believe in the supernatural, but it seemed I had no choice. I couldn't deny what I had just seen or heard. I knew my criteria for what I considered 'real' had just been altered.

It also occurred to me that this creature might very well be the one taking all of the missing people. I had to find out if any of the other families knew about this game. I had to find a way to talk to them.

The only possible person who could now connect me with any of them was Bill. But, if I told him about what I had just experienced, he would probably reverse his opinion of me, and I had just convinced him I was normal.

As I thought about everything I had experienced since being in Abilene, I wondered if any of these things were connected. How did Micah, the homeless preacher, fit into any of this? And what purpose did the creepy, dilapidated church play in this mystery?

Then it occurred to me that it was already Tuesday again and that was when they had met the week before. I wanted to know if this was a weekly occurrence, so I knew I had to do another stakeout at the Smith's house.

The thought of returning to the abandoned church made me feel anxious, but I knew if the Smiths went out there again, I would have to go, too. I recalled the long, terrifying night I spent out there. I did not want that to happen again.

Before I would begin the stakeout, I decided to get a charger for my phone that didn't require my car to be running. I didn't want to take any chances. I also needed a flashlight and a few other things which would be handy if stranded in the middle of nowhere.

Since it was late when the church started the week before, I figured I had time to find another room and settle in before I went to Dennis and Janet's house to begin my stakeout.

It didn't take me long to find another motel on the south side of town. The room was nicer than the other one, perhaps because it wasn't haunted. And when I saw the beautiful bed, I plopped down on it. I thought how nice it would be to just close my eyes for a few minutes. I knew I should have set my alarm because my few minutes turned into two hours. When I woke up, I knew I might have missed the opportunity to see if Dennis and Janet had gone out to the church.

I brushed my teeth and changed into some new clothes that didn't look like they had been slept in. I gathered my new stakeout gear and headed out to the car. I would go over to The Smith's house first to see if they were still there.

When I went to their house, it was evident no one was home. I wanted to kick myself for falling asleep when I should have been watching them. The only thing I could do at that point was to drive out to the church and see if they were there.

Since I knew I would probably be gone for hours, I decided I would need some sustenance, so I picked up a hamburger and fries with coffee. I hoped I remembered the way to the abandoned church. I wasn't paying close attention the night I followed Dennis out there. I had been more concerned about being noticed.

After I turned off onto the Potosi Highway, I remembered we turned on a country road soon after. After I passed some places that looked familiar, I took a turn and hoped for the best. I drove a ways and realized it wasn't the right road. I backtracked to where I started and went to the next exit. If it wasn't the right one, I'd probably be out of luck since it was getting late.

After I drove a few miles down the road, I was pretty sure I was on the right one. I knew it was about another mile or more to the turnoff. But as I started down the lonely country road, I noticed something in the distance I never expected to see. A large fire was burning, and I had no doubt it was the church.

Chapter 22

The fire was in the same area where the church was, so I was almost certain it had to be what was creating such a large blaze. But I needed to know for sure, so I headed towards the fire. I wondered whether there would be any fire trucks coming to put it out. I doubted the fire department would even know about the fire in this isolated area unless someone reported it. I seriously hoped that would not have to be me.

As I got closer, my suspicion was confirmed. I parked my car a safe distance away and got out to watch the fire. I walked closer and as the fire lit up the night sky, it illuminated the surrounding area, and I could easily see there was no one anywhere in the vicinity. It almost seemed like the fire had started all on its own. The fire was roaring hot, but it looked like the building was almost consumed, so I hoped it would burn itself out.

I couldn't imagine why someone would set a building on fire and then leave. In West Texas, fires are very dangerous because of the dry conditions. No one in their right mind would do something like this. The fire could easily spread to the dry grass and brush.

It became apparent no one was coming to put the fire out. I didn't know what to do. I wondered if I should try and call someone. It would be risky if I gave them my name and it would be suspicious if I didn't. And they would probably wonder why I was out there in the first place. They might even blame me for starting the fire.

But it would be irresponsible for me to not call and possibly dangerous to the surrounding ranches. So, I took out my phone, but once again I had no signal. I was almost relieved because I didn't want to be the one to report it.

I still felt like I should do something so I decided to leave and call 911 when I could get a signal for my phone. I wasn't even sure how to tell the fire department where to find the fire, but no doubt they would be able to see it.

The fire seemed to be gaining ground because the wind was picking up and catching sparks. The sparks were igniting surrounding brush and a Mesquite tree. When I saw the tree go up, I thought it best to leave because the fire was spreading. I got in my car to leave, but as unbelievable as it sounds, the nightmare from the week before happened again. My car would not start. How could this happen twice in the same place? I had never had trouble with my car starting before.

It was uncanny this happened twice in the same place. And even more improbable was the startling fact, the fire was spreading quickly and getting closer to my car. I realized I needed to get out of there immediately. I looked through my car and took out everything I thought I might need. I got out all the identification papers and then wondered if I should try and take off the license plates. If I didn't, they might be able to track the car to me.

How could I have been so stupid? Because of my curiosity, I got too close to the fire and it looked like I was going to get burned—literally. I put everything I could in the plastic bag I had brought for my stakeout supplies. I quickly opened my trunk to see if there was anything in there I needed to save. It became apparent, if I didn't leave soon, I would not be able to save myself.

I jumped in one more time to see if the car would start. It was completely dead. This could not be a coincidence. I didn't have time to think about it. I had to get out. The breeze was kicking up and the fire was spreading faster. I started running for the road carrying my belongings with me. I wasn't in the best shape, but I thought I could outrun the fire. I was wrong.

Chapter 23

It seemed very probable the fire was going to catch up to me, especially after I tripped and fell twice in my haste. I didn't realize fires could spread so quickly. The smoke seemed to be encircling me so I couldn't see where I was going. I gasped for air.

The horrible thought came to me that the authorities would probably blame me for the fire since I was the only one out there. And, even worse, I wouldn't be able to defend myself if I was dead. That would be a tragedy to me because I always wanted to die with a good name.

Then, another thought popped into my mind as smoke was engulfing me. Was this somehow connected to the demon thing that spoke to me in that video game? Was this the revenge of 'the souch'? I couldn't believe I was even considering that possibility, but this almost seemed like it was planned— just for me.

The creature had told me I would regret not playing the game with him, but I knew in my rational mind it was impossible for a character from a video game to have planned this. But as I dismissed the idea as absurd, the fire encircled me. It seemed impossible to comprehend something like this could happen, but the reality was—I had no way out!

The smoke was getting thicker. I was stumbling around trying to find some way to get out of a certain, fiery death. I was gagging as I struggled to breathe. My eyes were burning so much, I had to shut them. I couldn't see where I was going, so I fell on some sharp rocks. When I hit the ground, I noticed I was able to get more air closer to the ground, so I started crawling. The gravel was tearing into my flesh with each movement, but I had no other choice.

I was panicking, but I didn't how to stop since I believed I was facing certain death. I kept struggling to move forward, even though it felt like my hands and knees were raw from crawling over the gravel and rocks.

I wondered if anyone had spotted the fire by then, so I tried to cry out in case anyone had showed up, but I coughed more than I yelled. I knew I had to try and cry out again, because if anyone was out there they wouldn't be able to see me through the smoke. I yelled again as loud as I could.

As I screamed for help, I kept crawling but I couldn't see anything in front of me. I bumped into a big cactus which made me pay dearly for my blunder. I could feel each prick of the cactus as the needles entered various parts of my body. I painfully realized what I had done. The needles went into my face, fore arms and chest. The pain from all I was experiencing was excruciating.

At that moment, I decided I couldn't go on. I couldn't breathe, I couldn't move without great pain, and I couldn't get away from the relentless smoke. I had enough energy for one more cry, so I cried out to the only one I thought might be listening—-a God I had refused to believe in most of my life. I knew instinctively, if He was real, He was the only one who could help me. "Please, don't let me die like this. Help me!" I pleaded as I gasped for air. I then put my head down on the ground and gave up.

It must have been seconds later when strong arms reached from out of the smoke and grabbed me. They started pulling me out. I must have been close to losing consciousness because there was not any pain from being dragged on my raw knees for some distance.

The next thing I knew, the old farmer who had found me the last time I had been stranded, had apparently rescued me again. He looked down at me and asked, "What is it about this place that keeps drawing you back, mister? You look like death warmed over."

As I thought about what he said, it was kind of funny— "death warmed over." I thanked him for pulling me out of the fire, but he assured me he had done no such thing. "I was driving home and saw the fire. I figured someone had finally burned that old church down. I was surprised no one had done it sooner. You didn't burn it down, did you?" he asked me.

"No sir," I coughed, "I didn't." I was struggling to talk, but I felt like I had to explain why I was there—again. "I was driving out this way and saw the fire. I drove closer to see if anyone was out here. And then, just like last week, my car wouldn't start, so I tried to outrun the fire. I thought I was a goner because it caught up to me. But then someone pulled me out. Is the fire department here because I'd like to thank whoever it was that saved me."

The old man shook his head and said, "I don't know who saved you, but he must have left. As far as I can see, we are the only two people around."

His words shocked me because I knew someone pulled me out. It was dark and smoky, but the fire illuminated the landscape. If there was anyone else around, they had either gone back into the darkness or they had gone up in smoke. After all I had been through, I wouldn't doubt either possibility.

I was filthy and bleeding and knew I needed some medical aid. I asked him if he could take me to a local doctor or to a clinic. He said there were no doctors or clinics close by, but he informed me he had been a medic in the war and he could help me. "I can even do stitches if you need some. I have a first aid kit at my house."

That did not sound like a good option to me, so I asked him if he could just let me use a phone. I told him my cell phone wasn't working and I would call someone to pick me up. The only person I could think of who would do that would be Bill, my only friend in town.

"You can use my phone. Come on, I'll help you into my truck." He then helped me stand up and I staggered to his truck. My knees were so raw it hurt to move and my hands were just as bad. As we drove down the road to his house, I looked back and noticed the fire seemed to be slowing down. I asked him if we should call the fire department and he told me he'd take care of it.

He wasn't much of a talker, but I knew he was curious about why I was out there again. I decided to relieve his curiosity. I told him the truth that I worked for a magazine and was doing a story on the families of the missing people.

"So you are one of those media people who hounds these poor folks after all they have been through?" he surmised.

I assured him I was not like those people. "I want my stories to honor the missing—not exploit them."

"I'm sure you have their best interest in mind," he said sarcastically.

"Well, I'd like to think so. I guess if I were honest, I'd have to say I am out for a story, too. But if the story helps to honor the missing, then doesn't it accomplish a nice thing for these people? They don't want their loved ones to be forgotten so this is how I can help them," I explained patiently to him.

"If that is true, then what are you doing out here, in the middle of the country? None of those people are out here, are they?" He had a good point.

I wanted to tell him the truth about how I had followed one of the families out to the church and saw them doing some type of ceremony there. But when I started to say it, it didn't sound right. It kind of sounded like, I was stalking them. I couldn't think of a good response, so I just told him I had been trying to find someone and got lost.

"If that's your answer, then I guess we don't have anything more to say." And with that, he didn't say another word until we got to his house. How could he know I wasn't telling the truth?

When we pulled up to an old farmhouse, he told me, "Go inside and I'll show you where to wash up and I'll get some bandages for you. Then you can use my phone and be on your way." I knew he was perturbed with me because he somehow knew I was lying to him.

I couldn't stand his aloof judgment. "Alright, I'll tell you. I was following one of the families I had interviewed. They drove out to the abandoned church, and that's why I was out there last week. I went to the window of the church and looked in and there had to be about thirty people in there doing something." He looked at me in a strange way, so I said, "OK, maybe it was more like twenty. They had a lantern lit in the middle of a table and they were sitting around it. I couldn't be sure what they were up to, but I don't think it was a pot-luck dinner."

He looked at me like he was disgusted with me. I had seen that look a million times from my father. He finally said, "So apparently this family you were following didn't want you to honor their loved one?" He had me there.

"I guess it would seem that way," I agreed. "But what you don't know is the guy who put me in touch with this family, found out we went to high school together. He used to bully me back then and thought I was a loser. Apparently he still is a bully. He told me to get out of town and told the family to stay away from me."

I continued my explanation. "They had planned to help me before he got to them. I understand they don't know me, so naturally they'd trust him over me. But that's what I'm up against. He has a lot of power in Abilene, so I have to deal with some pretty big obstacles to get anyone here to speak to me."

He seemed a bit more sympathetic after he knew I was telling him the truth. "And who might this powerful man be who turned this family against you?"

I was reluctant to tell him, but it seemed like things were going better since I opened up to him. "Joseph Bardon—he's a sergeant in the police department."

He looked at me with surprise and smiled, "I know Joseph Bardon. He is my nephew."

Chapter 24

Whoever said, "Reality is stranger than fiction," must have lived in Abilene. I couldn't make this stuff up. What were the probabilities that the uncle of my high school nemesis would be the very one who would offer me kindness? I looked at the old man and said, "Are you pullin' my leg?"

He smiled and said, "He's a mean old cuss but he's my brother's son. If you knew my brother, you'd probably understand why he was so mean. I haven't seen him much since my brother died a few years ago. Never was close to my brother, or his son, and never wanted to be honestly. My brother and I pretty much hated each other, so I tried to avoid him. He made my life miserable while I was growing up. I don't think his son fell too far from the tree."

I wholeheartedly agreed, "No, I don't think he did, sir."

For the first time in my life, I felt validated. Someone else in the world could relate, literally, to the maniac I went to high school with. It was amazing to me that his very own uncle didn't like him.

"My name is Jake." He reached out to shake my hand, but I showed him the shape of my hand and he pulled his back and nodded. I felt warmth emanating from this man that comforted me. I felt he was someone I could trust even though he was related to my arch enemy.

"My name is Henry. Henry Pike. I write for a magazine called *Ragweed*. It's an on-line magazine, so you probably never heard of it." I figured, since he was older and lived out in the country, he probably didn't use a computer and never heard of an on-line magazine.

"So you don't think us country folks go on-line? I have heard of *Ragweed*. I have actually read a few of the articles, and they weren't that bad. Not sure I ever read any of yours though," he said.

I was surprised by his answer and explained, "I write under the name, 'Oh Henry'. How did you start reading *Ragweed*? Do you have a subscription?"

"No, I don't. They were offering a trial membership, so I thought I'd check it out. I decided not to keep it though," he explained.

"I see. Well, after tonight, I just might give you a free, life-long subscription," I smiled.

"That sounds like a nice reward for saving your life," he said sarcastically.

"I thought you said you didn't pull me out of the fire?" I reminded him.

"True. I didn't actually pull you out, but I'm the one taking you home and taking care of your wounds, aren't I? I'm being a Good Samaritan. Have you heard that story, Henry?" he asked.

"Yes, I have. I'm not as much a heathen as you might think," I said smugly.

"That remains to be seen," he replied. "Now get out of my truck before you bleed to death all over my seat."

"Don't think anyone would notice," I surmised as I looked at the mess inside his truck.

He shot right back, "Well, I might not have let you in my truck if it was a real clean, fancy one." I could see his point, and I told him I was glad he had a crummy truck. I liked this man and he seemed to like me, too.

We went into his modest home and a very little dog came up to greet us. "This is quite a watchdog you have here, Jake. He might scare off a mouse if one broke in."

Jake explained the dog was his friend's, but they had to move and couldn't take the little dog with them. Jake agreed to keep him, so they could visit him when they were in town.

"What's his name—Goliath?" I asked, trying to be funny.

"His name is Cooper, Henry," Jake informed me. I wasn't much of a dog person, but he was very cute. I would have liked to pet him, but my hands were almost raw, so I didn't.

Jake went into the kitchen to get some bandages. He came out with some pretty dishtowels that someone had embroidered. I looked at him with surprise and said, "I'm not going to let you use those nice towels for bandages."

"Why, are they not fancy enough for you?" he joked.

"That's just the thing, Jake, they are a little too fancy to stop my bleeding. Don't you have any ace bandages?" I asked.

"Fresh out," he replied sarcastically. "I don't use these towels. They just sit in my kitchen drawers and are useless. My wife made them a long time ago, and I know she would have liked for me to use them to help someone who is bleeding to death."

His sarcasm and wit were refreshing to me. "OK, apply the embroidered bandages."

He helped me to the bathroom where I washed up. Then he put some ointment on my raw knees and hands. He put the nice embroidered towels around my wounds and wrapped tape around them to hold them in place.

"There you are, as good as new." He stepped back to admire his work.

"Well, I guess so, if you think the cactus needles in my face were there before," I responded.

He went and got some tweezers, and then roughly pulled them out of my face, chest and arms. "You sure have a gentle touch," I grimaced.

"Well, you wanted them out, so I took them out. If you don't like the way I did it, you can do it next time," he said smugly.

I looked at myself in the mirror and replied, "I look like a half wrapped mummy with holes in my face. I can't go out in public like this."

"Well then, I guess you'll have to stay here for a few days," he said nonchalantly.

It kind of surprised me that he was so quick to let me stay in his home when he didn't know me. I figured he was probably enjoying the company, but I had to wonder if he had any ulterior motives, like turning me in to his nephew or stashing me out back in some hidden bunker.

I thanked him and explained how I needed to get back to town because I had a lot of work to do. "If I was going to tell someone how to pick me up here, what would I say?" I wondered.

He said he understood and then proceeded to give me such detailed instructions it made my head spin. I finally just asked him for his address and hoped Bill could use a GPS to find me.

Chapter 25

Bill seemed surprised to hear from me and even more surprised when I told him I needed him to come pick me up. When he asked me where I was, I tried to explain to him, "I'm somewhere out in the middle of nowhere near Potosi." As soon as I said it, I turned around and saw Jake standing there listening to my conversation. I hoped he didn't mind me describing his home as being out in the middle of nowhere.

Bill told me he didn't see that well at night and wasn't sure he'd be able to drive out in the country so late. I didn't want to push him, so I told him I'd find another way. He assured me he'd be happy to come the next morning. I wasn't sure I could wait that long. The thought of spending the night with someone I didn't know, out where I had been trapped twice and almost died, wasn't an appealing thought.

I told Bill I'd let him know if I decided to wait until the morning. After I hung up, Jake told me he would be happy to take me into town the next morning. He said, "I'm out here all alone, Henry. Please don't feel like you'd be putting me out to stay tonight. I'd be happy to have the company." Cooper seemed to agree with Jake as he came up to me wagging his tail.

Jake sounded so sincere I decided to take the risk and stay. "OK, Jake. Thank you for your hospitality. I guess it would make the most sense for me to stay here tonight. Are you sure it's OK? You don't even know me."

"I think I have a good sense of who you are, Henry. And, like I said, I would enjoy the company. I don't get too many visitors since my wife passed away," he confided.

"How long has she been gone?" I asked.

"It's been about fifteen years now," he said.

"That's a long time," I replied.

"It seems like yesterday to me. I can still see her flitting around the kitchen doing her magic. She was a great cook," Jake reflected.

"I'm sorry, Jake. It must be hard to lose someone you're so close to. I never got married, so I really can't relate," I admitted.

He seemed surprised. "A nice looking guy like you never found a woman?" I tried to remember if anyone had ever told me I was "nice-looking" besides my mother.

"No, I never did. I always hoped that would happen, but I guess it's too late now," I said sadly.

"As long as you're still breathin', it's never too late," he stated loudly. "You just need to get out in the world more and meet some people, instead of wandering around out here in the middle of nowhere," he said with a grin.

He showed me where the towels were and then showed me the spare bedroom where I'd be sleeping. I thanked him, and he then asked me if I was hungry. I hadn't even thought about it, but I never got to eat my hamburger, so I was pretty hungry.

"I have some turkey in the refrigerator. Would you like a sandwich?" he asked.

I told him I'd love one and I engulfed it in seconds. He made another one for me and I felt satisfied then. He asked me if I'd like some ice cream, and that sounded good. He scooped out a few dips for me. It was hard for me to hold the spoon because my hands were so sore, but I managed.

It felt so peaceful to be in this man's house and in his presence. I couldn't figure out why because he had the same blood running through his veins as the man I hated. I was glad I decided to stay the night.

118

We talked a little about current events and he seemed to be very knowledgeable about what was going on in the world. He was full of surprises. But, his relationship to Bardon was the biggest surprise. I hoped he was telling me the truth because I didn't want to wake up the next morning in handcuffs.

I finally started feeling tired as the adrenaline from the night was wearing off. I asked him if it would be ok for me to hit the hay. "Do you need me to read you a story?" he teased.

"No, that's OK. You probably need to go to bed since I imagine you have to get up early, and feed the chickens, and milk the cows," I quipped. I enjoyed our friendly banter.

"I got rid of all my animals a few years ago, Henry, so I will probably sleep as late as you city slickers do," he said smiling.

He didn't seem like the type that would sleep in. I told him I hoped he didn't snore. He laughed and said, "I hope I don't either, but I can't say for sure. I guess you'll have to let me know in the morning. Good night, Henry. Make yourself at home."

I told him good night and went into my room. I wished that my phone would work, but there was still no signal. It could be a long night especially if Jake snored. His room was right next to mine.

As soon as my head hit the pillow, I was out. I never realized how peaceful it was to not hear anything other than the night sounds of the country.

But about four in the morning, I woke up to the fact that Jake did snore— like a freight train. After that realization, it was a long time before I fell back asleep. Every time I moved, it hurt. My knees and hands were throbbing with pain. I took three more aspirin, and hoped it would numb the discomfort.

As I tossed and turned, I kept thinking about how I almost died that night in the fire. I wondered who started the fire and who pulled me out. The whole thing seemed surreal. But the experience did put life into perspective. I realized I had a lot of regrets, and I didn't want to die without trying to resolve some of them.

I thought about what Jake said that I should get out in the world and try to meet someone. I had kind of resigned myself to a life of loneliness. It was my biggest regret, but I had never considered doing anything about it.

As I reflected on the time I had been in Abilene, I realized nothing had happened the way I wanted it to, but somehow it had all worked out. It seemed like I found myself in just the right place at just the right time to meet just the right people.

Even though what happened to me that night was terrible, I was glad I met Jake. He seemed like someone I'd like to keep in touch with. And there was Bill, too. They both seemed like they might become good friends of mine. They would be the friends I'd call the next time I came to town.

It seemed like everything that had happened to me, since I arrived in Abilene, had a purpose. It often appeared like my paths had been orchestrated. But if they were, who or what was orchestrating them?

Chapter 26

When I woke up around seven that morning, it took me a minute to remember where I was and why I was there. But it all came flooding back as I started to move—the fire, the brush with death, the pain.

When I tried to sit up, pain shot through my legs and went straight up my back. My entire body seemed to be impacted by my narrow escape from the fire. I reached for my phone on the night table but it slipped right out of my hand. My palms were so raw, I couldn't completely shut my hands to hold onto the phone.

The clock on the wall said 7:10. I figured Jake must be up. I hoped he could take me into town so I could get some things done. I felt a sense of urgency for some reason, but as I tried to stand up, pain screamed from every raw nerve of my banged up knees. I fell back on the bed wondering if I would even be able to walk. My knees were two big scabs.

I yelled out to Jake so he could come help me up. I yelled again, but still no response. Where was he? At that moment several scenarios went through my mind and none of them were good.

With a big rocking motion, I managed to sit up on the bed. I tried the motion again to get up on my feet. It worked but the pain was very unpleasant. I shuffled to the door and tried not to bend my legs in any way.

The door creaked open and I yelled out again to Jake, hoping he was just hard of hearing. There was still no response other than Cooper running over to me. He jumped up for me to rub his head and I felt bad ignoring him. I shuffled over to the window to see if his truck was in the driveway but it wasn't there. I became more nervous.

I shuffled to the house phone to call Bill to come get me but there was no dial tone. That was when I started to panic. I shuffled back to my room to see if I could pick up my phone, but it had fallen behind the bed.

I was at a very big disadvantage with my painful knees and hands and no phone and no transportation. What could I do? I was in the middle of nowhere at the home of a family member of my biggest enemy. It did not appear to be a good situation. But, before I totally lost my composure, Jake walked in and I exhaled a sigh of relief.

He seemed surprised to see me up. He gave me a friendly greeting, "Good morning, Henry. How are you feeling today? I went to our little country store up the road and grabbed some eggs and bacon. I thought I'd make us some breakfast."

"That would be great." I replied much relieved. "I guess it's much easier to buy the eggs and bacon than having to raise the chickens and slaughter the hog," I joked.

Jake smiled, "Yes, it certainly is. I did enjoy raising my own food back in the day but it was just too much work. And since I am fresh out of farm hands, I decided to live like everybody else. I might get around to selling this place one day so someone could raise some food on it, but it's where I grew up so it makes it a little harder."

"This is your parent's home?" I asked.

Jake responded, "Yes, they lived here for almost forty years before they sold it to me. They decided to move into town with my brother Joey. He had a big house and he made part of his house into an apartment for them. Being in town made it easier for everyone because of all the doctor appointments they had. It was really the nicest thing my brother ever did— letting my parents live at his house."

He continued divulging his history as he got out a skillet and started our breakfast. "When my wife and I first got married, we didn't have much money, so we lived here with them and just never left. Miriam and I were older when we got married. I was in my late forties when I met her. She was a little younger. We never had any kids, so it was nice to have the company of my parents. I helped Dad with the farm and my wife helped my mother with the cooking and cleaning."

"We lived with them for about seven or eight years before they decided to move. They just basically gave us the house, which I don't think my brother liked too much, but he didn't need it. Anyway, since I grew up in this house, it's kind of hard to let it go. I know the land is just wasting away since no one is using it. Someone could have a nice ranch out here," he reflected as he started cooking the bacon.

Jake apparently liked talking about himself, and I enjoyed listening to him, so I kept asking him questions. "So how many acres do you have here, Jake?"

"I have about twenty acres—it's plenty of land to have a ranch or to grow a crop. I just lost the interest to try and do anything like that. But, I really don't want to move into town," he explained.

"It certainly is peaceful, but don't you ever get lonely being out here?" I asked.

"You mean living out here in the middle of nowhere?" he grinned. Apparently he would never let that go.

Then he answered my question, "Sometimes I get a little lonely or bored, but then somebody will come out here, in the middle of nowhere, for some unexplainable reason, and his car breaks down on the side of the road. Then the very same person comes out the next week and almost dies in a fire, because he can't seem to stay away from this place, and I have to rescue him again. So when someone like that comes along, it kind of relieves the boredom, I guess." He laughed and I laughed, too. I imagined I had brought some measure of excitement to his life.

Then he decided to ask me a few questions. "What kind of place do you live in, Henry? Do you own a home?"

"I live in a townhouse in Fort Worth. I've lived there about eleven years now. I like it because I don't have to worry about a yard or any maintenance. I travel a lot, so I don't want to be tied down to a house."

"I guess you don't want to be tied down to a woman, either?" he asked.

"Well, I just never had much time for socializing. I'm always working it seems." I realized it was a lame excuse as I said it.

"One day you might regret that, Henry," he said thoughtfully.

"I regret it now, Jake." And I did. I felt like I could be honest with him.

"So what are your plans, Henry? Would you like for me to take you into town?" he asked.

"If you wouldn't mind, I would sure appreciate it," I said.

He asked me to sit down to eat, so I slowly lowered myself painfully into the chair, keeping my legs as straight as I could. We ate a hearty, country breakfast. He had made some biscuits the day before and warmed them up. They tasted homemade, not like the ones I usually bought in the can. He poured some white, creamy gravy over the biscuits. The breakfast was heavenly.

After breakfast, we set out for town. We drove down the country road that was becoming unpleasantly familiar to me. I could see what was left of my car. I asked him if I could get out and look at it, but I forgot how much it would hurt to try and walk. I just stood near it and looked at what was left. It was still warm to the touch but was burned to the point no one would be able to recognize it, hopefully. "I liked this car. It was the first car I ever bought new," I said sadly.

"How long did you have it?" Jake asked.

"I only had it two years and planned to have it many more," I said, as I looked at the smoldering shell of my car.

"That's a real shame, Henry. Well maybe you can get another new one?" he said hopefully.

I realized I probably should take some pictures of it and of the church, so I could show the insurance company where the fire started. I asked him if we could drive by the church so I could take some pictures. As we drove up to the church we could see little puffs of smoke still rising from the ash. I took a few pictures of the ruins and then we headed to town.

I wondered how the fire went out, so I asked, "Jake, did you ever get a chance to call the fire department?"

He acted surprised when I asked him. He hesitantly responded, "I took care of it."

I was almost certain he had never called them and decided to push the issue. "You know, I tried to use the phone this morning and it didn't work," I said wondering how he'd respond.

"Sometimes, the phone works and other times it doesn't. It's as fickle as a woman," he explained. I didn't want to doubt him and remembered it had worked the night before when I called Bill.

If he was lying about calling the fire department, I decided I really didn't want to know. I was tired of not being able to trust anyone and I wanted to trust this man. He was someone I wanted to keep as a friend.

Then he looked over at me and confessed, "Henry, I never called the fire department. I'm sorry I lied to you, but I didn't think you would understand. I knew the fire would burn itself out as soon as it hit the road. When a fire is low like that, it will stop at a gravel road, unless the wind is high and it wasn't last night."

I was glad he told me the truth, but I knew there had been a strong breeze the night before which spread the fire to my car and then entrapped me. I was surprised he hadn't noticed.

"Really?" I asked puzzled. "I could see the wind whipping up when I was close to the fire last night, Jake. That's why it spread to the tree and towards my car and even caught up to me," I reminded him.

He looked at me and said, "Please don't ask me to explain this, Henry." He paused a moment and then looked back at the road. He spoke very quietly when he said, "It wasn't the wind."

Chapter 27

J ake kept his eyes on the road and became very quiet after making such a surprising statement. I kept looking at him expecting him to continue, but he seemed finished with his shocking revelation.

"Jake, you can't just say something like that and not explain what you mean. Please tell me what you're talking about," I pleaded.

"Henry, you don't want to know, trust me. I know there are many unexplainable things going on around these parts right now, and, unfortunately, I have discovered some of the reasons why. I don't like the answers I've found, Henry, and you wouldn't either. All you need to know is there is a world within this world which we can't see—at least not with our natural eyes. And let me assure you, that world is as real as this one," he stated hesitantly.

"What are you saying, Jake?" I asked, skeptically.

He paused a minute and then looked over at me, "Henry, some creature or devil from that unseen world started the fire at the church, and I think it was trying to kill you."

I looked at him in disbelief as I thought about what he had said. I really was amazed he even believed in things like this. "What are you saying, Jake? Are you saying there are spirits drifting around here starting fires and trying to kill people?" I asked incredulously, expecting him to make a joke.

"Yes," he simply replied.

"I didn't take you for one of those 'types'," I said. I expected him to be offended and hoped he would try to defend himself.

"Well, you were wrong, Henry. I didn't start out being one of those 'types', but when you come face to face with one of those spirits, you become one of those 'types'. So it may sound unbelievable to you, but it has become very real to me, regrettably," he explained.

"So how do you know one of these spirits was trying to kill me, Jake?" I was terrified to hear his explanation because all I could think about was the creature Teresa called 'the souch'. My greatest fear was that thing was going to come after me.

Jake gave me a stern warning. "You are putting your nose into places where you are not welcome, Henry. The one thing they don't like is being exposed. And when you attempt to uncover all that is going on here, you will uncover their secret existence and they will respond——and they do not respond kindly," he emphasized. "You must understand what I'm saying, Henry, and not go into this blindly. They are going to try to stop you."

He then looked at me with the seriousness of a mortician, "I have no doubt they will kill you if they can, Henry. After you get all your car business taken care of, I suggest you go back to Fort Worth and forget about this story. I'm saying this for your own good, I really am," he declared.

"You seem very afraid of these ghosts, Jake," I countered. I hoped he would return to his jovial manner and quit talking like this.

"Let's just say I have a healthy respect for them, Henry, and leave it at that," he responded.

"How did you learn about these beings, Jake? It seems like you know a lot about them," I surmised.

"Much more than I'd like to know, Henry," he confessed. "I am hoping they will never find out I had this conversation with you. That's why I didn't say anything until we got into the truck and left my house. I think they are stronger out where I live, and I think that church may have something to do with it."

Jake continued to explain, "I use to go that church when I was young. It was your typical Sunday morning service. There were about fifty people or so that attended and they were all decent people," he explained.

"One morning we heard a young mother screaming outside after the service. We all ran out to see what was wrong. She couldn't find her little girl. We all started searching for her and we all just thought she had wandered off somewhere. But we never found her. She blamed the church for her little girl's disappearance, and told everyone the church was evil. It seemed like a darkness came over the whole church after that and it eventually just dried up. So we quit going to church, mostly because there weren't any other churches close by at the time."

"Then when I got older, I heard rumors that people were having séances in that old church. I remember my parents talking about it. They were very upset the church was being used for something devilish. Even after they quit having the séances, I always felt there was something going on in the church that no one could see. It would give me the creeps every time I drove by it, especially at night."

"Nobody used the church after that, well, I guess until now. Apparently people think that god-forsaken place is some kind of portal for spirits. Maybe it is?" he pondered.

"So, that was what those people were doing that night I saw them sitting around the lantern?" I deduced.

"It wouldn't surprise me, Henry. These people are desperate to get some word about their loved ones and they'll go to any lengths to get it—even to the dead."

Jake continued, "But it's not just the old church where these things are happening—it seems to be everywhere. Just a few months back, I went to a family picnic out by Tuscola, and I noticed two of my cousins gossiping about one of my nieces who had just recently married. They were wondering how long the marriage would last and were badmouthing her new husband."

Jake clarified, "Those women have been gossiping for as long as I've known them, so this was nothing new. But this time, there was something new. While they were talking, I could see two spirit-like creatures on them. Each woman had a dark looking creature attached close to their mouths." He paused for a minute as he was apparently remembering the incident.

"And what happened, Jake?" I asked. I was wondering if he had seen the same dark spirits I had.

"I didn't know what they were, but they looked kind of like leaches. They were very dark, but you could see right through them. I couldn't believe my eyes. And you know, Henry, it looked like these things were feeding off their words—off their gossip—as it came out of their mouths. It was sickening to watch, but my cousins didn't seem to have any idea they were even there. I thought maybe I was hallucinating from the heat," he grimaced.

"I might be crazy, Henry, but I swear to you, when I saw those women a little later, those dark creatures had grown larger. It made me sick to my stomach. I wanted to tell them, but I knew they wouldn't believe me, so I just walked away."

"I decided to leave after that. On my way out, I saw one of my elderly aunts, so I stopped to talk to her for a few minutes. I always enjoyed visiting with her, but I didn't that day. I asked her how she was doing, and she told me she was having quite a 'spell'. She told me her stomach was giving her fits from all the greasy barbeque. She kept saying over and over how sick she felt and all she wanted to do was go home."

"As she continued to complain, I happened to look down at her feet and legs. I could see something like black specks forming on her legs. She had on a dress, and I could see those black bug-like creatures crawling up her legs. She didn't seem to notice them, so I reached down to swat them off. Henry, my hand went right through them and they remained on her legs. She asked me what I thought I was doing and I told her I saw a bug on her leg. She looked down and said she didn't see anything. I felt like I was the only one who could see these creatures," he moaned.

When he told me this story, I recalled the thing that had attacked me in my motel room. And even though I could feel it, I couldn't grab it. It surprised me that none of these people could feel these creatures on them like I had.

Jake continued, "At that point, I had enough of my family and these disgusting beings. I was walking towards my car when I heard another one of my cousins, come out with some colorful language. As he continued with his loud, profanity ridden story, I saw something dark hanging out of his mouth and I knew—it wasn't barbeque." He shook his head in bewilderment.

As he talked about these experiences at the picnic, I thought of the day I was at Teresa's house and how I kept saying I felt sick, even though I lied about it initially. I realized I kept getting more nauseous as I kept saying how I felt. I wondered if my words brought on that queasiness. I never thought our words could have that much power.

Jake continued, "For some reason, these spirits seem to be coming into our part of the world in droves. It's like someone left the door open 'upstairs', or 'downstairs' in this case. They are flocking to us like vultures, and our words seem to be what they feed on. Our words are the only invitation they need, Henry. And any bad or negative words seem to draw them like flies to rotting meat."

As he said this, I remembered what Bill told me the street preacher had said about our words. I came right out and asked, "Do you believe in God, Jake?"

"I sure do. I always have. And when you realize these devilish spirits are real, you are real thankful to know there is a Spirit who is good," he reasoned.

"Maybe, Jake. I don't know. It all seems too farfetched. I never believed in any of these things, until I came back to Abilene," I declared.

"Well then, I guess it's a good thing you came back, Henry," he said smiling.

"Jake, how can you live around these evil spirits? Obviously you are afraid. You can't keep living like this," I stated.

"It seems like if I leave them alone, they leave me alone. I keep thinking things will get back to normal one day, and they will go back to the dark place they must have come from," he said hopefully.

We pulled up in front of the car rental place and Jake looked at me and said, "It was nice to meet you, Henry Pike. I'm sorry it has to end like this."

I looked at him puzzled. "I'm glad I met you, too, Jake. What do you mean, 'It has to end like this'?" I asked.

"I'm sorry, Henry, I just think it's best if we don't stay in touch," he said sadly.

I looked at him like I was losing my best friend. "I don't think we have to go to that extreme, Jake. I really enjoy talking to you, especially about all of these things. And what if I have more questions?" I reasoned.

"Henry, I have already risked everything trying to help you. I could get in trouble from both sides of the fence if anyone, or anything, finds out. I really can't think of any more I could tell you anyway. Just be careful, Henry. Think about your words before you say them," he exhorted.

His decision made me sad because I had hoped Jake Bardon would become a good friend of mine. As I got out of his truck, he looked at me and was very serious. His parting words were what sounded like a proverb, "Life and death are in the power of the tongue, Henry. Choose life." And with that he was off. I would never see him again.

Chapter 28

When Jake drove off, I felt disappointed by his decision. I felt he was overreacting to these spirits and I didn't want to lose his friendship because of it. His life seemed so limited by his fear, but then I realized, my life wasn't much different from his. We were just afraid of different things. I was afraid of his nephew, and he was afraid of supernatural beings.

While I sat in the car rental place waiting for my car, I considered the warning Jake gave me. I knew it was something I should take seriously. I needed to be more mindful about my words. I reflected over my life and knew I had spoken some horrible things over myself. And unfortunately, many of those negative predictions had come true. Apparently, my words had affected my life.

The woman behind the desk told me they would have a car for me in a few minutes. I thanked her and went back to my thoughts. If what Jake said was true, then everyone I knew had brought great harm to themselves by the words they used.

My father had said so many negative things over my life, it was easy to see why I was such a mess. And he wasn't the only one speaking negative things over me; I was constantly putting myself down. My words had, for the most part, been prophetic. Nearly everything I believed about myself and my future had come true.

My deep thoughts were interrupted by a rental car pulling up. The lady told me it was mine, and I thanked her. I moved the seat back as far as I could before I got in. I had decided to rent a larger vehicle where I could keep my legs and knees stretched out as much as possible while driving.

As I drove back to my motel, I continued to think about the words I had spoken over my life, as well as the words my father had spoken over me. It was evident how much harm can be done to children when their parents constantly berate them. It is definitely a subtle form of child abuse.

My sister managed to escape most of the negative proliferation of words spoken by my father. His words were usually aimed at me or my mother, but he still spoke some harsh things to her. He thought she'd get pregnant before she graduated from high school because she was a pretty girl. And he never thought she was smart enough to go to college.

But, Carrie did not give in to my father's projections and predictions of how her life would turn out. She rejected his negativity and would counter it with her positive attitude. I often made fun of her and called her a "Pollyanna," but in hindsight, I could see she had been the smart one.

She would playfully try to tell my dad to see the glass half-full instead of half-empty. He would often seem amused that she had the guts to stand up to him, and sometimes it helped to curb his toxic words—at least for the moment. Apparently her positive way had served her well because she was very happy in her life with her family, faith, and teaching job. I had often made fun of her, but I should have been more like her.

I decided I would call her (something I rarely did). She answered my call immediately and seemed pleasantly surprised. She didn't ask me if anything was wrong, but I'm sure she wondered since I rarely called her. I asked her the usual questions about how she was doing and how her family was.

After some polite conversation, I told her where I was and what I was doing. She was shocked. "Henry, I can't believe you are in Abilene! I remember you told me you'd never set foot there again," she laughed and then said, "Never say 'never'."

When she said that I chuckled realizing she had inadvertently brought up the very reason I had called her. "Carrie, I was just thinking today about how you always had such a positive attitude growing up. I know I made fun of you a lot, but now I'm starting to realize how important our words are. It is so important to speak good things over your life like you did. Your life turned out well, just like you always said it would."

"I remember when we were growing up how you would usually brush off problems and didn't worry much about anything. I, on the other hand, would anguish over every little thing. How were you so positive when our family was so negative?" I begged to know.

"I never really thought I was so different from you, Henry, but it did seem like you saw everything in a bad light. You were always thinking the world was out to get you and everyone hated you. I never could understand how it helped you to think like that?" she responded.

"Well, obviously, it didn't help me. I wouldn't be where I am today if I had been more like you, Carrie. I guess dad's opinion of me didn't help. He always liked you, Carrie. He seemed to despise me. I think that's where I got my beliefs about myself—it was from him," I reflected.

She replied. "Henry, I don't think our father liked himself too much. You remember his father treated him badly and really wanted nothing to do with him most of his life. Our dad was a hurting person who hurt others—especially his family. I never believed he thought much of me, either."

"He seemed to like you more than anyone else in the family," I reminded her.

"No, he didn't, Henry. He wasn't as hard on me as he was you, but he had very few good things to say about me. I don't remember him ever telling me he loved me. Did he ever tell you, Henry?" she asked.

I was surprised by her statement and started thinking about her question. I actually did remember an incident that prompted him to say it. "Yes, he did once. You remember when I had that car accident where my car flipped over a few times. It was after I had moved to Fort Worth and had lived there a few months. He came to see me in the hospital. When he left, he leaned over my bed and told me he loved me. I was so shocked when he said it. It was almost worth losing my car just to hear him say those words."

As I thought of that incident, I was trying to remember if he had ever said it any other time. And then it hit me like a ton of bricks— I had never told my father I loved him.

"Well you are one up on me, Henry, because he never said it to me," Carrie responded.

As she continued to share memories of our dad, I realized I may have misinterpreted my father's contempt for me. He certainly was not the picture, perfect daddy, but neither was I the perfect son. Perhaps it was my disdain for him that made me think he felt the same way about me.

My sister still managed to interpret the world in a totally different way than I did, even though she didn't get what she needed from our father, either. She was still able to care about the flawed man who was our father, not letting his pain define her life. She apparently understood his actions and words better than I did.

As we wrapped up our unusual conversation, I thanked her for helping me to see some things I needed to see. She told me how glad she was I had called. "Henry, I miss you. Let's talk more often. And I would love for you to come see us soon."

"I will, Carrie. I'm sorry I haven't been the greatest brother. I plan to change that," I promised.

As we hung up, I had the disappointing revelation that I had been the culprit in my life all along. All those years I had blamed my father for everything wrong with me, but it was really me who had messed up my own life. I had blamed the bullies in school for my social inadequacies, and though they were wrong to do what they did, it was my reaction to them that dictated the rest of my life. I only had myself to blame.

There was now much regret and sadness as I faced these truths about myself. The question was: What would I do with the rest of my life? Would I let this make me feel more defeated, or would I change how I reacted to what life threw at me?

I decided then and there to change my perspective on life. I had recently heard a great saying, "What you believe about something makes it true—at least to you."

It doesn't matter if what you believe is right or wrong, it becomes your reality because it's what you believe. I had always believed I was a loser, unworthy of love, and I had unknowingly fulfilled those beliefs by how I lived.

As I pondered my past and my future, I decided I would make the effort to change my beliefs, my actions and my words. I knew if I didn't, my life would stay the same and I didn't want it to stay the same. I wanted to really live my life and have no more regrets! I knew this meant taking risks, but what did I really have to lose? I knew I wasn't going to change overnight, but I was not going to continue going down the same road I had always chosen—the path of least resistance.

With these new revelations, I felt a little more hopeful about the rest of my life. And after all of the emotional upheaval and soul searching I had done the last two days, I realized how very tired I was. My knees and hands were hurting and my whole body felt like lead. I needed to sleep for a few hours, so I could get back to the story I had come to do. I took a long, peaceful nap. I had not slept so soundly in weeks as I did that day.

Chapter 29

Bright light was shining in through my curtains as I woke up, which I found strange since it was late afternoon when I laid down for my nap. I got up to shut the curtains and almost fainted from the pain. My raw knees quickly reminded me of all I had been through the past few days. I groaned as I hobbled over to the curtains to see why it was so bright outside. I was totally disoriented, which was not unusual for me when I sleep soundly.

Even though I thought I was taking a short nap, I somehow had managed to sleep until the next morning. I must have been more exhausted than I realized. I knew my weary body needed the rest.

After washing up and putting on some warm up pants, which were the most comfortable and easiest pants to put on, I shuffled down to the hotel restaurant to get some breakfast. The last time I had eaten was with Jake when he had made me that wonderful breakfast, so I was hungry. After I got my food at the breakfast buffet, I looked up at the TV hanging on the wall. As I started to take in what I was seeing, my empty stomach started churning.

I moved closer so I could hear what the reporter was saying. Words were flying by on the bottom of the screen—something about unusual fires out by Potosi. I wondered if he was referring to the church. But the reporter said "fires." Was there another one?

He was standing next to a smoldering building as he continued his report. This couldn't be the church because it was still smoldering. Where was he?

Fear started to creep up my spine and into my consciousness. Surely it could not be. I prayed he was not standing next to what once had been Jake's house. "Oh, God!" I cried inside with anguish, "Please don't let this be Jake's house."

The reporter talked about the early morning fire and how someone driving down the road had seen the blaze and called the fire department. He continued his disturbing report: "There were no survivors from this blaze. Authorities tell us they have recovered only one body, but they are not sure how many people lived in this country home. We will have more updates at twelve. In other news...."

I looked at the TV in disbelief. Maybe my imagination was in overdrive. I went to the newsstand and bought a paper to see if there was any more on the story. The article had the additional information there had been another fire in the same vicinity within the last few days. I felt unsettled and full of dread.

My thoughts started racing as I began to realize the implications. If it was Jake's house, those "evil creatures" had found out he talked to me and they were taking revenge on him. And the horrifying realization followed—they would come after me next.

I couldn't believe all of this was happening. I had to know for sure if it was Jake's house. I had to go there, but I knew there would be police and firemen out there, too, so I had to be careful. And I had no doubt Bardon would be there, as well.

It grieved me to think Jake may have paid with his life in order to help me. I felt sad as I remembered our short lived friendship.

I went back to my room immediately—almost in a panic. How could I protect myself from something that, a few months ago, I didn't even know existed?

My initial thought of going out to Jake's house was being replaced by sheer panic. I decided the risk of driving out there was too high, especially since his deranged nephew would probably be there. I believed the only sane thing to do was to get out of Abilene fast. Fear was taking control of my mind.

Then, I started to rationalize my actions as I got out my suitcase and began to pack. I was taking Jake's advice and leaving. He knew he was risking his life when he tried to help me, so I didn't want him to die in vain. I started panicking, packing, and planning all at the same time. What would I say to Sid? How could I explain to him that I quit the story I had begged him to let me finish?

But as I continued to frantically pack, the thought of the little girl came back to me. I remembered how desperately I wanted to help her in my dream. I had resolved to help her and all the missing, if I could. But instead, I was running away in fear. That was exactly what I had done all my life. I had already forgotten the promises I made to Carrie and to myself that I was going to change my life and not let others tell me how to live—including bullies and evil supernatural beings.

I didn't know if the little girl was real or a figment of my active imagination, but I did know I was probably the only one who could help the missing because of the information Jake had shared with me. I doubted anyone else knew what was really happening in Abilene. If I left, I would be giving in to what I knew these sinister spirits wanted. They would win and then what would happen to the missing people?

It was like a light came on in my head and it suddenly illuminated the darkness swirling around me. I was letting those evil beings win. I was letting fear take over my life. I looked around my room, wondering if one of those dark spirits was nearby. It almost seemed like something, or someone, was churning this fear up in my mind.

Perhaps, that was how it worked? These spirits of darkness whisper fearful things into your ear until you become afraid. Then you start repeating their fearful words or acting on them, and all the while these demons are cheering you on.

Could it be possible those spirits put everything in place in order to scare me? Hoping I would act on the fear? Hoping I would leave and let them stay hidden?

As I considered all of this, defiance rose up in me. If those spirits were close by, I would make sure they heard what I had to say. "I will not leave. You are not going to scare me. You are not going to win."

Those spoken words encouraged me. I was through being intimidated by anyone. It was an amazing feeling. Fear was not going to be a factor in my life anymore. I was not going to be bullied anymore by demons or anyone else. I was tired of cowering to whatever life threw at me and it was going to stop.

I put my things back in the drawers and decided to do what was right and see if my friend, Jake, was still alive.

Chapter 30

As I lowered myself into my rental car, it occurred to me that I couldn't just show up at Jake's house because there would be people there. I would have to find a place where I could see the house, or what was left of it, without anyone noticing me. I remembered seeing a small hill in the distance, when we left his house the morning he drove me back to Abilene. I also recalled the hill was north of the house and I thought I could find it. I knew I would need some binoculars.

I went to a local store and bought the binoculars, and then drove to the area near Potosi which was becoming way too familiar. I drove slowly as to not kick up any dust. It took me about thirty minutes to find the right spot. I pulled the car as close as I could to the bottom of the small hill overlooking the area where Jake lived.

It was hard to ascend the hill trying to keep my legs straight, so I used a large rock to lower myself down to a sitting position. Trying to keep my legs parallel to the ground, I used my hands to push myself up the hill. I was thankful for the embroidered towels wrapped around my hands, as they were strong and cushioned my movements.

As I scooted up the hill on my butt, my knees, and hands were screaming in pain. I finally wiggled up to the top and then turned over on my stomach, so I could easily look through my binoculars. It took me a few seconds to get them adjusted, but when I did, I could see wisps of smoke coming from what once had been Jake's house. My heart sank as I realized my friend was dead.

My head dropped to the dirt in sadness and tears fell from my eyes. Jake had given his life to help me. It was almost too much to bear. His sacrifice inspired me to think there must be a purpose for my life, and I determined at that moment, his death would not be in vain. One way I knew I could honor him, would be to finish writing this story and warn people about these evil creatures.

Fear kept trying to grip me as I realized that, by pursuing this story, I was literally 'playing with fire'.

I made myself look at Jake's house again. The binoculars gave me a good view of who was there, and my nemesis stood out from everyone else because of his size and my disdain for him. I watched him as he walked boisterously back and forth, probably yelling at everyone there, bossing their every movement. I doubted he cared that much that his uncle had died in the blaze, but I was sure he pretended he did.

No doubt they were thinking arson as they looked over the remains of Jake's house. I wished I could tell them who started the fire but knew they would never believe me.

As I panned out over the area, I saw there were also people walking around where the church had been. I was sure they were scouring the area looking for clues, but I knew those spirits wouldn't leave any.

But then I saw someone looking at the shell of my car. Surely there was no way they could trace the car back to me. There was little left of the car, but I had watched enough dramas to know they have ways of figuring these things out. I got a knot in my stomach thinking of the possibilities.

Fear rose up in me again. How could I explain why my car was there? And if they thought I started the church fire, would they pin the fire at Jake's house on me, too? My mind started racing as I grappled with the potential for a very bad situation.

My focus had to stay on my purpose. I could not allow myself to worry about what might happen. I looked at my old car one last time because I knew I could never risk coming back. As I looked it over with the binoculars, I forced myself to believe there wasn't enough left of the car that could point to me. They would hopefully conclude it was just an abandoned car.

I couldn't believe those demons had killed my friend. And I had no doubt they would come after me, too. The best thing I could do for everyone was to figure out how to defeat them.

As I began my slow, painful descent on my butt trying to keep my legs as straight as possible, I noticed movement near the large rock. My first thought was a rattlesnake and I wondered what I would do if it bit me. I would probably pass out before I could get back to town.

I decided to scoot sideways away from the rock while keeping my eye on it. As I started to move sideways, I saw movement again and realized, if it was a snake, I would have heard the dreaded rattles by then but there was no sound.

With each inch I moved, I kept looking at the rock wondering what I would soon have to face. After reaching the bottom of the hill, I tried to push myself up, but I couldn't bend my knees. How was I going to get up without using the large rock as leverage?

As I pondered my predicament, I saw a dark, shadowy, snakelike being emerge from behind the rock. It moved very close to the ground. It was long like a snake and slithered like a snake, but it wasn't like any snake I had ever seen.

As I tried to wrap my brain around what this thing was, it continued its slow, calculating movement towards me. I had never seen anything like it. Terror was flooding my mind as I looked at it helplessly, trying not to imagine what it would do to me.

There would be no point in yelling for help because there was no one nearby. I was about to give in to total fear and panic when I saw something in the distance. I didn't want to take my eyes off the snake, but I had to see what else was moving towards me. Could it be another dark nemesis coming to gang up on me?

But the figure looked like a regular man. He walked quickly towards me, and I could only hope he was there to help. The shadowy snake looked over at him as he approached and immediately left. The snake seemed afraid of this man.

Whoever he was, I was grateful he showed up when he did. I was surprised he was able to scare the spirit snake off, especially from a distance.

When the man reached me, the sun outlined his head, which made it hard to see him. But when he reached down to help me up, I could see his face clearly and knew immediately who he was. It was the crazy prophet/ preacher/possible serial killer standing over me in a deserted place, and I couldn't even stand up—much less run.

Considering who I believed this man to be, I wondered if I would have been better off with the snake.

Chapter 31

I t was a surreal moment to look into the eyes of the very man I believed was behind all the disappearances. When he reached down to help me up, I took his hand without thinking, because I knew I needed his assistance to get up. But when his hand clasped mine, I felt something like electricity flowing from his hand into my hand, even with the thick towel wrapped around it. It shocked me, and I let go as soon as I got up on my feet.

"What was that?" I asked, referring to the power I felt from his hand.

"I'm not sure I know what you are talking about?" he responded.

I decided to overlook his weird handshake because I thought there were more pressing issues at hand. No doubt he could sense my uneasiness being near him. I didn't want him to know how afraid I was, so I tried to act as normal as I could. I said, "Thank you so much for helping me up. I was out here exploring the area, and I fell when I was coming down the hill."

"Well, it was a good thing you already had the bandages on," he said, somewhat confused as he looked at the embroidered towels taped around my hands. He couldn't see the bandages under my warm up pants, although I was sure blood from my knees was beginning to seep through.

I realized what I told him sounded rather absurd so I tried to think of another lie to explain the last one. "Yes, well I already had these bandages from a previous accident, but I didn't let that keep me from going out today."

He looked at me like I was as ridiculous as the lies I was telling him. "Yes, I can certainly understand why you would want to come out here and explore this area," he said sarcastically.

I knew he didn't believe me, so I finally confessed, "Actually, I had just gone up the hill to see the house that had burned down. I thought I might know the man who lived there."

"Was it his house?" he asked.

"Yes, unfortunately it was," I responded.

"I'm sorry to hear that," he said.

I doubted his sincerity. I tried to think of something else to say, but I felt helpless around this man because I didn't know what he was capable of. And I certainly didn't want him to know I thought he might be the prime suspect in the case of the missing. The only thing I wanted to do was leave, as I nervously eyed my car. But, unfortunately, he was between me and the car.

He just stood there looking at me, and I felt like I had to say something. I decided if I could only ask him one question it would be how he scared that snake thing away. If he had some kind of secret to keep these spirits away, I certainly needed it. They seemed intent on killing me. I asked him, "Why did that spirit-like snake, or whatever it was, leave when you came over to help me?"

"Because I know who I am," he responded. "I have the power to trample on snakes and scorpions."

His answer surprised me. "Who gave you this power?" I asked, with great curiosity.

"The Son," he replied simply.

I had no idea whose Son he was talking about, but I asked him anyway, "Can I get this power?"

"Yes, it is available to anyone," he informed me.

That was encouraging to hear, but he was making me work for every ounce of information. "OK, so how do I get this power?" I asked him somewhat annoyed.

"You must ask The One, who conquered these evil creatures, to save you and live in you," he replied.

"I need to ask someone to live in me?" I asked confused.

"Yes, that is how you have His power," he explained.

This man was getting on my nerves with his lofty, mystical answers. He certainly sounded crazy like everyone said, but I couldn't deny the fact the snake left when he showed up.

But then another question preempted all the other questions I had for him. It suddenly occurred to me how odd it was for him to be out there in the first place. It was also a very strange coincidence he happened to show up the same time the snake did.

And then another troubling question followed that one. I wondered if he might have had something to do with the fire at Jake's house. I had to ask him, "Why are you even out here in this deserted place?"

"I come out here precisely because it is isolated. That way I can be alone and hear The One who is always speaking. It is much harder to hear Him in the midst of many people," he said thoughtfully.

That didn't seem like the answer of a serial killer, but I knew they often come across as very nice people, at first. Since he was willing to answer all my questions, I decided to take advantage of the opportunity.

"Are you a pastor?" I asked.

"No, I just preach to whoever will listen," he said.

"Are you the one they call 'the prophet'?" I asked.

"Some might call me that," he responded.

"What is your name?" I was hoping he would give me his real name but I was certainly not expecting the response he gave me.

"You know my name, Henry," he said as he stared right at me.

His answer gave me chills. How did he know my name? And why did he think I knew who he was? I nervously asked him, "How do you know my name?"

"Let's just say someone told me," he replied.

"OK." I said apprehensively, wondering who in the world he was talking about.

"Is your name Micah?" I asked.

"Yes," he said.

It was shocking to me that I was having this conversation with the very man I was convinced had to be the perpetrator behind all the missing. I knew I had to confront him if I was serious about finding these people.

"And weren't you arrested several times on suspicion of murder?" I ventured.

"Yes," he replied. "I was."

I didn't expect him to be so forthright. I realized I was pushing my luck, but I wanted to ask him every question I could while the opportunity was staring me in the face.

"And weren't you also arrested for disturbing the peace?" I asked.

"Peace that can be disturbed is not really peace at all, Henry," he explained.

That kind of made sense to me, and I wondered if these little nuggets of wisdom were what drew Elias and maybe others to him. I decided to really provoke him to see how he would respond. "You know, most people think you are crazy."

"Henry, you are the one seeing spirit snakes," he said with a bit of a smile which surprised me.

He had a good point, but then I wondered, "You saw it too, right?"

"Yes, I did see it. I see them all the time," he said.

"You aren't afraid of them?" I asked.

"No," he replied. "I have more power than they do." He mentioned his power again which I really wanted, but I decided not to ask him about it again. My main goal was to find the missing.

"I find it interesting that all the families who have a loved one missing, know who you are," I stated, wondering how he would respond.

"Many people listen to me when I speak," he said. "What are you trying to say, Henry?"

"Just that.... you seem to be the common denominator with everyone missing, Micah, if that is even your name," I said deliberately.

I probed further, "I was doing a search on some of the events in Abilene from the past few years, and I happened to see your picture at one of those events. You were at the Art Walk, Micah, and the date on the picture was before the first person was reported missing. And you actually looked like a relatively normal person in that picture," I added purposely. I had to wonder if I was a very stupid man accusing him of being a serial killer out in the middle of nowhere.

"Yes, I was there, Henry, but I was not normal. I had all anyone could want back then but I found it can all be taken from you. I ended up with nothing, but found everything," he proclaimed.

"And what was it you found?" I asked with great curiosity.

"Truth," he responded.

"What truth?" I asked.

"There is only one Truth, Henry. If you search for it, you will find it," he guaranteed.

"I have been searching for truth all my life and I have never found it," I declared angrily.

"Keep looking and you will," he said. "It's a promise."

I was getting fed up with his super spiritual, pie-in-the-sky answers, so I decided to ask him what I really wanted to know. "What happened to all of the missing people, Micah?"

"Why do you think I would know the answer to that question, Henry?" he asked.

"Because you seem to know a lot of unusual things, Micah, and ten people missing without any clues is pretty unusual!" I stated loudly.

He tempered my agitation by asking me a question, "Henry, have you ever heard of Enoch?"

His question threw me because it was so unexpected. I regained my composure and responded, "No, does he live in Abilene?"

"When you find out who he is, we'll continue this conversation." He turned around and started walking towards the road. I was dumbfounded. I wasn't through talking to him, but he had ended our question and answer session without my consent.

As I watched him leave, I realized it was strange he hadn't hurt me or kidnapped me. If he truly was the guilty party, his reaction was a mystery, especially since I had just implied he was the perpetrator.

I wondered where he was going or if he had a car. I doubted I would ever see him again. I wanted to run after him but I could barely walk. Within a few minutes, he disappeared from my sight.

Chapter 32

When I tried to walk to my car, my knees stuck to my warm up pants, which wasn't pleasant. I hobbled to my rented vehicle, thinking I would drive and catch up to Micah. I ripped my shirt on the car door as I plopped into the seat, but thankfully the car started.

Micah did not have much of a head start on me, especially since I had a car. As I drove in the direction he walked, there was no sign of him. The land was flat and sprawled out in every direction with few diversions, other than some cactus and Mesquite trees. Where was he? Was he some kind of supernatural person, too?

Then I remembered a movie I had seen where a mad man had built an underground hiding place where he would take people he had kidnapped. He would put them in this underground dungeon where no one could find them. Could it be possible for someone to dig something like that in the hard West Texas ground? They would probably need some special type of machinery, but I was sure it was possible. Perhaps he was hiding all the missing in such a place.

Could I have possibly just discovered the answer to the mystery of what happened to the missing? An underground bunker would be an ideal hiding place. It would also explain how he happened to be around when the snake came after me, and how he had managed to just disappear off the face of the earth as I continued to search for him.

If there was a hidden bunker, it had to be in the proximity of where I last saw him. It would no doubt be camouflaged, so I would have to drive slowly if I would have any chance of seeing it. I brought out my binoculars and peered into them every few minutes for any indication of a possible underground shelter in the vicinity. I looked for something sticking out of the ground like a breathing pipe or some type of aberration in the landscape, but everything looked normal as far as West Texas terrain goes.

After driving around the area for quite a while, I realized I might have to get off the road and out of my car if I was going to be able to find a hidden bunker. I was tired and thirsty, but I knew if I left the area, I might not ever find it again. My knees protested greatly as I pushed myself out of the car and walked stiff legged around the vicinity trying to locate a possible hole in the ground.

After thirty minutes of hobbling around in the hot sun, I couldn't take it anymore. If he had a place out there, he had done an incredible job of hiding it. I hated to give up, but the thought of dying of thirst did not appeal to me. And the possibility of the shadowy snake coming back kept creeping back into my thoughts, as well.

But as I was about to get back in my car, I noticed some movement next to a cactus about twenty yards away. I almost jumped out of my skin thinking it might be another spirit snake, but as I watched it a few minutes, I realized it was some type of animal from this world. I was nervous to get close to it, but I wouldn't feel right leaving it there if it was hurt.

The binoculars were dangling from my neck, so I used them to see what I might be dealing with. As I peered into them, I could see a little animal curled up by the cactus. It looked like a small fox.

As I hesitantly inched closer, the animal lifted up his head and looked at me. I recognized him instantly. It was Jake's little dog, Cooper! I couldn't believe he had survived the fire.

Somehow he had escaped and ended up over a mile from the house.

He was a mess. Part of his hair was singed, and he looked very lethargic. I had to get him help quickly or I knew he would die. I had to wonder how he got as far as he did, and how he managed to survive most of the day without water and very little shade.

I gently picked him up and he groaned. I carried him carefully to my car and put him in the seat next to me. What in the world was I going to do with a dog with everything else I had going on? I wasn't sure how I could care for him or if the motel would even let me keep him.

Unfortunately, I didn't have any water to offer him, so when I got back into town, I stopped at the first convenience store and got a bottle of water. I poured some in my hand and hoped he would drink from it but he didn't. I realized he might be too far gone. I had to find a vet for him.

I went back in the store and asked the people inside if they knew of a vet close by. A woman who was shopping there said she had a great vet and told me how to find him. She then looked me over and asked me if I needed a doctor, too. I realized I probably looked as bad as Cooper with my bloody pants, torn shirt and embroidered towels on my hands.

I told her, "Thank you, but I'll be OK. I just need to take care of my dog first." She seemed impressed, and I was surprised I referred to the dog as mine.

It wasn't hard to find the vet. I pulled in hoping he would still be there. He wasn't, but they were open and I brought Cooper in. They immediately took him and put him on an IV. I could tell they considered it very serious. I asked them if they thought he would be ok and they said they weren't sure. They looked me over and asked if I needed a doctor. I told them I had a mishap while out hiking and that was how I found the dog. They seemed to believe me which was a relief.

They took my information which I was a little hesitant to give. I felt vulnerable letting these people know who I was and where I was staying, but I had no choice. I wanted to do all I could for this dog. It was the least I could do for Jake. I really wanted his little dog to make it.

I asked them if I could see the dog before I left, and they let me go back where he was. It made me sad to see this little animal hooked up to an IV. He wasn't moving, but I saw his eyes look at me when I walked in and, surprisingly, he wagged his tail just a little. He seemed to be saying, "Thank you for saving me." At that moment, he won my heart.

Chapter 33

It made me sad to leave Cooper alone in the animal hospital, but I knew I had no choice. If he was going to make it, he would have to stay there for a while. As I left, I told them to do whatever they needed to do to save him. They assured me they would.

As I headed to my motel, there was a lot on my mind. It appeared I had a dog for the first time in my adult life. And I had just met face to face with the man I thought was responsible for hiding or killing ten people. But, I couldn't help wondering, if he was the one taking these people, why didn't he take me?

It felt great to take a long shower and have some dinner. I was very tired after being in the hot sun all day. I watched a little TV but found it boring. TV just couldn't compete with real life anymore. I had more adventures in the past few weeks, than most people do in their entire lives. Who would have thought my life would become so exciting.

But adventures come with mishaps and tragedies. I felt great sadness realizing Jake was dead. He was someone I would have been honored to call my friend.

Then I thought about Bill and wondered how he was doing? I called him and asked if he would like to have dinner the next night. He said he would. I knew I couldn't tell him much about what had transpired the past two days, but it would be nice to see him. I imagined he was curious about why I had called him the night before sounding so desperate.

As I lay wide awake in bed that night, I thought of all the things that happened in just two days—-meeting Micah, losing my friend, and finding his dog. It had to be two of the most eventful days since I had been in Abilene.

I wondered where they would have the funeral for Jake. I knew I couldn't go so I would have to pay my respects to him in another way, like taking care of his dog. I hoped Cooper would make it through the night.

As I started to doze off, I thought of Micah and all the things he said to me. I questioned if he was a killer or just crazy. In my brief experience with him, he didn't seem like a bad person because he helped me. He probably saved my life from that spirit-snake thing.

He had a power I wanted and needed to protect myself from these spirits who I seemed to be encountering more frequently. I wanted to be able to trample them like he said. Micah seemed very confident about what he believed. I would like to be that confident in my beliefs, but after all I had experienced in Abilene, I had no idea what I believed anymore.

As I drifted off to sleep, I remembered him talking about a man called Enoch. I wondered who he was and how he was connected to any of this. The next day, I decided I would do some searching and see if I could find him. But first, I would go to the hospital to see how my dog was doing.

My night was flooded with dreams. I would fall asleep and have one dream after another. Sometimes they would wake me up. I didn't remember all the dreams I had that night, but I did remember one. A man came up to me who was wearing a robe. He had long hair and looked like one of those paintings of Jesus.

This Man said, "I am the Way, the Truth and the Life. Come to me." He put out His hands to me and then He disappeared. I immediately woke up. I was so impacted by this short dream. The Man in this dream spoke of being "The Truth". I pondered how someone could be 'Truth'. Was this what Micah was talking about when he said he had found "The Truth"?

As I contemplated the significance of that dream, I finally fell back asleep. But the next dream I had was the last one that night. After I woke up from it, I couldn't go back to sleep.

Cooper was barking continuously in my dream, and it seemed he was trying to warn someone about something. Cooper ran into an empty house that looked abandoned. I ran in after him but didn't see anyone. But when I looked up, I saw the evil character Teresa called "the souch". He was crouching upside down from the ceiling.

The souch jumped down on me and knocked me to the ground. He hissed at me and drooled something all over my head. He was hideous and the smell that came from his mouth was horrendous. I tried to get up, but I must have hit my head because I felt dizzy. I tried to crawl on the ground, but I could barely move. And then, I smelled smoke. I knew somehow that creature had set fire to the house where I was.

Cooper was still barking but I couldn't get to him. I felt like I had been drugged. I couldn't move and I knew I would die if I didn't get out. I tried to get closer to Cooper because I desperately wanted to save him. But as I started moving towards him, a firm hand grabbed me and pulled me out the door.

At just that moment the whole house was engulfed in flames. I turned around to tell whoever helped me to get my dog out of the fire, but no one was there. I could still hear Cooper barking but I couldn't stand up. I called to him to jump out the window. I kept yelling and yelling for him to come. I was so afraid he wasn't going to make it. And then, surprisingly, I saw Cooper jump out of the window, and I reached up to catch him. As he was about to land in my arms, I woke up.

When I woke up I looked all around for Cooper but then remembered it was a dream. I was sweating from my vivid dream. I had to wonder if my dream was what happened to Jake. Why couldn't Jake get out unless there was something wrong with him? Was "the souch" the one who started the fire at Jake's house? Were my dreams messages to me from somewhere or someone? It was all too much for me to consider.

I was exhausted from the tossing and turning and dreaming all night. I pushed myself up to wash my face. I saw it was around six in the morning, so I figured I would just stay up. After I dressed, I limped down to the lobby for some breakfast.

There were only a few people in the lobby. I was grateful for the small crowd. I sat close to the TV to see what they were saying about the fires.

The reporter said they had no suspects, but did mention the man who died in the fire was related to a police sergeant in Abilene. He then said, "Jake Bardon had lived in the house for many years, and investigators believe he was the only casualty. They are not sure what started the fire or the fire about a mile down the road at an abandoned church, but feel they are related. Further investigation will continue. In other news...."

The shock was wearing off and reality was settling in; Jake Bardon was dead and I would never see him again. I looked down and felt such sadness. I left my half eaten breakfast and went up to my room to get ready to go out.

All I could think about was Cooper. I wasn't sure if I could take it if he didn't make it. I got in the car and drove to the animal hospital. I tried to prepare myself for any bad news. I walked in and got a nice "hello" from the receptionist. She said the dog was doing much better and would be OK. I almost let out a Texas yelp but restrained my excitement. I was so thankful to hear he was OK. "Can I see him?" I asked.

She took me in the back and as soon as he saw me, his little tail started wagging, this time with more energy. I was so glad to see him. I reached down and petted him, and he licked my fingers. His head was up and he looked like he was trying to stand up. I told him to settle down because he needed to rest. Then, I looked at the nurse to see if she thought I was crazy telling a dog "to rest" but she just smiled at me.

I asked her when she thought I could take him home, and she said the doctor felt he needed to stay a little longer. "It's a good thing you found him when you did or he wouldn't have made it," she informed me.

"Yes, I'm surprised I even saw him because he's so little," I said.

"Are you going to keep him?" she asked.

"Yes, I believe I will, unless he has an owner looking for him," I said, knowing that wouldn't happen.

"Ok, sir, feel free to stop in any time to see him. He seems to pep up when you walk in," she said.

"He doesn't get that excited with everyone?" I asked.

"No sir, you are the only one who gets that kind of reception from him," she smiled.

Most dogs never seemed to like me but this one certainly did. It made me feel kind of special. I suddenly understood why people love dogs so much.

Chapter 34

My heart felt lighter knowing Cooper was going to make it. I even whistled a little as I got in my car. I wanted to do some research on the things Micah said, so I decided to go to the library and use one of their computers.

The library was more populated than it was the last time I was there and fortunately, there was a different lady at the front desk. I asked to use a computer and I gave them my guest library card. I logged in and did a search on "Enoch". I was surprised to see he was a character in The Bible. And I was also surprised to learn he was related to Noah of Noah's Ark fame. He lived a very long time—three-hundred-and-sixty-five years!

The information I found on Enoch was scant. The passage simply said, "He walked with God, and then he was no more." I gulped and reread this several more times—"he was no more." I reread the context of this and it was short and to the point. "Enoch walked with God and he was no more; for God took him."

Wow! Was Micah implying this was what happened to all of the missing people? Did he think God took them? Surely not. But, why then did he tell me to find out who Enoch was?

This was over my head. I needed to find some expert's opinion on this. I looked up some other articles on Enoch and they all said basically the same thing. But there was one theologian who felt Enoch would be one of the prophets who would stand before the temple in the last days. Woo! This was some wild stuff.

I wondered if anyone else had thought of Enoch when people started disappearing off the face of the earth. Why would God take these people? Were they all walking with God? I wondered if God had taken anyone else besides Enoch.

That question led me to another search, and I found out it happened at least one other time to a man named Elijah. As I read about him, the article said, "Like Enoch, Elijah did not die. He was taken up to heaven in a chariot in a whirlwind." This was fascinating.

After discovering these two men had vanished off the earth, I had to find out if this could have happened with the missing people. It seemed at that point anything was possible.

I knew one person who might know the answer—Micah. But how was I going to find him again? The only idea that came to mind was driving out to the area where I had last seen him. Hopefully, he might still be there. I was relatively sure he was not the villain in this story but I still wanted to be sure.

The day was very hot, and I dreaded being in the blazing sun again, especially in a place I had come to loath after all that had happened there. But, I didn't know how else to find Micah, and he told me we would talk when I discovered who Enoch was. I drove out again to the lonely hill close to Jake's house. I went to the very spot where I last saw Micah.

The heat was too much if I turned the car off, so I just sat there in the air conditioning with my motor running. I knew it might overheat the car and the last thing I needed was to be stranded out there again. Jake wouldn't be there to rescue me anymore. I sat there for about ten minutes, and then drove around the area. There was no sign of anyone. I wasn't sure how to summon Micah.

The heat was so bad it made the ground appear to have steam rising from it. I decided to get out of the car and go up the hill to see if anyone was searching through the remains of Jake's house. It was a little easier for me to walk because my knees and hands seemed much better. I was surprised at how fast they were healing after only a few days.

As I got out of the car, I saw the large rock where the dark snake had been and I hoped it wouldn't come again. I used the rock to help me sit down, so I could scoot up the hill as I had the day before. When I looked over the remains of Jake's house, all I saw was the typical yellow tape they put around crime scenes, but no one seemed to be there.

Then I looked at the church area and saw the same yellow tape around the burnt timbers. But the one thing I didn't see was my car. They had removed it. This made me nervous because I was wondering if some forensic scientist was going over it with a fine tooth comb. They might find something that would link me to the car.

I tried to push down those thoughts and remembered my resolve to think of the best possible outcome rather than the worst. My back side was getting hot, so I turned over to scoot back down. As soon as I flipped over, I saw Micah standing at the bottom of the hill. How did he know I would be there? For some reason, it didn't really surprise me.

He watched me scoot down the hill and then offered a hand to help me up. He pulled me up without too much pain, but I was kind of disappointed I didn't feel the electricity again. He said, "You just can't stay away from here, can you, Henry?"

His words reminded me of what Jake said when he found me next to the burning church. "Apparently not," I replied. "I was hoping you might be here, Micah, but meeting you would be so much easier if you had a cell phone."

Micah let out a hearty laugh. "Perhaps Henry, but I learned the distractions of this world do not help me spiritually," he said. "What do you need to ask me, Henry?"

"Do you believe these people were taken by God?" I asked.

"I assume you read about Enoch," he responded.

"Yes, I did, and that's what happened to him and to Elijah," I added.

"You did your homework," he said, obviously pleased I had followed through on his request. "Enoch came to mind when this started happening in Abilene. I have asked about it often. The missing people may have been taken out of this world, Henry, but I'm not sure they ended up where they were hoping to be. Because of their desperation and lack of knowledge, they may have been tricked by the enemy," he said. "In the last days, the enemy will fool many people."

I was taken aback by his words, "last days" but decided to ask him about that later. "So what are you saying, Micah? Do you think these people wanted to leave this earth, but they might have ended up somewhere they shouldn't have? " Hoping for some insight into his implication.

"I think it is a possibility," he suggested.

"Why did you tell me about Enoch unless you believed the same thing happened to the missing people?" I asked.

"The spiritual world is not like ours, Henry. The way you enter it is through your words and beliefs. Ask and it will be given to you. Seek and you will find. Knock and the door will be opened to you," he explained.

I had no idea what Micah was talking about. "Are you saying the way into the spiritual world is by what we say?" I asked skeptically.

"If you believe what you say," he confirmed. "These people may have been fooled into believing and asking for something they didn't really want," he supposed. "There have been many deceitful spirits in this area over the past year. I don't understand why, but I can only assume it has something to do with the last days being upon us," he concluded.

There was that "last days" remark again. It was making me uncomfortable. "I don't understand any of this, Micah. It is all so foreign to me," I confessed. "If that is what happened to these people, how in the world could anyone rescue them?" I asked.

"Henry, would you like help in understanding these things?" Micah asked.

Finally I was getting somewhere with this man. "Yes!" I said emphatically. But, the way he helped me was totally unexpected.

He came closer, placing his hands on my head and said, "You will dream dreams and have visions of what has been and what will come. The path to rescue those who are missing will be illuminated to you."

He removed his hands and looked at me. "You will be shown what you need to know."

He started to turn around and leave, but I wasn't through talking to him. I felt like I could spend days with this man and it wouldn't be enough. "Micah, I need the protection you have from these spirits. How can I get it?"

He turned to face me and said simply, "Ask Him."

"Ask who?" I asked, desperately wanting to understand all of this.

"Ask the One who conquered darkness and the evil ones who live in it. Ask the One who is light," he said simply.

The one thing I knew for sure was I wanted what Micah had. "I want you to show me how to find this light, Micah," I pleaded. I wasn't sure if my request would lead me to God, or to a hidden underground bunker where ten other people might be. But something inside of me wanted what Micah had, and I was willing to risk everything to find it.

Chapter 35

Micah didn't lead me off to an underground bunker; instead he knelt down and told me to do the same. I didn't even think about my knees as I knelt down on the hot dirt. There was no pain, but I didn't realize it until later.

"Tell the One who created you, that you want Him to live in you and be your Lord. He will take away any darkness in you, and He will fill you with light," Micah explained. "Tell Him you are sorry for all you have done against Him and you want to follow Him for the rest of your life. Give yourself to Him. He will come and dwell in you forever."

The words that came flooding out of my mouth did not seem like my own. I knew they were coming from somewhere deep inside. I hurled the words up into the deep blue sky, "I am sorry I have not believed in You. I do believe now. I am sorry for all the wrong things I have done. Show me the way."

Tears were flowing out of me uncontrollably, but I had no desire to stop them. "Set me free from the darkness I have lived in all my life. Please give me Your light. Protect me from the darkness and the ones who move in darkness. Thank You for giving Your Son in my place. I give my life to You."

I felt light headed and bowed down into the dirt where I gently fell prostrate on the hot Texas ground. Micah placed his hands on my back and my head, and said, "He is now Yours and, Henry, you are now His." He said some other words I did not understand.

He lifted his hands off of me and stood up. I was then totally unaware of my surroundings. All the pain, rejection, and grief poured out of my heart. Tears fell from my eyes like rain gushing through gutters, washing away years of loneliness and regret. The pain from my past was gone as if it never was. The anger, the bitterness and the hate left my heart as love flooded it. All my past, all my grief, all my mistakes were rescinded. The tears fell until nothing was left undone. I had poured it all out and I was free of it all!

I felt so clean. It was a joy I had never known before.

As I looked around to share my joy with Micah, he was not there. I looked all around for him, but he was nowhere to be seen. Why would he leave me at such a vulnerable time? Micah must have felt I didn't need him anymore, but there were so many things I still wanted to ask him.

Even though I was disappointed Micah left, I was too happy to care. I felt like I had been given a new life. I didn't think it would have been possible for me to be any happier.

There was so much joy bubbling out of me, I didn't know what to say or do. I looked up and shouted, "Thank You!"

I got in my car and went back to Abilene a new man!

It was something I had never imagined would happen to me. I wanted to embrace everyone I saw and tell them about this amazing experience. It was such good news!

When I came into the city limits, I decided to drop by and see my dog. That thought made me smile. Every thought made me smile. I walked in and they said, "Your dog is doing so well, the doctor said you could take him home today. And he was so impressed with your kindness in helping the dog, he told me there would be no charge."

It seemed like my life was already turning around. I thanked her so much and told her to thank the doctor. She prepared Cooper to leave, and then handed me my new dog. She asked me if I knew what I was going to call him. I told her, "Yes, his name is Cooper."

She thought that was a great name. While she was talking, I heard the bell on the door behind me ring as someone came in. I turned around and was surprised to see the woman who had first told me about the vet. She came walking in with her dog. She was surprised to see me, too and said, "I see you took my advice."

"Yes, I did and look how well it turned out. He is as good as new." I said smiling from ear to ear. I felt as good as new, too. I'm sure my joy was evident.

She laughed and said, "Well, I wouldn't say he is quite to the state of 'new' yet, but he looks like he's going to be fine."

As I looked down at him, I had to agree. It would take some time for his hair to grow back in where it was singed. And he still had a bandage on one of his legs. "I guess you're right, but we are both going to be just fine," I said with great assurance.

Then I thought about the fact that Cooper was going to need some dog food and a collar. I asked her if she knew of a good pet store where I could get some supplies. She suggested one close by, but I'm sure it was obvious to her I was a novice dog owner. She asked if I needed some help in shopping for my new dog.

I looked at her in shock. I didn't know what to say, so I didn't say anything. She told me, "Just wait here a few minutes. I have to pick up some medicine for my dog and I will be right out."

Her few minutes turned into twenty minutes, and the longer I sat there, the more the old me started having negative thoughts that she probably changed her mind. But just as I was about to leave and save her the trouble, she came out. She waltzed out of the doctor's office, looked at me unapologetic for keeping me waiting and said, "Let's go to the pet store." I stood up and followed her out like a little puppy.

I followed her in my car to a pet store only a few minutes away. When we walked inside, I decided it might be nice to introduce myself, "I really appreciate you taking time out of your busy schedule to help me out. My name is Henry."

"It's nice to meet you, Henry. I'm really not that busy," she said smiling. "And what is your dog's name?"

"It's Cooper," I replied.

"Oh, I love that name. How cute!" She petted him, and then started telling Cooper what I needed to buy so he would be properly cared for.

Over one-hundred dollars later, I walked out with a cage, a bed, expensive dog food, dog treats, rawhide bones, a collar, a leash, and of course, several dog toys. "I never knew it was so expensive to have a dog." I commented.

"Just wait until you start getting the vet bills," she joked.

I walked her out to her car. "You were so sweet to do this for me. I appreciate it so much."

She then looked at me like no other woman ever has and said, "Well, you could take me out for dinner to show me how much you appreciate it." She smiled at me and I almost fainted.

With a confidence I'm not sure I had ever displayed before, I said, "OK, where would you like to go?" She told me about a great Mexican restaurant not far from there.

Of course, it was my favorite restaurant, and then I remembered it was Bill's, too. I had totally forgotten we were supposed to have dinner that night. I told her I had to make a quick phone call and asked her if she would watch Cooper for me. I called Bill and explained the situation and he understood completely when I told him a woman was involved.

When I came back, she asked me, "Did you have to cancel your plans with another woman?" I looked at her surprised, but then she laughed. I realized she was teasing me. Normally that would have made me feel uncomfortable because I had always been so insecure, but for some reason it didn't bother me.

Then I thought to ask her, "What is your name? I don't think you ever told me?"

"I don't think you ever asked," she laughed. "My name is Irene, Irene Duncan." Then she introduced me to her dog. "This is Sugar and she is the sweetest thing in the world."

"Well then, that's the perfect name for her," I exclaimed as I reached down to pet her. "It's great to meet you, Irene. I'll see you at the restaurant."

Her name was Irene and she was the prettiest thing I had ever seen. (Please note: I'm not one for rhymes, but I couldn't seem to help it.)

Chapter 36

Irene and I had a wonderful dinner, and the restaurant even let us sit outside with our animals as long as we kept them secured. She asked me a little about myself and I told her why I was in Abilene. She seemed impressed by my occupation. She didn't ask too many questions about the story for which I was grateful. I knew better than to tell a woman a lie, so I was glad she didn't ask me anything I couldn't answer.

But she did ask me how I got hurt and why I had the bandages on when I came into the store. I tried to think of an honest way to tell her. I said I had been investigating a story and someone came after me. (I was referring to the church and how the fire came after me.) I explained I was trying to run back to my car and fell on a gravel road which banged up my knees and hands. She seemed to believe me, and I felt OK about my explanation.

Then I decided to tell her I had been in danger several times when trying to talk to people to interview them. I told her about the Texas mafia and some of my other exploits hoping she would be impressed with my macho job. It seemed to work.

Irene told me a little about herself and said she had grown up in Abilene. I thought we had to be close to the same age, and I wondered if our paths had ever crossed. I was not surprised to find out we went to the same high school, because there were only two in Abilene back in our day, but I was very thankful to find out she had graduated a few years after I had.

She told me she was a social worker and I could see her being very good at it since she was so positive and kind. She told me a little about her family and I was hanging on every word she said.

After an hour or more of finding out everything I could think to ask Irene about her life, I knew I wanted to spend more time with her. She was lovely in every way, and she seemed to like me. I couldn't believe how things seemed to be going my way for once.

Life seemed to have a magic to it that I had never experienced before. But the magic almost disappeared when she said, "I would love to hear the story about how you found this little animal out in the middle of the desert." She reached down to pet Cooper. "What in the world were you doing out there?"

How was I going to respond to her question? How could I explain why I was out in an isolated area without lying? I knew she had probably heard about the fires, and I didn't want to give her any reason to suspect me.

I had to think fast so I said, "It happened the same day I got hurt. I was on my way home when I saw something moving under a cactus. I got out of my car to see what it was and, at first, I thought it was a fox. But when I got closer, I could see it was a little dog. I don't know how he got there because there was no one around. I knew if I didn't take him, he would have died." I felt good about this explanation, too, because it was basically true.

She thought it was wonderful I had found him and saved him. And then she suggested, "Maybe you should report finding him, Henry, in case he belonged to someone out there."

And then I said something I would regret, "He must have been abandoned because there were no houses anywhere close by." I felt bad because I knew it was the last thing Jake would ever do. And then I realized I had just lied to her.

She shook her head saying, "I can't imagine how anyone could abandon a dog, especially one this small and cute."

My dishonest explanation made me feel horrible. She seemed to notice my change of mood and asked me what was wrong. I gave her the excuse I was just tired after all I had been through. Irene seemed to understand and accepted my excuse. We continued to have a nice conversation in spite of my guilt.

But the most surprising thing that night happened as we were about to go home. Irene looked me in the eyes and told me the most amazing thing. It was music to my ears. "From the first day I met you, when you came into the store asking if anyone knew of a vet, I knew you were someone I wanted to get to know. I thought you were a very special man to care so much for another living thing. It seemed like you were totally unaware of your own wounds and could only think of the dog. I appreciate kindness in others, but I don't see it that often. I was about to give up meeting a man who cared more about others than himself. So, after I met you that day, I hoped I would see you again. I even said a little prayer that I would."

This beautiful woman was talking about me! She was referring to me. She had actually prayed to see me again. I couldn't believe it. I laughed with joy and said, "Well, I guess your prayers have been answered."

"I guess they were," Irene said as she gazed into my eyes. I smiled at her and she smiled back. I thought my heart was going to explode.

After dinner, I walked her back to her car and she told me she'd love to see me again. I loved her confidence and it helped me to feel more confident, too. We decided to meet the next night at a steak house not too far from there. We thought it best to leave our pets at home for our next get together. I was glad I had bought the cage.

It didn't seem like I was the same person anymore. Something happened to me out there under the wide open Texas sky. I liked the new me.

Somehow my dysfunctional life had made a complete turnaround, and I believed my life might actually turn out good for the first time in a long time—really for the first time ever.

As I drove back to my motel, I felt so happy. I had to wonder why it had taken me so long to believe in the One who loves me.

Chapter 37

When Cooper arrived at his new temporary home–my motel room–he seemed relieved to curl up on my bed. He was trembling a little, so I decided he could sleep with me that night so he would feel safer.

It was getting late and I wanted to go to sleep, so I would be rested for my date the next day. It was almost like I had forgotten about the story or any of the other amazing things that had happened in Abilene. All I could think about was Irene. I had never felt this way before about anyone and it was wonderful. I could finally understand why people would do anything for love.

As I lay down on the bed and petted Cooper, I realized I hadn't fed him. Irene would be surprised to know her caring man had forgotten to feed his dog. I just wasn't used to taking care of anyone but myself.

I jumped out of bed, and poured some food into one of the dishes I had bought for Cooper and gave him some fresh water. He looked up when I called him but he didn't move. Apparently he was too tired to eat.

As I jumped back in bed, I realized how glad I was to think about something besides the story I had been obsessed with for the past few weeks. Sid was expecting a submission soon and there was still much I needed to do to finish the article, but getting out of Abilene was no longer part of the motivation. I was starting to like Abilene.

As I drifted off to sleep, I thought of Irene and Cooper. They both had become very special to me in such a short amount of time. Cooper snuggled close to me and I petted him, thankful to have him in my life. Then we both drifted off to sleep.

But sleep wasn't peaceful for me that night, and I'm sure it wasn't for Cooper, either. I tossed and turned most of the night battling vivid thoughts of the fire that had killed my friend and what he must have gone through. I felt tormented by these impressions.

I finally got up and turned on the TV. A man on one of the religious stations was talking about how to find peace in this world and my ears perked up. He said if we kept our thoughts on the One who created us, we would be at peace. That sounded good to me and I decided to give it a try.

But the harder I tried, the more I kept thinking about Jake and what he went through. The painful truth was—he had died because he had tried to save me. How could I feel peace with that awful truth swirling in my head? Instead of peace I felt guilt and fear and pain. I was surprised I was struggling with all of this after asking the One who is light to fill my life. I felt like there was darkness all around me.

Thoughts started pummeling my mind: "This God stuff isn't working. I thought I would be protected when I asked Him into my life, but it sure doesn't look that way. Nothing I ever do works out. Apparently, I can't even give myself to God the right way."

As I was becoming more and more agitated and angry, I thought about Irene. "She will probably dump me as soon as she gets to know the real me. It's only a matter of time. I can't fool her forever into thinking I'm a good, kind man. I'm a loser. Why would she want to be with a loser? I'm going to break up with her tomorrow and save her the trouble."

I started pacing back and forth while muttering about Micah and all of his lofty ideas. I got more and more upset with every thought and every word I was speaking. The anger was rising up in me. I was about to start cursing and yelling at God, that is, until I saw a dark figure in the corner of my room. The sight of it didn't scare me this time, but its presence jolted me back into my new reality—my words and my actions were drawing this thing to me.

This realization made me even angrier, but this time my anger was directed at the right source. I yelled at this evil presence, "How dare you have the audacity to come into my room. You have no right to be here because I belong to the One who is light. There is no darkness in Him, and now there is no darkness in me, either. Now get out and stay out!" And with those powerful words, the thing faded before my eyes. I felt like I had just won a battle.

There was a confidence in my voice I had never heard before. I knew it had to come from knowing the One I had given my life to and who I was in Him. Apparently this evil spirit recognized it, as well, because it obeyed me.

Feeling much safer, knowing who was watching over me and the authority I had in Him, I went back to bed. It made sleeping much easier and more peaceful. I soon drifted off to sleep, and I was sure Cooper was thankful, too.

The rest of the night, I dreamed about things that were nice—like Irene. I dreamed she told me she loved me and I was beginning to think I loved her, too, even though I had just met her. Could I feel something so strong so quickly? I guess it could be what some would call "love at first sight."

The next morning I hopped out of bed refreshed after only a few hours of sleep. Cooper was wagging his tail, and I thought it would be fun to take him for a walk. So I did and it was fun. I realized I was part of a whole new breed of people—dog owners. But when he pooped out on the lawn of the motel, I wondered what I was supposed to do with it. Should I just leave it there? I didn't want to touch it, so I did leave it there, but I was pretty sure I wasn't supposed to. I would ask Irene. I realized this might be one of the downsides of owning a dog.

The dog had to be hungry, so I poured some new food into his bowl and put him in the cage while I went to get some people food. I called Irene while I ate and asked her what one does with poop? She explained it to me as I ate my breakfast.

When I got back in the room, I wondered how long I should leave Cooper in the cage. I decided to work that day in the room, so he could roam around. I had a lot I wanted to get done before my date that night. I felt new energy tackling the story.

I typed up all of my notes from the past few days. I hadn't been keeping up with my journal because I had been rather busy trying to survive. I spent several hours typing up all the notes I had and everything I could remember.

Micah's words were even more penetrating as I typed them up. He had warned me about my words, just as Jake had done. "Life and death are in the power of the tongue. Choose life." It was becoming apparent that our words dictate our lives to a great extent.

As I typed the warning, I remembered the night before, when I started getting so angry. It was almost like that evil spirit was feeding me thoughts, and I fell into its trap like most people do. As the thoughts poured into my mind, I started repeating them out loud. I could just imagine that evil presence cheering me on as I became more and more agitated. If I hadn't realized what was happening, I might have said something or done something I would have regretted forever.

As I reflected on this, I wondered how I could convey how powerful our words are to other people. Most people had no idea their words could mean life or death depending on how they used them. It was a radical concept, but I knew it was true from all I had experienced. My job was to report the truth no matter how unbelievable it might be.

Then I thought of Irene, and wondered if I might lose her if she knew all the crazy things I was starting to believe. She told me she was a believer in the Holy One, but I was pretty sure not every believer believed what I believe. I knew I had to tell her sometime but I thought maybe it could wait. I wanted her to know I was normal before she thought I was crazy.

Bill floated into my head then and I knew I needed to speak to him. When I cancelled my dinner with him he seemed to understand, but I hadn't talked to him since. I realized I wasn't being much of a friend to him.

Irene was the only person I wanted to think about. She was amazing and she liked me. It was a miracle to me, and I knew it was due to the powerful change in my life—which was really the greatest miracle.

I started thinking about my date with Irene and thought about what I should wear. I decided to go shopping and get some new clothes. I took Cooper for a quick walk and remembered to bring a plastic bag for his poop like Irene told me. I left Cooper in his cage, and I was off to the mall. I couldn't remember the last time I felt so happy.

And since I was totally obsessed by Irene, I forgot to call Bill–again.

Chapter 38

The mall wasn't very crowded, and I was glad because I wanted to get in and get out. I went to the department store where I bought my last pair of pants which were, unfortunately, destroyed the night of the church fire. If nothing else I would get the same pair.

As I headed towards the store, I saw a man coming towards me with a large hump on his back. He was bent over in pain. When he walked past me, I realized the hump was not a physical anomaly, but a grotesque spiritual being. It was a demon! I could see the repulsive thing moving around on his back. It appeared to be connected to him somehow.

I watched in disbelief as the man walked away from me. He seemed oddly unaware of this thing on his back, but I could see it as plain as day. Others were walking past him oblivious to the man or his hump. They obviously couldn't see it. I wished I couldn't see it either, but I could, so I had to do something about it. Anger rose up in me as I watched it inflict pain on this unsuspecting man.

Jake's vivid description of the evil beings he saw at his family picnic came back to me. He had described them like transparent leaches, but this thing looked more like a dark blob. I knew whatever they looked like, they were our enemies. If I was going to learn how to fight these evil spirits, I was going to have to study them as much as the idea repulsed me.

Since I had just seen the one on the man's back, I decided to try and observe this creature. I walked quickly over to the man. When I caught up with him, I tried to stare at the man's back without appearing obvious. From what I could tell, the dark foe appeared to be latched onto the man's back somehow.

Because I was not looking at the man but at his back, I was startled when the man asked me if I needed something. I was embarrassed, but decided to ask him if he was in pain.

The man thought he understood why I was looking at his back. He responded, "That is so nice of you to ask. Are you a doctor?"

I told him I wasn't, but it didn't stop him from telling me all about his aches and pains. As he detailed his medical history, I could see the evil mass on his back moving around. It was sickening. I tried not to stare at it, but it was difficult.

After his exhaustive account of all he had been through over the past few years, he said, "I had been having a lot of pain in my back. It started small, but I knew there was something wrong the minute I felt that twinge. I kept telling my family something was seriously wrong with my back. They thought it was all in my head, until I ended up in the hospital where the doctor told me I was going to need back surgery. Now, my family knows I wasn't making it up," the man proudly stated. He seemed pleased to know he was right, even though it meant he had to have surgery.

As he talked, I watched the being on his back as it appeared to be sucking something out of the man's back. I then realized why Jake described them as spiritual leaches. I had to wonder if this creature was sucking the life out of the man. Whatever it was doing to this unsuspecting person, it was beyond despicable. It was so nasty. I was almost sorry I had decided to look at it.

The man hurried off when he saw his wife, so I continued walking towards the department store. But before I got there, I noticed a young man who had something dark hanging off his face. It was close to his mouth. I started following the teenager trying to hear what he was saying to his friend. After a few minutes, I realized he was making fun of some people directly in front of them.

Both of the boys were snickering but the one with the dark thing hanging off him was making biased comments about the people's ethnicity. He also used the Name above every name like it was a curse word. He didn't realize he was actually cursing himself. The dark globule hanging near his mouth appeared to be feeding off his bad words. This must have been what Jake saw at his family picnic.

At that point, I sat down on a bench flabbergasted from what I was witnessing. Nearly every single person who walked past me had some kind of spirit attached to them. Some spirits appeared larger than others, but it seemed everyone had at least one. It was unbelievable to see how far reaching this epidemic of spiritual decay had become.

When I had first started seeing these evil spirits, they were either attacking me or someone close to me, but that had changed. I was seeing them more often on people I didn't know. It had to be because Micah had put his hands on my head and told me I would have dreams and visions and answers to my questions. His prayer had somehow made these spirits more visible to me. It was not a gift I wanted, but I knew it might help me to figure out what was going on in Abilene.

This would be a good horror movie if it wasn't really happening. I watched people walk by me with dark globules hanging from them. There were even young children with small, dark spots on their arms and legs. I saw teenagers with dark blobs on their heads and bodies. And there were some older people who looked like they were totally encased in darkness. These people were clueless. It was overwhelming. How could I help them?

Few people believed Micah when he tried to warn them about the power of their words and I knew they probably wouldn't believe me either. It was frustrating to know I had the Truth that could set them free, but I doubted most people believed they were in bondage in the first place.

As I was beginning to feel very overwhelmed by the prevalence of these spirits, I suddenly remembered the wonderful fact that I had a date that night with a beautiful lady. This thought lightened my somber mood.

With that happy thought, I walked back to the department store to get what I came for. I wanted to forget about these evil entities that seemed to be taking over the world. But, as much as I tried to ignore them, I couldn't—they seemed to be everywhere. I knew I had to warn people about their existence as soon as possible.

The written word is powerful, but people have to read it for it to make an impact. I realized our magazine, as much as I loved it, was not a well-read publication. I knew I needed to reach more people than the small readership *Ragweed* draws. It was at that moment I got the idea to write a book.

The thought of writing a book was daunting, but it would have a better chance of reaching more readers. I already had enough information to do several articles for my magazine, but I had not finished editing them. Instead of doing the articles, I decided to approach Sid about the idea of a book. I realized he might not agree to it, but warning people about these evil spirits would be worth risking my job.

As I went into the department store, several grotesque creatures rode by me on their unsuspecting transports. I ignored them and looked for some clothes to wear. These things were so distracting to me I could barely concentrate. The same lady was there that waited on me the last time and she asked me the same question, "Don't you want to try these on?"

I gave her the same answer as the last time, "No thank you. I have to be somewhere soon."

The whole time she rang up my purchases and bagged my items, I watched a dark figure on her chest staring at me like it was daring me to do something. I could have sworn it had a smirk on its ugly face.

The woman looked up and noticed I was staring at her chest. She was embarrassed. Then I got embarrassed and quickly left. As I walked out of the store, I saw people coming in who seemed to be encased in a black substance. I thought they were probably near death. It was all too much to endure.

As I was leaving in haste to get away from the proliferation of spiritual beings, I heard something from deep inside my being say, "Tell the woman on the bench in front of you that I love her and My plans for her have not changed."

Immediately, I saw the woman. I went over hesitantly and saw she had a dark spirit moving around on her head. I sat down near her and told her what I had heard. She looked at me surprised, and then she shocked me by bursting out crying. I felt uncomfortable with her response but she told me, "I felt like I had gone too far this time and He would never have anything to do with me again. You have no idea how much your words have helped me today. Thank you so much."

She smiled at me, and I knew the words I had been given to tell her changed her whole outlook. It felt good to give hope to someone. As I walked away, I turned around to look at her. The dark spirit that was there before was gone. The words I had spoken to her had helped her to change her mind—literally.

I knew I could send these evil creatures away from me, but I was beginning to understand, I could do it for other people, too. If words brought these spiritual creatures to people, then words could send them away.

These spiritual beings seemed to thrive on lies and fear. They apparently flourish in darkness and do not want to be uncovered. When someone like me can see them, they want to bring fear into my life so I will leave them alone.

It suddenly became obvious; they cannot tolerate the Truth because it uncovers their lies. And they hate the One who is light because He reveals their evil presence.

Speaking the Word was the spiritual weapon I needed to fight these evil enemies. I knew it had to be the key to win this battle.

The Truth is powerful—to the one who says it and to the one who hears it.

Chapter 39

My new clothes made me look like a new man—-which I was. I walked into the steak house to find my girl but she wasn't there yet. I told the hostess I needed a table for two and then I sat down to wait for her.

As I watched the door eagerly, I saw a middle aged man walk in alone. But he wasn't really alone because he was carrying a dark, foreboding spirit on his head. I apparently could not escape this new reality. "Oh no, not now." I thought to myself. I didn't want to deal with this, I just wanted to enjoy the night with Irene.

But my heart told me something different and I knew I had to talk to him. He sat down next to me as we both waited to be seated. I turned to him and asked, "Hi, how are you tonight?"

He smiled at me and responded, "Oh, I'm OK. Thanks for asking. And you?"

I knew he was just being polite. I could have chalked it up to—at least I tried—-but I decided to pursue the truth. "I know I might be overstepping my boundaries, but I just couldn't help but wonder if you might be struggling with something?"

He looked at me like he was puzzled and said, "Is it that obvious?"

"No, it's not obvious," I said, as I watched the evil presence swirling over his head. "I just saw something in your face," I explained, not really knowing what to say without mentioning the spirit.

"My wife died a few months ago, and today would have been our anniversary. This was our favorite place, so I thought I'd come here tonight to honor her. But, life isn't worth much without her," he said sadly.

"So you were going to have dinner alone tonight, and then what?" I asked, hoping I wasn't being too pushy.

"I was going to go home to my empty house. There is nothing left for me now. Life is too painful without her," he confided. What he was really saying was he had planned to end it all that very night, which I had already suspected.

In my spirit, I could feel a Father's heart turning towards this man. I knew He wanted me to tell this broken hearted man how much He loved him, and if he could hang on a little longer, life would become livable again. So, I told him.

He looked at me in disbelief and started weeping. I was totally shocked and wasn't sure what to do, especially since we were out in public. But I knew the man needed a hug, so I hugged him as he poured out his heart to me. He told me I had given him hope that night.

As he thanked me profusely, Irene walked in. She was shocked to see this man crying in my arms. I was embarrassed, but in her eyes, it cinched the deal for her. I didn't know it then, but she decided at that very moment she wanted to spend the rest of her life with me.

He asked me my name and shook my hand. I introduced him to Irene, and he told her what a special man I was. With that sweet gesture he left, deciding not to go through with his last supper.

She looked at me in disbelief and asked me if I had set that up to impress her. I asked her if it worked and she laughed. We got our table and talked for two hours straight. There was so much to know about this delightful woman.

She wanted to hear more about the man I had been talking to and how that had come about. I tried to explain it to her without mentioning the spirit. I simply said, "I felt in my heart I needed to reach out to him." I was hesitant to explain everything to her not knowing what she might think, but I knew I would have to tell her eventually if we were going to move on in our relationship.

As risky as it was, I decided to tell her a little of what I had been through since I had arrived in Abilene. I told her about the dark thing on Bill's head, and how I had seen the same thing on the man who had been weeping in my arms. And then I told her about being attacked in my room. I started to tell her about the 'souch incident' at Teresa's house, but decided to wait. She didn't say much and I was getting nervous. I questioned if I had revealed too many bizarre episodes for one night.

Irene smiled and said she had to go to the restroom. As she walked away, I wondered if she was going to come back. I wished I hadn't told her about all those things. It was a lot to take in and I started thinking I should have waited a little longer, at least until she knew me better. I was so hoping I hadn't blown it.

But she did come back and with a surprising response to my stories. She told me she had a few of her own. She revealed to me she had only told her closest friends the things she was about to tell me. I felt honored and very curious to hear what she had to say.

"OK, Henry, I can't believe I'm telling you this. I was on a road trip with my mother. We were driving on a road in Oklahoma and it was dusk. I saw something in the sky way out in the distance that seemed to be going straight up. This was about thirty years ago, so not many things could do that except a helicopter. I kept watching it as it started moving toward us—mind you I was driving this entire time. As we came into Idabel, the thing was almost overhead."

I had to interrupt her right then to ask her why she had been in Idabel, explaining my grandparents used to live there. She was surprised to hear that, especially when I told her I went there a lot when I was young. She informed me they were just passing through on the way to see her grandparents in Camden, Arkansas. I realized I had rudely distracted her from her story. I told her to continue.

She tried to get back into her excitement about telling me the extraordinary story but I knew I had disturbed the flow. It was apparent I needed to work on my listening skills.

She continued, "I got out of the car to see this flying object better. My mother would not get out because she was scared, but I noticed there was a man right next to me who had also gotten out of his car to see it."

"It was very large and metallic, shaped like an oblong triangle with lights in each corner. It made no noise and it moved very slowly. The object was just above the trees as it went right over my head. I was terrified and fascinated all at the same time. But, then I got nervous. I was afraid it might beam me up or something, so I quickly got back in my car."

"Later that night I was listening to the radio and they said several people had seen the same object in the sky, but they explained it away saying it was an airplane refueling. I knew that was a cover-up. I couldn't stop thinking about it. I do believe there are things out there we just don't understand. I have no idea what I saw that night but I never forgot it." She looked at me waiting for my response.

I burst out with, "Wow, you saw a UFO! That is so cool. I always wanted to see one but never have. You are one up on me, Irene."

"But do you believe me, Henry?" she asked in the sweetest way.

"Of course I do, Irene. Why wouldn't I?" I reassured her. But as I said those words, I realized if she had told me the same story a few months before, I wouldn't have believed her.

"OK, then I'll tell you my other weird story. When I was very young, I woke up one night and there was a man standing by my bed looking at me. He was a dark figure, and I couldn't see his face. He had a big overcoat on and an old fashioned hat like men used to wear in the fifties. I wasn't terrified really, which surprised me. I clearly saw him standing there, but I can't remember what happened after that. It was so weird," she recalled.

"I thought about it recently, so I decided to look it up on the computer. I wanted to see if anyone else had ever mentioned seeing something like that and remarkably, a lot of people had seen the very same thing! That kind of creeped me out, but it was also comforting to know I wasn't the only one." She looked at me again, waiting for my response.

She then added, "You have to understand, I have never felt comfortable enough to tell anyone these things except my best friends, so you should be honored."

"You have no idea how honored I am, Irene. Thank you for sharing these stories with me and trusting me. I do believe every word you said. Believe me; I *know* there are things going on that we can't explain. I am starting to recognize there is an unseen world all around us and it seems it can interact with our world sometimes," I noted.

She agreed with me and said, "I'm so glad I told you, Henry, and that you believed me." Then her whole demeanor changed and she laughed, "Now what should we talk about?" She was so much fun. I felt like I could talk to her for days and still have a million more things to say to her.

We decided to go for a walk after dinner and went to a college campus close by. She told me her mother had actually worked at that college and showed me where her mother's office had been. Irene told me she had gone to the college for a year, but left when she wasn't accepted into one of their social clubs. She explained it was something like a sorority. She said it broke her heart at the time to be rejected like that, but it had ended up being a blessing. She left Abilene and went to Texas A & M for her college degree, where she had a great time and met some lifelong friends.

We talked about many other things, and then I asked her if she had ever thought about getting married. She informed me she had and said, "Yes, I've had a few proposals. I was even engaged a few times, but then the guy would ruin it and do something childish. I wanted to marry a man, not a child. I'm still waiting for the right one."

In my heart, I was hoping that would be me.

Chapter 40

Cooper and I went out for a walk when I got back to my room later that night. I reached down to pet him, and told him I thought I had met the girl of my dreams. He was more interested in finding the right tree than he was in my love life, but just sharing it with another living being made it more real.

I decided I would sleep better if I put Cooper in his cage, so he slept there for the night. He whined a little but finally went to sleep. I read for a few minutes and then decided to call it a night—a wonderful, glorious night.

As I drifted off to sleep, my last thoughts were of my first kiss with Irene. It was tender and sweet. We agreed to see each other the next night. I was thrilled she still wanted to see me. This was a whole new experience for me, and I loved every minute of it.

My good thoughts seemed to bring good dreams that night. The first dream I had was of my mother. I could see her from a distance but knew it was her. I ran over to her and hugged her. I told her how happy I was to see her again as she just smiled, delighting in my presence. She seemed very interested as I gushed on and on about Irene. As I described her, I realized how much Irene was like my mother. "She reminds me of you, Mom. She is kind and funny. She lights up the room with her smile just like you do."

My mother was thrilled for me, and told me she knew I would meet the right woman one day. She did always tell me that, but I never believed her.

We walked through this beautiful meadow and she shared with me what a wonderful place it was. I asked her if it was heaven, but she didn't answer. She seemed to radiate light from her very presence and I knew she was happy. She told me there was nothing but love there. There was no envy, selfishness, anger, hatred, or anything evil.

She also told me how important it was for me to forgive anyone I had anything against. Bardon immediately came to mind. I wondered if I even could forgive him.

My mother told me something unusual was going on in the spiritual world. She said I needed to be vigilant because spiritual beings were becoming more aggressive since we were coming into the last days.

There were those words again—"last days". I didn't like hearing them and wondered why everyone kept saying them. But before I could ask her, she continued with her warning, "Be careful, Henry, what words you say. Put a guard over your mouth. These evil spirits cannot read your mind, but they know what you believe by what you say."

She then gave me further instructions, "You have to warn people, Henry. Tell them they are opening the door to much destruction by their words."

As I started to ask her another question, my attention was distracted by someone beating on a drum in the distance. I looked at my mother and told her I would give the warning to anyone I could. I started to hug her, but I could feel myself waking up. I didn't want to wake up, but my mind finally grasped the fact there was someone banging on my door. Cooper started barking. It was three AM. Who could possibly be at my door?

I looked through the little peephole and saw Irene. I opened the door and took her in my arms. She was visibly shaken. "Henry, one of your spirit friends paid me a visit tonight. It scared me so much. I'm never afraid, but tonight I was terrified."

After she calmed down a little, I asked her if she wanted to go out and get some coffee and talk about it. She looked at me like I was silly. "Henry, do you know what time it is?"

I explained to her that truck stops are open all night. We went to the same one I had gone to before. When we sat down, the same waitress was there. She wasn't as bubbly, but she smiled at me and asked me if I ever got to talk to Carl's girlfriend. I told her I did, and it was very helpful to my story. I didn't tell her how much it traumatized my life.

Irene and I sat there and talked for hours about these horrible spirits. I told her not many people could see them so I was surprised she could. "I'm not sure if it's a blessing or a curse, but welcome to my world," I said glibly.

Because of all I shared with Irene, she had an understanding about how these spirits operate. She believed the spirit had entered her house because of something she said. She went on to explain, "I had been angry at one of my friends for posting something private about me on social media. I didn't want the information known." I wondered if the post had anything to do with me and our relationship.

"I know I shouldn't have but I called our mutual friend and told her what she had done," Irene said. "I knew it was wrong, Henry, as I continued to pour out all the things I disliked about this woman. But it didn't stop me."

"Honestly, the presence of that evil spirit in my house makes me realize just how wrong I was. I know now, the words I said brought that thing into my house. I will never gossip again!" she proclaimed emphatically.

After Irene told me her story, I told her about my dream. I shared the warning my mother had given me and how it was the same thing I had heard from others. Irene looked at me like she was surprised. "Henry, do you really believe it was your mother who spoke to you?" she asked. "It was a dream. People dream about their loved ones all the time but it doesn't mean they are literally there."

"I don't know, Irene, but it seemed so real. I have had so many weird dreams lately. This one was nice for a change because I felt like I got to see my mother again, whether it was literally her or not. She is the only person who ever believed in me—that is, until I met you."

Irene asked me to finish telling her about my dream. "My mother told me I must warn people to be careful what they say because they are drawing these evil spirits by their words. And now you know how true that is after what happened tonight, right?" I asked Irene.

Irene said her pastor had never mentioned any of this before, and she wondered why. She said, "I'm going to ask him about it Sunday."

It occurred to me he might be able to help me understand this spiritual world I had just discovered. I imagined he was knowledgeable about these spirits since he was a professional. Irene asked me to go to church with her Sunday and told me she would introduce me to him. I happily agreed.

We stayed at the truck stop until daylight when she felt better about going back to her house. I had a lot to do that day and hoped I could stay awake long enough to get it done. Even though I loved the fact Irene reached out to me, I knew I would be tired all day. I wasn't getting much work done. I was so distracted by her.

Because of the dream, I felt even more compelled to let people know about these spirits. Most people were blithely unaware of the spiritual world around them and the impact it was having on their lives. I believed my mother was trying to tell me–writing this story, was my mission.

Chapter 41

I rene decided it was safe to go back to her house when daylight made its appearance. She asked me if I would come in while she checked under the beds and inside the closets. I had never been in her house before so I was excited to see it.

Her house was nice and neat and she seemed very organized. I was thankful she had never been in my townhouse, since it was just the opposite.

It was interesting walking around her house seeing how she decorated her home. She had reminders everywhere of her favorite quotes from The Word. I thought it was a good idea, and decided I would put some of these quotes up in my townhouse when I got home.

There were pictures of her family scattered around. She had shared some about her family, so it was interesting to see their faces. Her mother had passed away a few years before, but she had quite a few pictures of her. Irene's father lived close by in a nursing home. Irene told me she would like for me to meet him. I thought that was a good sign.

After she declared her home was free of any spirits, I left so I could get back to Cooper and my story. She had to get ready for work, too. I kissed her good-bye and she stayed in my arms longer than usual. She kissed me again and thanked me for being her knight in shining armor. She certainly made me feel like one.

It was wonderful having this woman in my life, but it was not helping my career. I felt a heavy burden to get this book written and published as quickly as possible. Then I could get on with my life. It takes a lot of focus to write for long periods, and my focus constantly veered off to Irene.

I took Cooper out for a walk. I was getting inpatient with him to hurry and do his business, so I could get back to work. I would have liked to have gone to the library, rather than stay in the room, but I felt bad leaving Cooper in his cage again. I decided to spend the morning working in the room, so he could roam around.

Staying up late with Irene was taking its toll. I went down to the lobby for some coffee. I had a long list of things I wanted to get done. I needed to update my notes and revise them. Then I would begin the arduous task of putting it all together so it made sense. I wanted it to read somewhat like a novel to keep it interesting—hopefully.

Then I would need to get it to Kathy, the lady who does our editing, so she could correct all the mistakes I would make. All of this was going to take time. I wasn't shooting for the moon, but I wanted to make it flow and be thought-provoking.

The coffee helped and several hours flew by as I focused on all that had transpired over the past few weeks. There was more research I wanted to do on these evil spirits. I felt very ignorant about the spiritual world because I had ignored it for most of my life. All I really knew was what I had experienced and what Jake and Micah had told me.

But I understood my greatest challenge would be to convince people these spirits exist in the first place. It was obvious most people think they only manifest in horror movies.

Around lunch time, I had to stop for a break and I made myself a bologna sandwich. I gave Cooper some treats and decided to keep going since I was getting a lot done. But around three, my energy was sagging and my focus was gone. I thought it might help to take a nap for a few hours. I felt good about the progress I had made, so I made sure to save all the work I had completed. I put Cooper in the cage and set an alarm to make sure I wouldn't sleep the rest of the day.

As soon as I closed my eyes, I fell asleep because I was so tired, and of course, I had a dream. Surprisingly, I felt tired even in the dream. I couldn't escape the exhaustion I felt, even in my sleep.

My mother was in the dream again and I was glad to see her. But, because of my weariness, I told her I would talk to her later. I explained to her I just needed to sleep and rest for a while.

In the distance I saw a bed in a room that looked very much like my childhood bedroom. I put my head on the pillow and my mother sat down beside me on the bed like she used to do when I was a boy.

"Mom, I'm so tired. I don't want to save the world. Could they find somebody else?" I whined.

My mother looked at me with sadness and said, "People need to hear what only you can tell them, Henry. You have been given eyes to see what few others can. But, no one is forcing you to do this. It is your choice." Her voice then softened and she added, "Whatever you decide, Henry, know I will always love you."

As she spoke to me, I could feel myself drifting off. But her soft voice suddenly became alarmed and she started shaking me. "Henry, get up." I told her I had to sleep a little longer, but she shook me harder and said with more force, "Get up, Henry!"

The seriousness of her voice forced me to react. I sat up and looked at my phone. I was surprised I had already slept for an hour. I noticed a strange odor that I had never noticed before. I looked down at Cooper and he was sleeping soundly in his cage. Nothing seemed to be amiss.

My curtains were shut to block the light, but when I opened them, I saw a shocking sight. Right by the door to my room, there were flames blazing! It was a roaring inferno horribly close to my only exit. I grabbed Cooper's cage and got out of my room by the skin of my teeth. At the very moment I ran out, the fire engulfed my room and everything in it.

My heart was beating out of my chest as I realized how close we had come to being hurt. If I hadn't left the room when I did with Cooper, we would have both been in those flames. But at that same moment of relief, I realized my computer was still in the room—the computer I had just filled with hours of work. I thought about trying to run in and get it but knew I would be seriously burned.

The fire department arrived soon and put the fire out. The room next to me, where the fire seemed to originate, was not being used so no one knew how the fire could have started. But, I had a pretty good idea. No one was hurt, but I lost my computer and phone. I didn't care about the clothes or any of the other items I had, but all the work I had done for the last few days was probably lost.

My thoughts turned to Jake as I watched them douse the last remnants of the fire. I thought of how close I had come to sharing his fate. I understood more than ever, those evil spiritual beings were trying to kill me. If it hadn't been for my mother in that dream, I probably wouldn't have made it out.

As I stood outside in my underwear talking to the firemen and motel employees, a news truck showed up wanting to interview someone about the fire. I knew better than to let them plaster my face on the six o'clock news, but there wasn't any way I could escape since the fire truck was blocking my car. I walked into the lobby carrying Cooper. People from the motel kept asking me if I was OK. An ambulance came and checked me out and I was fine physically—emotionally I was spent.

I asked the motel if I could use their phone and I called Irene to tell her what happened. She was so upset and said she would be right over. I also called Sid and asked him if he could wire some money to me since I also lost my wallet. He felt terrible, and told me he would send some money as quickly as possible.

Irene offered to get me some clothes and shoes, so I could go out and get everything else I needed. She came back with some basketball shorts, a t-shirt, and some sandals. It was sufficient to go out in public, but it was the last thing I would have picked out.

Then she drove me to the location where I could pick up the money from Sid. She also took me to my cellphone carrier to get a new phone. I had lost all my contacts. I was so angry for the inconvenience. I told Irene I knew who set the fire. I explained to her it would have probably killed us, if I hadn't been warned in a dream to get out. She seemed surprised but didn't say anything. I knew my supernatural life was becoming a little too much for her. I knew it was for me.

This battle was becoming too difficult and I was weary. I realized I was in great danger from these evil spirits. I knew they wouldn't be content to just come after me—they would come after anyone I loved. I didn't want anything to happen to Irene, so I told her that it might be best for her to stay away from me for a while.

She looked at me in anger and said, "You're not getting rid of me that easy. You need me, Henry Pike, if you are going to get this story written. I have a good friend who can put you and Cooper up for a few days until you find a place."

I told her I couldn't stay with anyone because it would endanger them. I would just get another room at the motel. She could see my point, and, fortunately, the motel offered me another room for free since they believed it was their negligence which caused the fire. I'm sure they were afraid I might sue them. I was glad for their offer and accepted it, even though I knew they were not to blame.

Irene took me to the pet store, so I could get some food for Cooper and then to the mall so I could buy some decent clothes. I went to my 'preferred' department store to buy more pants and shirts. The same lady was there and she blushed when she saw me. She must have thought I really liked to shop for clothes; it was the third time I had been there in two weeks.

I picked out the same pants and shirt I bought for my date with Irene. I knew they fit and I liked them. She didn't ask me if I wanted to try them on because she knew I didn't. I barely looked at her or the beast on her chest, which had grown since the last time I saw her.

We went to another store where I found some socks and shoes I liked. Then I remembered I also needed underwear, deodorant, toothpaste, and all of my toiletries. Then, our next stop was the car rental place. They did have extra keys for the car for which I paid a small fee.

It was all a huge inconvenience and I kept complaining about it until Irene got annoyed and said, "Henry, you and Cooper could have died in that fire. I know you lost all your work which is terrible, but you should be thankful you're alive."

Her words were true and I knew it, but my feelings were all over the place. I felt defeated and tired. I just wanted to give up. And then it hit me like a ton of bricks. Those evil, deceitful spirits were behind all of it. They were, no doubt, behind the fire and they were feeding me every depressing, discouraging thought I was having. And, unfortunately, I was listening.

Chapter 42

Irene had been with me the whole day helping me out with everything I needed. She also took me out for dinner later, but my exhaustion got in the way of adequately thanking her. All I could think about was going to sleep.

I was too tired to do anything. I knew I needed to buy another computer, but I didn't have the energy to shop for one. I was glad to have a phone again, but I only had two contacts in it—Irene and Sid. I didn't know Bill's number by memory and I felt badly I hadn't called him.

Irene dropped me off at my motel and I kissed her goodbye. I asked her if she wanted to shop with me the next day for a computer. I usually enjoyed shopping for a new computer with all the latest features, but I wasn't looking forward to it this time. I just needed to get one and get back to work.

My new motel room was much bigger and nicer than my old room and the bed was larger and much more comfortable. I realized this was what a few more dollars could get you.

Cooper and I went out for a very short walk with his new leash. I fed him in his new bowl and was thankful I didn't have to buy a new cage. The only thing I could think about was going to sleep. The whole day had been exhausting. As soon as I got him settled, I went to bed.

I quickly fell asleep and slipped into another dream, which had apparently become my new bedtime routine. In this dream, I walked into a rather small room where five people were sitting on a bench on one side of the room. It was like they were all waiting for something. There were no windows or doors. I looked behind me to see how I had entered the room but there was no door behind me—only a wall. I wondered how I got in and wondered even more how I was going to get out.

As I ran my fingers up and down the wall trying to feel for a crack where a hidden door might be, I noticed the five people were just sitting there watching me. I stopped my search to ask them where I was. One young woman stood up and walked over to me.

She spoke slowly, "I think I might have made a mistake. I thought I was going to heaven, but this doesn't seem like heaven. I hope it's not the other place. It's not bad here but there is nothing to do. I'm very confused as we all are."

Then she turned around and pointed to the others. I looked over at the other four people as they sat and stared at me. They reminded me of people I've seen sitting on their porches just passing away the time. I was surprised by how lethargic they all seemed.

She continued, "There was a man who met me here when I first arrived and told me to be patient. He said others would join me and we would be free of all the pain on earth until the end of time. That sounded good to me. I asked the man if this was heaven, but he didn't answer. Then he walked out through a door. After he left, I tried to find the door, but there was no opening anywhere. I don't think this is heaven, do you?"

I told her I had no idea where we were. She then began to tell me about her sad life and why she believed she ended up in the room. "I had once been so happy. I was getting married and everything was perfect. I had never thought I would find true love, but then I met my fiancé. I loved him so much, but apparently he did not feel the same way about me. Right before our wedding, he broke up with me. He wouldn't even talk to me when I begged him to tell me why. He just brushed me off like a crumb on the table."

She started crying, "I always had this nagging thought that one day he would get tired of me and dump me. And that was exactly what happened. I kept telling my friends I knew he was going to break up with me, but they just told me I was being paranoid. But when he ended our engagement, they realized I had been right all along."

"I didn't want to live anymore after he left me. I put some of the things I saved from our time together into a box. I put a newspaper clipping about our engagement and some pictures of us, and my engagement ring in there. I also put a broken, ceramic heart he had given me in the box. It was broken because I had thrown it against the wall after he ended our engagement," she smirked.

"The box represented a coffin to me because it contained the remains of broken promises and a future I would never have. I was going to bury it along with my dreams, but then it occurred to me I should mail it to my fiancé instead. I wrote a note to him telling him how much he hurt me. I put it in the box, but I never got to send it to him. It's still under my headboard in my bedroom. I wish he had seen the contents of that box. I wanted him to know how much pain I was in," she lamented.

As tears were rolling down her cheeks, she continued her sad saga, "I wanted to be free from the pain in my heart. I wanted to find a way to escape. I wanted out. And one night, when I didn't think I could live another day, I cried out in desperation to be taken out of my sorrow. It was the next day when I woke up in this place, but this was not what I had in mind."

I tried to be sympathetic to her, but I was starting to feel a little claustrophobic as I stood in the small room listening to her tale of woe. I told her I was sorry how her engagement ended, and then I asked what her name was.

"My name is Jodie," she said. The list of missing people materialized in my mind and I remembered reading about Jodie. She was a musician and had played in the City Orchestra as a violinist. Her wedding had been cancelled right before she disappeared. She was one of the first to be reported missing. I couldn't believe she might actually be one of the missing people.

How could I be dreaming about this woman I had never met? She was standing right in front of me, telling me her life story with heartbreaking details. I knew it was a dream, but it didn't seem like a dream except for the exceptionally small room.

I didn't know if I was literally talking to the real Jodie, but if I was, I wanted her to know many people cared about her and were looking for her. "Jodie, you may not be aware of this, but nearly everyone in Abilene is looking for you. No one knew what happened to you or any of the other people who are missing, but no one is giving up."

She looked at me puzzled, and I remembered Jodi was one of the first to go missing. She was the next person reported after Mary. "Did you know you are one of ten people who are considered missing in Abilene?" I asked her.

She told me she didn't know and then she wondered out loud, "There are other people who are in a place like this?"

"I'm not sure where they are, Jodie?" Then I asked, "Are the other people in here from Abilene, too?"

Jodie looked over at the others on the bench, and told me only two of them were from Abilene. I was surprised and wondered if the other two were missing from somewhere else. I asked her to introduce me to the bench warmers.

We walked over to the other people and she introduced me to Barry. I shook his hand but his handshake was very limp. I asked him how he had ended up there. He stood up and proceeded to tell me.

Barry then gave me a presentation of his ministry that sounded like something he had rehearsed many times. "I am the director of a mission in Dallas where we reach out to runaways. We go to the bus stops and train stations to try and intercept the runaways before the pimps do. These kids are naïve because they think they are leaving their homes for a better life, but they don't realize there are always people watching to exploit them. We offer them shelter until something else can be worked out."

This sounded like a wonderful mission, and I was surprised someone like him would end up in such a horrible place. He seemed to read my mind and proceeded to answer my question. He and his wife, June had started the mission and both had served faithfully for many years helping to rescue many young people. But his wife and many others did not realize Barry had been embezzling money from donations designated for their mission. He had been able to avoid suspicion since everyone thought he was such a good man.

He went on to tell me, "I even stole money from some of our donors while staying in their homes. It was in the home of an elderly couple where I was first suspected. I usually stayed with them when doing fund raising in their area."

"I had asked the elderly woman where I might buy a gift for someone I was about to have lunch with. She told me about a store not far from where she lived. I thought she probably went there often to buy gifts. So while she was making lunch, I looked on her desk and saw her checkbook. I thought she would never notice if I used one of her checks to pay for the gift. Since she was an older woman, I figured she'd just chalk it up to forgetfulness."

"I was wrong," he said sadly. "A few weeks later when I was on my way back to Abilene, she called me and asked me point blank if I had used one of her checks to buy a gift. I told her I would never do such a thing but she was pretty sure I had. She knew she hadn't written the check and her husband couldn't have since he was an invalid. She said I was the only one who would have had access to her checkbook during that time period."

"Then she added she never shopped at the store she had suggested to me. She only told me about it because it was near her house. I knew then, I was in trouble," he said sadly. "I started to panic and wondered if any of the others might figure out I had written checks on their accounts, as well."

I interrupted him and asked, "There were others?"

"Yes, unfortunately, there were quite a few," he admitted. "I was afraid she would press charges and I kept imagining what would happen if this got out. My reputation would be ruined and it would destroy the mission we had worked so hard to build."

"When I knew I could not convince her I was innocent, I started crying and begging her to forgive me. She hung up on me after telling me she was appalled by my behavior. I was so distraught that I pulled the car over to the side of the road and wept. I believed my life was over," he mourned.

"All the years of taking whatever I wanted had caught up with me. Somehow I had convinced myself I was entitled to it. It all came crashing down on me. I didn't have the strength to tell anyone. I wasn't sure if they would forgive me because I wasn't sure I could forgive myself," he revealed.

"All I knew was I wanted out of the mess I had made. I begged for deliverance from my situation. I'm not sure what all I said, but when I stopped and opened my eyes, I found myself here. I wasn't sure if it was an answer to my pleas or the punishment for my deeds," he confessed.

He looked at me in all sincerity and said, "I know this is not heaven, but I would rather stay here forever then go back and face what I have done. Hopefully, the lady I stole from will never report it since I am missing."

This respected man was irrational to steal from people who trusted him, especially just to buy a gift. I thanked him for his candor, but I didn't know what else to say. He seemed to prefer to be stuck in a little room forever than go home and face what he had done.

Jodie walked over to me and asked if I'd like to meet the other man from Abilene. She introduced me to Carl and I recognized his name immediately.

"Carl, it is so nice to meet you!" I gushed, like I was meeting him at a party. "I met your girlfriend, Teresa, not too long ago."

He seemed surprised and asked how she was. I told him she seemed to miss him very much. He responded, "Really? I'm surprised she even noticed I was gone since all she does is play this stupid video game all the time. It seems to be all she cares about."

I gulped as I remembered the terror I experienced from that game. He continued telling me about her preoccupation with the game and how sinister it was. I pretended I didn't know what he was talking about.

"I cared about Teresa, but she became obsessed with this game. I had never seen anything like it. I hated the game, but I played it with her because that's all she wanted to do. I suggested we do other things but she never wanted to, so I would give in because I really liked her."

Then what he said surprised me, "I'm kind of glad I don't have to deal with it anymore. I was tired of fighting with her about it all the time. It seemed like the game had taken over her life. As crazy as it sounds, I sometimes wonder if that stupid game had anything to do with me ending up here."

I decided not to tell him I didn't think it was crazy at all. I felt badly for him, but he seemed rather content to sit in the room rather than deal with his girlfriend and their problems.

Jodie walked up to me again and I thought she would introduce me to the other two people but she didn't. I asked her, "Where are those two people from?"

One was a young man and the other a middle aged woman. She said, "I'm not sure. They never talk to us. I don't think they talk to each other, either."

It seemed intolerable to me that these five people could just sit in that small room all the time with nothing to do. They all seemed to be in a daze. They were sitting passively in this unbearable 'waiting room' bemoaning their past rather than figuring out a way they could get out and go home. It seemed to me, they didn't care anymore and had just resigned themselves to their new horrible home.

My curiosity got the best of me so I asked, "What do you do to pass the time in this room? Do you eat? Do you exercise? How can you survive in here without any food or water?"

Carl opened up and said, "We mostly talk about our old lives. We miss our families back home but the idea of going back is too difficult. I know we all hope to be in a better place one day. I think this room is where we wait to get into heaven."

Jodie piped in and said, "Most of us have been here for a while now and nothing has really changed. The only thing that ever changes is a person will show up out of nowhere— like you. I guess you'll find out what it's like since you are here now."

"No, no," I said emphatically. "I'm not staying here. This is a dream. I will wake up soon and I'll be back in my motel room," I explained.

"That's what we all thought when we first came. We all thought it was just a dream. I hate to break it to you, but I think you will be waiting here with us for a while," Carl said. Then he thought to ask, "What is your name, by the way?"

"My name is Henry, but I'm not supposed to be here. You guys are the ones missing. I'm just doing a story for my magazine about all of you. I have to leave now so I can finish it," I desperately explained to him.

As I turned to start searching again for a hidden door, fear was starting to overcome me as I wondered if their horrible plight was about to become mine.

Chapter 43

Fear was taking hold of me as I frantically moved my fingers all around the walls of the insidious 'waiting room'. The walls seemed like they were closing in on me as I desperately sought a way out. I was losing my composure as I started yelling at myself to wake up. I didn't care what the bench warmers thought as they sat there and watched me make a fool of myself. I had to get out.

I started screaming, "Wake up, Henry! Wake up!" But, my yelling did not jar me awake like I hoped.

When I finally calmed down and quit yelling, I could hear something groaning in the distance. I listened intently to know where the sound was coming from because it appeared to be outside the room. The others didn't seem to hear it, but I definitely did. The groaning suddenly turned into growling which sounded like a dog. When the barking started, I knew there was a dog outside. I thought it might be guarding the waiting room entrance.

The barking got louder and louder. The intensity of it finally broke into my consciousness and woke me up. I jumped up in my bed and quickly realized it was Cooper who was barking. He didn't bark often, so I was thankful he decided to start that night.

I let Cooper out of the cage to see what he was barking at. He jumped up on the bed and into my arms. Apparently something had scared him because he was trembling. I held him tightly for a few minutes which helped to calm him down.

It then occurred to me, it was probably me who scared him since I must have been yelling in my dream. My yelling had not worked, but Cooper's barking did. His barking freed me from that horrible nightmare. I was so glad to have him in my life.

It was 4:20 in the morning and I was wide awake. So was Cooper. I decided to put him on the bed next to me and turn the TV on for some background noise, but I couldn't go back to sleep. The horrible dream wouldn't leave my thoughts. What a disturbing feeling it was to be trapped in a single room with nothing to do except relive your heartaches.

It was just a dream, but their stories seemed so real to me. I couldn't have made up what they told me in my wildest dreams. I had to wonder if the missing people were trying to get a message to me.

Then, I remembered what Jodie told me about the items from her cancelled wedding. I questioned if there would be any possibility those things might actually be under her head board in a box. I imagined her parents and the police had gone through her room and possessions with a fine tooth comb. But, if it was really there, they might have missed it.

It would be quite a risk to try and tell them, or anyone, about the dream. But if those things were there, then it would prove I actually talked to her. But if they weren't, who knew what they would think?

Even if I really did talk to those three people, it didn't accomplish anything. I wanted to rescue these people not dream about them. And the dream didn't offer any mystical answers for their whereabouts. Their only known location was in my dream, which certainly wasn't helpful. Even if I did know their location, how could I get them out of a room with no door? It was all too bizarre to contemplate. I was just thankful it had been a dream—actually a terrible nightmare.

It made me wonder if I would dream about the other missing people. I decided I should get up and write down what Jodie had said, just in case. Since I was up, I decided to make some coffee with my fancy, in-room coffee maker they had failed to put in my last room.

When I finished writing down the dream it was around six in the morning. It felt like old times to write down my notes on paper instead of a computer. I would have to decipher them later when I got my new computer, so I could type them up.

Irene picked me up later for lunch and I couldn't wait to tell her about my dream. She listened to every detail but seemed hesitant to be as excited as I was about it. She thought it was unwise to put so much importance on a dream. "Henry, do you really believe you met some of the missing people in a dream? I have to say, this is one of the more bizarre things you've told me. Don't you think it's a strong possibility your active imagination could have conjured up these people and their stories?" She smiled as she said it but I knew she was concerned.

She was probably right but it seemed so real to me. I tried to explain to her, "Irene, I felt like I actually talked to each one of them. You have to understand, there is no way I could have made up all the details they told me, even in my dreams."

Irene then asked me an interesting question, "Have you checked to see if those people you met look like the people they claimed to be?"

Even though I had a list and a brief history of the missing people, I had no idea what they looked like. I decided I would do a search on them when I got my new computer and see if I could find some pictures of those three people.

Irene continued with her concerns, "Henry, I'm worried what will happen if you try to tell people about this dream. They are either going to think you are crazy or they might even think something worse. Are you sure you want to take that risk?"

I appreciated her concern and told her, "Irene, I don't think I'm going to tell anybody else, at least not right now. I just wanted to share it with you."

She smiled at me and said, "I think that is a good idea, Henry."

She was right. Perhaps I was putting too much stock in a dream, no matter how realistic it seemed.

Irene was still worried. She said, "Henry, I think you have become too involved with this story. It's great that you care so much about these people, but it's like you can't get away from them, even when you're asleep. Maybe you should take some time off and go back to Fort Worth and just rest. I don't think you can do that here."

Her suggestion sounded wise, but I was hoping she wasn't trying to get rid of me. I realized I really was too immersed in the story, so I decided to take her suggestion to step back and pause for a few days. I asked, "Irene, would you mind keeping Cooper for me if I went home for a few days?" She happily agreed.

The next morning, I packed the few clothes I had and stopped by the computer store to pick up my new computer before I drove back to Fort Worth. I called Sid and we planned to have dinner later that night.

Sid and I met at one of our favorite restaurants near the office and caught up on everything. He asked me about the story and I decided to not share the dreams with him. I told him it was going well, and I should have something for him soon. I also decided to not mention the book idea.

When he continued to ask me more questions about the story, I started to feel agitated. I understood why he wanted to know but it was the last thing I wanted to think about. I just wanted to take Irene's advice and step away from it for a few days. I told him I would be submitting everything to him in a week. I knew I should finish the articles I had been assigned to do. I would write the book after I finished my assignment.

After dinner, I went home and watered my plants and looked at my stack of bills. I took my new computer out of the box and decided it would be relaxing to play with it for a while. I had heard it was one of the best on the market. I would learn all of its features, so I could get back to writing in a few days. Then I would be ready to tackle the story when I returned. But, I would soon find the story did not stay behind in Abilene.

The first night I was home, I had another dream. And if I thought the plight of Barry, Carl, and Jodie was bad, I was soon to find there were worse scenarios I could dream about.

Chapter 44

In my new dream, I found myself on a dark street in a town I didn't recognize—at first. There were a few street lights but they seemed to be growing dimmer by the second. As the streets got darker, I could see shadows moving around in the dim light.

The seeds of fear started taking root in my mind as I tried to get a handle on where I was. I started walking faster and faster. I could hear rustling behind me. Something was following me so I instinctively started running. I knew I was in a dream and I wanted to wake up. But then, I had the horrible realization–I didn't have Cooper near me to bark if things got out of hand.

As I ran down the street, I started stumbling because it was hard to see where I was going. I had to find a place to hide. I saw a few dark houses with no lights inside. They did not look inviting so I kept running until I saw a building that looked strangely familiar. When I got closer, I realized it looked like the school I went to as a kid.

The classrooms and walkways were not enclosed but open to the outside just like my old elementary school. I frantically checked every door hoping to find refuge but they were all locked. They were not only locked, but when I looked inside the windows, they were empty. There were no desks or furniture in any of them. I wondered if the school had closed.

Since there seemed to be no refuge there, I decided to leave. I listened to hear if anyone was still following me, but I couldn't hear anything. My body was so tired from running. I just wanted to find some place where I could rest for a few minutes. Once again, I felt the exhaustion in my dream that I was experiencing in my waking life.

Then I remembered there should be some bathrooms in the annex if this was my old school. I hoped they might be open. I had often taken refuge in the boys' bathroom to escape the teasing I received even in elementary school. I quickly walked over to the annex, turning around every few seconds to be sure no one was behind me.

Unfortunately, the doors to the bathrooms were also locked. As I started to leave, I stepped over a large grate that covered a drainage hole. It was there to keep the area free from flooding during heavy rainstorms. As I walked across it, a hand quickly reached out from under the grate and grabbed my leg! It was like something from a horror movie. I couldn't get free as hard as I yanked and pulled. I was way beyond terrified trying not to imagine what was on the other side of that hand!

I yelled for help even though the place looked deserted. But, between my screams, I heard someone saying my name. I looked around wondering who would know me in that god forsaken place. But then I realized, whoever was holding onto my leg, seemed to know my name. "Henry! Henry, help me! Please, help me," he pleaded.

I looked down in the dim light into the hole where a man was looking up at me. I couldn't make out who he was but his voice sounded familiar.

"Who are you?" I yelled at him.

The man spoke with desperation, "You don't remember me, Henry? I taught you piano when you were a boy. Please help me get out of here."

It couldn't be. I had tried my best to forget about this man and what he had done to me. This couldn't be happening, even in a dream. What evil had conjured up this sadistic nightmare and put him in it?

The man looking up at me was the very one who had instigated my descent into darkness. When I was a boy, he was the one who gave me piano lessons, but he also taught me much more—things I didn't want to know.

He was the man my father had hired to give me lessons but after a few weeks, he asked I come to his house instead of him coming to mine. I didn't mind the short walk and thought he was a good teacher. He had initially insisted I call him "Brother Brian" and told me I was like a little brother to him. But his intentions were anything but brotherly. After a few weeks at his house, I could not fathom how I would survive his "lessons". His inappropriate affection made me question everything about myself.

My fragile self-esteem was in tatters and I thought about killing myself rather than my father finding out what was happening. Brian insisted he would have no other choice but to tell my father what was going on, if I didn't cooperate with him. I had no idea how to stop what was happening, but I knew I would not survive if I didn't. I finally begged my mother to let me quit. I knew it would disappoint my father greatly. It was the first thing I had ever done that seemed to please him, but I couldn't take it anymore.

My mother was surprised because she thought I loved the piano and I did for a while. I think my mother knew something was going on so she finally convinced my father to let me stop. He looked at me in anger and told me I could quit. He also called me a "quitter" and added he didn't think I'd ever amount to anything. I never went back to Brian's house and never talked to him again. I also never played the piano again.

The piano gave me the only connection with my dad that I felt was positive. It was the only time I ever felt my father was proud of me. When I quit, it seemed to break that fragile connection with my father. And it was all because of Brian.

As I looked down at this man who had brought such destruction to my life, an intense anger rose up in me. I yelled back at him, "Oh, yes. I remember you. I remember how you betrayed me and abused me when I was just a boy. How could I forget? You destroyed my life. I never felt like a normal person after what you did to me. Now let go of me!" I hated this man and had no desire to help him.

"I am so sorry for what happened, Henry. I have always regretted it. I had struggled with that problem for years but it had a tight hold on me. I kept trying to convince myself I wasn't really hurting anyone. But, I guess I hurt you," he said sadly.

"I guess you did!" I yelled at him. "Now get your filthy hands off of me!"

He continued to hang on to my leg as he lamented his pathetic plight and I felt trapped, much like I did when I was forced to take piano lessons from him. I continued to yell at him to let go of me while he continued his self-loathing,

"I hated myself so much for the way I was, Henry. I despised myself and begged to be delivered from my horrible life and the torment I constantly lived in. And someone apparently heard me one night, because when I woke up the next day, I was no longer in my house. I was taken from my life of torment there but I didn't realize I would end up in a worse place. This is more awful than anything I could have ever imagined. Where am I, Henry?" he asked.

"I don't know and I don't care. This is what you deserve for all the horrible things you've done!" I screamed at him.

"Perhaps I do. But don't you understand, Henry? If you don't forgive me, I will never get out of this place. You must forgive me," he begged and then he started to cry. "I can't even die the right way."

He continued his sad saga as I was trying to free myself from his hold. "I'm not even sure how I died? I have been here a long time, Henry, and you are the first person I have seen. You are my only hope of ever getting out of here," he pleaded.

When I looked at him underneath the grates, I could see his face more clearly. He was dirty and older, but I could still make out his face, the same one that had haunted my dreams as a boy.

When he taught me piano, he had never used his last name, so I hadn't recognized his name when I saw it on the list of those missing. If any of the missing deserved to be in such a horrible place, it would be him. But why was I in the same place?

He called out again, "Henry, please. What am I going to do if you don't help me? I wish I could go back and change the mistakes I made, but I can't. Will you leave me here forever?" he cried.

This place was evil, but then again, so was he. Maybe he deserved what was happening to him? But I didn't want to be the one who would seal his fate. As much as I hated this man and wanted to leave him, it was hard to think about him staying in that horrible situation forever.

I knew I had no other choice, so I said, "Please let go of me, Brian. I do forgive you, OK? So let go of me." But he wouldn't.

"No, you don't mean that. You are just saying it to get away from me," he assumed.

"How can I help you, Brian, if you don't let go of me? I have to get someone to help me or find a way to pry this grate up," I reasoned.

"No, I don't believe you. You will never come back once I let go of you," he stated. "You quit taking lessons from me and didn't even bother to tell me. You never even said 'goodbye'. You were conniving when you were a kid, so how can I trust you now?"

His words evoked a response in me I didn't know I was capable of. I looked at him with all of the pent up rage I think I ever had and then I let it all out. "I was conniving?! You sick pervert! You ruined me in every way! I thought you were someone I could trust but you only wanted to use me!" I yelled. And with that incredible burst of anger, I yanked my leg out of his hand.

He screamed, "I'm so sorry, Henry! I know what I did was horrible. But, it had nothing to do with you; it was me. I did use you, but please forgive me and help me. I will do anything I can to make up for the harm I did to you."

"Can you give me back forty years of my life?" I yelled at him. "You made my life a living nightmare and now you are in a nightmare. It sounds like a just reward to me."

And with that I ran from him feeling perfectly justified. He did not deserve my help. But my resolve softened as I heard him continue to scream. I kept running until I couldn't hear him any longer.

Chapter 45

Brian's screams were growing silent as I ran further away from him. I wondered if he died or just gave up. I didn't realize how much I hated him until I saw him. Seeing him again evoked feelings of repugnance as I recalled his perverted, piano lessons. I could feel my body tense up as the unwanted memory taunted me.

Why should I help him? He deserved to be in this dark place. I continued to run down the street, as far from Brian as I could get. As I ran, I remembered my mother's words. She told me to forgive. But how could I ever forgive someone like him?

It would stand to reason, if that school was the one I attended, then I should be close to my childhood home. I went to the street where my home should have been, but all I could see was a very rundown house which looked like it had been covered with soot. I couldn't tell from all the bushes and dirt if it really was my old home.

When I walked up to the house, I tried to open the front door. The door knob broke off in my hand and there was dark goo on it which oozed onto my hand. I wiped my hand on my clothes but the goo wouldn't come off. I hoped it wasn't toxic, but whatever it was, it caused a big stain on my hands and whatever I touched. I wanted to find some way to wash it off as it was very sticky.

We had always kept the back door open when I was growing up, so I wondered if it might be in the dream. I decided to try it, but as I walked into the back yard, a swarm of flies greeted me. I swatted at them, but they swarmed all over me as I tried to feel for the back door. I couldn't see anything with the flies in my eyes but when I pushed on what seemed like a door, it opened into the house.

When I rushed inside, I brushed away the last remaining flies. But, as I breathed a sigh of relief, I gagged from the odor emanating from the house. It smelled like Teresa's house but much worse. It seemed to be a mixture of urine, feces and vomit.

I had to run outside to be able to breathe, but then the flies attacked me again. I almost swallowed one since I had my mouth open. I gagged and coughed to get it out. I tried to take a few deep breaths before I went back inside, but flies were all over my face. I ran back in slamming the door behind me.

There was a rag on the counter, so I covered my nose and mouth with it as I proceeded to walk quickly through the house. As I glanced around, the house looked similar to mine when I was a boy except for the smell and the soot.

When I saw what should be my mother's room, I ran inside and shut the door. It had always been a refuge for me throughout my young life and it was again. There I could finally breathe. I took deep breaths of the sweet air I found there. Her room had somehow remained untouched. It was just as she had left it. If only she had been there.

I walked over to her bed and fell on it, exhausted from running. I was so tired and knew if I shut my eyes, I might not ever wake up, but I couldn't help it. As I curled up on her bed, I kept hearing sounds coming from inside the house. It seemed like someone was yelling and cursing. I got up to lock the door but it wouldn't lock. If someone came, I knew I didn't have the strength to fight them. I got in bed again and covered my head with the covers. It was how I used to hide from monsters when I was a boy. I hoped it would still work.

Even the fear of someone in the house could not keep me awake. Exhaustion like I had never known shrouded me. There was no other choice but to allow myself to sleep.

As I succumbed to a deep sleep, I found myself in another dream. The bizarre reality was—I was in a dream within a dream. I tried to fight it not knowing what it would mean, but I just didn't have the strength. I let myself go wherever it would take me. I was losing consciousness of where I was. I felt lost and totally disoriented questioning if either nightmare would ever end.

As I became more aware of my surroundings, I found myself on another street. I was too tired to walk anywhere so I sat down on the curb and hoped it would all be over soon. I didn't know where I was or what I was supposed to do and I was at the point of not caring.

There were no people anywhere, which was eerie. I felt like I was in a ghost town. I didn't know if I could take any more surprises and pondered the likelihood of someone literally dying in a dream. I thought I might be the first.

Just then, I heard another voice calling out for help. I was thankful to hear a human voice, even in distress. I ran in the direction of the voice and found a bizarre situation. A middle aged man seemed to be hanging from the roof of what looked like a church. He was secured to the roof by his hands which were tied with a rope and his feet were tied to part of the wall. He was almost completely naked and in each of his hands there were long white papers. He didn't seem to be in pain, but he was apparently very uncomfortable. He was wiggling, trying to free himself from his strange predicament.

When I ran up to him, he stopped wiggling and spoke in a low, raspy voice. He asked, "Please find a way to help me. If you can get me down, I will give you anything—whatever you want," he promised.

"I don't want anything except to get out of this place," I told him. But I realized I should probably try to help him. "I'll go see if I can find a ladder." But when I ran behind the church to look for one, I saw the building was in shambles. It had fallen down and all that was left was rubble. The church was made out of large stones so it would be too difficult to sift through the debris to find anything. The only part of the church still standing was the front where he was hanging. I was surprised it had not fallen down, too. It reminded me of a movie set with a false front.

There did not seem to be anything I could use to climb up and set him free. I was afraid to try to climb up on the wall because nothing seemed to be holding it up. I didn't see any way to get him down. I told him, "I'm sorry but I can't find anything to climb up to reach you. Do you know a place where I could get a ladder?" I asked.

"No, there is nothing left here. Just forget about it. You can't help me. No one can help me. Just leave me alone," he said pitifully.

I had to ask, "How did this happen to you? And how did the church fall down?"

"Evil people destroyed it and they tried to take me down with it. They didn't realize who they were dealing with. I wasn't going to let them come in and ruin what I started. But even though I protected the church, everyone still blamed me when it fell." He went on to assure me none of it was his fault. I doubted that was true.

He continued justifying himself, "I did so much for those people and this is how they repaid me. They just left me here in shame. They should be the ones hanging here."

No matter what he had done, I found it hard to believe people would just hang him out to dry like that. I asked him who put him up there. He responded, "I'm not sure. It could have been any number of people." It was apparent this man was not well-liked.

I asked him his name and he told me it was Jonathan but everyone called him John. I was trying to remember if he was on the list Sid had given me. Then I remembered who he was.

John had been accused of embezzling money from a business he worked for. He had also swindled a few people out of their houses. And he had been accused of rape, but he was never convicted. I hadn't realized he was also a church leader. He had been a busy man, but apparently not with 'the Lord's work'.

The long papers dangling from his tied up hands were unusual. I asked him what they were but he wasn't sure. I walked closer to be able to read the writing closest to the ground. It looked like a laundry list of sins: adultery, seduction, lies, stealing, and an unfamiliar one—"wolf in sheep's clothing." I asked him about these charges, but he had no idea why these things were written about him. He certainly didn't appear to have any remorse about them if they were true.

It looked as if there was no way to get him down and I wasn't sure what else to do so I said, "I'm sorry, but I have no idea how to help you."

He told me again, "Just leave me alone like I said before. No one can help me."

He seemed so hopeless. I imagined if these allegations were true, he had taken hope away from many people who had trusted him. I didn't know what else to do, but as I started to walk away, a thought occurred to me. I went back and suggested to John, "What if you were to ask for forgiveness for some of these things on the lists, then maybe you would be set free?"

His response to my suggestion was, "I told you before, I haven't done anything wrong. I was falsely accused of all these things. Don't you understand? Just go away and forget about me, like everyone else."

As he continued to speak, I saw the lists from his hands grow longer. I walked over and read the newest word added: unrepentant. I looked up at him and could hear him blaming everyone else for his plight. I decided not to interrupt him and just left.

The darkness was palpable, and I was hoping to wake up from this lonely, gloomy place. But, as I stumbled down a deserted street, I could hear someone else screaming, and this time it was a woman. I ran in the direction of the screams and saw a woman standing under a traffic light. I told her she should get out of the middle of the street or she might get hit by a car. She looked at me and harshly told me to mind my own business.

I had no problem with that suggestion so I started to walk away. But, as luck would have it, she changed her mind and decided to engage me in a conversation. "I've never seen you before. Why are you here?" But before I could answer, she asked me, "Do you have a car?"

Her question reminded me I did not have a car. My car was a charred mess but I decided not to explain all of that to her. I simply told her I didn't have one available. Then I asked her why she needed a car. She said, "I need to go see my baby."

"Where does your baby live?" I innocently asked.

"She doesn't. She doesn't live anymore because I killed her!" She screamed like a person who had lost her mind.

I was taken aback by her reaction. "I'm sorry. How did she die?" I asked.

"Oh, you didn't hear? "She asked sarcastically. "It was in all the news. I had a few drinks like I always do. I was OK to drive. I had done it many times. I put her in the back seat and I buckled her in. She should have been OK, right?" The woman was slurring her words like someone who had too much to drink. "But the car ran into a pole somehow. I was fine— but she wasn't," she explained.

Then I remembered reading about this woman. She had a mental breakdown after being in a wreck where her daughter had died. She had once been a very successful accountant, but after the wreck happened, she couldn't work and ended up homeless for several months before she disappeared.

I walked back to where she was standing and asked her if her name was Belle. She was surprised I knew her name but then she became suspicious. "Are you a cop?" she asked.

"No, I am a reporter for a magazine. But, I heard about your accident, Belle." I tried to sound as compassionate and kind as I could. "You didn't intend to hurt your daughter, Belle. It was an accident. You have to forgive yourself."

Belle looked at me like she was listening. She seemed touched by my sympathy.

I asked Belle how she ended up on the dark street. "I have no idea how I got here?" she said. "I probably got so drunk one night, I just wandered over here somehow, but now I don't know how to get home." She started giggling and finally said, "I just remembered, I don't have a home." And with that, she started laughing hysterically.

Then she said as she laughed, "You know what my friends call me, right?"

I said, "No, I don't. What do they call you?"

"They call me 'the Belle of the Ball' because I'm always a blast at parties. Everyone wants me at their parties because I'm so much fun. Everyone loves me then. I don't know where all those people are now when I need them," she said and then she started snickering again.

I tried to talk to her but she wouldn't stop laughing. I figured she was probably laughing to keep from crying. This place seemed so dark and hopeless. I wanted nothing more than to wake up.

Chapter 46

This nightmare was the worst one since I began my life of dreams. I wondered every night where I might end up when I shut my eyes. It was sometimes terrifying to go to sleep, but I had to believe I was being shown things I needed to know. That belief kept me sane and able to handle all the reveries. I had to believe there was a purpose for my strange 'night life'.

The most unusual aspect of this particular nightmare was the realization that I was dreaming within another dream. It was difficult to contemplate, but I knew if I thought too much about it, I might panic. I had learned from my experience in the 'waiting room' that panic can make things much worse.

One thing that seemed to plague me in every part of my life was exhaustion. It was becoming my constant companion. I couldn't escape it even in my dreams. I felt like I had been wandering dark streets for days, which caused me to feel more tired than usual. Since I had found some reprieve in my childhood home, I decided to return to it if I could still find it. I hoped if I rested for a while, I could figure out how to get myself out of the nightmare. I just hoped if I fell asleep, I wouldn't find myself in another dream.

I finally arrived at my soot covered childhood home and was relieved it was still there. I went in the back yard and fought off the flies as I rushed inside. I didn't bother with a rag since I knew where I was going. I burst into my mother's room and slammed the door so I could breathe.

But when I turned around, I saw myself curled up on my mother's bed. That was too weird even for a nightmare. I let out a shriek. But, unfortunately, my loud scream didn't wake me up or the other me on the bed.

This whole dream within a dream situation was very disconcerting. How was I going to wake myself up from either dream? And what would the other me do when he saw me? The question itself was too weird.

It was very uncanny to see myself in this dimension. I tried to fix this glitch in my dream reality. I walked over and shook myself hard. It didn't work, so I started yelling at my other self, hoping to stir myself awake, but it didn't happen. I started to wonder if the other me had died. I yelled one more time with all my strength, but the figure on the bed did not move. Then I started to panic, which I knew was the wrong thing to do.

But before I completely panicked, I decided to try one more thing. I remembered what I had done a few times when there was no one else I could turn to. I cried out to the One who sees in secret. I couldn't imagine a more secret place than being in a dream within a dream.

I yelled out, "Help me, please. Get me out of this crazy dream. I'll do anything You ask if You get me out of here." But as I shouted out to Him, I realized I was begging Him to help me and I was full of fear. I had learned He was not receptive to those kinds of prayers because my words did not suggest I trusted Him. I had to calm down.

He obviously knew where I was and He could rescue me. I didn't have to beg, I just had to ask and believe. "All knowing Father, who sees in the secret places, take me out of this dark place. Thank You for hearing my prayer," I calmly requested.

Then I remembered the cries of those I had just left behind. I felt like a hypocrite. I made a promise to Him, "If You help me and show me the way, I will come back and rescue these people who seem to be trapped in this spiritual nightmare." At that moment, I didn't realize I was saying "Yes" to my calling.

Immediately I jumped up in my bed. I looked around and was so relieved to be back in my townhouse in Fort Worth, safe and sound. I had never been so happy to be home in my life! I got up, even though it was very early, and wrote down everything and everyone I had just encountered in my dreams.

Later that morning, I called Irene and told her I was having bad dreams at home, so I decided I might as well go back to Abilene. I really missed Irene and wanted to get back to her. I also missed my barking dog.

Before I left, I used my new computer to look up any more information I could find on the missing people. I wanted to follow up on Irene's suggestion to see if I could find any pictures of the missing people. I realized I would be disappointed if I found out their pictures didn't match their names. I believed I had met the actual people but I had to know for sure.

As I put in some of their names, a notice would pop up that the information requested had been removed from the page, especially when I would look on social media. Apparently a lot of material had been removed by the families because of so many snoopy reporters—like me.

But then, I found an article on the embezzling church leader and his arrest. I read the article and found one picture that had been in the newspaper. I recognized him. He was the same man I had seen hanging from the church. I was flabbergasted. It had really been him.

There was also an article about the missing man who had the mission in Dallas. They had posted a picture of him when he had first gone missing. They had found his empty car out by Hamby. When I saw Barry's picture, I knew he was the same man I had met in the 'waiting room'. I was thrilled to know I had actually met some of the missing people. I had not made these people up in my dreams.

The last picture I found was of Jodie. It was her engagement picture that had been in the newspaper. It was her. I had met the real Jodie and she had poured out her heart to me. At that moment, I knew her box of sad mementos would be under her bed just like she said. I was literally meeting the people who were missing.

Chapter 47

When I got back to Abilene later that day, Irene and I had dinner together. I couldn't wait to tell her I had checked out the pictures of the missing like she suggested and discovered they were the people I had talked to in my dreams. I decided to build up to it, instead of blurting it all out at once.

The first thing I told her about was the horrible, confusing dream within a dream. She listened as I told her the horrific details of the people I saw there and their horrible situations. And I told her I had actually encountered a man from my past in that dream. I didn't go into great detail but I did tell Irene he was someone who had hurt me deeply when I was a boy.

I opened up a little by telling her, "This man I stumbled on was someone I hoped I would never have to see again. He made me question everything about myself. But I don't feel like I'm that man anymore, Irene. Something happened to me when Micah prayed for me that day out in the desert. I received healing in every part of my being. It was there I found the truth and it set me free from my past. Nothing has been the same since."

Irene had tears in her eyes as I shared this with her. She was so thankful I was free from the pain of my past. I knew I would eventually tell her all the details.

She finally said, "Henry, you are an amazing person. I know you have been chosen to help these people, whether it's through dreams or some other way. And it sounds like, in the process, you are being helped, too." I had never considered that before but she was right.

"Thank you, Irene. It means so much to me that you believe me. I don't know what I would do without you. I'm sure it is helping me to confront all of these issues as I dream about them. I just wish I could find someone who could help me figure out how to help these people," I said.

"I wish I could talk to Micah. He prayed I would be shown what to do and I believe that is why I am having all of these dreams, but I still don't know what to do to help the people I'm meeting," I lamented.

Irene then suggested I talk to her pastor. "Maybe he could help you, Henry. He knows a lot about spiritual matters."

I agreed and told her I needed to talk to someone instead of trying to figure all of it out on my own. Then I asked her, "Are you sure I can trust him?"

She said she had known him a long time and trusted him completely. I asked her if she would talk to him first. She called him right away. He told her he could meet with me the next day. It was all set.

Irene and I met the next day at her house. She kept Cooper while I met with her pastor. I kissed her and told her I was so glad she was in my life. She told me she felt the same way.

The secretary gave me a warm greeting when I walked in and told me the pastor would be with me in a few minutes. As I sat down to wait, it brought back memories of my time in the 'waiting room'. My hands started to get clammy and my heart started to race. I remembered how helpless I felt in that tiny room which wasn't much different from the one I was sitting in. I got up and started pacing hoping he would come out. The secretary asked me if I was ok and just when I was about to bolt out the door, the pastor came out.

The pastor gave me a firm handshake and smiled. I was relieved. He told me any friend of Irene was a friend of his. He then asked me how I knew her. I told him how I met her because of my dog and that we had been dating for a few weeks. He was surprised because he hadn't heard she was in a relationship. I told him I was very surprised, too.

He told me to call him Sam, but I felt uncomfortable saying only his first name. He told me he wasn't my pastor, so I didn't need to call him pastor. I could see his point. He then asked me what I needed to talk about. He seemed nice enough.

I told him a little about myself and about the story I was writing on the missing. I told him I wanted to honor their memory. But then things took a strange turn.

"I started seeing some strange apparitions. One of them literally attacked me in my motel room," I explained, eyeing him curiously for his response.

He didn't flinch as I revealed this first bizarre incident. That encouraged me to continue. I proceeded to tell him about all the other experiences I had with these spirits. I told him about Micah and what he said to me. And I concluded by telling him how I had asked the Savior to save me.

Pastor Sam seemed very interested in all of my stories and only asked for clarification once. But when I started talking about the dreams I was having and how I had met several of the missing people in them, he had a shocked look on his face.

"I realize the way I met them is a little unorthodox since it was in a dream. But I truly believe someone gave me these dreams to help me find them. The man I told you about, Micah, he prayed for me before he left. He said I would be given knowledge and understanding of how to help these people. So, I believe that is why I'm having all of these dreams," I reasoned.

He looked at me with a frown, and then asked me, "So, you met all ten of the missing people in your dreams?"

"No, I have only met some of them, but I have no doubt I will meet the others eventually. They asked me to help them, Pastor, but I need someone who understands these things to help me. I need your guidance on what I can do to rescue them," I stated hopefully.

"So, you are saying you know where these people are?" Pastor Sam asked with considerable uneasiness.

"No, I don't know where they are literally," I explained. "They are in some type of spirit world from what I can gather.

I think they ended up there because of some words they spoke in desperation," I said warily. I realized how bizarre it sounded as I tried to explain it.

"I see. And when did you last speak to these people?" Sam asked.

"Well, I didn't literally speak to them, except in my dreams," I clarified. "I know it sounds unusual, but I have heard people do receive instructions in dreams, isn't that right? I am thinking that is what is happening to me possibly. But, I don't know much about spiritual things since this is all new to me. That is why I thought maybe you could help me." I tried to lay it all out for him clearly so he would understand why I was there.

"OK," he said hesitantly. "So, your main interest here is helping these people. Is that right, Henry?" he asked.

"Yes," I stated firmly.

I was starting to feel very uncomfortable with the way he was talking to me. "You said they spoke some words and ended up where they are now?" he asked for clarification.

"I am learning that the words we speak over our lives seem to govern what happens to us to a great extent. And it appears the effect of our words is intensifying in this area of the world for some reason. I don't understand it, but I do know our words are very powerful," I explained.

"So, you are saying they all wanted to leave their lives at first, but then changed their minds?" he questioned.

"Yes, apparently," I confirmed. "They were all sad or disillusioned with their life and wanted out of it. But when they ended up wherever they are, it was not what they were hoping for," I explained.

"OK, I think I understand." Pastor Sam then asked, "Are there any requirements in order for them to be returned?"

"I'm not sure what you mean?" I said. "One of them did tell me something that is provable if her family would be willing to check it out. It would be impossible for me to know this information unless I had actually talked to her," I reasoned.

"Oh, I see," he assumed. "That was a smart idea. Otherwise, they might think you are a crackpot making all of this up for attention." His words and the way he said them made me wonder if he was thinking the same thing about me. Then he added, "We have had quite a few of those as you may know," he explained and then smiled.

"Yes, I've noticed," I smiled back, somewhat relieved he explained the accusing statement.

"Listen, Henry, I am going to do some research on this phenomenon you just described and see what I can come up with so we can help these people. Could you give me an hour to do some research and then could you come back around five?" he asked.

"Yes, I could certainly do that," I said very much relieved to think I might finally have some help with my new found quest. "Thank you so much, Pastor." I shook his hand and told him I'd see him in an hour.

Irene was happy her pastor had been so helpful. "I knew you guys would hit it off," she gushed. "He has always been there for me, Henry. I'm glad to know he is going to help you. I knew he would." I believed this was another good sign for our future.

We hung out in the park for a while and took a walk with Cooper and Sugar. I told her I really appreciated her 'puppy sitting' Cooper, and she told me how much she enjoyed him. "He is so cute. I really like him, Henry. He and Sugar get along so well."

She dropped me off again at the church and told me to call her when I was finished. I walked into the office but the secretary had apparently gone home. I sat in the waiting area wondering what information the pastor had discovered through his research. He opened the door and told me to come in. When I did, I was not expecting what awaited me.

Three men in black suits grabbed me, threw my head down roughly on the pastor's desk, and handcuffed me. One of the men read me my rights and they whisked me off to their unmarked car. As they pushed me out of the pastor's office, I yelled at him, "Why did you do this? I was telling you the truth."

He followed us outside and yelled back, "I believed you, Henry. That's why I did it."

Chapter 48

I t seemed nightmares never end in my life. This had to be the most dreadful one ever because I wasn't asleep. I had never been arrested before and never dreamed I would be. The police seemed to think they had caught their man. Pastor Sam must have believed me when I told him I met the missing, but he apparently did not believe the dream part. I decided right then, he would never be my pastor.

I wondered how my girlfriend was going to take my arrest. Would she still trust me after her precious pastor suspected me to be the villain who had kidnapped ten people? I wanted to talk to her but they had not offered me a chance to call anyone. I didn't know if I should use my one call for Sid, who would surely stand by me and get a lawyer for me, or Irene, who may not.

Some guards walked in and roughly brought me out to a bright room and sat me down, chaining me to a table. A few minutes later a man came in and sat down. He talked to me kindly, asking my name and what I was doing in Abilene. The way he spoke to me, I thought maybe he realized they had made a mistake. But that was just his warm-up act.

He soon became more aggressive and offensive. He asked me where the missing people were. I told him I had no idea. He said, "That's not what we were told. We received information you had recently spoken to several of them."

"No, I didn't literally talk to them. I had a dream where I talked to them," I tried to explain.

"You expect me to believe that?" he yelled. "Where are they, Mr. Pike?"

"They are in a spirit world of some kind," I tried to explain.

"Is that because you killed them?" the man asked.

"No, it's because they asked to be there," I said, knowing he was not buying anything I was saying.

"Did they ask you to take them there, Henry?" he countered.

"No, I have no idea who they asked or how they got there, but I do know they want to come back," I said.

"I see. Did they have some requests on what they'd need to come back?" he asked suspiciously.

"What are you implying?" I asked. "Are you asking if there is a ransom on them?" I wondered.

"Is that what you are saying, Henry?" the detective asked.

"No, I'm not saying that." I then realized I was probably incriminating myself and should have asked for a lawyer when I was first brought in. "I want a lawyer," I stated emphatically.

"You will be appointed one," he said.

"No, I want my own lawyer," I stated.

With that, the man got up and knocked on the door. Some large men came in and took me back to my cell. I asked them if I could make a call but they ignored me. I sat there for a while wondering what was going to happen to me. As I reflected over all I told the pastor, I realized it did sound pretty crazy and probably incriminating, as well. I should have never trusted him or anyone, including Irene.

Finally a man came to the cell and told me I could have one call. I decided to call Sid.

"Sid, you'll never believe what happened to me," I said, trying to sound lighthearted. I wasn't sure how to break the news to him.

"You figured out who the perpetrator was who took all the people?" he said excitedly.

"No, but you're close. The police think they found the guy. They think it was me, Sid! They just arrested me," I said, praying he wouldn't get real angry.

"You're kidding me, right?" he hoped.

"No, Sid, I'm not kidding you. Please help me. Could you get a lawyer for me? A good one. And could you call my girlfriend, Irene?" I asked.

"You have a girlfriend?" he asked surprised.

"Yes, it's kind of a recent thing, but this may put a bit of a damper on our relationship. Could you call her and explain to her they have made a big mistake. Tell her you have known me a long time and I would not be capable of doing anything like this," I pleaded. Then I gave him the number.

He told me he would and he would find a good lawyer in the Abilene area. I thanked him and they took the phone away from me. It was going to be a long night.

Chapter 49

Since I was such a high profile suspect, they decided to put me in a cell alone. There didn't appear to be anyone in that area of the jail. They must have thought I was extremely dangerous.

All I had were my thoughts to keep me company. I paced back and forth trying to rid myself of all the nervous energy coursing through my body. As I paced, I pondered my fate. I went over everything I had done and said over the past few months and wondered if they had a case against me.

After what seemed like hours, a man brought me a small meal, pushing it through a wide slot in the door. There was a napkin and some flimsy plastic utensils included with the meal. I ate the food even though it was horrible. It was the only way I could kill some time.

The man came back in about thirty minutes and took the garbage. I had no idea what time it was but I knew it must be late. I asked the guard for the time. He said it was around seven thirty. I couldn't believe it. I was thinking it had to be later. How was I going to survive doing nothing in an enclosed space for endless hours?

There seemed to be nothing else I could do except lay down and try to sleep. The bed was so hard, I felt like I was lying on boards even though there was a thin mattress. There was also a small, thin pillow. I always liked to sleep with two pillows, but I doubted room service would bring me another one.

When I turned on my side, my shoulder felt crushed as I tried to place my head on the pillow. I doubled it, but it didn't help. I was pretty sure I'd have a cramp in my neck the next day, but I knew that was the least of my worries.

I tried to imagine what Irene was thinking. I knew she must have talked to her pastor by then and he probably told her to stay away from me. He may have convinced her I was guilty or crazy at best. But, I had told her nearly everything I told the pastor, so why didn't she think I was crazy? I hoped she wouldn't listen to him, but since she had known him for years, I was pretty sure I knew who she was going to believe.

Then I thought of Cooper and hoped she would care for him. She told me she liked him and I was glad he was with her. Perhaps she'd find it in her heart to keep Cooper. I felt so sad. In my weariness, I fell asleep and mercifully slipped into yet another dream.

I found myself in a field of bluebonnets mixed with roses. It was breathtaking. I had never seen this combination in all my years but it was a beautiful sight. And the aroma they created was strong and pleasing. I realized I had smelled it before. I remembered the same pungent smell in Elias' apartment when Bill first opened the door. I wondered if Elias would be the next person I would meet.

Bluebonnets were my favorite flower and I loved how they could turn an otherwise dull landscape into fields of beauty. And roses held my favorite scent. It was a lovely blend and I savored the moment as I looked out over the fields of blue and red.

I knew I was in a dream, but I was thankful to be temporarily out of my drab cell. I was free. I could go anywhere I wanted in the dream. I ran through the fields and picked a few flowers, thinking I would give them to Irene. I knew she would love them, but then I remembered she probably hated me.

When that thought hit me, I became so sad. And then the weirdest thing happened. I watched the flowers wilt right before my eyes. It was like the flowers were affected by my thoughts and my emotions. Were my thoughts so toxic they could cause flowers to die? I had come to believe only my words had power, but apparently, in that place my thoughts did, too.

As I looked around, the flowers were gone and there was only the brown landscape. I realized my thoughts were going to dictate the dream. I had to keep my thoughts positive which would not be easy since, in the real world, I was in jail for murder.

If it was going to be a pleasant dream, I had to think positively. Finally, I thought of a positive way to look at what was happening to me. The media attention I was sure to get from being arrested, would certainly garner a lot of publicity for my book. I believed this was as good a way as any to look at my unbelievable situation.

I opened my eyes and looked out over the fields hoping to see the bluebonnets and roses again, but instead, I saw butterflies everywhere. They were fluttering over fields of wheat and it was beautiful to behold. It gave me a sense of joy. I realized this could be fun. Looking for the best in any situation would seem to make life more tolerable.

As I walked through the field of wheat, I watched the butterflies flying all around me. They were beautiful. I studied their intricate wings as they continually landed on me. I had never taken the time to study nature before, but I promised myself I would, if I was ever able to go out in it again.

The butterflies seemed to be congregating at the top of a hill so I ran up to them. They all scattered as soon as I arrived, but when I looked down, I could see a town close by. I hoped it was not like the last town I dreamed about with people in holes and tied to churches.

When I reached the town, there were people milling about just like normal. They were buying and selling. They all seemed too busy to stop and tell me where I was. But, out of the crowd, a young woman came up to me and asked if I was visiting. I assured her I was. She asked me to follow her because she had someone she wanted me to meet. I was hoping it would be Elias.

As we walked to what looked like a regular home, I was excited about who might be inside. When we walked in, the girl introduced me to a man I would soon learn was the dentist, who was the last person to be reported missing.

He shook my hand and told me how happy he was to meet someone from Abilene. I started to tell him I lived in Fort Worth, but decided it wasn't important. I told him my name and he told me his name was Robert Darby. "Dr. Rob is what most of my patients call me," he said.

Dr. Rob seemed like a very nice man for a change, and I looked forward to hearing his story. I asked him how he happened to end up wherever we were.

"I was a dentist for a long time in Abilene and loved my job. But when I was younger I made some horrible decisions. I was fresh out of dental school with a ton of debt to repay because of student loans. I worked in a practice for a while, but then had the opportunity to buy a place where I could open up my own practice. It was a great price and a perfect location, so I jumped on it. I knew financially it would be a stretch, but I didn't want to lose the place," he explained.

"It took a while but I got a nice practice going but my bills were piling up. I had a lot of young patients and got an insidious idea. I wondered how much harm it would cause, if I told parents their children had a few cavities in their baby teeth, even though there were no cavities. I wouldn't be hurting anyone and they would eventually lose those teeth anyway," he reasoned.

He continued his detailed story but I didn't mind because I had no place to go anyway. "So after a few years, I had filled enough pretend cavities to get myself out of debt. It seemed like a perfect plan because no one knew except me, and I believed I wasn't really hurting anyone."

"But one day, many years later, a young man confronted me in church. He told me he knew what I had done to him when he was young. I questioned him like I didn't know what he was talking about— but I did," Dr. Rob said sadly.

"The young man had said, 'I went to you for a check-up and you told me I had three cavities, just like I usually did every time I came in, but you said you'd fill them at another visit. I told my parents and they set up the appointment but we couldn't keep it for some reason. My parents forgot about it, and I didn't remind them because I didn't really want to go.'"

Dr. Rob continued as he remembered the young man's words. "'Five months passed before my mother remembered and called for an appointment. But you must have just thought it was a regular check-up, since we hadn't been in for a while. You told me my teeth looked great and that I had no cavities. Then I knew you had been making up all the other cavities, because none of my friends ever had as many cavities as you claimed I did.'"

"The young man yelled at me, 'My parents trusted you and you scammed them!'" Dr. Rob recalled. "He then told me he started going to another dentist and he rarely had cavities after going to him."

Dr. Rob said sadly, "I was mortified. He had figured out my scheme."

The dentist looked at me and recalled the harsh words the young man then said to him, "'You are a criminal and I should report you. I thought you were a good man because you are a leader in our church, but you are nothing more than a crook.'"

The dentist shook his head, "He was right. I was a criminal. The young man left and I never saw him again. But his words penetrated my heart and I knew I had wronged him and so many others. I couldn't stand the guilt and shame I felt."

"So I decided to make things right with as many of my old patients as I could find. I knew it would be quite an undertaking, but I had to do it. All of them were adults by then and many had moved away, but I located a lot of them and sent letters to them. I told them what I had done and asked them to forgive me. Some wrote back and told me they did. Others I never heard from, but I felt good that I was trying to make things right," Dr. Darby concluded.

When he said that, I wondered if he had actually ended up in heaven. It seemed like a much nicer place than the other dream locations I had visited. "Where are we now?" I asked. "Is this heaven?"

"No, it isn't," he answered. "I really don't know where we are, but it's not heaven. The people here are so driven and they are stressed out to the max. All they think about here is how to make themselves happy. I don't want to stay here. I would really like to go back home."

"How did you get here?" I questioned.

"I don't really know," he admitted. "The last thing I remember happening before I came here was I heard one of my old patients had died in a car accident. She died before I could ask her to forgive me. I was devastated. I remember weeping and feeling so sorry I never had the chance to get her forgiveness. This woman probably died thinking I was a criminal. I was tired of trying to undo all the harm I had done. I gave up at that moment and remembered saying very loudly that I just wanted to go somewhere far away and rest forever."

"And then you found yourself here," I surmised.

"Yes. I guess this is the faraway place where I will rest forever. This is not how I pictured it," he said. Then he asked, "Do you know a way I could reverse my wish?"

"I'm working on it," I said. "Do you happen to have a 'get out of jail free' card I could use?" I asked.

He looked at me funny and I realized I had reached a new low when I sounded crazy to a person in a dream. And with that realization, I woke up.

It was the first morning of many I would wake up to bars. But the bars weren't the worst thing I woke up to that first morning.

Chapter 50

My first morning in jail was made all the more horrible by being greeted cheerfully by Sergeant Bardon. He walked up to my cell with some of his guard friends and peered in to gawk at me as I sat helplessly in my cell. Suddenly I knew how zoo animals must feel.

He grinned from ear to ear as he relished my pathetic plight. I knew he was delighted to have me in this predicament. He said, "Well good morning, Putrid Pike. How are you this fine morning? How are your accommodations? I hope they meet your standards. I'm sure they do since you don't have any," he laughed boisterously. The other men joined him in his glee.

His desire to hurt me had no limits, and I knew he was just getting started as he began his painful bombardment of insults. "I knew you were a loser, Henry, from the first day I met you. But I have to say, this is a surprise! I guess I underestimated just how low you could go."

"I was just reminiscing about all those years we spent together in school and it made me laugh as I remembered how inept you were at everything. Do you remember those awards they used to give out in high school? You probably do because everyone secretly wanted one. I received several awards: 'Most Popular', 'Most Likely to Succeed' and 'Most Valuable Player.' I was trying to remember which ones they gave you, Henry?

But then I remembered, they didn't give you any," he said with delight. He let out another roar of laughter.

But he wasn't through. "I thought of some awards they should have given you, Henry: 'Most Likely to Fail in Life' or 'Most Likely to Become a Serial Killer'. And you definitely deserve the 'Worst Loser in the History of Abilene' award." He snickered at his stupid jokes.

"One thing I do know, Henry, you will become the most notorious graduate of our high school. You have been a 'nobody' all your life and now you will be known all over the country. I hope you are proud of yourself. It is certainly not a proud day for this City to have produced someone like you. But you will pay for your crime. And I, for one, will enjoy every minute watching you go down," he pompously declared.

Finally he was finished with his barrage of insults and turned around to be let out. As he did, I noticed something moving near his head. It was a huge, dark creature swirling around him. This creature appeared to be in the midst of a feeding frenzy as it consumed the torrent of Bardon's negative, insulting words. It reminded me of a shark feeding off the carcass of a whale.

After he left, I felt like someone had literally beaten me up. All of the pain from my past was gurgling back up from the pit of my stomach, like acid reflux. He had opened up the wounds again with all his cutting remarks. How could words hurt so much?

When he left, I curled up on my bed and started crying like a little boy. I didn't care if anyone saw me. I felt like giving up. I felt like I had lost everything—my girlfriend, my dog, my job, and my dignity. I didn't think things could get any worse— but they could.

Soon after Bardon's visit, I had another one from my new lawyer. They took me into the room where they had first questioned me and chained me to the table. My lawyer walked in and introduced himself, "Hi, Mr. Pike. My name is Mike Milner. Your boss, Sid Goldman, called me as soon as he learned of your arrest. He had heard of my reputation because of several high-profile cases I've represented in this area. I have won eighty-five percent of my cases, Mr. Pike. I would like to say one-hundred percent but I'm an honest lawyer. I have represented some of the most notorious people in Texas."

When he said "notorious people", I realized I was probably the newest member of that group. "I guess this case would require someone of your stature, Mr. Milner. You can proceed," I said trying to be funny.

He smiled, but was not amused. He continued. "Could you please tell me how you ended up where you are now, Mr. Pike?"

I gave him a brief history of my tragic life, and then told him how I had ended up in Abilene again. I told him a little about Sergeant Bardon and how he had made my life so miserable in high school and how he was repeating the effort. I told him every detail I could think of except for the supernatural incidents. I thought I might save those for later.

Mr. Milner seemed all business so it was hard to know how to read him. I wasn't sure how he would take the dreams and spirits and other strange things I had been through, but I knew I had to bring it up. "Mr. Milner, I don't think they really have any evidence against me. The only thing they have is what I told a pastor about some dreams where I talked to the missing people. I don't think they can lock me up because I had some weird dreams."

Mike Milner looked at me and spoke very seriously, "Mr. Pike you are right. They can't lock you up for having dreams," he paused for a moment, "but the thing is--they have much more than just dreams against you. Once you were arrested, they tested your DNA against some blood samples they found near the church and in the deceased man's truck. Their forensic report put you at both locations," he revealed. He then looked at me to see how I would react.

Panic flooded my mind. "What are you saying?" I asked incredulously. "They found my DNA in some blood around there? How is that possible?" I was trying to grasp what he was saying and what it meant.

"Yes, Mr. Pike, they did. There is no question you were there. The important question is—why?"

Mike Milner seemed to fade away from my consciousness as memories of those nights near Potosi came flooding back. The first night I was there, I remembered falling several times as I ran back to my car after hearing that horrible scream. Then the second time I was there, I had scraped my knees and hands trying to crawl out of the fire. I did leave my blood out there in many places and they had found it.

I also remembered Jake kidding around the same night, telling me to get out of his truck before I bled to death all over it. It was true; I had bled all over the place out there! I had never even thought about it. How stupid was I? At that moment I understood two things: There was no denying the fact I had been out there, and I was in a horrible predicament.

No doubt they would probably figure out the charred car by the church was mine, too. For the first time since I was arrested, I lost all hope. The preponderance of evidence made me look very guilty.

Mr. Milner came back into my awareness as he asked me again, "Why were you at these locations, Mr. Pike?" When I looked up at him, all the energy I had drained out of me. I had nothing left. I couldn't even talk. What difference would it make if I even tried to explain myself? No one was going to believe me. They were going to pin the fires on me and probably think I was responsible for all the missing people, as well.

I had literally been framed by demons. Even that sounded absurd.

Chapter 51

Mike Milner kept looking at me waiting for my response. The fact I didn't respond probably made him think I was guilty. It didn't matter anymore. I had nothing to lose so I figured I might as well tell him everything. I asked him, "What do you think about the supernatural, Mr. Milner?"

"Well, I certainly don't get asked that question very often, Mr. Pike, but I'm sure there are things out there for which we have no explanation. But, I have never personally witnessed anything out of the ordinary," he said carefully.

It became clear at that point, Mr. Milner was not a believer in the supernatural realm. I realized that might be a problem considering my only defense would be trying to convince the court supernatural occurrences are real. I knew I needed someone who would believe me. Even though this attorney had a great reputation and a lot of experience, I wondered if he was the right one for my situation.

"Mr. Milner, I'm going to need a lawyer who, first of all, believes I'm innocent and secondly, he needs to believe I'm telling the truth when I tell him about some very real supernatural occurrences I've had. I have experienced phenomena that cannot be explained by our natural minds. I used to be just like you, Mr. Milner, in that I didn't believe in any of it. But, that has all changed," I explained to him.

He seemed surprised by my requirements so I recapped, "What I need is an attorney who will believe me when I tell him the most unbelievable stories of what I've been through. Most of my defense is going to depend on it. I'm not sure you can do that, Mr. Milner?"

"Mr. Pike, it's not my job to believe you. It's my job to be sure the jury does," he explained.

I thought about that and realized he was probably right, so I told him, "OK, but I need you to be open minded as I tell you the rest of my story."

He told me he would be open minded, but he added, "Mr. Pike, I need you to tell me everything. I don't want any surprises when I get into court, so you cannot keep anything from me. Do you understand?" he asked very seriously.

"Yes, I understand. Could you please call me Henry?" I asked.

"Yes, I can do that, Henry," he complied.

"Can I call you Mike?" I asked.

"No," he replied simply.

I then began to unfold the unseen world I had become so familiar with over the past few months. I was sure Mike Milner had never heard of anything like it. I told him about the spirits I had started to see in various places and how I had been attacked by one. I told him about the spirit who had threatened me at Teresa's house. I told him about the fire by the church, and how I became trapped even though it didn't make any sense in the natural world.

Then I told him about my friend, Jake, and how he had tried to save me. "You have to believe me when I tell you, Mr. Milner; I would be dead if it weren't for him. He saved my life more than once. The last thing I ever wanted was for him to die. He was my friend even though we had just met. He was afraid of those demons, but he honestly believed if he stayed out of their way, they'd leave him alone. I'm beginning to see, Mr. Milner, they don't leave anyone alone. They are after all of us."

"I see," he replied, like I hadn't just shared the most astonishing story ever. "Do you have any proof of these things you are telling me about?" he wondered.

"Well, it matters what you consider proof. They don't leave fingerprints. They are not of this world so they don't really leave any tangible evidence. There seems to be only a few of us who can see them. One of them is dead and I don't know where one of them is. My girlfriend can see them, too."

"So, one of the people who could see these ghosts was Jake Bardon, who is now deceased?" he clarified.

"Yes, that is correct," I verified. "There is another man who can also see them."

"Great." Mike replied. "How do we get in touch with him? I need to talk to him."

"I'm not sure how to get in touch with him," I confessed. "The few times I saw him was out near Potosi. He would just kind of show up out of nowhere." I realized how crazy it must sound to him.

Mike seemed perturbed by my answer, and impatiently asked me if there was anyone else. "Henry, we need a real person to testify— not one who appears and disappears." I started to remind him that Irene had seen one in her house, but then I realized he had already lost his patience with me and we were just getting started.

"Mike," I said his first name intentionally, "I don't think it's going to work out for you to represent me. I know the things I'm telling you sound crazy, but they are true. And I can't help the fact that the man I was telling you about is not easy to contact. I'm going to need an attorney who can accept the crazy things I tell him. I know you are not that person."

He looked at me in amazement that I would actually turn down his services. He got up, put on his suit coat and knocked on the door. There were a few awkward moments as he stood there waiting to get out since I had just insulted him.

When he left, I had no idea what I was going to do for an attorney, but I knew I had made the right choice. The guards came in and brought me back to my cell. I asked them if I could make a call and they asked me who I wanted to call. I told them I had fired my last lawyer and needed another one.

They brought me a phone a few minutes later and knowing I might regret it, I called Irene. I was surprised when she answered since she wouldn't know the number I was calling from. "Hi Irene, it's me, Henry. How are you doing?" I asked.

She sounded so sad and tired. "Henry, I'm so glad to hear from you. How do you think I'm doing? The love of my life has been arrested. And the news reports are saying authorities believe you are the man who started the fires in Potosi. How am I supposed to be doing, Henry?"

All I heard from what she said was, "I am the love of her life." Then I wasn't sure how to respond since I got distracted by those words. She interrupted my thoughts with, "Henry, are you still there?"

"Yes, I'm here, Irene. Please know I'm not a killer or an arsonist. I have apparently been framed, Irene. I know it looks bad but I'm telling you the truth. Please don't give up on me," I pleaded.

And then I said it—the three words I had wanted to say since I met her came flowing out of my mouth—I love you. I shocked myself when I heard myself saying it and I know I shocked her. She didn't respond, but I was glad I said it because it was the way I felt. I had wanted to say it so many times.

The silence was deafening after my emotional confession, so I quickly filled it with, "How is Cooper doing?"

She responded, "He is fine, but he misses you."

"Can you keep him for me, Irene?" I asked hoping she would say yes.

"I will right now, Henry. I hadn't planned on having another dog, but I do like him and he gets along well with Sugar. I will keep him until you get out," she promised. That was a major relief. But the greatest relief was she hadn't written me off yet.

I asked her if she knew of any good lawyers and I told her about firing mine. She did know of one from a previous job. She said, "I have heard he is a good lawyer. A few of my co-workers used him and thought he was someone you could trust."

When she said the word "trust", I tried to be lighthearted by joking, "When you say he's someone I can trust, you don't mean like in the same way I could 'trust' your pastor, right?"

She laughed a little and said, "Henry, I'm so sorry. I had no idea he would do something like that. I think he was just trying to protect me."

"I'm sure he was, Irene. I can't blame him for that," I responded.

Then I asked her, "Could you call this lawyer you told me about and ask him to get in touch with me?" And while I was asking for favors, I decided to ask for one more, "Irene, do you remember I told you about a man I met a few weeks ago whose son was one of the missing. He is probably the only friend I have in Abilene besides you. But, unfortunately, I lost his number when I lost my phone. Do you think you could find his number somehow and let him know what happened?"

She told me she would be happy to do those things. I gave her his full name and suggested she call the bowling alley if nothing else.

"When can you have visitors?" she asked.

"I thought I could now," I said.

"No, they told me I couldn't come right now. They are worried about security because the media is going crazy outside the jail. It's like a circus. You probably aren't aware of how much attention this is getting," she informed me.

"I'm not surprised, Irene. It is a big case. At least maybe I'll get some great publicity for my book." I laughed.

She laughed, too and said, "Well, hopefully some good will come out of this, Henry. I'll see you as soon as I can," she promised.

After we spoke, I knew I could conquer the world if Irene was by my side.

Chapter 52

Irene's lawyer referral called me later that day and said he would meet with me the next morning. I assumed he would not have the expertise Mike Milner had, but hopefully he wouldn't be so sophisticated that he couldn't believe my stories.

I slept well that night and was rested when Bardon came the next morning. He started in with his onslaught of insults, "Too bad they didn't have 'Predator of the Year' awards back in high school. Just picture it, Henry, your plague would read: 'Putrid Pike—Predator of the Year'!" He then burst out laughing as did the five guards behind him, who had apparently accompanied him for the laughs. I could just picture Bardon and the boys at the precinct coming up with these *hilarious* anecdotes.

But that particular morning, I decided to do something I had never done before. I stood up to Bubba Bardon. I got up from my bed and walked over to him. "So Bubba, does it make you feel more important when you make fun of someone? I read an article about bullying and it said that bullies are typically very insecure people. It makes them feel better about themselves when they put others down. Is that true, Bardon? If it is, then apparently you are still very insecure, because you're still just as much a stupid bully now as you were in high school."

Bardon and I locked eyes, but I didn't look away. The steel bars between us helped to increase my confidence and I didn't back down. He seemed shocked and furious all at the same time. I then said to him, "You are going to have to find your worth somewhere else, Bardon, because I'm not going to listen to your moronic jokes anymore. Maybe you can find some other prisoner to berate."

He turned around, pushed through the guards, and went out the door without a word. It seemed my confrontation left him speechless. I couldn't believe it. I had just taken Bardon down a few notches and it happened right in front of a nice group of guards who would surely tell others about it. I couldn't have hoped for a nicer start to my day.

After breakfast, I met my new lawyer and liked him immediately. He introduced himself, "Hi, my name is Marco Gonzales. I will be your new lawyer." I told him to hang on before we made that decision. But after talking to him for a few minutes, I knew he was the right man for the job. He didn't have the famous cases behind him but he did appear to be a humble man who knew the law. And he had a kind way about him. Those were two qualities I liked in a lawyer, or anybody for that matter.

But there was still one more thing we had to settle before I signed on with him. "What do you believe about the supernatural, Mr. Gonzales?" I inquired.

He didn't look at me like I was weird or crazy. He just simply replied, "I think it's fascinating. I have seen things I cannot explain but I know they happened. Just because we can't see something or feel it, doesn't mean it's not real. I believe in God and He is supernatural."

Then he added, "And, by the way, you can call me, Marco." And with that, Marco Gonzales became my new lawyer.

Marco and I went over my history. I told him about the weird events I had experienced since coming back to Abilene. He seemed very interested in my stories and kept saying, "Fascinating" and "Wow."

He asked me some of the same questions Mike Milner had, but he didn't get inpatient with me. He didn't scoff when I told him I believed I had been framed by demons. He seemed to believe me when I told him how they almost killed me in a fire. He didn't deny the possibility that people could talk to us through our dreams. He seemed to understand when I told him how much I cared about Jake and how I found his little dog. And he was happy for me when I told him about Irene and how this dog seemed to be the one who brought us together.

He said, "You should write a book, Henry."

I responded, "I just might do that, Marco."

He then got serious with me and said, "Henry, the jury will want to link you to the arsons since your blood was found at both locations. This is plausible evidence and you will appear guilty to them. So we will have to give them a believable explanation as to why you were there."

He looked at me with concern because he knew my defense was going to be challenging due to the unusual circumstances. "We have to find a way to help the jury believe your explanations. I'm not saying we should minimize the supernatural events, but we have to explain them in a way they can believe them. Do you understand what I'm saying, Henry?" he asked.

"Yes, I'm afraid I do, Marco. This has been my concern all along that no one is going to believe what happened to me. But I do recognize, and I hope you do as well, it might be my only hope to be acquitted," I told him.

He asked me who could corroborate any of these stories. I gave him some names of people I had interviewed and talked with: Bill, Dennis, Janet, Teresa, the waitress at the truck stop, and of course, Irene. Then, I thought about it for a minute and told him maybe he should scratch Teresa off the list. I wasn't sure she would be the best witness based on our last visit, but my main concern was 'the souch' might come with her.

Then I told him about Micah, and how he would be the best witness because he understood the spiritual world, but I didn't know where to find him. I recounted many of the things Micah had shared with me. I also told him how I had suspected Micah of taking the missing people at first.

Marco asked me, "How do you know he didn't, Henry? Maybe he did based on what you told me."

It was hard to explain how I knew Micah wasn't guilty. I just knew he wasn't. And there was the huge fact that my whole life changed for the better after I met him. I asked Marco if he would try to find him and he promised he would try.

For the next three days, Marco and I would meet for several hours to discuss my case. I was starting to feel a little more confident. He told me he was going to try and contact all of the people I gave him, so he wouldn't be around for a while.

He said, "I'll see you soon, Henry. In the meantime, do whatever it is you do and talk to some people in your dreams. Ask them for some ideas on how to explain all of this to a jury." I laughed and told him I'd do my best.

When I talked to Irene again, I told her how much I liked the attorney she recommended. She was so happy he was working out. I warned her she might have to testify in my trial. She told me, "Henry, I will be there anyway, so I would be happy to support you. I know you're innocent and soon, everyone will know."

I appreciated her confidence and positive attitude. I hoped it would rub off on me—and the jury.

That night, I fell asleep quickly but it would not be a peaceful sleep. I realized I was in another dream. I found myself in the same town where I discovered the butterflies, but this time the fields were covered again with bluebonnets and roses. I was careful to not think anything negative so the flowers would remain. They were beautiful and the aroma was delightful and refreshing.

I ran through the flowers enjoying every moment of the freedom I felt, knowing on the other side of this aberration was my cell. I went up over the hill and down into the town I had found in my last dream.

The young woman came out of the same house and motioned for me to come in. I wondered if I would then meet the other missing people, but when I followed her in, there was only one man sitting there.

When I saw him, I recognized him immediately. Because of the pictures Bill had shown me, I knew it was Elias the second I saw him. I hugged him and told him I was a good friend of his father. Elias seemed quite surprised by my reaction and said, "Well I'm glad to hear my father has a friend." He smiled at my apparent joy in meeting him. I felt so relieved to finally talk to him.

Unlike the others I had met, I felt like I knew this man. We talked for a few minutes about his father and his family. Then we talked about bowling. It was like meeting an old friend. I also remembered the wonderful aroma I smelled as I entered his apartment in Abilene. The very same scent lingered in the room as we talked. I asked him how he ended up in the weird little town.

Elias said he had become so despondent about his dependence on drugs, he just couldn't go on. "I would do well for a time but then fall right back into it. I was tired of the battle and tired of hurting my father and my family. I even thought about killing myself, but knew it would also kill my dad. I was so mad at myself for what I had done to my life."

At that point, I couldn't help but ask the lingering question, "Elias, I found a little bag of pills in your bag. I wondered if you might still be using after I found it."

He looked surprised, "You found those? I hope my father doesn't know."

I hesitantly told him, "I'm afraid he was there when I found them, Elias."

"He was probably upset, right?" he asked, already knowing the answer.

"Yes, he was. But, he is much more upset about losing you," I told him.

Elias explained, "A friend gave them to me and told me they would help me if I became too despondent. I don't know why I even took them because I knew they were only a temporary fix. I needed something lasting."

Elias continued, "I had heard of a rehab in Fort Worth that sounded promising. I thought I'd go check out the program and see if it was right for me. I knew my father wouldn't want me to go, so I was going to leave later that night after he went to bed. I had planned to leave him a note and explain where I was going and why. In the note, I told him how sorry I was that I hurt him and my mother. I also told him I wanted to start over, but I couldn't do that in Abilene. I hid the note until I decided for sure I was going. I guess he never found it?"

"He never mentioned it to me if he did," I said. "Where is it?"

"It is on the top shelf of my closet. It's inside my Bible. When he reads it, maybe he will understand why I wanted to leave. He never knew how hard it was for me every day. I was just so tired of fighting this addiction," he revealed.

Elias sighed and continued, "I was so frustrated and upset the night I had planned to leave. Nothing was going right. I started crying and saying to myself how much I hated my life. I wanted out. I didn't want to go on the way I was. I felt so trapped. So I just cried out, 'Take me out of this bondage.' It was like a plea I made to whoever might be listening," he explained. He looked at me with tears streaming down his cheek.

"And that's when you ended up here?" I asked.

"Yes," he responded. "Can you help me? I want to go back home," he said tearfully.

"I don't know," I answered honestly. "But, I will try."

And with that I woke up in my cell. I couldn't wait to tell Bill I had met his beloved son.

Chapter 53

I t continued to amaze me that I had actually met eight of the missing people. And even though our introduction was made through dreams, it seemed almost as authentic as meeting them when awake.

My next step was to figure out how to rescue them. I had told many of them I would try to help them, but I had no clue how to accomplish that feat.

I found myself wishing I could talk to Micah so I could ask him all my questions. He was not afraid of spiritual issues like Irene's pastor was. I also wished I had access to a computer so I could do more research on these evil spirits, but I knew that probably wouldn't happen. Then I wondered if there might be a book I could read with some answers on these spiritual matters.

It then occurred to me that there was such a book, and I felt certain they would allow me to have one. So, I asked for a Bible to read and they readily brought me one. Perhaps they thought I was going to 'get religion', when in actuality, I was trying to solve a mystery.

My questions were many but one of the hardest to fathom was: "How did the missing end up in a spiritual world without taking the usual path—death?"

I read again about Enoch and Elijah who were taken from the earth because they "walked with God". But, what I knew about the missing did not indicate they had been walking with God. It seemed more likely they were walking away from Him. It would appear they were taken from earth, but I was fairly certain it was not God Who took them.

The next few hours I poured over the Word and asked for guidance. It looked like I was being shown things I needed to see, and I was thrilled to think someone in the spiritual realm might be helping me.

There were so many stories in the Book of how people were led by supernatural means. It was encouraging to find out other people had dreams that directed them and many of their dreams foretold the future. I had not realized dreams were such an integral part in the history of His people.

I was fascinated by everything I read and never knew how exciting the Word of God could be. I found some passages about our words and how they can impact our lives. It said, "The power of life and death are in the tongue." I remembered Jake said something similar to that, and I realized this was where he found those words. Even though this Book was written thousands of years ago, it seemed very relevant to what I was going through.

A guard interrupted my reading and told me I had a visitor. I wasn't expecting my attorney so I could only hope it was good news. It was. They finally allowed Irene to visit me. I was so happy to see her.

When I saw Irene on the other side of the glass, I could not take my eyes off of her. She was more beautiful than I had ever seen her. She seemed happy to see me, too. I wanted to hug her so much.

She showed me a picture of Cooper on her phone and it made me realize how much I missed the fur ball. She caught me up on a few things and then I said, "Irene, I think I might have figured out what happened to the missing," I said excitedly. "Based on my time with the missing and all I am learning, I believe these evil spirits may have somehow tricked these people into believing they could get free of their situations by taking an easy way out."

I looked at Irene to see how she was responding. She did not appear too excited about my theory but she was still listening so I continued.

"These spirits may have tempted these people into saying things they shouldn't have. In their desperation, they must have cried out for relief not caring how they got it. I believe their cries were the only invitation these evil spirits needed to make it happen. I think that may be how these people ended up in their spiritual prisons," I concluded.

Then I told her about the dreams I had since being incarcerated. "I met two of the missing who seemed to be better off than the others. They were in a town where things seemed kind of normal. The first person I met was the last person to go missing. He was the dentist. But, the last person I dreamed about was Elias. It was him, Irene! I knew him as soon as I saw him because his father had shown me several pictures of him," I said excitedly.

Apparently my excitement was not transferring to Irene through the glass barrier that separated us because she did not respond the way I hoped. She seemed sad and I asked her what was wrong.

She said with irritation, "What do you think is wrong, Henry? I'm looking at you through a glass wall with guards all around us. And all you can talk about is these dreams you keep having. I just don't know what to think about all of this, Henry." She started crying. I felt so helpless watching her cry and not being able to comfort her.

Then she said calmly, "I'm sorry, Henry. I know you are innocent, but I don't think anyone else believes you are. They keep saying on the news that the authorities believe they have in custody the culprit behind all the missing people. It's all so overwhelming. I almost got mobbed by the press when I tried to enter the jail today. A policeman had to come out and help me get in the building. I never dreamed I would be dating a man in jail, Henry."

"I never dreamed my girlfriend would be dating a man in jail, either." I smiled at her and my ability to joke about it seemed to help. "I'm so sorry, Irene, that you have to go through all of this. I know somehow it will all work out. I have decided to believe for the best. And I know these people I'm meeting in my dreams are real. There is a plan for all of us, Irene. I just have to understand what it is."

She agreed and said, "You are right, Henry, and I believe you are going to help these people. Now tell me more about Elias. I really want to hear about your time with him."

Irene seemed more like herself so I continued telling her about my time with Elias. I wondered if she had spoken to his father. I asked her, "Did you get a chance to talk to Bill, yet?"

Irene's countenance fell again as I realized she had not talked to him. I was disappointed and I knew she could tell. "Irene, I'm so sorry if I'm asking too much from you. I feel so helpless in this place," I admitted, but I knew it was hard for her, as well.

But I softened as I told her, "You have kept me sane throughout this ordeal. I could never thank you enough for believing me and for being here for me." And then my heart spilled out of my mouth again, but this time I said it to her face, "I love you, Irene." I seemed unable to contain how I felt about this woman.

There was another awkward moment of silence, but I decided not to fill it with a question about Cooper. Instead I held my breath as I awaited her response. And then she said the words I had longed to hear, "I love you too, Henry. Being here for you is exactly where I want to be."

My breath returned and her words washed over my heart like warm, soothing oil. They were words I had longed to hear for years but never thought I would. My heart ached to hold her as I looked longingly through the glass barrier.

Our special moment was interrupted by a guard telling us our time was over. She put her hand on the glass and I did too. It was just like I had seen in the movies. "I'll be back," she smiled, as she quoted one of my favorite movies.

"I'll be here," I smiled back. With that, she left but I knew I would see her again because, after all, she loved me. And knowing that made my heart soar and gave me renewed strength. And God knew I needed strength to face what was ahead.

That night I hoped to meet the other two who were missing as I fell into a deep sleep, but I didn't remember any of my dreams the next day. The next few days I woke up refreshed but fresh out of dreams.

Each night I hoped to go somewhere to escape the drudgery of my cell, but I found no relief. So I used my time the best way I could, reading the Book I knew had the answers. There were quite a few interesting things I discovered. One of the most surprising things I learned was—the name *Abilene* is in the Book.

I also found the story of Joseph who had many dreams of the future and they all came to pass. But his family hated him because of his dreams. I hoped that wouldn't happen to me when I revealed the things I saw in my dreams. There were other dreams where people were instructed to do something or warned not to do something. Dreams seemed to be prevalent throughout the Book.

And there were some interesting passages about The Son of Man. I read that after He died on a cross, He went to a place and preached to many people who I assumed were dead. I tried to envision where they were when He preached to them. And after He was raised from the dead, The Word said He would appear and disappear to His disciples. When He disappeared, I tried to imagine where He went.

There were many surprising spiritual scenarios, but I wasn't seeing the one that would help me. I realized time was of the essence if I was going to find some kind of rescue plan for these people. I wasn't sure if I could rescue them, but I knew I had to try. There had to be an answer and I figured the best place to find it would be in the spiritual Handbook I held in my hands.

I asked again for guidance. A few minutes later I saw what might be a clue. The Son spoke about entering heaven through a narrow way and He warned that many would try to enter another way. There seemed to be no doubt when He proclaimed—"I am the only way."

Perhaps these eight people had tried to enter another way? If they came in the wrong way, it might explain why they ended up in the wrong place.

The thought of them being trapped in these spiritual worlds forever was unthinkable, no matter what evil they had done on earth. But what could be done to get them out? How can people be rescued if they can only be found in a dream?

I got on my knees and asked the One Who sees in secret to show me the answer. He knew where they were and He had the answer. It would be shown to me just like Micah said. I knew He would not want these people trapped in these spiritual prisons. And I also knew it was not His will that I was trapped in a jail cell, either.

Chapter 54

Because I had not had any dreams in several days, I was getting nervous. I needed answers and I needed them fast. I decided to try and go to sleep early right after dinner, hoping a full stomach might induce some dreams. I knew it also had the possibility of inducing gas.

In my estimation, time was running out for all of us. There were two of the missing I still had not met, and I could only hope they would have some answers for me.

The idea of figuring out how to rescue people trapped in a vast spiritual world was daunting, to say the least. I had found several examples in the Word of people leaving this earth in their natural bodies, so I knew it was possible. But there was no indication they had ever came back.

As I hoped to fall asleep on my full stomach, my thoughts were keeping me awake. I would try to replace them with more peaceful truths from the Word, but the questions and doubts were persistent: "What am I doing? Do I really believe I've talked to these missing people in dreams? Look at where I am. Look what believing this mumbo jumbo got me—a little room with bars."

These fears were certainly not conducive to falling asleep. Every time a fearful thought came into my mind, I would say out loud something in the Word to counteract it like: He is my refuge and strength; I can do all things through Him who strengthens me; and I will give Him my burdens and He will give me rest.

There were so many new truths I was learning. But, my favorite one I found was—If I keep my mind on Him, He will give me peace. It didn't say He might give me peace, it said He *would* give me peace. It was a promise.

As I poured these words of faith into my mind, the fear subsided and I fell into a deep sleep. And then it happened. I was in a place I had never been before. It was the brightest place I had ever seen. There must have been a thousand suns shining down on me, but the light was coming from everywhere, not just the sky. The light poured into my body and filled me with warmth and peace. It was a glorious feeling.

Although I could not really see anything in front of me because of the intense light, I decided to step out in faith. I felt there was someone next to me leading me. I couldn't see anyone, but I could feel His presence. I was not afraid because I knew I was not alone.

And then it was like I stepped through a curtain into a land of vivid colors and sights. Before me, there were meadows as far as I could see and there were trees and streams and fields of flowers of every possible color, and some colors I had never seen. The flowers seemed to be dancing in a slight breeze.

This field was far more brilliant than the one I had seen before in the little town where I met Elias. And the scent, emanating from these flowers, was intoxicating. There were birds everywhere. They were singing, and I was pretty sure they were in harmony. There were animals everywhere running carefree. Some of these animals would be considered very dangerous on earth, but I instinctively knew they offered me no harm.

It took a while to make my eyes look away from the beauty before me but when I did; I could see a hill close by where a beautiful house stood. As I got closer, I could see the house was huge and ornate. There were no fences or gates around it, just acres of grass. There were children playing in the yard.

They were running and laughing. I knew this place would be considered a paradise by anyone's standards.

As I walked towards the door, a little girl ran up to me and said, "They told me you would be here today."

I looked at her in shock wondering who "they" were. She continued to energetically tell me who she was, "My name is Kim." She reached out her hand to shake mine. I shook her hand excitedly because I knew who she was. She was the little girl in my dreams who had been asking for help!

"It's nice to meet you, Kim. My name is Henry. I believe I have heard of you—didn't you once live in Abilene, TX?" I asked playfully.

"Yes, all my life," she replied.

"I used to live there, too. I was born there." I hoped being from Abilene would make her feel more connected to me, but she didn't seem to have any hesitation in trusting me.

"So how did you end up here, Kim?" I asked with baited breath.

As she began telling me her story, I looked at her in amazement. She was the reason I had stayed in Abilene and pursued the story of the missing. It was the dream of her asking me for help, which gave me the resolve and desire to follow through when everything had fallen apart.

And here she was, standing in front of me. She was talking to me like it was an ordinary, casual encounter. But, this encounter was anything but ordinary. It was perhaps the most amazing meeting I had ever had. This was the very girl I had tried so hard to reach in my dream and, then I almost lost my composure as I realized–I had finally reached her!

It was so hard to take it all in. I knew my thoughts had distracted me long enough, so I tuned back to her story hoping I hadn't missed anything important.

"I was so sad without my grandmother and I wanted to be with her. She was my best friend. My parents didn't know how much I missed my grandmother, but God did. I told Him nearly every day," she explained.

"How did you tell God?" I asked.

"I wrote prayers to Him every day in my diary. My grandmother always told me how much God loved me, so I knew, if I asked Him, He would let me see her again. And see, it worked. He answered my prayers," she said gleefully. I wondered if her grandmother would show up next.

"But when I first came here, I was afraid. A man came over to me and told me I was 'too early' and I would have to go back. But, when I begged him to let me see my grandmother, he told me he would allow me to see her for a moment. I wasn't allowed to talk to her, but I got to see her. When I saw how happy she was it made me so happy. My grandmother smiled at me, and I knew I would see her again one day. But now I am ready to go home to my parents. You came to bring me home, didn't you?" She asked me with confidence.

Her question threw me off guard. I didn't know how to respond to her hopeful question. I desperately wanted to tell her I was there to bring her home, but instead I had to tell her, "That is my hope, Kim. I haven't quite figured out how to do that yet. Did the man happen to tell you how you would get back?"

"No, I don't think so. He said a lot of things, but I don't remember him telling me how it would happen. He just said I had to go back," she said thoughtfully.

"I see," I said with disappointment. At least I knew it could happen since the man told her it would.

Then I thought about the diary. I wondered if her parents had found it yet. I asked her, "Do you think your parents found your diary?"

"I doubt it," she responded. I always hid it in a special place, so no one knew about it."

"Could you tell me where it is, Kim? I could tell your parents and then maybe they could understand what you had been going through," I suggested.

She seemed hesitant. I tried to reassure her, "Kim, I won't read it, I promise. But if your parents read it, it might help them find a way to get you home."

That idea seemed like a good idea, so she said, "OK. I keep the diary in my bookshelf near my desk in my room.

It's inside a hollow book. It looks like a big book, but it's not. My grandmother gave it to me a few years ago and told me to keep all my important things in there. She said no one would know since it looks like a big, boring book. I keep my diary and some other things inside it."

I smiled at her and said, "Thank you for trusting me, Kim. I'll tell your parents as soon as I get back," I assured her. I knew if they found the diary, they would know I actually spoke to their daughter.

"Can you please take me with you?" she asked again.

The look she gave me broke my heart. "I'm sorry, Kim. Believe me, I would if I could. It's complicated because I'm not even sure how I got here, much less how I'll get back. But when I figure it out, I'll do all I can to get you home," I promised.

"OK," she said sorrowfully and started to cry. "If it would help, you can read my diary, too."

I hugged her tightly. I felt so bad that I couldn't take her with me. But, suddenly she broke away from me and said, "I just remembered something else the man told me."

I held my breath and waited for her to gather her thoughts, hoping her new memory would be helpful to both of us.

"I remember I saw other children playing when I first got here. I asked the man if they were just visiting, too. He told me they lived here. I didn't think it was fair because some of them were younger than me. I asked him why they were not 'early' like me. He told me the Father did not want any of his children to come 'early', but things happened to them back on earth, which were not His will. The man said because I didn't die on earth like they did, I would have to go back."

As I thought about what she said, I realized this might be part of the answer I had been searching for. I asked her if the man had said anything else.

"Yes, I remember he told me I would just have to wait until someone prayed," she said.

"Prayed? I'm sure many have been praying for you, Kim. Did he say what they are supposed to pray for?" I probed.

She started to explain it, "The man said they would have to ask for–" but as she began to tell me, I could feel myself slipping away from her. "No!" I cried. "Wait! Wait!" I could see her stretch out her arms to me like she was trying to pull me back, but it was too late. I was ripped from her presence and found myself back in my horrible cell again.

A guard was banging on the bars, "Hey, Pike, are you alive in there?"

Apparently I had been asleep for several hours. And because the guard had never seen me fall asleep early before, he had to be sure and wake me up to see if I was alright.

I couldn't believe he had to feign concern at such an inopportune moment in my dream. He laughed when he saw me glaring at him for his ill-timed interruption. It seemed very much like it had been planned.

Kim was about to tell me something significant. My only hope was to go back to sleep and hopefully continue where Kim and I left off.

My anger at the guard made me very tense. It certainly wasn't helping me fall back asleep. I knew the guard's timing had to be orchestrated by some spiritual entity he was totally unaware of, so I tried to forgive his poor timing. I went back to bed and shut my eyes, but I never could go back to sleep. It was a long, miserable night.

Chapter 55

It is never pleasant to be wide awake at three thirty in the morning, but it is especially unpleasant when you are laying on a hard mattress in a cold jail cell, behind bars, accused of one of the biggest crimes of the century.

Apparently my short nap after dinner was keeping me awake all night. I was not allowed to have any lights on after eleven, even though no one else was in the ward with me. So, I had nothing better to do than to lay awake all night with my thoughts.

The time I spent with Kim was replayed over and over in my mind. I tried to imagine what she would have said if we had not been interrupted. She had said "someone needed to pray something". There were a few possibilities and I brought each scenario to its logical conclusion, as if logic had anything to do with any of this. I knew it would be helpful if I could write it all down.

Around six, a guard brought my breakfast, so I asked him if I could get a notebook. Later that day he brought me a notebook and a safety pen. I had never heard of a safety pen, but it is very limp and flexible which made it very hard to write with. I finally wrapped a couple of pages from the notebook around it to make it sturdier. It didn't really help.

The notes would be quaint but they would help me to remember and keep my thoughts in order. The dream with

Kim was the most significant one I had, and I wanted to process it and learn all I could from it. If her parents could find her diary, I believed it might offer some clues on how to get her back.

And if they believed I talked to Kim and wanted to help them get her back, perhaps the jury would, too? If they believed that, then they might believe my explanation of why I was out at the church and Jake's house. The only hope I had of convincing the jury my stories were true, were if the things people told me in my dreams were accurate. It would prove I had spoken to them.

I realized this could also have a downside. It would prove I talked to some of the missing, but it might make them wonder how I had access to them to get this information. If they didn't believe the dream part of the story, they might come to the same conclusion Irene's pastor did. It could make me look guiltier than I did already. It wouldn't necessarily help me to convince the jury of my contact with the missing, if I couldn't find a way to bring them home. It was quite the dilemma.

Since I lost my journal I kept on my computer, I decided to once again go back over everything I had encountered from the moment I arrived in Abilene. I made cryptic notes with the stupid pen. I hoped I could piece together all the dreams and what the missing had told me.

I had gone over it all with Marco, but I kept thinking I was missing something. I hoped he had been able to talk to some of the people on the list I gave him. I hadn't heard from him in a few days which concerned me.

Hours passed more quickly because of my new project. It kept my mind focused on the story and not on my fears. The only connection I saw between the missing was that they were all unhappy in life. Some of them ended up in better places than others, but I knew they were all trapped and wanted out.

The next day, Marco finally came back. He told me he had been working feverishly at his office to wrap up some things so he could focus just on my case. He knew it would require his total effort.

He asked me how I was and I truly felt better about everything. I had a peace inside of me which was unexplainable. Marco and I both knew the peace had to be supernatural considering the circumstances.

It seemed like I was living more in the supernatural world than I was in the regular one. Since I knew the spiritual world was real, it held much of my attention, especially since it offered a great distraction from my jail cell. Irene and Cooper were the only two strands still keeping my feet on the natural ground.

Marco was very interested in the connections I was trying to make out of all the dreams, visions, and experiences I had since arriving in Abilene. He thought the notebook was perfect since it was a good way to keep it all in front of me.

He was fascinated when I told him about the various dreams I'd had since I had last seen him. And he was very interested to hear about my theory on how the missing may have ended up where they were. He was amazed when I told him I had finally got to meet the little girl I had first dreamed about. He listened intently as I told him my ideas on what she might have said next if the guard had not interrupted us. I realized how fun this conversation would be if my life didn't depend on the outcome.

Marco informed me of when the court case would begin. The jury selection would begin soon. They were thinking of moving the case to another town due to the amount of people affected in Abilene. I was surprised, but understood why. I realized I would more likely get a fairer trial somewhere else. I then thought of Irene and wondered out loud if she would still visit me if they moved it too far away.

My thoughtful attorney told me not to worry. He had talked to her a few times and felt she would be willing to travel. He said, "You put quite a spell on that woman. She is lovely and seems very committed to you."

His words made my heart leap and I told him that had to be supernatural, too, because I never dreamed it could happen. Then again, most of my life over the past few months had seemed like a dream.

The trial of the century was moved to Midland. It wasn't too far, but far enough from Abilene that hopefully there would be some unbiased people there. I was transferred to Midland in the dead of night, so no one would shoot me when I was removed from the Abilene jail. I wasn't aware there had been numerous threats on my life.

I had tried to tell Irene to be cautious who she talked to and urged her to be careful if she came to the jail to visit me. I didn't want anyone to get any ideas of hurting me by hurting her. She told me she believed there were always angels around her, so I shouldn't worry. I wouldn't doubt the probability of the angels being there, but I still worried.

The Midland jail was more comfortable to me since no one knew me there. At least, I didn't think anyone did. A day after I arrived, I had the most wonderful visitor—my sister. Carrie found out I had been arrested and called the Abilene Jail. When they found out who she was, they told her I had been moved to the Midland facility. I had never been happier to see her.

She smiled at me and asked me how in the world I had ended up in the mess I was in. I asked her, "How long do you have?"

She laughed and told me, "I have all the time in the world for you, Henry. You are, after all, my only brother."

Then I asked her how open minded she was about the supernatural. She looked at me very surprised and said, "Try me. I guess we'll find out." She smiled again and that gave me the strength to tell her about the crazy things that had happened since I had arrived in our hometown. She was very happy when I told her about Irene which was the nicest part of our conversation.

Once in a while I would check her reactions to some of the bizarre things I was pouring out. There were a few moments I was sure she was struggling to believe my stories. After I had finished by explaining how I had ended up in jail, I looked at her and asked, "Carrie, don't hold back. Please tell me what you are thinking. I need to know if this story will be believable to anyone else."

She looked at me with concern and asked me if there would be any way I could tone it down some. "Henry, this is a lot to take in. Isn't there some other way to explain how you were framed for this crime? I want to believe you but, honestly, it sounds pretty far-fetched," she said hesitantly.

What she said discouraged me because I had told her the truth, as unbelievable as it was. I'm sure it showed on my face. Carrie looked down and started crying. "Henry, I want to believe you. I really do. Maybe if I have more time to process everything. I'm sorry."

She stood up and put her hand on the glass that separated us and said, "Henry, no matter what, I still love you and you will always be my brother."

As she was let out of the visitor area, I felt disheartened in a way I could never describe. If my own sister didn't believe me, how could I expect anyone else to?

Chapter 56

There were few times in my life where I had felt as defeated as I did after my sister left. Negative thoughts started pummeling my mind: "You are losing it, Henry Pike. Do you really think people will believe demons framed you for these crimes? Even your own sister doesn't believe you. Everyone will think you are crazy. You have lost the support of your sister. No doubt, your girlfriend will leave you when you end up in prison; then you will have nothing."

The thoughts were becoming louder and more insistent. It was a constant barrage of doubt and fear. I felt like my mind was about to explode when all of the sudden, a man casually walked by my cell.

At first, I thought I must have imagined it because I hadn't heard anyone come into the ward. And it's usually obvious when someone comes in because a buzzer sounds when the door unlocks and then it clangs loudly shut. But I thought it was possible I missed it, since I had been so distracted by my own troubling thoughts to notice.

I walked over to the bars to look down the hall to see if I did imagine it or not. I could see someone at the end of the hall. There were no other people locked up in this ward so I wondered why he went down to the end of the hallway.

But when he turned around, I could see he was pushing a mop. I watched him as he continued his mopping back and forth across the hallway. It was almost mesmerizing to watch him as he cleaned his way towards my cell.

I was hoping he would stop and talk to me for a few minutes. I had become desperate for human interaction since I was usually isolated. When he got closer to the cell, I was happy when he stopped and looked at me. He spoke to me in a friendly way, "How are you today?"

"I have been better," I replied back.

"I'm sure that's true," he responded. He smiled at me and went back to his cleaning. He seemed like a very pleasant man, and I longed to have a conversation with him.

I asked him, "And how are you today?"

"I have never been better," he replied.

"Well, that's good to hear," I answered. This wasn't as stimulating a conversation as I was hoping for. I was wondering what question to ask so he would stop his incessant mopping and talk to me. I finally just asked him, "How long have you worked here, sir?"

"Not long," was all he said in response.

"Oh I see. What did you do before you came here?" I knew I appeared needy as I tried to engage this man in some type of meaningful dialogue.

"Well, let's see," he smiled as he thought for a moment, "I worked as a messenger for as long as I can remember. The cleaning business is new," he replied somewhat amused.

"Oh, I see. Do you work for the prison?" I asked.

"No I don't. I was just assigned to work here today," he revealed.

"Oh, OK." I was running out of things to say. "What kind of messenger were you?" I asked, hoping to get him to open up about something. "Did you work for a company in this area?"

"I work for the One above," he stated.

His answer surprised me, and I could not imagine who he was referring to. "Would that be the warden?" I asked.

"No, Henry, He's not the warden," he replied.

When he said my name, I wondered how he knew it since we had not introduced ourselves. But then I figured, since I was the infamous suspect in this well-known case, he had probably heard about me in the news or something.

"So you've heard about me?" I asked kind of basking in my apparent fame.

"Not until today," he said.

"Oh, really?" I was surprised. "So you didn't know who I was until you were assigned to clean my cell area?" I asked.

"Yes, that's right," he stated. Apparently he was getting as tired of the conversation as I was because he finally opened up and told me why he was really there. "Henry, I was sent here to remind you of who you are."

"Who I am?" I asked puzzled. "I know who I am. I am Henry Pike, a journalist who has been wrongly accused of a crime."

"No, you are much more than that, Henry. You have forgotten—this world does not define you," he reminded me. "You have forgotten all the things you have learned, Henry."

"What am I forgetting?" I asked wondering what he was referring to.

He looked at me with the most piercing eyes I had ever seen. "You have forgotten you have an enemy and you are still listening to his whispers—to his lies. You must fight his lies with the Truth you have learned. The enemy is the source of your pain—but the Son is the source of your peace."

It was like someone hit me up the side of the head! He had to be from the unseen world! How else could he have known about the struggle I was having right before he showed up? He had to be some kind of supernatural person. But he looked like a normal man, not like the grotesque creatures I was used to seeing from the spirit world.

But I had to know for sure so I asked him, "How did you know?"

He explained, "Not all spirits are bad, Henry."

"Are you an angel?" I asked in amazement.

"I told you, I am a messenger. I am a messenger who cleans up the mess people make because they believe lies. You must learn to trust and believe the One you gave your life to," he exhorted.

This was too much to take in. This had to be another dream. I seemed to be awake, but I had to know for certain. So, I whacked my head on the iron bars to make sure I wasn't dreaming. I wasn't. It hurt—a lot.

My unbelievable visitor looked at me very puzzled. When I realized what he must be thinking, I knew I had reached a new, all-time low—an angel thought I was crazy.

"You have to understand," I tried to explain, "I have had some pretty crazy dreams these past few weeks and I wanted to make sure I was awake before I continued this conversation."

"Henry, who do you think gave you those dreams?" he asked.

My head was pounding but his answer managed to surprise me. I still couldn't believe these dreams were actually instigated by someone. "You gave me the dreams?" I asked.

"The people who are missing are trapped, Henry. You will be shown the way to rescue them. As you see, this will not be an easy task, but it is of the utmost importance. You cannot give up, no matter who believes you or who doesn't."

I looked at him wondering how I, or anyone on earth, could help these people. Without even asking him, this spirit man seemed to know what I was thinking, "The One who has all power has given power to those who trust Him. He has given them the authority to command principalities in the heavens and on the earth. All should be in agreement with Him—as it is in heaven so should it be on earth."

"Why would He give us so much authority?" I asked. "Doesn't He know what we're like?"

"Yes, He knows. But all along, it was His design for men to rule and reign with Him," he explained simply.

"I don't know if I'm the right man for this job. I can't even convince my own sister that any of these things happened, how will I convince a jury?" I reasoned.

He assured me, "You will have the ability of Heaven to help you, Henry." I wasn't convinced that would be enough.

"Tell Marco to contact the families of the missing people you spoke to. He must give them the information you received in the dreams. When they understand you have literally talked to their loved ones, they will start to believe you and they will want to talk to you," he explained.

The sad fact was, I knew Marco had already tried to contact some of the families, but none of them wanted anything to do with him—or me. It was understandable. They thought I was the villain in the story.

The messenger/janitor said, "Give him the information and tell him to mail a letter to each family. When they see the evidence, they will believe."

"But there is still one I have not spoken to, "I told him.

"You will," he assured me.

"Do not be afraid, Henry. Only believe," he exhorted.

I looked down for only a moment wondering what else I wanted to ask this spirit man, but when I looked up—he was gone. The bucket and the mop he left behind.

Chapter 57

The night I met the messenger janitor, I expected to have an encounter with the last missing person—Mary. But, it didn't happen because I couldn't fall asleep. I couldn't sleep because of my anticipation about meeting Mary. It was a long, dreamless night.

But the next day, I did have another visitor. It was the one I had been longing for since I had arrived in Midland. Irene came to visit me and I couldn't wait to tell her about the angel messenger. My excitement caused me to overlook her somber mood.

"Irene, he just walked by my cell like it was no big deal. I didn't even hear him come in. And then he was mopping the floor, so I thought he was the janitor. He knew my name and knew what I was thinking. He told me the most amazing things. He told me I needed to convince the families I met their loved ones," I said enthusiastically. I rambled on and on about every detail concerning my encounter with this spirit being.

Irene apparently did not share my enthusiasm and asked, "Henry, how can you be sure he was an angel?"

Her answer dumbfounded me. She had always believed me before. "Irene, I told you why I believed he was. He couldn't have been a normal person because he knew so much about me. I'm surprised you are questioning this? I have always told you the truth about all the weird things that have happened to me," I paused and then added, "And you have always believed me."

She smiled a sad smile and responded, "Henry, you have not always told me the truth. You didn't tell me the truth about Cooper. You knew the dog belonged to the man who died in the fire." Then she paused for a moment and said, "Why did you lie to me? Honestly, I don't really understand why you were even out there, Henry? It is just so hard to believe that fire at the church started by itself."

"Irene, I never said the fire started by itself." I then looked around to see if any of the guards were listening and reminded her quietly, "I told you, demons started the fire—all of the fires." As I repeated my explanation, I realized how crazy it sounded. Then I noticed she wasn't looking at me the way she usually did.

"And the fire in your motel room is now being questioned, Henry. The Fire Marshall recently discovered the source of the fire began in your room, not the room next to you like you told me. Everything is starting to sound so suspicious when I stop and really think about it. I never had before because I wanted to believe you, Henry. But, now..." She stopped talking and looked at me.

"Now, I'm feeling so confused about everything. Please tell me the truth, Henry? How did those fires start? Did you have anything to do with them? Did you start the fire in your motel?" It seemed like she had already made up her mind as she poured out her accusing questions.

As she continued to demand answers, my heart was breaking. I questioned what precipitated her doubts. I wondered if her pastor had anything to do with her change of heart. I asked her if anyone had put these questions in her mind.

"I can think for myself, Henry. These questions are just logical to ask. And when I think logically about everything you've told me, none of it makes any sense," she stated loudly.

How ironic. I finally quit thinking logically and then Irene decides to start. Irene's tragic change of heart was almost more than my heart could bear. I couldn't believe she thought I was capable of such cold-blooded acts.

I couldn't sit by and let her think these things about me. "Irene, I did lie to you about Cooper and I'm sorry. I didn't know what you would think if I told you I knew the man who died in the fire. You didn't really know me very well then, so I didn't think you would believe me if I told you what actually happened," I explained desperately.

"But I did believe you, Henry. I believed all your stories because I desperately wanted to. You were the kind of man I had always hoped to meet. At least, I thought you were. Now I'm beginning to think you may not be that person," she said in a sad, low tone.

"Irene, please know that was the only time I lied to you and I just explained why I did. Please, don't leave me now. I need you more than ever," I pleaded. I looked in her eyes as they filled with tears.

She choked up as she said, "I'm sorry, Henry. I can't do this anymore. I will always care about you, but for now, I have to distance myself from you. I will take care of Cooper until I can find a good home for him. I truly wish you the best. Goodbye, Henry."

As she walked to the door to be let out, I started to cry out to her and beg her to reconsider, but I knew it would be pointless. She had made up her mind and I didn't want her last memory of me to be begging her to stay.

Irene didn't look back as she waited to be let out of the visitor area. I tried to control my emotions until she left, but I could not stop the tears. Irene and my sister had both given up on me. They were the only two women in the world I loved and they no longer believed in me. The guards took me back to my cell where I cried until there was nothing left in my heart.

Once again, I felt hopeless. It seemed everyone was turning on me—my sister, my girlfriend and the whole town of Abilene. And it appeared I was losing my little dog, too. Even if I got out of jail, what would I have to go back to? My life seemed worthless, which really wasn't much different than it was before. I was a loser then, and apparently I would remain one.

In the midst of feeling totally dejected and defeated, I remembered what the messenger had said the day before when I had similar thoughts. He had asked me if I remembered what I had learned. Apparently I had not as I was still in the same place I was the day before. Would I ever learn?

At that very moment, my determination came back. I decided I was not going to give in to self-pity. I was going to win this case and then I would win Irene back. I was not going to let her walk out of my life without fighting for her.

Then I said very loudly to whatever spirit might be lurking about, "I will not listen to your lies of defeat and self-pity anymore. I know who I am, and I know what I have to do, and I will do it! I have The Almighty on my side."

New resolve came into my heart again and I decided I was not going to let anything or anyone deter me—not Bardon, not Irene, not Carrie, and certainly not any demon from the abyss. I would prevail because I was telling the truth and I would continue to tell the truth—whether anyone believed me or not. From then on, I would only believe and speak good things over my life.

With my new resolve, I felt peace come back into my mind. I finally was able to calm down and rest. It was then I realized how tired I was after my emotionally draining day. As I so often did, I decided to take a nap and it was just what I needed. As I drifted off into a peaceful, drowsy, dream state, I met the last of the missing.

Chapter 58

I immediately recognized I was in the same place where I had met Kim in the last dream. The scent of the flowers was intense and the brightness of the area was reassuring. I knew Mary had ended up in a good place.

There was a large house in front of me, so I walked over to the house but there was no door. I stood there for a moment and decided to just walk in. I entered a large living room where I saw a pretty woman sitting in a chair near a roaring fire. She looked to be in her twenties and she was having tea. She asked me if I would like some and I told her that would be nice.

She introduced herself, "Hello, my name is Mary. They told me you'd be here."

Her introduction surprised me because I thought Mary was an older woman, but I decided it would probably be best to not ask her age.

It was like she could read my mind and she answered my question even though I didn't ask it. "People are not old here, Henry," she explained and then she started laughing.

Her laughter was so contagious and joyful, I found myself laughing, too. I asked her where we were.

"Where do you think we are?" she asked with a twinkle in her eye.

"Heaven?" I said. I presumed it was the answer, but I really wanted to hear her say it. She just smiled at me.

I felt so at peace sitting there, I found myself thinking I never wanted to leave. She looked at me and apparently read my thoughts again because she said, "You have to go back, Henry. You are just visiting. But, do be sure and come back when it is your time. I believe you know the Way."

I gave her a knowing smile. "Mary, I talked to your family not too long ago and they told me all about you."

When I mentioned her family, she seemed delighted and asked, "How are my dear ones?"

"They are doing well, Mary, but they miss you. They have been diligently searching for you because they believe you are still alive. They will be so happy to know you are," I exclaimed.

"Oh, I am very much alive here," she responded. "But I cannot be alive anymore on the earth, even if I wanted to be. You see, I died in transition when I came here."

"Really?" I asked surprised. "I didn't know that could happen?" I felt silly after saying that since I didn't know any of this could happen a few months ago."

"Well, Henry, apparently it can," she started laughing again and I laughed with her. It felt so good to laugh again.

"I am glad to see you are happy, Mary. I guess that means you were able to forgive yourself for what happened to the little girl?" I assumed.

"You heard about that, too? They told you everything." She chuckled again. "Yes, I knew it really wasn't my fault, but I felt so guilty that I hadn't offered to take the little girl for the night. But, if I had..." Then her voice trailed off as she got up and went into another room. When she returned, a little girl was with her. "If I had, then neither of us would be here."

Mary introduced me to her, "This is Eden. She is the little girl." I gasped as I began to understand what she was telling me. This was the little girl who had died. And they both were in heaven together.

The little girl looked up at Mary and then at me. She was radiant. She laughed at my reaction and said, "Mary is so nice. I am so happy here. I was never happy when I was with my momma. I loved her but she was always so sad and she always brought sad people home with her. But, no one is sad in my new home," Eden declared as she skipped away.

How wonderful it was to know Eden was alive in this amazing place. And she was free from all the pain in her life. It was so comforting to know this was where little children come when they leave the earth. It was unfortunate an evil man had caused Eden to come "early" to heaven, but she seemed to have no remorse at her untimely arrival. It was a glorious ending to such a tragic story.

Mary asked me to tell her sons about her joy and to not be sad for her. I promised I would but I said, "Mary, I don't know if they will believe me."

She thought for a moment and then said, "I know a way you can convince Dennis. Tell him to go to my house and look in his hiding place. He and I are the only ones who know about his secret hiding place he had as a boy. There he will find the birthday present I bought for him before all of this happened. He had mentioned how much he liked it one day when we saw it at the mall. He will know I bought it for him. That should convince him."

I promised her I would let him know as soon as I was able. Then I asked her, "Mary, before I go, do you have any idea how I can get all of you back home?"

"Henry, I told you I can't go back. This is where I belong now, and even if I could, I would never want to go back," she explained.

"But what about the other nine people, Mary?" I asked.

Mary seemed surprised. "There are others?" she wondered.

"Yes, nine people were reported missing after you," I informed her. "People from all over the country have tried to find out what happened to all of you, but no one has found any clues."

"I did not know about the others. Are they here?" she asked.

"No, they did not make it here," I told her. "Well, except for one who came 'early'," I explained.

"I hope no one took them," she said hopefully.

"Mary, I believe all of them are still alive. I have met them in my dreams and they seem to be in some type of spiritual holding area. Some of these places are horrible," I told her.

She thought about what I said and then suggested, "They could have gone the wrong way."

"The wrong way?" I asked.

"Yes. If they were trying to get here, they may not have known there is only One Way to come," Mary said confidently. "You have to go through the Son. He is the only door to heaven. He paid for our entrance with His blood."

"Oh yes, when He died on the cross," I said rather proudly. I felt thankful I had learned this truth. Then I added my own thoughts, "I remember reading this very thing you are telling me, Mary. I had never heard before that a person could be an entrance or a door, but I just read recently that He is the narrow way. It also said some try to enter another way," I stated. "I came up with a theory that maybe the missing were tricked into believing there are other ways to eternal peace. I think you just confirmed my theory, Mary!"

"Henry, I don't know if they were tricked or not, but I do know there is only one way to the Father. You must tell people the truth when you get back. People seem to think they can come to Him any way they want but they are wrong. If that was true, then why did His Son have to pay such a horrible price?" she asked.

"The way to heaven is paved with His blood. Promise me you will tell everyone you can," she asked, with an urgency that was noticeable. Her insistence made me realize how important this was, and I assured her I would.

As I woke up from the intense dream, her words continued to echo in my mind. "He is the only way into heaven, Henry. He is the way, the truth, and the life."

Chapter 59

It was good to see Marco when he came the following day. I had not seen him for a few days. He told me he encountered a lot of challenges when trying to contact the people on the list I had given him. He wanted to go over his progress and update me about the trial which was looming over us.

As far as the possible witnesses for the defense, his success was limited. Marco had been able to talk to the waitress at the truck stop. He thought she might be a good witness for us. He had not been able to contact Bill, which concerned me. Marco had driven out to Teresa's house, even though I had asked him not to. He said he knocked several times but the house looked abandoned. I didn't bother to tell him that was the way it normally looked. And he looked around the Potosi area for Micah, but he did not see anyone fitting his description there.

When I asked him about Irene, he informed me she had been subpoenaed by the DA. That did not sound promising. I didn't tell Marco we had broken up. Then I asked him about Dennis and Janet. He said they had not returned his calls. It didn't appear Marco had much to show for all his effort.

Marco told me the jury selection was almost complete and the trial would begin soon. This was not good news, since we really didn't have a great roster of witnesses for the defense.

Even so, I was excited to tell him about the dream I had the day before involving Mary. "Marco, I met the last missing person yesterday. She is in heaven and so is the little girl who had been murdered. They both seemed incredibly happy."

"And Mary had the same theory I did. She wondered if the missing people might have gone the wrong way when they tried to find relief from their situations. She thought they may have gone through the wrong door." My mind was racing with all I wanted to tell him.

Marco was puzzled about what I was trying to say. I tried to explain it all to him again as he just nodded. Like Irene, he was not sharing my enthusiasm about any of it. He was all business that day, and I was annoyed by his inability to appreciate all I was telling him.

He apologized and explained he was frustrated about the case. The lack of success he had when trying to contact the people on the list had upset him. He also had been listening to the news reports about my case and that had discouraged him, as well. I tried to understand what he was going through even though it was my life in the balance, not his.

Since Marco had not been too successful in his efforts, I knew we needed to try what the angel had told me the day before. "Marco, I need you to do something for me. I want you to contact the four families whose loved ones I met in my dreams. I need you to give these families the information I received from them," I asked.

He seemed surprised by my request and reminded me he had already tried to contact them. I told Marco I needed him to try one more time. I didn't explain how I got this directive because I thought he might balk if I told him an angel told me to do it. But I persisted until he agreed to do it. Marco looked at me with all seriousness and said, "Henry, I know you believe you really heard this information from these people, but what if you are wrong? No one will believe anything else you say."

He was right and I knew it was a big risk. I asked him, "Marco, what other choice do I have? I can't think of any other way to prove any of the things I learned in these dreams. But even if one of those families starts to believe me, perhaps the other families will, too." I explained. "And then maybe the jury will, as well."

"Ok, Henry. I will try," he said reluctantly.

"Please do more than try. My life depends on this, Marco," I pleaded.

"I'm sorry, Henry. I will do my very best. I will start contacting them," he reassured me. "I will go back to Abilene for a few more days and spend some time with my family. And if they do contact me, I will be there and can meet with them," he said.

I thanked him and told him I was counting on him. He smiled and said, "Don't count too hard, Henry. You are asking for a miracle."

"I know, but miracles still happen, especially in Abilene," I smiled hopefully.

Marco went back to Abilene and sent a registered letter to the four families I gave him. He wrote a letter personally to each one of them and basically told them, "Please check on this information given to me by my client, Henry Pike. If you find the information accurate, I ask that you would please contact me." Then he gave them the information I had received pertinent to each family. He also notified the DA's office and sent them a copy of the basic letter.

"It is a great plan," I told Marco when he called me to explain how he fulfilled my request. "They will no doubt read the letter and I can't imagine they wouldn't check out the information. If the information is accurate, I'm sure they will call you. And if it's not, then I am really no worse off than I was before."

I was thankful the messenger angel told me to do it. And I was also thankful Marco trusted me enough to try it. I wasn't sure what the next step would be, but I assumed I would be shown what to do when I needed to know.

All I could do was wait and hope. I hoped for the miracle, Marco assured me we would need, for the plan to work. And I kept hoping I would have another dream or a janitor would walk by again or for any help to know how to free these people from their captivity. I knew He would show me eventually, I just hoped it would be sooner than later. But I would not allow myself to fall into fear again.

Every hour, I read and tried to fill my mind with positive thoughts from the Word. I would say the passages out loud over and over. I could tell it was affecting the way I thought in a good way. It was like I was rewiring my brain to think the way it should have before it was tainted by the world. I was renewing my mind.

Three days passed and I had not heard anything. I was hoping Marco would call to tell me what was happening, but he didn't. I knew he needed some quality time with his family before the trial started, but it was hard to keep my thoughts positive when I was in the dark. The only people I saw were the guards who gave me my three meals a day. They were not looking for a conversation, so after a while, I quit trying to engage them in one.

But there was a positive aspect from the isolation I was experiencing. I was able to immerse myself in the Word like I never had before. I was committing as much of it to memory as I could. These new passages I learned were the ammunition I needed to destroy any old thoughts that would still try to pop-up.

I spoke these words over and over, every day and every night. I knew His words were true and I believed they were the only truth I needed. I would implant them in my mind until they replaced the unbelief I had lived with all my life.

Then I had only one thing left to do—believe.

Chapter 60

Marco finally came back from Abilene. He sat down across from me and he seemed upbeat. I asked him why he had not contacted me while he was gone. He said hesitantly, "Henry, I just needed to separate from the case for a few days—and from you. I'm sorry, but sometimes all of this was too much for me. I felt burned out and we hadn't even started the trial yet. But now I'm re-energized and ready to conquer the mountain."

It was nice Marco had the luxury to separate himself from this case and from me. I wouldn't have minded a reprieve from the constant battle I felt raging around me. But I couldn't go anywhere and I didn't have a family to surround me with love, so I had to find my strength somewhere else. I had started finding it in the Word and was surprised just how much the Book could help me with whatever I was going through. It seemed like anything I needed was in there; I just had to look for it.

I knew I could feel sorry for myself if I wasn't careful and I could easily get annoyed with Marco for his insensitivity. But I also knew that was what my enemy wanted. He would like nothing better than to get between us. I had to take the high road and get over myself if we were going to win this case.

Marco then told me he had heard from one of the families just as he was leaving to come back to Midland. I couldn't wait to hear what they said. "It was Kim's family who contacted me. They found the evidence you gave me, Henry. Can you believe it? They found the diary! They had no idea it was there." Marco was elated. He added, "They are wary, but they are ready to listen."

I knew this confirmation by Kim's family was something Marco needed to hear as much as I did. We both needed to know I hadn't imagined all of this.

"What a relief" I yelled. I was almost as shocked to hear this news as Marco probably was. It was all true. The little girl in my dreams was real and I had actually talked to her. Not only had I met her, she had given me information that proved to be accurate. It was amazing to ponder. I had believed it was real, but I finally knew for sure.

"Now that someone believes you, Henry, what is the next step? What do we tell this family who desperately want their little girl back?" Marco asked hopefully.

I ignored Marco's question and asked him, "Marco, do you realize what this means? I actually talked to this little girl in a dream. Do you understand how remarkable this is?"

Marco looked at me like he was in a daze. He shook his head and said, "Yes, it truly is amazing, Henry. I'm so happy for you. Now you can be sure you actually talked to at least one of the missing."

Even though he was happy to know what I had told him was true, it was obvious something was wrong. I asked, "Marco, it seems like there's something bothering you. Can you please talk to me about it?"

"Henry, what is your plan to get these people back?" he asked with concern. I wasn't surprised by his question.

"I have been seeking the answer to that question since you left, but I haven't been shown the answer, yet." I hesitantly informed him. "But I know He will show me," I assured him.

This was not what Marco wanted to hear. "Why did you ask me to do this, Henry, if you have no idea how to get these people back? For some reason I assumed you would know what to do if we got this opportunity."

"Yes, that would have made sense," I agreed. "I know the plan has some holes in it, but I was just following orders," I explained.

"Someone told you to do this, Henry?" he asked. "Who?"

I was hesitant to tell him because it seemed everyone had quit believing my supernatural explanations for things. I didn't want to take that chance with my lawyer so I simply said, "Please just trust me, Marco. I don't want to explain it right now."

He almost seemed relieved that he didn't have to absorb any other bizarre explanations. I was relieved, too, that I didn't have to give him any.

"What about the ones you didn't get any information from? What about their families?" Marco wondered.

"I'm assuming they can be brought back the same way the others can. But there is one who will not be coming back," I revealed.

"Please just tell me it's not Kim," Marco begged.

"No, it's Mary, the older lady. She told me she had actually died when she was in transition. She is the only one I know for sure who can't come back," I clarified. I was aware as I attempted to explain all of this to Marco, that it all sounded so unbelievable.

"Well, hopefully she'll be OK in the place where she went," Marco said thoughtfully.

"Yes, she will be. Remember, I told you she was in heaven. She and Kim are both there, but Kim can't stay. A man told her when she first arrived that she would have to return because she came 'too early'. Since he told her she had to go back, I assume there is a way for it to happen," I reasoned.

Marco looked away and shook his head. "You know, all my life I have believed in God and in heaven, but when I hear you talk about these things, it doesn't seem real anymore. It sounds like science fiction or fantasy," he said.

"I know. I sometimes feel the same way but that is our natural mind trying to explain away a world we have never experienced—until now. Trust me, Marco, it's real. It's more real to me than my jail cell with bars. Most of us just don't have 'eyes' to see it," I suggested.

"Did you send a letter to Bill?" I asked hopefully.

"Yes I did, but I haven't heard from him. I hoped he would be the first to contact me since you told me you were friends," Marco responded.

I knew I had not been a great friend to Bill after I met Irene. I wished I had stayed in touch with him. He probably didn't trust me anymore or believe I really cared about him or his son. He probably thought I just used him to get my story. But hopefully he would read the letter from Marco and realize I met Elias. Then I knew I would have another chance to make things right with him.

Marco got up to leave and told me he would let me know if he heard from any of the others. He looked at me with great seriousness, "You had better find the answer soon, Henry, if we have any chance of this working." And with that he left.

Was I premature in my request for Marco to contact these people? Maybe I should have had the answer before we made this bold move. The messenger had not specified when I should do it, he just told me to do it.

When I returned to my cell, I got on my knees and asked the One who knows all things to show me what I needed to do next.

Chapter 61

The trial was beginning in a few days, but there were still too many holes in my defense. Marco had worked feverishly to establish my whereabouts throughout the past year when the first nine people were reported missing. I had kept receipts for tax purposes from most of the places I stayed while doing various stories for *Ragweed*. These receipts from hotels and restaurants would verify my exact time in those towns, which I hoped would be enough to convince the jury I had not been in Abilene during the past year.

But even with all of this documentation, some of these assignments still put me within driving distance to Abilene. The DA could probably argue it would have been feasible for me to drive to Abilene and kidnap a few people, even while staying in another town. It would actually have been a great alibi for me—if I needed one.

It was not easy to come up with all of this documentation. We were literally trying to establish my whereabouts on an hourly basis over the past year, especially on the exact days when those nine people were reported missing. Of course, I had been in Abilene when the tenth person disappeared.

My personal journal, which I kept on my computer, would have been helpful in establishing my innocence. The things I wrote in my journal, about my fears and anxiety of what was happening in Abilene, would have probably demonstrated my innocence to the jury. But the hard drive did not survive the intense fire in my motel room.

The journal would have been such an asset in this trial. I had written notes in my journal from all the places I had gone over the last year or two. There were entries about the articles I was writing and there were more personal entries, as well. My journal alone would have probably proven my innocence. It certainly would have revealed 'the real Henry Pike' to the jury.

It was still so hard to believe I had actually been framed for these crimes. And not only was I framed, I was framed by sinister beings from the netherworld. It was hard to believe these spirits were so intelligent and yet so evil. There were things they couldn't have known about though, like how I decided to talk to Irene's pastor. And because he was the one who turned me in, it almost seemed like he was part of the plan.

Pastor Sam was, no doubt, behind Irene's change of heart towards me. I was sure he had filled her mind with doubts about my innocence. I realized what I told him would have been difficult for anyone to swallow, but I had erroneously thought a pastor would naturally believe in spiritual occurrences. It was obvious I still had a lot to learn about those who call themselves "believers". It seemed many of them don't really believe, especially in the supernatural.

It was hard for me to sleep the night before the trial. I kept waking myself up tossing and turning on my uncomfortable mattress. I was desperately hoping I would have a dream or a visit from someone to tell me the plan of how to rescue the missing. I especially wanted to give some hope to Kim's family, but there were no dreams and no visitors.

The next morning, they cuffed me and brought me into a room where a barber was standing. They attached me to the chair as he washed my hair and gave me the best shave I ever had. I looked in the mirror and looked like a new man. I knew I was a new man on the inside but, after his touch up, I looked the part.

The guards then brought me to the showers. It had been a few days since I had a shower and it felt wonderful. I enjoyed every minute of it. Then it was back to my cell where they gave me a suit to wear with a shirt and tie. They also gave me socks and dress shoes. All the attention and new clothes helped me feel more positive about my trial. I knew my feelings had nothing to do with the truth, but being treated like a human being and looking like one certainly helped.

They escorted me in chains to a van where they took me to the courthouse. The press was there trying to get as close as they could to the van. There must have been fifty or more reporters with their cameras and other paraphernalia. The guards warned them to stay away from me. There were six guards who surrounded me as they walked me up the steps. In a strange way, it was kind of a rush to see all of those reporters trying to take pictures of me.

When I walked into the courtroom, the seats were all full, but the one person I was hoping to see was missing. Irene apparently had chosen not to attend the opening day of my trial. But, I knew she would be subjected to all of it soon enough since she would be called to testify.

As I glanced over the crowd of people, I saw Sid and was happy to see him. He waved and I tried to wave back but the chains prevented it. I looked for my sister but couldn't see her. I wondered if anyone else was there I knew.

They took the demeaning chains off of me and I sat down next to Marco. Marco shook my hand and the first thing he asked me was if I had any dreams or visitors the night before. I was sad to tell him I had not. I knew he was disappointed, but it wasn't like I could just conjure something up.

I looked over at the jury and scanned their faces. I could only hope they were compassionate people with open minds. The judge walked in and I was glad to see the judge was a woman. I always believed women were more compassionate. We all stood up and she sat down. And with that motion, the trial of the century began.

Chapter 62

During the opening arguments, I observed the prosecuting attorney seemed pretty confident, which was not a quality I like in someone who is trying to convict me for murder. He told the jury he could connect me to the fires and murder of Jake Bardon. And he assured the jury, I was the perpetrator behind the ten missing people, as well.

Marco then presented his opening remarks, but he did not exude the same confidence as the DA. His lack of confidence made me nervous. Where was that bravado he had always demonstrated in our meetings together? I imagined he did not feel comfortable being in the national spotlight. It made me question my decision to fire Mike Milner.

The words of the angel messenger then came back to me. I slapped myself mentally and told myself to believe the best no matter what. Pain comes when I believe the worst. Peace comes when I believe the Truth. The Truth would be revealed; I just had to be patient.

The first witness the District Attorney called was the forensic officer who had analyzed the DNA of my blood found near the crime scene. I knew this would not look good for me but I prepared myself to listen to his testimony.

The forensic scientist revealed his findings to the jury. "We found the fire was due to arson. An empty gasoline can was discovered out in a field not too far from the house. It was determined the house had been surrounded with the gas because it had evenly burned from the perimeter to the interior."

"A body was discovered in the home which was the deceased Jake Bardon. Mr. Bardon's truck was far enough from the house that it did not receive any damage. In the truck there were several areas on the passenger side where blood was found. A sample of Mr. Pike's blood was taken upon his arrest which matched the blood found in the truck," the man said convincingly.

He spoke these words like they were just facts, because that was all they were to him. But these facts were devastating for me to hear again. I started to relive all the feelings I had the day I discovered my friend had died. Marco could see I was visibly shaken. I knew my reaction did not look good to the jury but the feelings blindsided me.

"About a mile from Mr. Bardon's home, another fire had occurred which had not been previously reported. Blood was also found on several of the rocks around the church which matched Mr. Pike's blood, as well. This fire was also determined to be arson," he concluded.

But, he wasn't finished. The DA asked him if there were any other findings and he said, "Yes, there was. A burnt shell of a car was found near the church which is believed to be the car of the defendant. We do not have conclusive evidence to confirm this, but the defendant had rented a car during the same time period of the church fire. It was determined that the house fire happened a day or two after the fire at the church."

The DA thanked him for the account of his findings and then the judge asked Marco if he had any questions. He did not—much to my alarm. I looked at him with surprise and irritation since he seemed to have no inclination to minimize the damage this forensic specialist had just done to my case. He told me later there was nothing more to be said about it. These were facts that could not be disputed.

Marco had emphasized to me, my best defense would be to tell the truth about why I was out there. I knew he was right, but I was not looking forward to revealing to the world that I had been stalking Dennis and Janet. I knew this information would embarrass Sid—not that he wasn't already mortified. How could he not be embarrassed when one of his journalists was on trial for murder and arson and for the disappearance of ten missing people? But, the person I least wanted to find this information out was Bardon. He would soon discover I knew his uncle and considered him a friend.

The situation suddenly hit me as humorous when I started to realize what would happen as the case progressed. All the things I tried to hide from Irene, from Sid, from The Smiths, and from Bardon–was about to be revealed to the whole world.

Chapter 63

The next witness The DA called up was the one I dreaded the most. I hadn't noticed him when I had entered the courtroom, but I knew he would be there. Sergeant Bardon stated his name and occupation and his relationship to the deceased man in the fire.

The DA then asked Bardon to tell them about his relationship to me. He told the jury he had graciously offered to connect me to a few of the families of the missing. And in the process, he discovered we had gone to high school together.

Bardon then proceeded to give detailed accounts of how weird he thought I was in high school. He related it to my trial by expressing his ridiculous notion that I must have been a sociopath in high school. He reasoned I must have been emotionally unbalanced back then, since I did not fit into his definition of a normal kid. Then he backed up his theory with incidents he remembered about my socially stunted life in high school. Memories I had tried so hard to forget. I felt shamed by Bardon's account of my pathetic past and was thankful Irene was not there to hear it.

The DA let Bardon degrade me and no one tried to stop him—just like in high school. I was upset with Marco again that he didn't object to Bardon's unnecessary description of my past life. But when he started questioning Bardon, I began to understand his reasoning.

"Mr. Bardon, could you please explain to the court how you reacted to the defendant's awkward ways in high school?" Marco kindly asked.

Bardon responded, "I guess I might not have been the most compassionate person back then." I snickered because the word "compassion" was not in this man's vocabulary.

Marco knew, from all I had told him, about the horrible things Bardon had done to me in high school and he was determined to reveal it. I wasn't sure if it really had much to do with my trial, but I enjoyed his exposé of Bardon's true character.

"Mr. Bardon, is it true that you bullied Mr. Pike relentlessly and made his life miserable in high school?" That was struck down as conjecture so he reworded it, "Is it not true that you did some things to Mr. Pike while in high school that could be considered abusive, Sergeant Bardon?"

Bardon looked up at the judge and then to the prosecuting attorney hoping for a reprieve from the question, but none came. "I suppose I was a little hard on him at times, but I was young back then. Kids do that to each other in school," he reasoned.

"Do they, Mr. Bardon?" Marco asked. "I don't believe it's considered the accepted norm for students to ridicule others or to push them down or to put them inside a locker and lock it. Would you consider that normal, Mr. Bardon? If so, I would question your ability to judge if someone is committing a crime in the town you are supposedly protecting."

The DA objected to the last statement and it was sustained.

It seemed Marco's statement went right over Bardon's head. Bardon shrugged his shoulders. And being who he is, he decided to say the first thing that came into his mind. It was the worst thing he could have said for his defense, but it was the best thing he could have said for mine.

"If he had been more of a man, he would have fought back," he said as he glared at me in a way I had never seen before. He was too rash to realize he had just admitted his guilt.

Marco jumped on the opportunity. "So by your own admission, you have just said you would not have bullied Mr. Pike if he had fought back. Is that true, Sergeant Bardon?" Bardon looked at Marco like he was in a daze.

Marco asked him again, "Sergeant Bardon, are you saying, if Mr. Pike had fought back, then he wouldn't have received all the abuse he took from you? Is that what you are saying, Mr. Bardon?" Marco asked.

"Yes. If he had stood up for himself, nobody would have bothered him," Bardon admitted after being badgered.

It seemed like the DA was in a daze, too, because he finally objected, saying he did not see how any of the questions related to the case. Marco explained to the judge that he was trying to establish the relationship Bardon had with the defendant. I wasn't sure if Marco really needed to go that far into my past, but it certainly was fun to watch Bardon squirm. The judge overruled the objection and told Marco to continue.

Marco did continue—with a vengeance, "Mr. Bardon is it not true that you used to stuff the defendant into lockers on a regular basis when you were in high school?"

Bardon snickered as did a few in the audience. The judge called for order and told Bardon to answer the question. He straightened himself up in the chair and reluctantly shook his head up and down. Marco told him he had to say his response out loud, even if he was ashamed of it. "Yes, I did do that a few times," Bardon admitted.

"Would you not arrest an individual for doing that to someone now, Sergeant Bardon?" Marco pushed.

"No, not for something that minor," Bardon assured the jury. He was finally catching on to what Marco was trying to do. "I would talk to them and maybe give them a warning," Bardon responded feeling very uncomfortable. I'm sure he felt like he was on trial instead of me. With every answer, he was convicting himself for his past crimes.

"I see, Mr. Bardon. It's a shame no one gave you 'a warning' when you were in high school," Marco exclaimed. This received an objection which was sustained.

Marco continued, "But even after both of you discovered who the other one was in high school, is it not true that Mr. Pike was still willing to work with you?" Marco asked.

"Yes, I guess he seemed willing," Bardon agreed.

Marco inquired, "Were you willing to work with him?"

"I would have," Bardon assured him as he squirmed in his chair.

"I believe when Mr. Pike asked you if he could interview more of the families of the missing, you said, and I quote, 'Are you out of your mind, Pike?' And then you said something to the effect, 'I looked you up in the yearbook and now I know who you are, Pike. You were a loser back then and you are one now. You left Abilene a long time ago and this no longer concerns you. You need to leave and never come back," Marco said with emphasis.

"Isn't that basically what you said to the defendant, Mr. Bardon?" Marco questioned.

Bardon took a deep breath and admitted it was. He explained, "I didn't want him bothering people who were already going through so much."

"And you felt qualified to make that determination, Mr. Bardon, is that right?" Marco asked.

"Yes, it's my job to protect the people of Abilene and I felt like that was what I was doing," Bardon concluded.

"I see. So, you really felt Henry Pike was a danger to people in Abilene?" my attorney pressed.

"No, not a danger, just a nuisance," he admitted. After Bardon realized what he said, he corrected himself. "Well, apparently he was a danger. Is he not on trial for the death of my uncle and for all those who are missing?" Bardon responded.

Marco had wanted the jury to hear Bardon say he did not really think I would commit these offenses and he had known me longer than anyone else in Abilene. Marco continued, "Sergeant Bardon, were you not surprised when they accused Henry Pike of these crimes?"

"Yes. Well no. Who knows what a loser like that is capable of? Maybe he killed my uncle to get back at me," he suggested.

Marco reminded him of what he said to me when he first found out I had been arrested. Bardon remembered. "Of course, anyone who knew the guy would be surprised. He is a loser, but I never thought he would kill anyone." This was the response we were hoping for from Bardon.

Marco asked, "Didn't you just suggest Mr. Pike might have been a sociopath in high school? Do you even know what that word means, Mr. Bardon?"

"Of course I do. I'm a police officer. And yes, I suggested it, but I wasn't really serious."

"This is a court of law, Sergeant Bardon, and you are not on the stand to offer your unprofessional opinion about anyone."

Then Marco went in for the kill. "I spoke to Dennis and Janet Smith earlier today and they said they had thought very highly of Henry Pike until you talked to them, Sergeant Bardon. They told me you said, 'Henry Pike is a loser. He is not someone you want to associate with. Just ignore him and hopefully he'll go away,'" Marco revealed.

"I might have said something like that," Bardon confessed.

"And when both Dennis and Janet protested, did you not say, 'Listen, I do not want either of you to have any contact with this man. You don't know him like I do and he will cause all of us a lot of problems. I don't want to hear you've talked to him again. Understand?' I believe those were your exact words," Marco concluded.

Bardon hesitantly agreed that he had said those things.

"No further questions, your Honor." And with that Marco concluded his interrogation.

When Bardon stepped off the stand, I felt validated for the first time in my life. It was a long time coming but it was worth the wait. My miserable history with Bardon had just been revealed to the world. The bully had humiliated himself in front of everyone thanks to Marco.

Finally, after all of those years, justice had been done.

Chapter 64

After Marco had succeeded in his effort to expose Bardon, the DA was not as eager to call up their next witness, Dennis Smith. The DA had originally thought he and his wife would corroborate Bardon's testimony against me, but now that didn't appear likely after Bardon had just confessed he had bullied them, as well.

The DA asked Dennis several questions about our meeting. Dennis said he was hesitant at first to talk to me, but then Bardon initially put in a good word for *Ragweed*, so he agreed.

Dennis continued, "Janet, my wife, liked Mr. Pike from the first moment we met him. He seemed like he really cared about the missing and their families. We had talked to several reporters in the past and they were all business. They just wanted a story, but Henry was different. He told us how he had helped solve a crime many years before and he wanted to help us solve this one. We didn't have anything to lose and no one else had given us any answers, so we were willing to cooperate with him. But then Sergeant Bardon told us to stay away from Mr. Pike, so we abided by his request."

After the DA had finished, Marco got up and continued the questioning. He asked," Mr. Smith, is it true that Henry wanted to talk to the other families?"

"Yes, he thought if he could talk to them, he could put all the missing pieces together and solve what happened to our loved ones," Dennis said.

"Does it make any sense to you, Mr. Smith, that if he were the one who took these people that he would offer to help you find them?"

"No, it would not," Dennis agreed.

"Did he seem like someone who would kidnap or murder these people, Mr. Smith?" Marco asked.

"No sir, he did not. Neither Janet nor I believed he had anything to do with any of it," Dennis concluded.

With that I almost jumped out of my seat for joy. I did not expect this man to stand up for me, especially since he had to know I had watched his house and followed him to the church.

Marco continued, "Mr. Smith, did you receive the letter I sent you a few days ago?"

"Yes, I did, Mr. Gonzales," Dennis confirmed.

"And what did the letter say?" Marco asked.

Dennis had it in his pocket and Marco asked if he could show it to the judge. At that point, the DA objected saying he was not aware of the letter. Marco told him he had sent notice to his office that he was planning to send a letter to four of the families and he had included a sample of the letter. The DA seemed perplexed. He glared at his assistant attorney as he scrambled through his folders. The judge asked to see the letter and Marco took it to her. She looked at it and then gave it to the court reporter that referenced it.

Marco then gave it back to Dennis and asked, with the court's permission, if he could read it. The judge agreed and Dennis read the letter Marco had sent them: "Dear Mr. and Mrs. Smith, I am writing you today as a representative of Henry Pike, who I believe you met several months ago. Mr. Pike asked me to verify some information he had received from Mary Smith. He realizes this is most unusual, but he believes he met Mary in a dream."

There were a few gasps and giggles throughout the courtroom as Dennis read the last sentence. The judge called for order and told Dennis to proceed.

Dennis read the part of the letter where Mary had given Henry a secret which would prove he had actually spoken to her. "Janet and I immediately went to my mother's house and checked the information given to Henry and it was exactly as he said it would be," he concluded.

When he said that, I almost yelled for joy. At that point, I had not heard that the Smiths had confirmed the information given to them. Marco told me later, he had only been informed a few hours before the trial started so he wasn't able to tell me about it beforehand.

"Thank you, Mr. Smith. So you did find the information given to Henry to be true? And this was something only you and your mother knew about, is that correct?" Marco clarified.

"Yes, we were the only two people in the world who knew the information she told Henry. There is no doubt in my mind that Mr. Pike spoke to my mother," Dennis said.

I could hear the gasps in the courtroom. Dennis believed I had actually spoken to his mother, even if it was in a dream. I was ecstatic. I then knew for sure, I had met at least two of the missing.

Dennis paused and looked at me and then at the judge. He continued, "Mr. Gonzales had asked for us to verify the information before reading the rest of the letter. After we checked it and found it to be accurate, we read the remainder of the letter."

"My mother asked Henry to tell everyone something she considered to be extremely important. When she could no longer bear the pain of this earth, she specifically asked the Son to bring her where she longed to be. My mother wanted it to be emphasized, there is only one way to go to heaven and she went the right way." Then Dennis added, "I believe my mother is in heaven now."

The judge asked that the last part be stricken from the transcript. Marco objected saying this was evidence that should not be tampered with. He continued, "These words are from a woman who had been declared missing. Should we not use her testimony because it may not be deemed politically correct?"

The judge thought about it a moment and then told the court reporter to leave it in. I was thrilled because the judge only made it more impactful.

Dennis continued, "My mother, Mary, told Henry how very happy she is and she wanted Henry to tell her family they should not grieve for her. She also told him it would be impossible for her to return, even if she wanted to, because my mother literally died when she was lifted out of her house that day. My mother understood this would be a lot to take in and believe, so that is why she gave Henry the information to prove he had actually spoken to her."

"When I received this letter, I was shocked especially when I read about our 'secret place'. No one even knew that little hole in the wall existed except my mother and me. And when I found the watch there, which I had told my mother I wanted for my birthday, I knew no one else could have orchestrated this. Not even my wife was there that day when I told my mother how much I liked the watch. This blew my mind, but it has given me great peace because I know my mother is in a better place. She is right where she wanted to be," he concluded.

"And what did the defendant ask for in return for this information?" Marco asked.

"Well, the letter said Henry wanted me to have peace about my mother," Dennis said.

"Would you consider that a ransom, Mr. Smith?" Marco asked.

"No sir, I would not," Dennis responded.

"And I believe you have already stated this information has given you great peace, is that correct?" Marco asked.

"Yes, it has," Dennis concluded.

"Does this give you hope for the others who are missing, Mr. Smith?" Marco questioned.

"Yes, it does," he replied. "I actually had a dream myself a few nights ago. And in that dream, the missing people were returning—-one by one. I can't say it was prophetic, but it seemed as real to me as us sitting in this courtroom."

I almost fainted.

Chapter 65

Court was done for the day and I was surprised I felt good about it. The letter to Dennis and Janet had been a godsend. It had proven to the jury that my dreams were not bogus. And I was pleased to know my information gave them peace about their mother. Marco knew Dennis' testimony was going to benefit the defense which was an unfortunate surprise for the DA.

Two of the letters had produced the right results. I hoped the rest of the letters would turn out to be as beneficial.

I thanked Marco for all he had done. "It was great how you went after Bardon when you questioned him. It showed the jury how he had bullied, not only me, but also Dennis and Janet. It was a great move." I knew it encouraged Marco that I pointed out his effort.

It was almost worth going through this nightmare to be vindicated for the harm Bardon had done to my life when I was young. It had affected much of what I had believed about myself for so many years. And it must have reinforced all the things I had told Sid about Bardon, as well. But, I knew I couldn't use Bardon as an excuse for failure any longer.

My jail cell offered some peace and quiet which I needed after such an emotional day. After I undressed, the guards took my clothes and shoes and told me I would be wearing them the next day. I joked, "Do you think you could give me a different shirt and tie? I want to make a good impression on the ladies tomorrow."

The guards laughed and simply said, "No." And with that they whisked my outfit away which I assumed I would be wearing for the entire trial.

I decided to take a nap, but shortly after I had fallen asleep, I was awakened by a guard telling me I had a visitor. I couldn't imagine who it would be, but I quickly combed my hair.

They took me out to the visitor center and there was a sight for sore eyes. Bill stood looking at me through the glass barrier. I couldn't believe he had come to see me. I was so thankful and hoped we were still friends.

We sat down and I told him it was good to see him again. He quickly got serious and said, "Henry, I was a little sad when it seemed you forgot about me after you met your new girlfriend. I understood that, but I also thought we were friends. It kind of looked to me like you had been using me to get your story and when it was done, so was our friendship."

I took a deep breath as he continued, "I reflected over all the things we had spoken about when we were together, and I knew you were not the kind of person who uses others. You were just in love with a woman and everyone else got tossed to the side. I did the same thing when I met my wife."

Bill continued and I listened waiting to hear where we stood. "I was surprised when your attorney sent me the letter, Henry. When I read the letter, it confirmed my belief in you and I knew you were just trying to help us like you said all along. But I really didn't expect to find anything that your lawyer mentioned in the letter. On the other hand, like the letter said, I had nothing to lose."

"I had the letter a couple of days before I checked on the things you said Elias told you. I was hoping beyond all hope that you did talk to him, but I couldn't bear the disappointment if it didn't turn out to be true," he admitted.

I shook my head like I understood, but I didn't. If I had received that letter, I would have checked the information first thing.

"I finally got the courage to check it out. I went in his apartment and looked on the shelf in his closet where he said the book would be and found the note inside it. It was actually there, Henry! No one could have known that except Elias!" he cried.

Tears were falling down his cheeks as he told me his surprise and delight in finding the note Elias had written. He then pulled it out and summarized it for me. "The note explained what Elias had been going through and how he knew he was slipping back into drugs. He said he didn't want to hurt me anymore, and so he was going to find help for his problem. He wrote about a rehab he wanted to check out. I guess that's why he had packed that bag."

Bill put the note up to the glass where I could see it. "Where is he, Henry? How can I get my boy back?" he asked with pleading, tear filled eyes.

The note was real. It was the first physical evidence I had literally seen and it was thrilling. I had actually spoken to Bill's beloved Elias. There was the proof—staring me in the face. I had literally spoken to three of the missing people. But, the excitement faded as I knew I had no rescue plan to give Bill on how we could get his son back.

"Bill, I am so glad you trusted me and believed in me. That means the world to me. And I'm sorry I let you down by not staying in touch. You're right. I was smitten by this girl, and she was all I could think about. It hurt my work on the story, too because I was so distracted. But I don't have to worry about that now because she dumped me a few days ago," I revealed sadly.

He seemed sad when I told him I had lost the love of my life. Bill told me, "She called me a few weeks ago and told me you had asked her to call. I believe her name is 'Irene'. Is that right, Henry?" Bill asked. I confirmed it was.

Bill continued, "Irene explained to me why you had not called me. She told me about the fire that destroyed your phone and your computer. I saw that fire on the News but I didn't realize it was your room," he explained. "This woman seemed to care so much for you, Henry. What happened?" he asked.

"She was listening to the wrong people, Bill. They put doubts in her mind about everything I had told her. But I can understand how hard it would be for anyone to believe all the crazy things I've been through. I guess it was just too much to swallow and she couldn't take it anymore."

I appreciated Bill's concern, but I really didn't want to talk about it. "I am glad we are still friends, Bill. I'll try to be a better one from now on," I sincerely said.

"Henry, I will be happy to contact Irene and tell her your dream about Elias was real. Then she will believe you were telling the truth. Surely that would bring her back to you," he thought.

His offer was tempting, but I decided to wait until I was hopefully acquitted for the crimes before trying to get her back.

"Bill, I wanted to tell you the minute I woke up from the dream about Elias. I was so thrilled to meet him because I felt like I knew him after all you had shared with me. We talked about bowling and we talked about you. He told me he was glad to know you had a friend. He's a great guy!" I gushed.

Bill looked at me like he hadn't heard anything I had just told him. He asked me again, "How will Elias come back?"

The hope in his eyes made it harder to say, but I knew I had to tell him the truth. "Bill, I believe there is a way, but it has not been revealed to me yet. When it happens, you will be one of the first to know," I promised.

After my heartfelt explanation, I saw him slump in his seat. "Henry, I feel like my hopes keep getting dashed. Why would you offer me this proof he is alive, if you don't know how to get him back?" he questioned.

I told him my attorney had asked me the same thing. "You have to trust me, Bill. It will come. We just have to be patient. I wouldn't have been brought this far if there wasn't an answer."

He shook his head in agreement. He stood up and said, "I do trust you, Henry. I'm glad you came to Abilene because I know there was a purpose. I believe I will see my son again," he said with tears in his eyes. He turned around quickly because he didn't want me to see him cry.

I felt like crying, too, because I had no clue how to rescue these people from their spiritual prisons. I knew the answer would come from the unseen world, but I felt helpless to initiate it.

The angel's words came back to me—"Do not fear, only believe."

Chapter 66

The night was long and I kept waking up every few minutes. I had prayed again for help. I could only hope I would have a dream, or a visitor, or a sign from heaven to show me the way. The anxiety kept me tossing and turning most of the night, which made dreaming impossible.

The night turned up empty with no answers, and I dreaded seeing Bill and Marco the next day with nothing to tell them. They were putting their hope in me, but I knew the answer would not come from me; it would come from the One above.

They both looked at me expectantly when I was brought into the courtroom, but I shook my head with disappointment as we all took our respective seats. Court began and we stood up as the judge walked in. She didn't look like she was having a good morning. I hoped it would not influence mine.

Bill was called up to the stand. He told the jury about the letter he had received from Marco. It was handed to the judge, but she only glanced at it. Bill went on to tell the jury, "I put the letter away for a few days because I honestly did not expect to find the evidence the letter suggested I would. After waiting a few days, I decided I had to know. I walked into Elias' apartment and looked on the shelf where he said I would find the book. Inside it, I found the letter Elias had intended to give me but he never got the chance."

Marco asked Bill to read the note. He did, and I imagined there were few dry eyes in the courtroom when Bill began to cry as he read the note. The anguish was evident as Bill labored through the words.

Bill looked at the jury and said, "Henry Pike did not take my son. He cared about me and my son, even though he had never met Elias. He was trying to find him and the others when he was framed for this crime."

Marco redirected Bill and asked him about the call he received from me while I was at Jake's house. "Yes sir, he did call me before the fire was reported out there. He sounded like he was scared. I didn't know it at the time, but I found out later he was in the house that burned down. All I knew for sure was he seemed very frightened."

Marco thanked Bill for his testimony.

The DA had a few questions for Bill, of course. "Mr. Major, I think we are all convinced that Mr. Pike has actually talked to some of the missing people, including your son. But, don't you think it's reasonable to assume he may have had access to these people by another means other than dreaming about them? Would it not be possible that he could have the missing people hidden away somewhere and that is how he gleaned this information. Wouldn't that make more sense than us believing he met them in his dreams?"

I wondered why Marco did not object, but later learned he believed Bill would be able to handle the DA's implications. He was right. Bill responded, "No, I don't think he has them all hidden somewhere. And if he did, why would they give up these secrets so their loved ones would think they were OK, if they weren't?" he asked.

"He could have threatened them," The DA suggested.

"Why would he? They would have just lied to him. The missing people who talked to Henry wanted their families to know they were OK and that is why they gave him this information," Bill concluded.

"OK, thank you. That will be all, Mr. Major." The DA dismissed him but Bill didn't leave.

"And why wouldn't he ask for a ransom if he took them?" Bill interjected without being asked. "All Henry has asked for is the chance to help us find them." The DA responded with, "No further questions. Thank you, Mr. Major."

Bill had stood by me. He was willing to go head to head with the DA on my behalf. He was a true friend.

The next witness called was the bubbly waitress from the truck stop. Her name was Lori Mason. Since I had never thought to ask her name, Marco had to figure it out. He found her by asking the manager who was working the night I met her. There were several women working that shift, but after talking to each one, he found the right person.

Marco asked Lori about the night she met me. She began by telling the jury, "He looked so tired that night. I don't know what he was doing up so late, but he was exhausted. He seemed very interested when I told him I knew of one of the missing people through my son, Joe. He wondered if I could find out the name of the missing man's girlfriend. My son knew it and gave me the name. But when I went to tell Mr. Pike, he was sound asleep. I had to wake him up to give it to him."

Marco asked Lori if she had ever seen me again at the truck stop. "Yes, he came in another night around the same time. But this time, a girl was with him. He told me the information I gave him was very helpful which made me feel good," she said as she smiled at me. Marco thanked her for her testimony and then it was the DA's turn.

The DA asked Lori why she thought I was up so late. She told him, "I don't know, sir, I don't pry into my customer's business. He said he was doing a story and I figured he was up late working on it. He did have his laptop with him."

The DA abruptly told the judge he had no more questions when he saw a man walk in from the back of the courtroom. The bubbly waitress hadn't contributed too much to my defense, but she did verify some of the things I had previously said.

During recess, Marco told me he had heard from Jodie's family and would meet with them later. He was hoping for the best.

The next witness called up was the forensic officer who had first testified. He had been the one who walked in when Lori was being questioned. The DA asked him about a recent finding. Marco objected because he was not notified about this evidence. The DA explained to the judge that he had just received word about the new finding.

The judge told the DA to proceed. The forensic officer explained, "About an hour ago, one of our men, who is still investigating this case, happened to find a large trash barrel quite a ways from the house. They went through the garbage inside and found some bloody embroidered towels. The blood on the towels matches that of the defendant."

Marco looked at me as he heard the man's new revelation and I whispered, "Jake used a few towels just to clean my wounds. These must have been the ones they found in the trash. He used the other ones for my bandages. He probably used around six towels altogether." Then I added, "Wouldn't this evidence be more compelling if it had been Jake's blood instead of mine?"

Marco understood what I was saying. When it was his turn to question the new discovery, he asked the officer, "Why would there be no blood from Jake Bardon on the towels if Henry Pike had killed him?"

The officer responded, "It is hard to determine what exactly killed Jake Bardon due to the condition of his body. But we did feel it was suspicious to find blood on these handmade towels. I doubt Mr. Bardon would have used towels like these to clean up someone's blood."

I knew different. Jake did choose to use them, but I had no way to prove it.

Court was dismissed early for the day and soon after I was taken back to my cell, Marco came to discuss this new evidence. I told him how I had protested when Jake wanted to use the towels, but Jake insisted because he never used them and he didn't have any bandages.

Marco told me I would need to explain that when I took the stand. I understood this new evidence did not help my case. The jury probably reasoned no one would use embroidered towels to clean up blood unless they didn't mean anything to the person using them.

Marco told me he had meetings later with the families of Kim and Jodie. Marco had already talked to Kim's parents over the phone but he had not been able to meet with them. And Jodie's family had just called him, so he wasn't sure what they had found in response to his letter.

I got up the nerve to ask him if Irene would be testifying and he said he thought she would be there the next day. I couldn't wait to see her, even if her testimony was not what I was hoping for. I just wanted to see her again. I got my chance sooner than I thought.

Chapter 67

The guards came to my cell and told me I had a visitor. I figured it was Marco, but thought he was rather early. It was not Marco; it was the love of my life standing in the visitor center. Her visage stopped me in my tracks. I stood and just looked at her. My eyes had longed to see her again.

She sat down and I waited eagerly to hear why she came. She said, "Henry, your friend Bill saw me in a restaurant last night and came over to talk to me. I think he might have followed me there." She smiled, so I did too. I was sitting on pens and needles waiting to hear what she had to say.

"He told me about Elias and how you had literally talked to him in a dream. Is it true Elias told you where to find a note he had written to his father?" she asked.

"Yes, it is true. I think I mentioned it when I told you I dreamed about him," I reminded her. I knew she hadn't been listening when I was sharing about the dreams and I didn't want to make her feel bad about it.

"You might have, I'm sorry. Well he wanted me to know so I would believe you and not think you are crazy. Those were his words." She smiled again, so I nodded and smiled back. It sounded like something Bill would say.

She continued, "Henry, I had already decided to stand with you through all of this even if we didn't get back together. I knew you could never do the things they are accusing you of, but I still wasn't sure what to believe about all the crazy things you've told me. I have to say Bill's story certainly helped me to reconsider the possibilities. It is amazing to know you actually talked to Elias!"

I interjected, "Irene, I knew it was a risk to tell you about all my spiritual escapades, but it meant so much to me that you tried to believe me. And it still does."

"Henry, I have to testify tomorrow and I will be truthful, but I might be a little biased in my testimony. They don't have to know that, but I wanted you to know that bias leans towards you," she revealed. She smiled again. I was so happy to know she was reconsidering her thoughts about me.

I wanted to grab her and kiss her. I wanted to tell her everything was going to be OK and then we could be together. But I knew that was still uncertain. All I could say was, "Thank you, Irene. That means the world to me."

This time when she left, she turned around and smiled at me. My heart melted.

After dinner that night, Marco came to share with me what the families had shared with him. He had met with them separately; nevertheless they both had basically said the same thing. I sat down preparing myself for what I might hear. I knew if even one of the things I told them was wrong, I might be facing prison.

Marco relieved me of my anxiety when he smiled at me. "They both found exactly what you said they would find, Henry! Did you hear me? It worked! The letters worked and now they all believe you," he happily exclaimed.

It was the news I had longed to hear. It was now substantiated that I had literally spoken to these four missing people and I had proof from all of their families. The news was all good that day.

"Henry, there is only one thing left to do. We have to get these people back to their families. Even with these testimonies on your behalf, you still have no proof you didn't kidnap the people. Like the DA suggested, the jury still might conclude you had access to these people where you could have obtained this information in some unsavory way," he explained.

Marco was right. I hoped the powers that be understood the predicament I was in. When I went back to my cell, I once again got on my knees and started praying. A guard interrupted me with my dinner. I was a little embarrassed he saw me on my knees, but it didn't matter. I was desperate. I got up and thanked him for my food. Surprisingly, he didn't leave like the other guards had always done in the past.

After he handed me the food, he just stood there. I asked him how he was doing and he told me, "I have never been better."

Those were the very same words the janitor had said. I looked at him intently, but he seemed like a normal guard other than the fact he was talking to me. I didn't want to assume anything, so I asked him, "So how long have you worked here?"

"Not long at all," he replied, which was exactly what the janitor had said. Was I going to have to come out and ask him if he was a spiritual messenger?

"So what did you do before you worked here?" I asked, hoping he would give me a little more information.

"I worked as a messenger for a very prestigious firm," he replied.

I knew then who he must be. "How prestigious?" I asked.

"The most," he declared.

"Thank God!" I shouted

"Yes," he responded.

He passed the heavenly messenger litmus test, so I went for it and asked him, "Sir, are you here to tell me something?"

"No," he replied surprisingly. "You don't need anyone to tell you anything, Henry. You already know. I just came to remind you."

"Please, spell it out for me," I begged. "Too much is riding on this for me to get it wrong."

"You won't, Henry. You have all of heaven behind you. They are just waiting to hear the word," he explained.

"The word?" I asked.

"How did the people get where they are now?" He was spoon feeding me, but I didn't care. I was going to find out all I could.

"They asked to go," I said.

"So what do you and their families need to do?" the messenger guard asked.

"We need to do just the opposite! We need to ask for them to return!" I shouted.

"These people are caught in a spiritual web, Henry. If they are going to be set free, then you and their families will have to ask for it to happen," he explained. Then he smiled and said, "But my firm happens to be in the business of setting people free."

"So when we ask for their return, your 'firm' will respond to our requests? Is that how it works?" I asked.

"Yes, that's the way it's been set up. You ask and we respond," he said glibly.

"And your people will fight for my people?" I surmised.

"Yes, and we always win, Henry. We've never lost a case yet, and we won't lose this one," he said confidently. "You see their ransom was paid long ago and their freedom is theirs for the taking. They just haven't realized it yet, so you have to tell them," he explained.

I wasn't sure what he meant by that. "What do you mean, 'I have to tell them'? I have to dream again and go back to each one?" I asked. The very idea of doing that was exhausting.

I was relieved when he said, "No, it will work just as well if you tell their families and they believe. As long as one of them believes, it will work."

"These people are in a spiritual world, Henry, and they will have to be rescued by spiritual forces," he explained. "Spiritual forces are not commissioned until you ask for them to be. The spiritual world operates with you—not separate from you."

I looked at him and smiled. I was so thankful I finally had 'the rescue plan', even though I did not totally understand how it would work.

"Thank you." I said with all the sincerity I ever had.

"You're welcome, Henry," he said.

"You just saved my life," I replied.

"Not me," he said. "That was also taken care of many years ago."

"Then I will thank Him tonight," I said.

"He would appreciate that, I'm sure." And with that he walked out the door—without opening it!

Chapter 68

When I walked into court the next day, I felt like a free man. Marco and Bill looked at me and both reacted like kids when I shook my head, "Yes!" They knew I finally had the plan to rescue the missing. We took our respective seats and Marco told me he couldn't wait to hear what I had to tell him.

After the judge entered, a new day in court began. The first witness was called up which was the father of Jodie, the young musician who had disappeared soon after her break-up with her fiancé. Her father, George, got on the witness stand, and Marco asked him if he had ever met the defendant, Henry Pike. George answered, "We never got to meet Henry, but the Smiths had told us about him. They were told to stay away from him so we never reached out to him."

Marco continued, "Did Henry ever try to contact you?"

"No, he never did, but we were aware he wanted to meet with all of us," George responded.

Once again I felt myself getting angry at Bardon for all the ways he had tried to mess up my life. Marco continued, "You received a letter I sent you a few days ago, is that correct, Mr. Balsom?"

George pulled the letter out of his pocket and it was given to the judge who handed it to the court reporter.

"Yes, we did and we were surprised to receive a letter from the defendant's attorney. We knew we might be called in to testify in this trial, but we never expected to get a letter like this one."

"Could you tell us what happened as a result of the information in the letter?" Marco asked.

"Yes. When we received the letter, it explained how Mr. Pike believed he had met our daughter in a dream. We have heard some pretty bizarre things since all of this happened, but this had to be the most outrageous. We didn't know what to think? But, even though we thought it was absurd, we decided to check on the information given us in the letter."

"I see," Marco said, "So you checked on the information even though you had heard some negative things about Mr. Pike?"

"Yes. We were curious about it even though we didn't expect to find anything," he responded.

"And what did you find from the information given in the letter?" Marco asked.

"We looked under her bed and found the package she said would be there. She had addressed the package to her ex-boyfriend–fiancé, I should say. The package was in the corner, underneath her headboard exactly where it was stated. We would have never found it unless we had taken the bed apart," he revealed.

"And what did you find inside the package, Mr. Balsom?" Marco prodded.

"Exactly what the letter said we would find. There was a wedding invitation, which had never been sent out since it had been cancelled. There was a newspaper clipping with the engagement announcement, and her engagement ring which was inside a little box," he explained.

"There was also a handkerchief with her initials embroidered on it. Penned to the handkerchief, she had written a note to her ex-fiancé, telling him she had cried her eyes out in that handkerchief every night since they had broken up," he responded.

"And there was a busted plaster heart which I think her boyfriend gave her as a gift. She might have thrown it at him because it was broken," he concluded. "Apparently, she had been planning to send this package to her fiancé before she went missing. Everything was just as it was stated in the letter."

"What did you think, Mr. Balsom, after finding these items?" Marco asked.

"I thought Mr. Pike must have really spoken to her," he replied.

"And did Mr. Pike ask you for anything in return for this information?" Marco asked.

"No. In the letter it was stated that Mr. Pike just wanted to help us get her back," George replied.

Marco finished his questions, "Thank you, Mr. Balsom. No further questions, your Honor."

The DA got up and only asked one question, "Mr. Balsom, it is obvious Henry Pike talked to your daughter to get this information, but have you considered he could have obtained it in other ways besides a dream?"

George seemed uncomfortable with the question but answered, "Yes, I suppose so. I certainly considered it. But why would he do that? How would that benefit him? He obviously had nothing to gain by telling me this information, unless he was trying to make a deal with me or get a ransom. But he never mentioned anything like that," George reasoned.

"No further questions, your Honor." Even though the DA chose to ignore George's last statement, the jury heard what he said and it made me look innocent.

The next witness they called was Sid. He went up and took the oath and Marco asked him what relationship he had with the defendant.

Sid explained to the jury how much I fought him about doing the story in Abilene. Marco asked, "If Henry was taking people in Abilene, then why wouldn't he jump on the chance to be closer to these people?"

Sid agreed. "It wouldn't make any sense if he was the culprit in these crimes. He never wanted to do any stories in Abilene so I always sent someone else," he concluded.

"Do you know why Mr. Pike did not want to do any assignments in his hometown?" Marco asked.

"No, he never told me why. I figured his past was his business," Sid explained.

Sid also told the court how I had always been a good employee, and he had never known me to do anything unscrupulous. He also said, "I've known Henry Pike for close to eleven years and I have never known him to do anything hurtful or mean to anyone. He is a great person and would never do the things he has been accused of. I know that for certain."

The DA then took his turn and asked Sid about my social life. "I don't think he really goes out much," Sid said hesitantly but honestly. "We have gone out for dinner and he comes to office parties, but I'm not sure who his friends are."

The DA continued his line of questioning, "Are you saying he is a loner, who stays to himself most of the time?" Sid seemed uncomfortable and said he wasn't sure. I was sure the DA was trying to make me look like a recluse to the jury.

Sid concluded his part in my trial and I felt he contributed to my defense. He had made a good point when he told the jury how much I resisted doing the story in Abilene. He had also been a good character witness for me.

The judge decided to call a recess earlier than usual. I was grateful because I was exhausted. I asked for permission to meet with my attorney, but it was denied. They said I could meet with him later. I knew he wanted the information I had to tell him, but I supposed there was no harm in waiting a little longer.

The guards whisked me away to a holding cell. Being exhausted and having nothing else to do, I quickly fell asleep and then had one of the worst dreams ever.

In this nightmare, some evil looking characters were walking towards me. It looked like they had clubs in their hands. There had to be ten or more of them and they surrounded me. They were laughing as they appeared to be whispering something to each other.

Then one of the grotesque creatures started yelling at me, "Henry Pike, do you really think you are some big savior to these people? You're no hero, Henry. You lost this case, Henry, and you don't even know it. We are much smarter and much more powerful than you are." They all laughed an evil laugh.

They continued to taunt me with a horrible revelation, "The people you were hoping to rescue have been taken to a place where you will never find them. The only one who escaped our grasp was the old woman who died. We can no longer reach her, but we have all the others. You will never find them now." They all started laughing again.

These evil beings continued to taunt me, "Everyone will be laughing at you soon. None of the missing people will be returned now. We won, Henry. We defeated you. You should have never tried to fight us." These ghoulish characters kept laughing and mocking me. Then, each one started to cackle like an evil witch. Their sordid laughs pierced my ears and my mind.

In an effort to block their taunts and laughter, I tried to put my hands over my ears which caused the handcuffs on my wrists to hit me soundly in the head which woke me up. I jumped up and realized it had been a dream—a horrible nightmare.

As I carefully lifted my fingers to my forehead where I had just clocked myself, I could tell I had been sweating profusely. At that inopportune moment, the guards came in to take me back to the courtroom. They both looked at me bewildered and asked, "What happened to you?" Then they both started laughing before I could answer. It was like they were joining in with the ghoulish creatures, laughing at my horrible new predicament.

As they brought me back into the courtroom, I wondered if what the grim creatures had said was true. Was it possible these evil spirits managed to move all of the missing? Could we have missed our opportunity to save them? Could they find a way to somehow sabotage my trial? Fear flooded my mind as I realized from experience—they definitely could.

Chapter 69

Since I was concerned about my appearance when I entered the court room, I glanced around to see if anyone was staring at me. I think my self-consciousness caused more reaction than the red bump on my head or the sweat that permeated my clothes and my hair. Marco looked at me oddly when he saw me.

"What happened to you in there? Did someone rough you up?" he asked.

"Yes, you might say that. I'll tell you about it later," I explained.

At that moment, the judge walked in and also looked at me in a strange way. I was hoping it was just my imagination, so I tried to forget about my appearance.

Kim's mother was the next witness to take the stand. Marco walked up to question her and went through the same inquiry he had done with the other witnesses regarding the letter.

When Marco asked Barbara Baldwin how she responded to the letter she said, "I immediately ran to the place where Kim said I would find her diary. I looked in her bookshelf and found the hollow book where she kept it. I had never noticed it before. I turned to the date she specified and found written in large letters, 'I don't want to live here anymore! I'm going to find a way to be with my grandmother today!'"

Barbara continued, "I was heartsick as I read my daughter's despair. I knew she was sad after her grandmother died, but I thought she would eventually find a way to deal with it. I didn't realize the extent of her depression over it."

"Then I read some of the pages before this entry where it looked like she was writing down prayers to God, asking Him to let her see her grandmother again. I always knew her grandmother was her best friend, but this outpouring of grief surprised me," Barbara explained.

"What did you think when you realized the information in the letter was correct?" Marco asked.

"Well the first thing I thought was Mr. Pike must know where she is, and that maybe he had taken her. I couldn't think of any other way he would be able to get this information from her. But as I read the rest of the letter more carefully, you stated Mr. Pike's intentions were to help us get her back. I thought it was strange because I wasn't sure how knowing this information could do that. He didn't seem to want anything from us, so I really didn't know what to think. But, it did give me some hope she was still alive."

"Do you believe Mr. Pike wants to help you and that's why he sent the letter like it stated?" Marco asked.

Suddenly her demeanor changed. "I don't know what to believe. All I know is I want my daughter back. If he can help me do that, then I will do whatever he asks," she said passionately. She seemed very agitated.

She looked directly at me and stated loudly, "I want my child back, do you understand? I don't know what this is all about or what games you are playing; I just want my daughter back. Do you know where my daughter is, Mr. Pike?"

I looked at her in horror as I remembered the dream I had in the holding cell. Questions began to flood my mind: Was it possible Kim was no longer in heaven? Could those evil spirits have taken her? Were those cackling creatures telling the truth about moving all the missing to another location?

As I pondered these possibilities, her mother started screaming at me, "Where is my daughter? You obviously talked to her. Please, tell me. I'll give you anything."

The judge called for order and told Barbara to stop talking to the defendant or she would be removed from the court. She started crying and shook her head that she understood. Her passionate outburst made me look horrible. Marco knew there was nothing more he could say or ask of her.

The DA walked up to her and obviously decided to capitalize on her outburst. "It does seem odd to me that Mr. Pike did not bring your daughter home after he ascertained this information. If he was truly trying to help, wouldn't he have rescued her and brought her back? Do you find that puzzling, Mrs. Baldwin?" he asked, knowing he had a good point.

Barbara answered, "I don't know. Perhaps, he couldn't for some reason?" She looked at me again and started to say something, but decided not to. She was wringing her hands, and I could see she was in deep distress.

The DA continued, "Mrs. Baldwin, you don't even know this man. You have never met him before. How could you assume the best about him?"

She responded, "Because I have nothing else. He is the only one who has given me any hope of ever seeing her again, and I'm willing to put all my dimes in his jar to get her back."

Once again the DA decided to not respond to her statement and told the judge he had no more questions. As hard as he tried, it seemed these families were giving me the benefit of the doubt. But because of the dream I had earlier, I was the one having the doubts.

It had been established that I had definitely talked to some of the missing people, but my intentions were still in question. I knew that had to be a lingering doubt in the jury's collective mind.

The next witness to take the stand was Pastor Sam. The DA asked him why he decided to call the police after talking to me. Pastor Sam said, "Mr. Pike told me he had spoken to nearly all of the missing people, so what was I supposed to think? How could he speak to them if he didn't know where they were?" he asked.

The DA asked, "Did he appear to be someone who would do something like this?"

"No," Sam said, "But neither did most of the other serial killers we know about. I also thought he might be a little crazy when he started talking about all of the dreams he'd had. Mr. Pike also told me about some supernatural experiences which sounded bizarre to me. I had never heard of the things he talked about. That was why I called the police. I figured if he was guilty, then I did the right thing and if he was innocent he would be released. And I was concerned about Irene's safety, as well."

The DA thanked him and then Marco came up and asked, "Why would a serial killer come to you for help, Pastor Sam?"

"I don't know?" he replied. "He could be mentally imbalanced or something? Who knows what goes on in other people's minds? But what made me take notice, was when he told me he had met some of the missing people. Should I have just kept that kind of information to myself?" he questioned.

Marco countered, "Did he not tell you he talked to them in his dreams?"

"Yes, he told me, but how weird is that? Was I supposed to believe something that ridiculous?" the pastor replied.

"I think if you check, there are quite a few stories in the Word about people having dreams and visions. It is actually quite prevalent throughout the book, if you read it. So maybe you should reconsider how weird it is, Pastor," Marco informed him. "Thank you, no more questions."

Marco's final statement to the pastor made him look rather ignorant for someone in his line of work. I breathed a sigh of relief that the pastor's testimony was over and it didn't seem that damaging to my case.

The court recessed for lunch. I was taken to the holding cell where they gave me a light lunch. The one thing I knew I would not do while waiting in there—was take a nap.

Court reconvened and Irene took the stand. The DA called her up as his next witness and I held my breath. She sat down and looked at me. I smiled at her. I had no idea what she would say, but I knew it could be the most damaging or the most helpful to my case.

The DA began the questioning, "Ms. Duncan, are you in a relationship with Henry Pike?"

This guy wasn't wasting any time to make that connection. I sat with baited breath wondering how she was going to answer the question.

"Yes, I am," She replied. I smiled at her with relief and she smiled back.

"Ms. Duncan, how long have you known the defendant?" he asked.

"Several months," she replied.

"How did you meet?" he asked. She told him about Cooper and the vet and how she had helped me buy supplies for the dog.

"I see. So did he tell you how he acquired this dog?" the DA asked. This would be a hard question for Irene, since I had initially lied to her about Cooper.

"Yes, he did," she responded. "He told me he found him under a cactus somewhere around Potosi." I hoped she wasn't perjuring herself but her answer was basically true.

The DA questioned her further, "Did you know Henry knew the dog's owner?"

"No, not at the time," Irene answered honestly.

"And did you also not know the dog's owner was killed in a suspicious fire?" the DA asked.

"I didn't realize it at the time," she answered.

"Does it not seem strange to you that your boyfriend failed to mention these things when he got his new dog?" he asked.

"He had just met me, so he didn't know how I would respond," she explained.

"I see, Ms. Duncan. Did it cross your mind that your boyfriend might have had something to do with the fire that killed Jake Bardon?" the DA probed.

"No, I would never think that because Henry would never hurt anyone. He is a good man who cares about people. But, he did tell me why he went out there. He was doing an article on the missing and had gone out to investigate the fires in that area to see if they might have any relevance to the story," she said with confidence.

"It sounds like Mr. Pike is more of a detective than a journalist, doesn't it?" he said sarcastically. "So you had no reason to suspect your boyfriend might be involved with the fires even though your pastor, whom you have known and trusted for years, told you he doubted Henry's innocence after he spoke to him at length. Is that right, Ms. Duncan?" the DA pressed.

Marco objected saying he was leading the witness. The judge sustained his motion. The DA said, "Let me reword that. Did your pastor talk to you after he had spoken to Mr. Pike?"

"Yes, he did. He told me he thought Henry might have something to do with the missing people, but Henry had explained to him that he had met these people in dreams. And that was the precise reason I had suggested to Henry he should talk to my pastor in the first place. Since Henry had met these people in a spiritual realm, I thought my pastor would understand and be able to help him. But, instead of helping him, he turned him into the police," Irene expounded as she glared at the pastor sitting in the audience.

"Do you think your pastor was just trying to protect you, Ms. Duncan?" he asked.

"I'm sure he was, but I didn't need his protection. Henry needed answers and this is where it landed him," she declared as she gestured at the courtroom.

"Did Mr. Pike ever talk to you about these dark creatures he had seen?" the DA enquired.

"Yes, he did. And, honestly, I wasn't sure I believed him until one night when I saw one myself. It was late one night when I saw one of them in my bedroom," she said.

"Is it possible you were just dreaming, Ms. Duncan?" the DA asked.

"No, I was reading a book and looked up, and there it was. I screamed and ran out of the house," Irene explained. "I went immediately to Henry's motel because I knew he would know what to do. And no, he didn't take advantage of the opportunity," she clarified as she heard some people snicker in the courtroom.

"He took me to a truck stop where we stayed until daybreak. Then he took me back to my house and went through every room with me to be sure nothing was there. He stayed with me until I was ready to go to work. He even walked my dog for me and made a pot of coffee. He was the perfect gentleman. And he told me what to do if I ever saw the thing again," Irene said.

"And what was that?" the DA wondered.

"He told me to speak the Word out loud at them. Henry said I needed to know the authority I had to tread on them. And he also told me, 'When we know who we are, they will do what we say'," she recalled.

"And did that work?" he asked.

"I never saw another one to find out," she said. "But, I'm sure it would."

He thanked her for her testimony and then Marco got up. "Why would Henry Pike risk everything to talk to you and your pastor about these dreams?" he questioned.

"Henry shared with me because he needed to talk to someone about everything he was going through. And he shared with my pastor because he wanted some guidance," Irene explained. "He wouldn't have wanted to talk to my pastor if he was guilty of this crime. Henry truly needed help to figure out how to rescue these people who seem to be in some kind of spiritual prison."

"Why do you believe Mr. Pike is innocent, Ms. Duncan?" Marco asked.

"Because I know him, and he would never harm anyone. He is one of the kindest, most gentle men I have ever met. Once I found him comforting a weeping man who had just lost his wife. Does that sound like a murderer to you? He is the kind of man I had always hoped to meet," she responded. With her closing statement, my heart soared and the third day of court was over.

Chapter 70

After I returned to my cell, the guards took my suit, which was disgusting since I had sweated so much in it. I asked them nicely if they could have it cleaned, but they just laughed and said room service was closed for the day.

Marco came to see me later and felt the day in court had gone well. But his real reason for coming was that he wanted to hear the plan I had received to rescue the missing.

The excitement I felt about it was diminished by the horrible nightmare I had in the holding cell. It had filled me with doubts and a great deal of fear, which dampened my enthusiasm about what the angel guard had told me. I tried to push my doubts aside as I told Marco what the heavenly messenger had said.

"A guard came to give me dinner yesterday but this time was different. Usually the guards just put my food through the slot and leave. But this time the guard stayed. He looked like he wanted to talk which made me curious," I said.

"We had the usual small talk, but then he said some of the same things the last messenger said, so I almost knew for certain he was there to give me a message. But I didn't want to come right out and ask him," I explained.

"What did he tell you?" Marco asked impatiently.

"He said something like, 'Words took the missing where they are and it would be words that would bring them home,'" I recalled as I summed it up in my own words.

Marco looked at me bewildered and said, "That's all he said? That doesn't sound like a plan, Henry, it sounds like a proverb. How can words bring those people back? It sounds too easy."

I responded, "It seems easy to us, but it cost one Man everything. I am beginning to learn the spiritual world operates on words. He gave us the ability to ask—'Ask and it will be given.' So, we need to ask."

"It does say that," Marco agreed. "It just seems too simple. I thought you would receive some elaborate plan on how to rescue them. This is all too weird for me, Henry."

"We can't get them out in a normal way, Marco. The messenger explained that to me. They are in a spiritual prison so they will have to be rescued spiritually. He also said the spiritual forces go into operation as soon as we ask. We need to ask that everything on earth will be the way it is in heaven."

"I hope you're right, Henry. You do seem to understand all of this better than anyone else, so I guess I will take your word for it," he stated. And then he laughed when he realized the pun he had made.

I laughed, too, but I knew I had to tell him something that wasn't funny. "Marco, you remember when you asked me if someone had roughed me up in the holding cell."

Marco responded, "Oh yes. I meant to ask you about it again."

"I had a horrible dream when I was in there." Then, I cautiously unfolded the ghastly nightmare.

"Henry, what are you telling me? Are you saying these evil spirits moved the missing people somewhere?! Is that even possible? How can we find them now?" he asked anxiously.

"I don't know the answer to any of those questions, Marco. But I never knew where they were in the first place, so I'm not sure if it makes any difference. I know the One who sees in secret knows where they are. The only thing we can do is what the guard, or messenger, told me to do," I replied.

Marco agreed and asked, "OK Henry, so what is the plan?"

I gathered my thoughts and said, "This is what I think we should do. Tell the families who have testified, to call their loved ones, their churches or anyone who prays. Tell them to ask the Lord of hosts for their loved ones to be returned."

"Henry, do you really think this is a plan? I think most of them have already done this," Marco responded.

"I'm sure they have prayed, Marco, but they probably did it out of fear and despair. I think they put more trust in the police and detectives to help them than they did in the One above all. Many of these families even turned to mediums for help. I know these people were desperate, Marco, but I have learned it does not please Him when people put more confidence in men than they do in Him," I said emphatically.

"They have to put their trust in Him alone and believe He will do it. When they ask and believe, then they will receive. But, the one requirement is--they must believe," I stressed.

My instructions to Marco were reviving my faith as I continued telling him what we needed to do. "Tell these families what will happen when they ask, Marco. Tell them the Commander of the armies of heaven will send out His angels of light and they will go into the darkness and find the missing. These angels will fight for their loved ones and they will win!" I said with more confidence.

Marco was looking at me like I was crazy and in the natural world I would be. But we weren't dealing with the natural world anymore. This was a battle which could only be fought spiritually.

As we talked more about how we would convey all of this to the unsuspecting families, Marco surprised me by saying, "I'm not going to tell them, Henry—you will. You will tell them in court tomorrow after you testify. Your words will be in all the news outlets and when people hear your instructions, I am pretty sure they will start asking."

It sounded like a good idea, but the doubt from that horrible dream was still clouding my confidence. I hoped I could fill my mind with faith filled words overnight and restore my belief. But even if I couldn't restore my confidence by the next day, I knew the plan would still work if the families and those who stood with them would ask and believe.

Marco seemed uplifted which helped me to feel more encouraged. Then he exclaimed, "When they start coming home, Henry, you will be able to go home, too. You'll get your life back and you'll be a free man."

In my heart—I already was a free man.

Chapter 71

The day had arrived when I would take the stand to defend myself in my trial. I was nervous and knew I had a lot to explain. There were huge holes in my defense and I would need to fill them. Explaining the unexplainable would not be an easy task.

The guards brought me my stinky suit from the day before, and I put it on even thought it was disgusting. I no longer felt good in it and it was not helping my confidence as I was brought into the courtroom.

But what was helpful was when Marco handed me a note from Irene. She gave it to him to give me before court began.

Irene wrote: "I believe you will be acquitted, Henry, and I am looking forward to having you back in my life. I am willing to see where our relationship will go. Cooper misses you, as does his present caretaker. I have contacted my church in Abilene and they will be going before the Father on your behalf, Henry. Love, Irene"

It was exactly what I needed to hear to begin that anxious day. I turned around and smiled at her. She smiled at me. I knew with her standing with me, I was as ready as I'd ever be to face what was ahead.

After the ritual of rising and sitting as the judge entered, I was asked to take the stand. I took a deep breath as Marco walked over to me. He would let me explain myself in detail to tie up all the loose ends, but the DA would be right behind him to undo them if he could.

Marco asked me to explain who I was and why I was in Abilene. It didn't take long for me to sum all of that up. He then asked me to explain my relationship with Jake Bardon. I told the jury, "After I had met with Dennis and Janet, I kept hoping to hear from them again. But since I didn't, I wondered if Sergeant Bardon may have spoken to them, which now I know he had," I said somewhat angrily.

"I decided to stop by their house to see if Bardon might come by." (I didn't want to tell the jury, or Dennis and Janet, I had been watching their house for hours.) It was a Tuesday evening when I drove by their house. As I did, I saw them pull out of their driveway, so I decided to follow them. They drove somewhere around the Potosi area to a little church," I explained.

Marco clarified, "So you found the church by following the Smiths there, is that correct?"

"Yes, I had no previous knowledge of the church before this," I explained. "I parked on the side of the road and went down to the old church where they were. I looked inside the window and quite a few people were gathered there. I never found out what they were doing, but it didn't look like they were having a church service," I surmised.

"It was on the way back to my car, when I stumbled a few times in the dark, which is why they found blood on the rocks there. And when I got back to my car, it wouldn't start. I had to spend the night in my car. The next morning Jake Bardon stopped to see if I needed any help. That was the first time I met him," I explained.

"The next week, I went out there again to see if the group was meeting. But instead of finding them, I found the fire. The church was almost consumed by the time I got there. And then it started spreading and somehow it spread to my car, even though I had parked quite a distance away. Unfortunately, my car would not start again which was why it was destroyed," I clarified.

"The fire spread quickly and I couldn't get away from it. I fell because of all the smoke, but found I could breathe better closer to the ground. So, I crawled on my hands and knees until Jake Bardon found me and helped me out of the fire." I decided not to mention someone else pulled me out.

"My hands and knees were all bloody due to crawling on the gravel and rocks. Jake took me to his house in his truck and that was why my blood was found on the passenger side. When we went in his house, he cleaned my wounds and bandaged me up. But, the only thing he had to bandage my hands and knees with were some embroidered towels his wife had made. I didn't want him to use them, but he insisted. He said she would have wanted him to put them to good use since he never used them," I expounded.

"He also told me he was Sergeant Bardon's uncle, which surprised me. He graciously offered to let me stay at his house that night, but I wasn't sure I could trust him considering who his nephew was. He let me use the phone, so I called Bill to see if he could come pick me up. He couldn't because he doesn't see well at night." I looked over at Bill and smiled.

"I ended up staying that night at Jake's house and I found out Jake Bardon was nothing like his nephew," I concluded. I realized this statement was quite an insult to the Sergeant, but I didn't care.

"Jake was a kind man and I enjoyed being with him. He had an amazing sense of humor, and I am very glad I got to know him. The next day, he drove me to Abilene, so I could rent a car. On the way there, he revealed to me that he was very afraid of these 'evil spirits' which he had encountered several times. I was surprised to find out he believed in the supernatural. He assured me he did after dealing with these 'devils' as he called them," I revealed.

Then I explained to the jury that I didn't believe in the supernatural, either until I started doing this story. "Jake told me he believed these evil spirits started the fire at the church. I was shocked when he told me this. But, based on all I have experienced over the past few months, I now believe he was right. And I also believe they started the fire at his house that killed him."

After explaining my theory of how the fires started, I glanced at the jury to see their reaction. They were just staring at me, like any group of people would, listening to a man talk about demons setting fires to churches and houses.

I continued with my testimony, hoping they believed at least some of the unbelievable things I was telling them. "Jake was afraid of these evil spirits. He was one of the few people I had met who could see them. He believed if he left them alone, they would leave him alone. But obviously, he was wrong. I found out the next morning, along with the rest of Abilene, that his home was the one which burned to the ground. I was devastated to think he had died in the fire."

As I continued my defense, I knew I was taking a long time, but I wanted them to know every detail so they would believe I was not making this story up. And I knew it might be hard for them to swallow everything I was feeding them, so I was trying to give them some time to digest this startling testimony.

"Jake had tried to warn me to leave Abilene and stay away from these spiritual nightmares, but I just couldn't do it. I was convinced these evil spirits had something to do with the missing. So I stayed even though I knew, at that point, what they were capable of," I acknowledged.

Marco interrupted, "So, you ignored Jake's warning, even though he seemed to be very afraid of these spirits?"

"Yes, I did. I am someone who finishes the job I start. I went to Abilene to do a story, and even though I was alarmed by his fear and his warning, I knew I had to finish my assignment. But, I do believe Jake paid with his life by warning me," I said, wanting people to know the heroic thing he had done for me. I also hoped my work ethic would impress the jury, Sid, and Irene.

Marco knew he needed to clarify with the jury that I understood how my story sounded. "You know this all sounds unbelievable to most people, do you not, Mr. Pike?" he stressed.

"Yes, of course I do. I wouldn't have believed it myself a few months ago," I assured him.

"Could you continue, Mr. Pike?" Marco urged.

"Since they had not released the identity of the person killed in the fire, I decided to drive back out to the Potosi area just to confirm it was Jake's house that had burned down. It was when I was out there, that I found Cooper. When I first saw him, I thought he was a little fox, but when I got closer I recognized him. He was very close to death. He must have jumped out of the window when the fire started. I took him to a vet that Irene had suggested and that is how I met her," I explained.

"Jake's death made writing this story even more compelling to me, because he died trying to help me. I knew I had to expose these evil entities for what they are—murderers and liars. And I wanted to try and help the families of the missing in any way I could," I concluded.

Marco interrupted, "Do you still believe these evil spirits had something to do with those who are missing?"

"I believe they did. I am learning what they are capable of and it is frightening. There is a lot of spiritual activity going on in Abilene and the surrounding area. It almost seems like someone accidentally left the gate open in the heavens, or the other place, and these spirits escaped." My last remark brought laughter in the courtroom. I didn't know if they were laughing at me or because what I said was funny.

"You can see why I was hesitant to talk to many people about all of this. I didn't think anyone would believe me, but Irene did. We both felt I needed some guidance about how to deal with these spiritual nightmares and how to rescue the missing. That is the reason Irene suggested I talk to her pastor," I explained.

Marco interjected, "So that is how you met Irene's pastor, Samuel Rash?"

"Yes. I was hesitant to tell him about the dreams and the evil spirits, but I thought he believed in these things, but apparently not like I do. I guess I can understand why he might have been suspicious when I told him I had spoken to the missing people. I did specify, though, that I had met them in my dreams. It was quite a surprise to find the police waiting for me in his office when I returned later that day. And the rest is history," I concluded.

But Marco wasn't finished. He felt like he needed to ask another question the DA might ask so I would have a better chance to explain, "Henry, tell us about the fire in the motel."

"Yes, that's when I lost all my notes and the documentation I had in my journal. I put everything in a journal I kept on my computer. I had been working all day on my notes when the fire happened," I said.

"By that time, I had already had some dreams of the missing and was trying to write down what they said to me. I was tired that day because the night before was when I had been up with Irene. I decided to take a nap and that's when the fire broke out. But fortunately, I woke up just in time to escape the fire. I barely got out with Cooper before it engulfed the whole room. The fire destroyed my computer and the hard drive was unsalvageable. My car keys, my phone, and all my money and clothes were consumed," I explained.

Marco continued, "So you believe these evil spirits started the fire, is that correct, Mr. Pike?"

"Yes, as unbelievable as that sounds. I can't imagine how else it started?" I presumed.

Marco asked me one more thing before letting the wolf in, "Mr. Pike, how sure were you that you had actually talked to the missing in your dreams?"

"I wasn't sure at all, except the dreams seemed so real and the people I met told me details about their lives. I knew the only way to know for sure would be for the families to check and see if what they told me was true," I stated.

"So you did talk to the other missing people, but they did not give you any way to confirm their stories, is that right?" Marco asked.

"Yes, that is true. I did see all of the missing in my dreams, but I wasn't able to get information from some of them."

Marco asked me to tell everyone what I believed they should do on behalf of the missing.

I swallowed hard and said, "Gather all who believe in the One true God and ask Him, the Commander of the armies of Heaven, to send forth His angels to fight for those who are being held captive. They are counting on us to pray them back. Gather in your homes and in your churches or wherever you can. Ask the Father of light to pierce the darkness to uncover your loved ones. Do it now and don't stop until they come home. They asked to leave this earth and now we have to ask to bring them back. He wants you to believe in Him to save them—not anyone else. Believe and you will receive," I assured them.

Marco thanked me and I dreaded facing the DA next, but the judge called for a recess. I was thankful I'd have some time to gather my thoughts before he would pounce on me.

Chapter 72

C ourt reconvened and I was asked to return to the witness stand where I had to swear to tell the truth again. The DA walked over to me and I could almost see him salivating with his questions. "Mr. Pike, can you tell us a little more about those you met in your dreams. There were four who gave you a lot of information but what about those who didn't."

"Yes, I can do that. I did see all of the missing at various times in the dreams, but there were some who were not in the best of circumstances which made it hard to talk to them," I explained.

"And what kind of things did you discuss when you could talk to them?" The DA asked sarcastically.

"Each one told me who he or she was. They told me a little of how they believed they got where they were. And then four of them were able to tell me some things that would confirm I actually spoke to them," I explained.

"Yes, I believed we have confirmed you actually spoke to those four people. But would you please tell us what prevented you from speaking to the other six people?" he asked.

"When I first met some of the missing, I did not think about the need to prove I had spoken to them. Jodie was one of the first people I met, and she did not specifically tell me information so I could prove I met her. I just remembered what she said about her fiancé and the box under her bed. Elias was the first one who actually gave me information so I could prove to his father I had spoken to him." I looked at Bill and he nodded at me.

"Then there were three people I found in horrible circumstances. I didn't really want to talk about it because I thought it might upset their families," I thoughtfully said.

The DA interjected, "Mr. Pike, I believe these families are already upset, so I don't think your testimony will alter that. Please continue."

I hated the district attorney's sarcasm, but I tried to answer as nicely as I could. "Well, one of them was tied to a church and he couldn't get down. There was a woman who was hysterically crying out in the middle of the street. She was screaming because her baby had died in a car accident. Her name was Belle. And the other man, Brian, was in a hole with an iron grate over it. So they really didn't tell me anything I could share," I concluded.

"I see, Mr. Pike. And you found there was no way you could help these people?" the DA asked.

"No, I couldn't or I would have," I explained.

"I'm sure you would, Mr. Pike. Moving on to events which happened in this world, did you happen to know the Fire Marshall just released his report today? He found the source of the fire in your motel began in your room. It was also deemed arson. Now how would you explain that, Mr. Pike, since you were the only one in the room when the fire started?" the DA prodded. He looked at me intently hoping to see me squirm based on the new revelation.

This new information was not something I was prepared for. I was not aware they had released their findings on the investigation and apparently, Marco was not, either. My heart sank because there really was no reasonable explanation I could give him, other than to say a demon did it.

"I do not know how it started because I was asleep when the fire started. Perhaps it was an electrical fire?" I suggested.

"As I said, Mr. Pike, the fire was determined to be arson," the DA rudely replied.

The DA continued his onslaught by questioning my sanity, "Mr. Pike, isn't it likely you have been hallucinating all of these things? Either you have imagined all of these things or you have invented these dream stories to cover up your crimes. So which is it, Mr. Pike?"

"No, I did not hallucinate or imagine any of this. And anyone who knows me knows I would never commit any of these crimes. I would never hurt anyone," I stressed, but I knew I was sounding desperate.

"That's what they all say, Mr. Pike," The DA responded. "Isn't it true that you told your boss how much you hated Abilene so no one would think you had been there in years?"

"I told him I never wanted to come to Abilene to do a story. I had not stepped foot in Abilene for almost thirty years before I came to write this story for my magazine," I said confidently.

"Really? Then how would you explain this picture, taken at the Art Walk a little over a year ago?" The DA then had a picture flash up on a large screen where everyone in the entire courtroom could easily view it. He pointed to the date and continued, "The camera caught you and a group of people staring at a painting. This picture shows you looking directly into the camera," the DA stated, as he pointed me out with a laser pointer.

In horror I looked up on the screen where the photo was projected. And there in vivid color was the very same picture I had found months before. But instead of Micah looking directly at the camera—it was me. "No, it can't be!" I yelled without thinking. "That is impossible."

The DA looked at me and waited for me to explain. I was horrified beyond words. I couldn't believe those demonic entities could do something like that. I had never shown that picture to anyone and the only person who knew I found it was Micah. I was speechless.

When I looked helplessly at Marco, he looked like he had seen a ghost. I scanned the room to see if they were as mystified as I was. I could see Bill had a stunned look on his face. Sid was shaking his head in disbelief. My sister, Carrie, had buried her face in her hands. And when I saw Irene, I could see she was crying. I knew in that horrible moment, I had lost.

The DA pressed harder. "Tell me, Mr. Pike, what have you done with all of these missing people? We know you hid these people and that was how you were able to obtain the details you told their families," he asserted.

I felt hopeless as he continued to lambast me with his accusations. Marco was not objecting to anything he threw at me. I looked at him. He had a look of bewilderment on his face. I knew the picture of me, still exhibited on the screen, had dispelled any faith he had left in me.

Energy drained out of me as I resigned myself to the fact that the trial of the century was not looking good for the defendant. The only thing I could do was tell the truth whether anyone believed it or not. "Like I already told you, I met all of these people in my dreams. That was how I learned the information I shared," I said with no emotion.

"Do you really expect us to believe that, Mr. Pike? Isn't it true that you killed Jake Bardon because he must have seen you doing something with these people?"

"No, it's not true. I cared about Jake. I would never hurt him. He gave his life for me." I felt like crying uncontrollably.

"Isn't it true, Mr. Pike that your motivation in all of this was to look like the hero to these poor, despairing people. You made them believe you wanted to help them when all along, you were the one who took their loved ones! And what a great façade you came up with to cover your involvement. You had your attorney send letters to these desperate families to convince them you only had their best interest in mind," the DA reasoned.

"It would have been a great cover if I needed one, but I don't. My intention is, and always has been, to do the story I was sent to do. And if I could do anything to help these families find their loved ones, I would," I said with a fevered pitch. I felt desperate because I knew the DA had me just where he wanted me. And with every question and accusation, he was digging my grave.

He finally stopped the torture and told the judge he had no more questions. I felt like someone had beaten the life out of me. I was asked to step down and I took my seat next to Marco. I felt like there was an unseen wall between us. I knew he didn't trust me anymore and I doubted anyone else did, either.

The closing arguments came and Marco tried his best to gather his wits about him, so he could try to generate some sympathy from the jury. "My client truly believes everything he has told you and the families. If he was trying to cover up a crime, don't you think he would have come up with something more believable than these supernatural stories and dreams? But he is not trying to cover up a crime. He was trying to do his job when these unusual events occurred in the process."

Marco continued his plea to the jury, "I ask you to consider that just because we can't see the unseen world around us, does not mean it is not there. Do not condemn an innocent man whose only crime was being assaulted by these spiritual villains while trying to write a story for his magazine. Thank you for seriously considering with an open mind that he is telling the truth." Marco finished my defense, but his argument no longer sounded convincing–even to me.

Then the DA made his closing argument and said, "Henry Pike has created an elaborate story to explain how he was able to talk to some of the missing people from Abilene. His only explanation of how he obtained this information was— he talked to them in a dream," he said with drama and a hint of sarcasm. "You must decide—is it more reasonable to believe he had access to these people through close physical proximity or through the avenue of his dreams. I know you will make the logical conclusion."

While the DA diminished any hope I had of winning the case, I felt my faith was diminishing as well. How could I continue to believe I had all of heaven behind me when it was obvious I had been deserted? As I sat in my chair helplessly listening to this man convince the jury I was guilty, I had to wonder what the people I loved thought of me.

Hope was leaking out of my heart as it was breaking apart. Only bits and pieces of what the DA said registered in my mind as it began to shut down. I was no longer able to process the reality of what was happening to me.

The DA continued his assault on my character. "There is no doubt, Mr. Pike is an arsonist based on the Fire Marshall's report. And due to the excessive evidence found in the Potosi area, Henry Pike was behind the fires there, as well."

"And because of the established fact he was with Jake Bardon hours before his body was found, it is obvious he murdered him and tried to destroy the evidence with the fire," The DA concluded.

"Mr. Pike tried to convince some of the families that he is a noble man who wanted to help find their missing loved ones. But, in reality, he is a cold-blooded, calculating murderer. Not only does he dare to raise the hopes of these families that their loved ones might still be alive, but he offers them no solution to get them back other than telling them to pray, which no doubt they have done a million times."

"His account of how he encountered the missing is ridiculous, and he insults our intelligence by asking us to believe it. None of his testimony is believable. All he has proven is he did speak to at least four of the missing people from Abilene. If nothing else, this proves his guilt by association and their continued absence. I ask you to find this man guilty as charged."

And with the DA's final nail in my coffin, the last day of my trial was over and it certainly was not a happy ending. Sentencing would be the following day if the jury had decided on a verdict by then. I doubted it would take them that long.

I was taken back to my cell where I wadded up my sweaty suit because I didn't care how I looked the next day. It didn't really matter anymore. I figured my attire for the rest of my life would be an orange jumpsuit.

As I pondered my fate, I knew I was in trouble. I paced back and forth most of the night. I felt like a wild animal that had just been captured after living free all his life. I was trying to come to terms with the realization that the world of steel bars and guards would soon be my reality.

There were no visitors that night. I imagined they all had abandoned me. I could understand why because I certainly looked guilty. I couldn't eat and I couldn't sleep. My thoughts were tormented by the DA's words and his attack on my character.

Then I remembered the horrible dream I had in the holding cell. Those evil characters had been right. Those disgusting creatures had won. Their laughter and taunting came back to me vividly. And their incessant cackling tormented my mind the rest of the night.

Chapter 73

The next morning, when I entered the courtroom in my wrinkled suit, I did not expect a good outcome. The judge walked in and she seemed all business. I knew she probably just wanted the trial to be over. So did I, but I doubted she cared as much about the outcome.

The jury walked in and the judge asked if they had made a decision. They had and the foreman stood. I was told to stand up, but I collapsed when their decision was announced—guilty on all counts! I felt like I was going to pass out. They hadn't believed anything I told them.

The judge looked at me while Marco helped me to stand back up. She told me she would hand down my sentence the next day. I couldn't believe the jury thought I was capable of such heinous acts. How would I survive in prison for a crime I did not commit? Or maybe she would just give me the death sentence? I would prefer to die rather than live the rest of my life in prison.

I heard Irene cry and I wanted to comfort her, but I wondered if I would ever hold her again. I was taken back to my cell where the inescapable conclusion was realized—-this would be my new home.

Marco came to see me soon after and it was obvious he was angry. "I am disappointed, Henry. You were more than just a client to me. I believed the things you told me. But I do not know what to believe anymore. Could you please explain to me how they found a picture of you in Abilene a year ago? Did you lie to me when you said you had not been in Abilene for over thirty years?"

"No, I didn't lie to you, Marco," I responded, knowing he didn't believe me. A picture is worth more than a thousand lies.

"Well, the jury obviously thought you were lying, which was understandable after they saw that picture of you. When the jury thought you lied about that, no doubt they assumed you lied about everything else. Did you?" he asked again, as he gave me a cold, calculating stare.

"I'm sure it looks that way, Marco, but I did not lie to you or them. That is the very same picture I found the night the dark spirit jumped on me in my motel room. I never told anyone about the picture, but it was the one that made me think Micah was responsible for all the missing people. He is supposed to be the one in the picture–not me," I explained. I didn't even bother telling him who I thought was responsible for altering it.

I asked him if he had talked to Irene and he hadn't. He said he had not seen her since the verdict was read. I wasn't surprised. I doubted Bill or Sid or my sister had stayed, either. Why should they? They had probably concluded I was a liar and a murderer along with everyone else.

It was truly a sad day. It appeared evil had triumphed over good.

It was obvious Marco no longer believed me and wanted to get on with his life. I knew he had done the best he could in spite of the odds. I told him, "Marco, thank you for all you did for me. I know it must have been hard for you to believe everything I told you. I only wish you still did."

With great sadness, I got up and waited to be let out of the visitor area. I sat in my cell wondering how I could ever survive in prison. I started to weep and didn't think I would ever stop. I could feel despair envelop me.

Then the negative thoughts started coming. I didn't fight them anymore because I didn't care anymore. Those evil spirits had won, so what was the point. I gave up and darkness flooded my mind like a tidal wave.

The guards brought me dinner but I didn't have an appetite. I curled up in a ball and went to sleep. The nightmares came all night, but I decided I might as well get used to them. Whether I was asleep or awake, my life had become one big nightmare.

The next morning, I woke up with a weight on me that was unbearable. I did not know if I would be able to endure what had been declared over my life. The sentencing would be that morning and I was hoping I would get the death penalty. My life was over anyway.

They came to my cell to give me my ugly suit to wear to my sentencing. I didn't even try to look good. The guards straightened my tie and told me to comb my hair. What difference did it make? Who was I trying to impress?

We went into the courtroom and no one talked. Marco didn't say anything. I could see tears glistening in his eyes which surprised me. I didn't think he cared that much about me. But then it occurred to me, he was probably just sad about losing such an infamous case. I didn't bother to turn around because I doubted anyone was left in my cheering section. It seemed the whole world had deserted me.

The judge walked in and we all stood. As she began to pronounce her sentence of doom over me, the rear doors opened and a court officer walked in. He handed the judge a piece of paper. She read it and looked at me.

The judge told me to sit down and said, "The sentencing has to be postponed until tomorrow." She got up and left quickly.

Great. I would have another endless day of worrying what the outcome of her decision would be. I looked at Marco for an explanation but he looked as puzzled as I felt. He had no idea what had just happened. I asked him again if he had talked to Irene and he had not.

As they were taking me away, Marco said, "Oh, I forgot to tell you that I heard from Bill. He had an urgent call and had to return to Abilene yesterday." At least Bill had a reason to leave, unlike Irene who left without even saying goodbye. Marco added, "I'm sorry, Henry. I'll try to find out why the sentencing was postponed. It's most unusual." Then they whisked me away.

I got undressed and threw the wadded suit on the bed. The guards took it and told me they thought it was a tough break how everything turned out. Even they felt sorry for me.

It was a long day and I ate little. I had no energy left to do anything. But, it did help some when my sister came to see me later that day. I was glad at least one person still cared about me.

Carrie looked haggard and I could see the trial had been hard for her. She had been there to support me throughout the trial, and had even offered to testify as a character witness on my behalf. Marco didn't feel it would benefit me since I rarely saw her. But it meant a great deal to me for her to be there every day.

"Henry, I am so sad how everything turned out for you. I know you are not guilty, even though it did seem they had a lot of evidence against you. Even so, I know you would never commit these crimes. It's obvious someone framed you. I told Marco we wanted to appeal the case. I'm not going to just sit by while they falsely accuse my big brother," she proclaimed. She smiled at me. I was very touched by her words.

I had never loved my sister more than I did at that moment. I told her, "Carrie, I thought everyone had abandoned me, but I'm so glad you didn't. You are the best sister anyone could ever want and I'm sorry I have not been the best brother. I'm also sorry you've had to go through all of this. I'm sure it's embarrassing to have such a notorious brother."

"You are a great brother, Henry, and I'm proud you are my family. We will need to be more intentional about spending time together in the future," she said with assurance. "I will see you soon, Henry." And with her positive proclamation, she got up and put her hand on the window and I put mine next to hers.

Her visit gave me some hope which I desperately needed. Hope—it's hard to live without it.

Chapter 74

Marco came to see me later that evening and he seemed rather cheerful after such a bleak day. We sat down in the visitor area and he tried to explain what happened that caused the postponement. "The judge received notice that one of the missing people had been found."

My ears perked up when he said this. "Who was it?" I asked tenuously.

"It was Elias, Henry. He turned up in a hospital in Abilene. He is in the detox ward but he is alive and well. That is why Bill left. He got the call and rushed home. I'm not sure but I think Irene went home to be with him."

I was shocked to hear this news. I was happy for Bill that he would have his beloved son back. And I was relieved to hear about Irene, too. At least she had a good reason for leaving. ˙

"Do you think they rescued him, Henry?" Marco asked enthusiastically.

"Who?" I asked.

"The angels," Marco said annoyed. "Henry, what is going on with you? I know the trial did not go the way you hoped, but those dreams you had were obviously real. They were proven in a court of law."

"Yeah, well it did me a lot of good," I said angrily. "Elias was probably in some stupor somewhere doing drugs and now he's found his way home." I refused to believe it could be anything else.

"Henry, you saw Elias in a dream. How could you not believe anymore when everything he told you was proven to be true? Somehow he has returned from that spiritual state of being. Someone must have set him free," Marco reasoned.

It was hard to believe anymore in my dreams or in the One who gave them to me. I was too disappointed in how everything worked out, and I didn't want to risk being disillusioned again.

"There was no identification on Elias when he appeared in the ER, and since he couldn't talk or explain how he got there, they took a blood sample from him. They discovered who he was by matching his DNA to a sample they had taken when he was reported missing. In a few days they will hopefully know more," Marco explained.

The news still didn't penetrate my emotions. I was cold and numb because of all I had been through. It was almost like it didn't matter to me anymore.

Marco had to leave, but he told me he would see me in court the next day. I told him I could hardly wait.

The next day, I got word from the guards that the sentencing was going to be postponed again. I couldn't believe I had to wait another day. Hours dragged by until Marco finally came to see me.

They brought me out to the visitor center. I glared at him expecting only the worst. But, Marco was smiling at me.

"Henry, you are never going to believe what I'm about to tell you. Kim showed up at her parent's front door last night! They are beyond thrilled. She is in perfect condition and she told her parents the most incredible story." He was practically jumping up and down.

He certainly had my full attention as he continued. "She told her parents she had been in heaven. She told them what it was like being there and how happy she was to see her grandmother. She also told them she met another lady there and her name was Mary." Marco was virtually dancing in his chair as he relayed this story to me.

"Mary told Kim she was from Abilene and a little about her life. They also talked about the sadness they felt after some people they knew died. Mary told Kim about the little girl and Kim told Mary about her grandmother. When her parents realized Kim was describing Mary Smith, they immediately called me," Marco said excitedly.

"They also said Mary introduced Kim to a little girl named Eden. They realized she had to be the little girl who had been beaten to death a few months before by her mother's boyfriend. Henry, there was no doubt in their minds that Kim had met Mary Smith!" Marco was ecstatic.

"Henry, do you understand what this means? Kim just verified everything you told the jury. But that is not the most amazing part of her story."

He couldn't wait to see my reaction to what he was about to tell me. "The last thing Kim remembered was talking to a man who told her he would do his best to get her home. She said he asked her a lot of questions but then he just suddenly disappeared. That must have been when the guard woke you up from your dream, Henry! Do you understand how remarkable this is? She was talking about you, Henry!" He was bouncing up and down as he shared this incomprehensible story to me.

As I watched his obvious joy, it caused me to snap out of whatever spell I was under. I couldn't comprehend it all, but it did register in my dazed mind when Marco told me, "Henry, I think they are going to reverse the jury's decision in light of everything that is happening. This is why the judge has not sentenced you yet. She wants to see if any of the others return."

It was almost too amazing to believe. It occurred to me to ask, "Do you think the families did what I told them to do?" It had to be the only explanation of why this was happening.

Marco then informed me, "Bill and Irene have been talking to every church in Abilene asking them to pray. Bill just called me and told me he would fight until you are released. He believes you are the reason he has his son back. Irene and Bill are in Abilene fighting for you, Henry."

The wonderful truth washed over me. Irene had not left me. She was fighting for me along with my good friend, Bill.

Good does triumph. Sometimes it just takes a while.

Chapter 75

Three days after I received that wonderful news from Marco, I was released from custody. The charges were dismissed after the missing started showing up at their respective homes. None of them could remember where they had been or how they got home.

Kim could not recall how she arrived on the front steps of her home, but she did remember every detail of her heavenly visit. She was the only one who did. Perhaps that was merciful considering what some of the missing had endured.

Over the past year, most of the missing people returned. There were still two who had not. Barry has not returned, and I believe it was because he did not want to come back. He did not want to face the consequences of his actions. Or, perhaps, his wife found out what he did and was too angry to ask for his return. I realized someone might need to talk to her about forgiveness.

And Brian has not come back, either. Since he had no family or friends, and there were probably many who hated him, I had to assume no one on earth had fought for his return. Since I have learned the spirit world desires our cooperation in order to move on our behalf, I realized someone would have to intercede for him. And, I knew in my heart, it would have to be me.

The missing returned over a period of several months. Whenever a report went out saying another one had returned, it helped the others to intercede with more belief. Belief seems to be the catalyst that gets things moving spiritually.

During that time, I learned of two people who were found in Sweetwater who had been missing for months. A young man and an older woman were discovered sitting in a church and they seemed to be in a stupor when they were discovered. They had no idea how they got there or where they'd been. I had a pretty good idea where they had been. They had to be the two nameless people in the 'waiting room'.

None of the missing people remembered meeting me except for Kim. Her account of what happened during her heavenly visit surely saved me. Even though the other people didn't remember me, their families told them all I had done to bring them back.

Most of the missing were thankful for a second chance at life and have flourished. Jodie was one of those who blossomed into a lovely person. She now understands how valuable she is as a person. She will not settle for anyone who does not treat her like the treasure she is, which I now understand is how every woman wants to be treated.

Her old boyfriend tried to get back together with her soon after she returned, but she decided she wanted nothing to do with him. She did give him the box under her bed but without the tearful note and handkerchief.

Jodie started playing the piano and violin in her church and people often comment how her music sounds so heavenly. She became a good friend, and we frequently go to the church where she plays. Their assistant pastor, Luke, has become a good friend of ours, as well, since he and Jodie started dating.

Elias also became a good friend of mine. We joined a bowling league and bowl every week together. His father never misses a game. He is our biggest fan. Elias is a great guy and he is now free from what once plagued him.

John, who I found tied to the church, did a great deal of repenting after he returned. He no longer had a church to go to so we invited him to ours. John didn't remember what happened to him while he was gone, but he did have a sense it wasn't good. He straightened up his life and tried to make things right with all the people he had hurt. Most of them chose to forgive him.

And I was glad to learn Belle had sought help for her drinking problem at a rehab center in Dallas. One day I went to visit her and Belle assured me she was working hard to get her life back. Belle told me she had asked for forgiveness from the One who paid for her sins, but she still struggled to forgive herself. Belle understands His grace and love is not based on her past and that comforts her. She remains grateful to have another chance at life.

The dentist, Dr. Darby, was welcomed back to his home and his practice. He continues to look for those he defrauded to ask for their forgiveness. But, more importantly, he learned to forgive himself, which has made his life much more joyful.

When Carl returned, he told Teresa in no uncertain terms, she had to stop playing the evil video game. Even so, she still seemed unable to give it up. He asked me for advice. We found some people at Jodie's church, who believe very much in the supernatural world, and they went out to visit Teresa.

After talking to her at length, they realized they had to cast a few foul spirits out of her and out of her home. And then they took the evil game to a barrel behind her house and burned it. Teresa was set free from the souch's spell. Carl and Teresa got back together and they recently invited us to their wedding.

It seemed with the souch's demise, there was not as much evil activity in and around Abilene anymore. And because people have become much more careful about the words they speak, it would appear the malicious spirits have moved on to better feeding grounds. But I'm sure they will continue to look for those who are unaware of the power of their words. They need to read my book.

Mary's family has welcomed me into their lives. They are grateful to know their mother is right where she wanted to be so they are at peace in her absence. They had us over for a barbeque one night and we were sitting around the fire pit.

As I watched the fire flicker in the breeze, it brought back the time I saw the people sitting around the lantern. I had to ask them what they were doing in that disreputable church the night I was there. I had an idea, but I wanted to confirm it.

Dennis shook his head as he explained, "One of the families had heard of people having séances in that old church, so we decided to go. It was wrong, but we were so frustrated with the lack of answers, we were willing to try most anything. We only went a few times and after being scared out of our wits more than once, we knew we were dabbling in something evil. When we heard the place burned down, I was secretly glad because I never wanted to go back."

Even though I suspected that was what they were doing, I was glad to finally know for sure. It was one less mystery I had to solve.

Tim, the mechanic, has also become a good friend and whenever I need work done on my car, I take it to him. He has taught me how to change a tire, but more importantly, he has taught me about the need to forgive. He told me, "The One who forgives us, commands we do the same."

Sergeant Bardon was one of the people I struggled to forgive. It was not easy, but I believe I am free of him because I did forgive him. He is still on the police force, as far as I know. One day I am sure I will run into him again, but I'm not afraid to see him anymore. Although, I think he might be afraid to see me.

I also had to forgive Pastor Sam for betraying me after I had gone to him for help. He did ask me to forgive him numerous times which made it easier to do. He decided, after being a pastor for thirty something years, it was not his calling. He resigned and went to a local college to teach. The last I heard, he was teaching a class on all the supernatural events found in The Word.

It is a work in progress, but I am working on forgiving Brian for all he put me through as a little boy and how it affected me as a man. I finally found the strength to start asking for his return and I feel certain he will show up in the near future. I'm not sure what I will do when I see him again, but I am glad to know he will be set free from his prison. He was right; I was the one who had to set him free.

My father was perhaps the easiest person I had to forgive. Through the process of looking back over my life, I realized how much my perception of him was wrong. Carrie helped me to see he had tried to do the best he could in the midst of his own pain. But because of my pain, I would often misinterpret and reject his feeble attempts at fatherhood. We were two hurting people who kept hurting each other. It was a painful awareness.

Perhaps the hardest person to forgive was myself for how I had sabotaged my own life and blamed everyone else for it. It made me sad to realize how much of my life I wasted believing the wrong things and speaking them over my life. I know regret is useless so I stopped looking back and will look forward to what's ahead.

I am looking forward to the next chapter of my life!

Epilogue

I t seems with all the publicity I got from my trial, I actually did end up on The New York Times Best Seller List. As a result, I have been very busy on my book tour for the past few months. I am getting used to the recognition, but being in the spotlight during my trial certainly cured me of ever wanting to be famous, or infamous, as the case may be.

The book has given me the platform I needed to share with a large audience two messages I feel are of the utmost importance. I felt a great urgency to warn people of the danger they face if they do not guard their tongues. Their words can either bless their lives or curse them. I hope those who read this book can understand why I believed the message was so important.

But the most important message I have is for those who want to spend eternity in Heaven. A lady, who happens to live there, wanted me to share with the world that there is only *one Way* to get to the place we call Heaven. The Way is provided by the Father and it is through His Son- *He is the Way, the Truth and the Life*. If you get nothing else from this book, I hope you will get that message. It is the most important message there is.

My life has been forever changed since I began my adventure in Abilene. From the day I met Micah to the day I pen my last story, I will see myself as a blessed man for He has made everything new.

And in case you thought I forgot about Bill, let me assure you that will never happen again. We are the best of friends. We often go out together to our favorite restaurant. Sometimes Irene comes, too. And Bill is going to be the best man in my wedding in April.

After my trial, Irene and I got back together and we decided we were made for each other. One night under the big Texas sky with a million stars twinkling above us, I asked her to marry me and she said, "Yes!" Then she added, "My life would be so boring without you, Henry Pike."

Carrie will be a bridesmaid along with some of Irene's friends. Carrie's children, who I have come to know and love, will be helping with the reception. And her husband, Jack, will be one of my groomsmen along with Bill, Elias, Sid, and Marco.

Our wedding will be well attended. Many of the people, once referred to as "the missing", will be special guests at our wedding. They told me they don't want to be called "the missing" anymore.

We will be having our wedding in a most unusual location—on the hillside where I first met Micah. It is where my life changed forever, so it is a very special place to me. I have a feeling he might be watching and rejoicing with us.

Irene and I will live in her house along with our dogs, Sugar and Cooper. And we will begin this new chapter of our life together in my favorite town in the world—Abilene.

The End—or the beginning—as the case may be.

CPSIA information can be obtained
at www.ICGtesting.com
Printed in the USA
BVHW03s0814060418
512672BV00001B/25/P